QUEEN OF THE NIGHT SKY

Also by Amalie Howard

The Starlight Heir

Praise for *The Starlight Heir*

"My newest obsession! A breathtaking, sexy romantasy full of twists and adventure."

—Rebecca Yarros, #1 *New York Times* bestselling author of *Fourth Wing*

"One word to describe Amalie Howard's new fantasy—ENTHRALLING! *The Starlight Heir* pulls readers in with lush worldbuilding and compelling characters, consuming all your attention and leaving you longing for more!"

—Jennifer L. Armentrout, #1 *New York Times* bestselling author

"*The Starlight Heir* glitters with magic, every page brimming with romance and adventure. Amalie Howard's lovable characters, gorgeous worldbuilding, and passionate storytelling are beautifully combined to create the perfect romantasy . . . I couldn't put it down!"

—Nisha J. Tuli, internationally bestselling author of *Trial of the Sun Queen*

"With stunning worldbuilding, clever banter, and engaging characters, Amalie Howard has created a fascinating story full of magic, royalty, rivalry—and just the right amount of spice. Readers won't be able to put this one down!"

—Brigid Kemmerer, *New York Times* bestselling author

"Vivid, gripping, and intensely romantic, *The Starlight Heir* is pure addictive delight. Amalie Howard has an electric way with beautiful

words and an incomparable knack for lush worlds. This is a gorgeously crafted fantasy that will leave an indelible mark on the soul."
—Thea Guanzon, *New York Times* bestselling author of *The Hurricane Wars*

"With its sumptuous worldbuilding, witty characters, and spicy romance, *The Starlight Heir* is Amalie Howard at her finest!"
—Danielle L. Jensen, *New York Times* bestselling author of *A Fate Inked in Blood*

Queen of the Night Sky

Starkeeper Book II

Amalie Howard

AVON
An Imprint of HarperCollinsPublishers

Without limiting the exclusive rights of any author, contributor or the publisher of this publication, any unauthorized use of this publication to train generative artificial intelligence (AI) technologies is expressly prohibited. HarperCollins also exercise their rights under Article 4(3) of the Digital Single Market Directive 2019/790 and expressly reserve this publication from the text and data mining exception.

This is a work of fiction. Names, characters, places, and incidents are products of the author's imagination or are used fictitiously and are not to be construed as real. Any resemblance to actual events, locales, organizations, or persons, living or dead, is entirely coincidental.

QUEEN OF THE NIGHT SKY. Copyright © 2026 by Amalie Howard. All rights reserved. Printed in the United States of America. No part of this book may be used or reproduced in any manner whatsoever without written permission except in the case of brief quotations embodied in critical articles and reviews. For information, address HarperCollins Publishers, 195 Broadway, New York, NY 10007. In Europe, HarperCollins Publishers, Macken House, 39/40 Mayor Street Upper, Dublin 1, D01 C9W8, Ireland.

HarperCollins books may be purchased for educational, business, or sales promotional use. For information, please email the Special Markets Department at SPsales@harpercollins.com.

Avon, Avon & logo, and Avon Books & logo are registered trademarks of HarperCollins Publishers in the United States of America and other countries.

hc.com

FIRST EDITION

Interior text design by Diahann Sturge-Campbell

Flying stars in a stream illustration © Vicgmyr/Stock.Adobe.com

Map designed by Nick Springer, Springer Cartographics, LLC

Library of Congress Cataloging-in-Publication Data has been applied for.

ISBN 978-0-06-335589-7

25 26 27 28 29 LBC 5 4 3 2 1

*To anyone who has been told you're too
much, too little, or too something,
you deserve the right to exist . . . exactly as you are.*

*Also, slay your demons; they're only holding you back.
Unless they're hot and have shadow magic, then do what you want.*

Realm of Terrania

Glacier Ocean

Verisia
Vora Bay
Lora
Verlea
Pix
Solis
Whispering Sea
Morien
Deadman's Canyon
Pila Range
Xersten
Isle of Bones
Indraloka
Ryndhr
Eskorit Plains
Bay of Pearls
Kaldari
Eloni
Veniar
Gray Range

Andala Ocean

Copyright © MMXXIV Springer Cartographics

Content Guidance

War, violence, blood, gore, torture, amnesia, death of people and fictional creatures, sexual situations, drug and alcohol use, profanity.

When the lightbreaker falls,
darkness will abound,
a king lost to chaos
by star-cursed song.
Such is the long shadow of day
and the bright star of night,
a soul-blooming spark
tethered to both earth and sky.
By the chosen's own hand,
the ill-fated shall die . . .
And as the night sky bleeds,
a godslayer will rise.

The Gods of Endara

Saru—god of creation and light

Fero—god of death

Mithral—god of the sun and spiritual fire

Darrius—god of shadow and sky

Anahima—goddess of wisdom, fertility, and war

Vara and Vati—twin gods of wind

Huma—god of harvest and rain

Zora—goddess of time

Ris—god of the afterlife

Everlean Magic

Kinetic—elemental, lightning, light, flora/fauna, weather, time, metal

Psionic—mind control, telepathy, telekinesis, illusion, dreamwalking, scrying, precognition

Corpus—shapeshifting, healing, animagus, beast speech, enchantment, spelled objects; *forbidden corpus magic:* necromancy, summoning, sanguimancy

Oryndhrian Houses

Imperial House—reigning king or queen of Oryndhr

House of Regulus—leaders and scholars

House of Fomalhaut—creators, curators, and performers

House of Antares—warriors and mercenaries

House of Aldebaran—farmers, craftsmen, and merchants

Order of the Magi—magical practitioners (formerly outlawed magical order)

Part I

To behold the simurgh is a most precious gift;
the brightest heart is but a mirror of its divine beauty.
—A testimony of the Royal Stars

Chapter One

Coban is hot. *Desert* hot.

I can't help the grin that breaks over my face as the dry wind hits my cheek when we step through the enormous shimmering portal. Of course, it's nothing like the first time I used a portal to travel to the capital city of Kaldari for Prince Javed's bride contest—or the last time, when I came back alone to say goodbye to my father and Amma.

Sands, the invitation that had changed my life seems like a lifetime ago.

I suppose it is. I'm a different woman now. A *magi*. Powerful in my own right with the magic of the stars at my fingertips. Silvery iridescence flickers over my knuckles as the simurgh inside of me stirs, sensing my joy.

We're here. Finally.

It feels as though a huge weight has been lifted from my shoulders. I breathe in the desert air like someone deprived of oxygen for years.

The noise of the village hits me then as cheers of welcome rend the air. The smell of sweet incense infuses the village as we step into the decorated market square. Connected garlands of flowers stretch across the space, and colorful yellow and orange marigold petals litter the ground wherever we tread. I can barely see over the heads of the men marching in front of me, but my heart knows that it's home.

Instead of the single runecaster and dozen guards I'd had before, I now arrive in the presence of the king of Oryndhr. King Roshan Acharia, First of His Name. Illegitimate son of the former sovereign, King Zarek. Brother to the deceased regent Javed, the despotic ruler who sought to bring back the worst of the old gods by using me.

Me, Suraya Saab, the prophesized Starkeeper.

The only natural source of true magic in Oryndhr for centuries.

As a result, we are accompanied by several dozen imperial soldiers, six runecasters, the full might of the entire kingsguard, and a handful of attendants. The guards are all armed to the teeth with jādū-forged weapons, not that we expect any kind of attack from the people of my simple village, but one can never be too careful.

I'm no longer the humble tavern girl who had never left the desert. In fact, I've seen enough of Oryndhr to make me want to settle down for a while and just enjoy the tranquility of being still. Though there doesn't seem to be any sign of that happening in the immediate future, not with this royal tour of the realm. It's a necessary show of strength to the four noble houses, that much is clear. Coban is the first stop, but the bigger cities are still to come.

I'm still hoping that I can get out of that; Roshan doesn't need me.

"Suraya! Sura, over here!"

I turn wildly, searching through the faces surrounding us, and ignore the barked warning of the commander of the guard—Hamid, formerly the leader of the now dissolved Dahaka—to propel myself into my father's arms. Amma is next, her round face already wet with tears. Mine are quick to follow as I inhale her delicious, familiar scent of wood, baking bread, and spices.

"Stars, I've missed you both so much!"

"My lady," Hamid says, looming behind me, narrowed eyes on my father. "Please get behind the guards with His Majesty. It's not safe."

I frown. "This is my home. I have nothing to fear here."

"It's the king's command," Hamid insists.

"Fine." I want to roll my eyes, but Roshan's protectiveness is nothing new. In fact, I usually enjoy having the gratifying sole focus of his attention, especially after we'd nearly lost each other, but sometimes it can be excessive.

With an apologetic look to Papa and Amma, I comply, moving closer to where Roshan is being greeted by the effusive alderman of Coban. The local representative takes both of my hands in his and bows. I don't remember him ever being so friendly to me, but being in the presence of royalty will have that effect.

As we are led to the village hall, once more surrounded by Hamid and his very efficient kingsguard, most of whom are trusted senior officers from the Dahaka, I glance over at Roshan, who is immaculately dressed in his ceremonial golden-threaded, amethyst-hued robes. My heart instantly beats a little faster. Sands, he's so handsome.

His dark hair is brushed back from his brow and his eyes are lined with kohl. An elegant dusting of gold shimmers across his high cheekbones, enhancing their sharpness even more. The faintest hint of dark stubble over his hard jaw brackets that sultry and very talented mouth—the one he'd used earlier that morning to my utter ruin—making me catch my breath. The memory of those lips nearly makes my knees buckle.

His head swivels, and his golden-brown gaze slams into mine.

"Stop it," he whispers. The mouth that I'd been thirstily staring at curls into a smirk.

"Stop what?" I ask.

"Ogling me like I'm a sweetmeat."

I can't help the snicker that erupts from me. "I was not." *I totally was.*

"Behave, my starling," he says softly, though his eyes convey the opposite. He loves it when I defy him, and besides, he knows what that directive does to me. I despise being told what to do, even by the man I've accepted as my sovereign, but in public, the rules of being the future royal consort apply, which means I must be demure.

Or at least *try* to be. That was the promise I made, anyway.

"As you wish, my king."

Edging out of reach, I lower my lashes as a tendril of my magic wisps across his shoulders, down his muscular back, and over his tight rear. He gasps, which he covers up with a cough, causing a solicitous attendant to dash up with a cup of water. Impishly, I don't relent, sending the sinful stroke of magic down his leg and then back up, winding my way around his knee, over a rock-hard flexed thigh... and higher...

"Sura." His warning is a gravelly rasp as my invisible, playful touch inches upward, nearly to where we both desire it the most. "Your family," he grits out.

"What about them, Your Majesty?" I ask innocently, and widen my eyes with concern. "They've gone ahead. Is everything well?" I fight the urge to bite my lip at the strained look on his face. We've toyed with my magic before in the bedchamber, though never in public, and the power I feel over my poor, tortured king in this moment is practically indecent.

With no one else the wiser, I shift to cup his rapidly stiffening length beneath his silk trousers and groan at the feel of him, even via my magic. Holding his gaze, I indulge in a long stroke. Roshan stumbles and hunches over, the back of his neck going crimson and the veins in sharp relief on his forearms.

"Your Majesty!" General Clem Jinn, one of my few friends and Hamid's second-in-command, shouts. "Guards, formation! To the king!"

As the guards form a defensive circle around us, I crouch down, peering up at him with a sweet, solicitous smile. He sees right through my act, glittering eyes that promise vengeance meeting mine.

"You don't like it when I behave, Ro," I whisper, my breath grazing his ear.

He chuckles. "Stars, what compelled me to fall in love with a magical sadist?"

"I don't know," I reply cheekily. "Why did you?"

I stand up to shoot a glance at Clem, who has hurried over but still stands a respectable distance away to respect our privacy, her face stern as she scans the surrounding area for threats. I'd met Clem during the games for the competition for the former prince's hand. Two outsiders, we'd bonded quickly, only for me to discover later on that she'd been one of Roshan's inner circle and part of the Dahaka. Her deceit had been a hard blow, but I understood the pull of duty and her loyalty to her cause above all else. It didn't mean our friendship wasn't real, and I'd chosen to forgive her just as I had Roshan.

I pat her shoulder. "It's nothing, don't worry. He has a cramp from an injury. Give him a minute."

She frowns. "When was he injured?"

"Er, yesterday?" My brain whirls. "During training."

"He didn't have training yesterday," she says. "He was in the forge, if I recall, with you. Did something happen there?"

I blink and inhale a suddenly shallow breath. Oh, something did happen. The king and I had thoroughly defiled almost every available surface in the castle forge to the point where I'd sustained temporary minor burns on my backside that had healed immediately.

Worth it.

It's my turn to blush when a smug Roshan stands and lifts his brows, finally able to rise without an embarrassing tent in his trousers. "Yes, Sura, did something happen?"

Clem's gaze dances between the two of us before she lets out an aggravated sound and rolls her eyes. "By the gods, can the two of you keep it in your pants for once?" she mutters, keeping her voice low so that no one else can hear.

"What can I say?" Roshan teases, winking at me. "She can't resist me."

"You're an arrogant pain in the ass." I must say it much too loudly, because someone gasps on the periphery as we resume our progress to the village hall.

We are separated once we enter, Roshan striding to the front to make his address to the townspeople. I choose to stay near the back, ducking into a quiet corner. I've heard his speech multiple times since his coronation in Kaldari: an acceptance of the transfer of power, the condemnation of the coup that had nearly decimated the Imperial House, and reassurance that the dark forces have been eradicated from Oryndhr.

For good.

It feels like a step in the right direction to rebuild and to restore the confidence of all the people in the realm. Coban was targeted specifically by the former king because of *me*, so Roshan's reassurances mean more than he knows. I wave hello to a few Cobanites, mostly old neighbors, some of whom stare at me openly. The notoriety I've gained for my part in the rebellion still makes my skin itch, but I'm used to the attention by now.

Who in Coban would have guessed that the Starkeeper would have been Suraya Saab?

Even after a handful of months, it's a heavy mantle to carry, and I still struggle with the memories of how close I came to giving in to the darker siren song of my magic. Like any power, it's shaped by the mind and hand of the wielder. Lost in grief and rage after Laleh's death and Roshan's betrayal, I'd almost descended into darkness myself.

With the amount of starlit magic I had in my veins, things could have gone very badly for everyone in Endara. Our entire world might have been destroyed. The risk is always there if I don't continue my lessons with Aran—Roshan's cousin and a practitioner of formerly outlawed arcane magic—to strengthen my skills.

Roshan has tasked him with training magic users from all the houses, instead of keeping all magic and jādū use under the control of the crown as his father had. Jādū is a finite resource in our realm, but it's like oxygen. It belongs to the people. Of course, there are regulations and laws in place around its use—never to harm—but we're making progress.

Sometimes, and especially here, in the familiar heat of my beloved desert, I wish I could go back to the old me and my old life, when all I cared about was not getting caught for forging illegal jādū blades. But Zora, the goddess of time, waits for no man. She keeps marching forward, no matter our secret wishes.

In recent months, I've become familiar with our pantheon of gods, not just Saru and Fero—the gods of creation and death—but others like Huma, the god of harvest and rain; the mischievous twin gods of wind, Vara and Vati; and Ris, the stern god of the afterlife. Goddesses like Zora as well as Anahima, the goddess of wisdom, fertility, and war, fascinate me. Erased over generations by the ruler of the Oryndhrian Imperial House who wanted to be worshipped as a god-king, it was no wonder they had forsaken us.

A deafening round of cheering jolts me out of my musings.

"His Majesty is charismatic up there," Clem says from where she's standing close to my side like an ever-present shadow. She is usually the one assigned to guard me, even though I've insisted time and time again that I don't need it. She's better off protecting the king.

I nod. "He was born to rule. Oryndhr is in good hands."

She glances at me. "And if he needs you, will you fight at his side?"

"The war is over, Clem," I say with a frown at her tone.

She doesn't answer for a minute, but her mouth flattens as her eyes continuously survey the room. "That doesn't mean our enemies are gone. We need to be vigilant, especially in Eloni and Veniar, and even with the Scavs."

"The Scavs?" I ask. "Their general is dead. They have no leader."

"For now. They have been confined to the northern Dustlands for the time being, but they won't be held forever. We can't underestimate them again." She pauses. "As compelling as the king is, he'll have to keep his crown with force, if necessary. There are many who would see him off the throne permanently, especially in the House of Regulus. A leaderless army addicted to Jade could be a boon to an ambitious enemy."

I shiver at the mention of the hallucinogenic drug that had almost felled me. *Twice.* I knew the houses were discontent, questioning the succession of the newly coronated king and hunting for creative ways to unseat him. But at her words, awareness skitters over my tight shoulders. "Regicide?" I ask.

Her face is grim. "Assassins are the greatest threat."

MUCH LATER ON and safe, thankfully, after too many hours of food, fanfare, and celebration, Roshan and I are finally alone. I've convinced him to spend the night in Coban instead of returning to Kaldari, and while the rooms above the tavern have to accommodate us and his personal guard, my father and Amma don't mind. My aunt loves having extra mouths to feed.

"So this is the workshop I've heard so much about," Roshan says, coming up behind me and wrapping his arms around my waist as I stare at the cold forge.

"Where all the magic happened," I say, and turn to face him. I take in Hamid and two other guards who are standing near the door, as well as the shadows of others outside the window. I wish we could be alone, but Roshan's title comes with . . . an armed entourage.

"Magic?" Roshan asks, bending to nuzzle my temple. "Tell me more."

"I am a master bladesmith, you know," I say, my body heating at the gentle touch. "People paid good money for me to forge their swords with jādū." I wrinkle my nose. "Remember my old boss Vasha? He said I had a way with the crystals." I lift a hand between us and wiggle my fingers. "I suppose my magic manifested in its own way even then."

Roshan presses his lips to my fingertips, unexpectedly taking two of them into the wet heat of his mouth. My breath hitches, every inch of me intently focused on that scorching point of contact. I'm mesmerized by the movement of his lips and tongue, shivering when his teeth graze lightly over my skin. Heat gathers in my blood as I raise my gaze to find his eyes smoldering with desire. With a tiny moan, I sink my teeth into my bottom lip, and his stare darkens.

He releases my glistening fingers with a soft pop and glances over his shoulder. "Hamid, wait outside," he says huskily, walking us backward until the backs of my legs hit my old workbench. The sound of the door closing is the only sign that we are alone. *Finally.*

"You were amazing today with the people. They needed to hear you say that they were going to be safe," I tell him, gasping as his palms slip under my thighs and he lifts me to sit on the bench. He slides his trim hips, still wrapped in his ornate ceremonial tunic and pants, into the space between my knees, making my pulse ratchet. "You were very kingly," I add breathlessly, when he tucks my legs around him and pulls me flush against his torso.

At this angle, we both suck in a gasp at the snug, perfect fit of our bodies. Roshan rests his forehead against mine, taking his sweet time as he slides his hands down my shoulders and gathers my wrists in his grip at my back. He runs his nose up the column of my throat. "I like you like this, my starling," he says. "At my mercy."

Grinning, I lock my ankles, and he lets out a groan. "And you're at mine, my king."

He crashes his mouth down, the kiss a near-violent tangle of lips, tongues, and teeth, rife with hunger and dominance. It's wet, hungry, and wild, but so *us*, and I meet him stroke for stroke, desperate to satiate the desire burning in my blood. He releases my wrists to cup my face, gentling the kiss as his molten eyes burn into mine. "Gods, you're beautiful."

"Ro, I'm aching," I whimper, and wind my fingers into the wrinkled silk of his tunic. The runes on my arms begin to glow with silvery radiance as the magic fires in my veins. "I need you now. Please."

He smirks. "When you beg so prettily, how can I say no?"

Our hands fumble gracelessly at the ties and buttons of our clothing. We're so lost in disrobing each other that we don't hear the door slamming open until an urgent voice pierces through the thick haze of desire. "Your Majesty."

"Shit," I say, grasping the ties of my tunic. "It's Hamid."

Roshan hisses through his teeth, covering me from view with his body. "What is it?"

"Two of our men are down, Your Majesty," Hamid says in a low tone. "There are soldiers here, we don't know how many yet, but they're fast and skilled. We need to get you back to Kaldari."

Fumbling with my clothing, I sit up quickly and hop off the table. "We're under attack? Here? Is my family safe?"

Hamid's dark eyes meet mine. "Men are already in the tavern. There are . . . hostages, but I don't know if any are your father or aunt. They're demanding to speak to the king alone. I suspect it's a thinly veiled ploy to draw His Majesty out."

"Ro," I say, stomach diving to my feet at the thought of Papa and Amma being in danger. *Again.* "I won't run and leave them. We have to do something."

His brow creases, but then he nods. "Hamid, take some men to the front. Have Clem man the windows. We can shut this down without any more casualties, if we are careful."

"It's too risky," he begins, but is shut down by a ferocious glare from Roshan.

"Ro, it's best if you go with Hamid," I say, and lift my palms, flickers of magic sparking between my fingers. "I'll stay behind and make sure they're safe."

"Not an option," he says, banding a thick arm about my waist. "You stay with me. We do this together or not at all." Sands, he's so stubborn, but the truth is I'd refuse to leave him, too.

"They're probably watching this entrance," Hamid says. "It's what I would do, and despite their skill, we don't know if we're dealing with seasoned assassins or simply disgruntled countrymen."

"There's a back way over there." I point to a small trapdoor in the rear of the workshop. "It leads to a storage room, but there's an exit near one of the old jādū mines."

"That'll do," Roshan says, just as shouts and sparks light up the night. Magic arcs into the air from crossbows, thudding into the wood of the building, and I can see the ice spreading on the inside from the impact. Someone crashes against the door, and the sounds of clanging swords ensue. Orange flames shoot into the sky as the earth trembles.

"Go now!" Hamid says as the doors rattle. I don't know when he locked them, threading a metal bar through the handles, but the workshop is secure for the moment.

The trapdoor is a tight fit for both men, but they manage to squeeze through before I yank it closed, throwing the inner bolts. Again, it won't deter anyone for long, but it will buy us some time. The storage room is pitch-black and smells musty and unused, but I know the small space like the back of my hand. We quickly clear the way, shoving bags of sand, old tools, and metal sheets aside, before pushing on the doors leading up and out. They're rusty and the creaking sound is loud. Hamid goes first—and the sounds of a scuffle instantly filter in.

"You stay here," Roshan tells me. "I'll go."

Furious, I yank at his shirt. "I'm the Starkeeper. You're the king, so you stay put. *I'll* go."

I'm out the door before he can argue or stop me with some horseshit overprotective chivalry. I'm the only one with natural magic here and he knows that. My starlight flies out of me toward the grappling shapes on the sand and identifies Hamid at the last second. It incapacitates the two other men immediately and soundlessly.

"Thanks. Are they dead?" he pants, limping back toward me.

"Unconscious," I say, and glance over his shoulder, my magic lighting their faces. Both men are unfamiliar—neither of them looks like he's from here. More sounds of conflict pierce the air, the noise of two swords loud in the night. "Roshan, the tavern!"

Panicked, I start to sprint toward it, ignoring his hushed warnings to wait. My magic crackles, the simurgh inside alert. There's no movement around the back of the inn, and I signal to the two kingsguard to stay in their positions at the door. Clem is crouched near a side window, her weapons at the ready, and I run silently over to where she is.

"What's the status?" I ask, just as she demands, "Where's the king?"

"With Hamid," I reply. "Behind me. How many assailants?"

"At least five," she says, "with a dozen hostages in the main part of the tavern. Aran is in there, too."

My stomach roils, though I know Aran can handle himself. While my magic is fueled by the raw akasha in my veins, he uses jādū—a crystal form of magic—to amplify his runes. He is a more than capable master runecaster.

Unless there are too many of them.

Clem had said at least five hostiles, but more could be hiding out of sight, biding their time. This whole offensive appears to have been orchestrated very carefully, which means whoever is the leader in there had to have had information from someone on our side who was privy to our plans. They had to have known that we were staying with a smaller contingent of guards. The knowledge is gutting—we have a traitor, and it could be anyone.

"And my father? Amma?"

"Both inside." She turns to Hamid. "You need to take the king to safety. I'll stay with Suraya and get the situation under control."

"No!" Roshan snarls. "The Starkeeper does not leave my side."

I flinch at his unusual vehemence, more so when his fingers fall and tighten over my wrist. Despite the words being similar to his ones earlier, they don't evoke the same feelings of warmth. The edge of anger feels more possessive than protective. But I have more pressing things to worry about than sifting through Roshan's mercurial emotions, namely my family's safety.

"Calm down, caveman," I mutter, and ease myself out of his hold. "No one's going anywhere until we can figure out how to defuse the situation. I'm the least exposed. My magic will protect me, so I can go in there and see what they want."

"*Suraya.*"

I stare at Roshan. "Do you have a better idea? They'll kill anyone else. What you three need to figure out is who leaked information. Barely anyone outside our inner circle and your war council in Kaldari knew that Coban would be our first stop or, even worse, that we would be remaining here overnight. All the cities of Oryndhr were told to prepare, but the order for the tour was only announced this week to the aldermen out of an abundance of caution. This assault was *planned*. These mercenaries are not disgruntled villagers. People in many cities hated the previous regime and were punished for it."

The three of them exchange dark looks.

I don't wait for Roshan's assent before slipping around the side to the front and boldly banging on the door. I can hear his growl of displeasure, but with him, it's always better to ask forgiveness than permission. He'd wrap me in wool if he could and tuck me away like a precious jewel. It would be sweet if we didn't have any other option. But there aren't enough soldiers to storm the tavern, and even if there were, the risk of innocents dying in the crossfire is too high.

"Open up!" I yell. "I'm not armed and here to talk!"

When the door cracks open, I walk in with both hands in the air to multiple weapons pointed at me. I'm not too concerned about those, but I am worried about the ones aimed at my father's head. Aran's, too; he's crouched down beside my father, blood spilling down his cheek from a nasty cut on his temple. I scan the room, relieved to find Amma sitting in one corner with no sign of injury or fear on her face. She looks utterly furious.

I smile at her before staring down each of the men. More than double the five Clem had initially counted . . . and there could be more hiding.

"Who are you?" I ask them, trying to determine which one's the leader.

One sneers, a man with a half-shaved head and long upper braid pointing a crossbow at my father. Him, then. "Where's the false king?"

I lift my brows. "The *false* king?" I echo. "He has a blood claim to the throne, and I seem to recall he's the one who saved your homes, lands, and families from being destroyed by a usurper god who intended to yoke Endara into subjugation."

"We have no quarrel with you, Starkeeper," the aggressor says, though his voice is belligerent with skepticism. Stories of my power have traversed the land, but men out here haven't *seen* it. Most of those who have are dead.

"But you see, if you have a quarrel with the *king*, you have one with me." I pull a nearby chair out, flip it around, and straddle it. "Now, let's be civil. I'm Suraya Saab. My father under your arrow is the owner of this tavern. Who are you, and what house are you from?"

I can hear his teeth grinding from where he stands. "I am Sandar of Eloni, House Regulus." He points at a tall man with golden skin and a thick auburn beard. "Alderman Rubias of Eloni, House Antares."

"An *alderman*, my stars, and you're both far from home," I say with an impressed expression. "What grievance do you have with King Roshan, pray tell, that you attack him in my home under my hospitality?"

"He's a bastard," the redhead grinds through his teeth, "and led the Dahaka. The rebellion stole from us for years. He's untrustworthy and undeserving of the crown."

I nod again. "Harsh words. But where were you during the battle of the capital? Where were all your men who find it so easy to prey upon unarmed villagers now? Does doing this—forcing people to their knees in their own homes—make you feel powerful?"

"Kill the bitch, Sandar, she's nothing but a traitor, just like her king," one of the other men growls from the side—a fox-faced grunt holding a glowing crimson mace.

Seeing me staring, he lets one of the red-hot points on the mace touch a hostage's shoulder, making the poor man at his feet groan. It's Cyrill, I realize, one of the tavern's regulars and the man who had accompanied my father to the capital to save me from Javed. Cyrill is kneeling beside my former childhood nemesis, Simin, one arm around her quaking shoulders. They'd been dancing earlier in the tavern, with Simin flashing her pretty new engagement ring. Silent tears track down her cheeks.

I want to send them a reassuring look, but I don't. I'm hoping to end this with the least amount of carnage possible, and even with the increased control I have developed in recent months, thanks to Aran's tutelage, my magic can still be volatile.

Because, if I'm attacked, my simurgh will defend me at any cost— that is a certainty. She is waiting alertly under my skin, flexing her wings with a flick against my senses as if to assert she'll never let anything happen to me.

"The Starkeeper is a lie," someone else says from the back.

With a slow lift of my brows, I let my magic roll along my forearms, the runes there lighting up in silvery symbols and spirals as the akasha in my blood makes itself known.

"Parlor tricks!" Alderman Rubias says, his eyes full of suspicion and contempt. "The monarchy is spinning stories to control us, to control the houses and diminish our influence. The House of Antares was on the brink of exposing the Imperial House's lies and the seed of their corruption."

"By 'seed' you mean the dead Queen Morvarid?" I ask. "Because as far as I know, she was the unhinged magi resurrecting a dangerous god."

His face twists at my sarcasm. "She was the prophet who meant to cleanse her house of the rot eating away at its very foundations," he shouts, a fanatical tone to his voice that makes me stiffen. "She was to usher in a new age for those who served! Who still serve!"

My breath catches at the last. Suddenly, the situation becomes infinitely more dangerous. Nihilistic arcanists are unpredictable. We'd known that there would be pockets of Morvarid's rabid supporters lingering throughout Oryndhr, especially in Eloni, but to be faced with them here in Coban is surprising. But it solidifies my suspicion that this incursion wasn't by chance.

"I was there," I say. "I know *exactly* what the queen planned to do and how she intended to do it. She embodied the rot you speak of, and yet here you are, praising her. What is it you think you can do in her name now that she's dead?"

He glares, and I can sense the darkness of his spirit, roiling within him. "Call in the false king. Tell him to surrender to his fate or we will execute everyone here, including your family."

"You know I can't let you do that," I say. "Because if you hurt a single hair on their heads, I promise you will find yourself in unspeakable agony."

He nods at someone I can't see, and I feel the blade at my neck a heartbeat later. Icy tendrils lace across my throat like eddies of frost, but there's something else imbued in the blade, not just ice. There's a power within ... some kind of underlying death magic. I quell the instant roar of my simurgh and the burst of akasha in my blood that wants to incinerate the steel at my throat.

Where and how would they have gotten a weapon like this?

Or better yet, from whom?

The man sneers. "You're flesh and blood like any of us, so pay attention. That blade will freeze your blood from flowing *and* eat away at your organs if you so much as twitch in a way I don't like. And the little light show on your arms means nothing, Starkeeper." He spits the name like it's a curse. "The oracle might need you alive, but trust me, we can bleed almost every drop of you and still keep you breathing."

Exhaling, I blink. *The oracle?*

My gaze drops to Aran's, and I see the alarm and suspicion spark in his gaze. This is new. Despite Roshan's hopes for a united peace throughout the realm, confirmation of an antagonist changes everything. *Who* is the oracle? I need to get the alderman talking.

"Such a good boy, following orders," I taunt, trying to keep my face neutral while my simurgh roils beneath my skin against the corrupted magic it can sense from the knife still pressed to my throat.

Soon, I promise her. "If you're not the true leader, then who is? This oracle? Maybe the grown-ups should be speaking."

"I *am* the starsdamned leader," Alderman Rubias hisses.

"Are you sure it isn't the oracle?" I press. "You seem uncertain."

His eyes shoot daggers. "No."

"Who are they?"

"You'll find out soon enough," he says.

I fold my arms, ignoring the razor-sharp blade cutting into the flesh of my neck. I don't do anything to heal myself, letting the blood drip down my skin.

The alderman's eyes snag on it and brighten. "See? The Starkeeper can bleed. Now, get me your king or we'll sever your spine!"

Knowing I won't get more out of him, I let my lip curl. "No."

It's the only thing I utter before I let my simurgh loose.

Chapter Two

Bands of iridescent magic shoot out of me, healing me instantly and sending the knife at my throat flying, while targeting almost every enemy within close range. It's not enough, however, as more enemies slink from the shadows. Maintaining my control, I let out a growl of rage when I see two of our guards get taken out by successive blasts of fire from one of the mercenaries, and I instantly restrain the man, knocking his crossbow from his fingers with a savage flick of my magic.

Easing backward, I dodge a sword coming at my head, fire magic enveloping the entirety of the blade. I pull my dagger from my waist and send my starlight along it. Metal crashes against metal, and I relish the skill of the soldier before his much weaker weapon snaps in half. He begs for his life, so I crack him in the temple with the hilt of my blade. I might be powerful, but I'm not a murderer.

A shrill scream from one of the hostages in the tavern has me swiveling, and I cry out in horror as a glowing mace cleaves through a woman's sternum.

It's the fox-faced prick who'd stood over Cyrill.

Rage pumps through my veins, but I know if I break, if I lose control over myself, I'll never be able to come back from it. I inhale, focusing my center . . . and leaning into the brimming wellspring of akasha. My simurgh shrieks and lances a silvery whip at Fox Face, snapping the weapon from his hands and cinching around his neck like a noose. His eyes bulge as she drags him toward us like a fly caught in my shimmering web.

Gods, the power is intoxicating, darkness hovering on the edge of the light, whispering for me to end them all. I can't bring myself to kill anyone—not even Fox Face—without a fair trial for their crimes, but I won't lie: His screams of terror are music to my ears.

No time to celebrate, though, because more armed men pour out of hiding and into the room, fresh weapons at the ready. My father wastes no time crashing his fist into the nearest mercenary, and magic flies from Aran as he mutters offensive spells while clutching the jādū crystal at his neck. Holding my web of magic firm, I rush over to Amma, who assures me she is unharmed, and nod urgently to Cyrill.

"Get them out of here to somewhere safe," I tell him. "We'll handle this."

"I've been wielding this pot longer than you've been alive, child," Amma chimes in, lifting a blackened iron pan at her side.

I snort and give her a kiss on her lined cheek. "Fine. Just don't get hurt."

My eyes bulge when she takes out a mercenary with a fair whack to the head and a vicious chortle of glee, then immediately turns and sneaks up on another. In seconds, he's slumped down to the floor.

I suppose I get my temerity from both her *and* my mother.

Within no time at all, most of the enemy are disarmed, incapacitated, and rounded up. The majority are alive, groaning as they wake groggy and angry. Roshan instructs his remaining kingsguard to take the assailants into the middle of the square, where I belatedly notice that a crowd has gathered—people who'd been in their beds and ventured out after the sounds of battle.

"You dare," Roshan roars to the bound men, his voice ringing across the silence. "Attacking your king without provocation is a crime."

I send a wink to Alderman Rubias. "How do you like my little light show now?"

"You are an abomination," he says, but fear flashes in his eyes. "And you're no king of ours," he adds to Roshan, and spits to the side for good measure.

"Ouch, such cruelty, sir," I say, putting a hand to my chest. "I'm a person, too, you know."

Unamused, he glares at me.

"For the crime of treason and murder as well as intent to kill, I sentence you all to death," Roshan says. Twisting in shock, I stare at him. That is not what I expected him to say. He turns, the usual gentleness in his eyes eclipsed by fury. "Execution by starfire."

His words are a detonation as blood thunders between my ears. Every eye in the square falls upon me, and I hurry to his side. "Ro. They deserve a trial," I whisper. "A chance to explain and atone for their crimes. You can't just slaughter them in the middle of the square! There are children probably looking through their windows."

Roshan bares his teeth, fire simmering in his stare. "They tried to kill you. Kill *me*. This is war, and I will give no quarter."

"The war is *over*. We should talk to them," I say quietly. "Find out who they're working for first. Someone ordered this. There's a leader. This oracle. Aran heard it, too."

His jaw tics, but then he turns to Hamid and Clem standing at attention behind him. "Secure the one with the braid," he commands. Hamid hauls the man called Sandar away from the others. The king gestures imperiously to me, but my feet are frozen to the ground. *Everything* is frozen. "Sura, now."

The knot in my throat thickens. "I . . ."

Roshan's mouth descends into a scowl. "They were going to kill your family. These mercenaries would have no mercy if things were reversed. They deserve death. This is treason, you know that."

With a tremor of hesitation, my eyes rove blindly around the square, settling on Amma, my father, people I knew growing up. I don't want them to see me as a monster, as some kind of horrific weapon of the king—but that is exactly what I will be if I do this. "Please, Roshan," I beg. "We should take them back to Kaldari for interrogation. It's the right thing to do."

He pulls me close, but the act is not meant to comfort; it's for privacy. His low words are emphatic, his grip on my arm just this side of firm. "No. It has to be now. Sura, I need your help to keep the peace, you know that. We need to send a clear message that any attacks against the crown will not be tolerated or the houses will run roughshod over us."

"Then tell Hamid and your men to do it. I can't murder innocents."

A muscle clenches in his cheek, that fire in his eyes darkening. "They're *not* innocent. And the message has to come from the Starkeeper. The houses and the dissenters have to know that you stand behind the crown, that your magic is behind the Imperial House. Behind *me*."

"Ro, you know I am, but . . ." My voice wavers. "Not in front of my family . . . please. I'm begging you. Don't do this."

Gods, his expression is so cold, so *disappointed*, that I feel a small part of me wither. "You agreed to stay by my side, Suraya. That's what this means. That you might have to do a small evil to fight for the greater good, to defend the throne we fought so hard for against my brother and the queen, against the Scavs."

"I know," I whisper.

Sighing audibly with a look of regret as though he understands my qualms, he presses his forehead to mine, voice softening.

"It's what Laleh died for. These men are not good men. They came here to hunt us all down, held your father, aunt, and my cousin at the ends of their weapons, and murdered villagers and loyal guards who protected you with their lives. Don't fail us now. We need to defend the people. They need you. I *need* you."

Defend the people...

Gulping past the boulder in my throat, I bury the small voice inside that wonders who defines the greater good when the history of wars is always recorded by the victors.

But maybe Roshan is right: they hurt us first and drew first blood, and I made him a promise to help him usher in an era of peace as the Starkeeper. Head down, I don't look at anyone as I make my way to stand in front of the men, fighting the coils of horror snaking through me.

What should I do? I beg my simurgh, desperate for clarity.

Whatever is in your heart of hearts.

With a silent sob, I wonder if she's channeling Vena. *Not helpful.*

She gives a soft chirp. *As we are not seers, we can only make a decision with the information we have at the time.*

"You're doing the right thing," Clem says when I walk past her.

Am I?

My simurgh gathers inside, the magic coalescing into a bright ball in my chest and blasting from the runes on my arms. I hear the gasps of awe and fear, and the subsequent cries for mercy.

Glancing over my shoulder, I meet Roshan's hard gaze. For a heart-stopping moment, I imagine I see deep purplish whorls clouding his eyes, but then it's an arrow to my own heart when he gives me a curt, emotionless nod.

I bite my lip so hard I taste blood as my starlight ignites in white-hot, iridescent ribbons of flame.

"Burn," I whisper.

My dreams are brutal.

I toss and I turn, but they have me in an inexorable grip, relentless and punishing.

Gods, their faces. The terrified cries of the villagers who'd known me as a child and saw me as one of them . . . and now see me as a stranger. An *executioner*.

Even though I'd been quick in actuality—my magic barely a flash before the two dozen armed assassins had crumbled to ash, borne away on a wind I'd summoned—in my nightmare, I smell their charred flesh and hear their pleas on an endless loop. Eventually, no evidence of them remains, except for Sandar, who stares at me like I am a demon incarnate.

I am, after all, the monster he believes me to be.

My eyes fly open, the first light of dawn slanting through my glass windows. The weight of their souls is a crushing burden. How many of them had been convinced that what they were doing was right? That attempting to assassinate the king was their purpose?

They brought the judgment on themselves . . .

Roshan's words from last night are little comfort. He'd ordered the death sentence, but I had fulfilled it. I draw my knees up to my chest, holding them tight with my arms. The remnants of my argument with the king do not offer any consolation.

"How does this not make us as bad as them?" I'd asked Roshan.

His expression had been unrecognizable. "I am the king of Oryndhr. My enemies need to understand the consequences of going against me."

"But you could have gone about this a different way. A humane way." I'd glanced to Clem for support, but she had shaken her head.

"He's right, Sura," she'd said. "We can't afford to be merciful when our foes are not."

"Merciful?" I'd scoffed. "Our response was monstrous."

"Sometimes you have to be a monster to kill the monsters," Aran had interjected, though I could see the sorrow on his face before he wiped the emotion away so Roshan wouldn't see it. That was telling— why would he hide his true reactions from his cousin? He was the king's chancellor, his *adviser*. And yet, even Aran had seemed unusually meek.

I'd known I couldn't convince them, and it was much too late to change anything, but I'd persisted anyway . . . perhaps out of my own monumental guilt. "But we're *not* monsters. Those are men who might have been led astray by a heretic. We don't even know who this oracle is. You have a duty to your people, Ro, even those who might be your opposition."

Oh, he hadn't liked that—me taking him to task in front of his trusted circle. "It's not your place to question my rule."

That had struck like the blow he'd meant it to be.

My face must have reflected my hurt, because remorse had leaked over his features. "Leave us," he'd told the others. "This is hard for me, too," he'd said once we were alone. "By the maker, you think I wanted to kill those men? I had no choice."

"There's always a choice."

"Ruling is not that simple, Sura." He'd raked a hand through his hair, the brief glimpse of softness in his expression disappearing. "Look, perhaps it would be better if we . . . both had some breathing room. You're upset, and I don't want to say something I don't mean. I'll go back to Kaldari, and you can stay here to visit with your father and aunt until the morning."

I'd frowned. "We promised to be honest with each other, remember?"

"And I *am*, Sura," he'd said. "Gods, I can't bear you looking at me like that. This path is paved with brutal decisions, and I need you with me. But I understand if you can't."

"You'd let me remain here?"

The words had slipped out, the hope in them at being released something I'd stupidly been unable to hide, and the bitter devastation on his face had hit me hard. It'd vanished in a blink, his features stiffening with practiced neutrality. "*Tonight*, Suraya. I'll give you tonight because we both need space. But you'll return tomorrow, and we will continue the tour as planned."

So magnanimous of him.

In truth, I'd appreciated the reprieve, even with Clem and a few guards staying behind. I needed the time to process my emotions separate from the king, and I'd fallen into a restless slumber in my bed immediately after Roshan left.

But everything aches: my body, my mind, my heart.

I need . . . *him*. My shadow god.

My eyes flutter shut as I curl back under the blankets, hoping that sleep won't continue to elude me. But my brain is still churning in a sour mix of bitterness, guilt, and anger that I can't seem to overcome. Eventually, however, I give in to utter exhaustion and dream of nothing until a devoted hand brushes over my hair.

At first, the light touch makes me think of Vena and then, achingly, of my mother—but the scent of smoky darkness and oud that accompanies it is deeply familiar. My silver-haired knight in stygian armor who always seems to appear in my dreams whenever I am distressed. I'm thankful for that, at least, even if my delusions are all in my head, though admittedly, my mysterious visitor becomes more substantial the more often I imagine him.

Even in my dream state, I feel my body instantly at ease with his presence.

"You came," my lips shape.

You called.

Usually his visits take on a more erotic slant, but these unhurried ministrations feel kind and compassionate, as if he senses—and by *he*, I mean my subconscious, clearly—that I am in need of solace and tenderness. I sigh in quiet gratitude as those long, gentle fingers graze my brow, ghosting over my fluttering eyelids. His mouth touches my brow in the sweetest of kisses. For the first time since the horrific execution, my chaotic thoughts abate.

His mystical presence lulls me into a placid state of somnolence, a thousand gentle shadows stroking me into quiet serenity.

Rest and release your burdens to me, Starbright. I am here.

I sleep. Finally.

A SCANT FEW hours later when I wake, the sun is bright in my bedroom, making me squint as I sit up. I inhale a deep breath of the warm air, letting it fill my tight lungs. Rising, I peer out into the desert from the window, the sand dunes rolling in shimmering bands of silver and gold as the morning sun crests over them in the distance.

But the beauty I can always find to cheer me up is absent.

All I see is blood. On my hands. On my *name*.

Futile tears trickle out of my eyes. I lay my head on the windowsill and count the dunes that I can see, but my childhood trick to calm myself doesn't work as well as it used to.

"Peapod?"

Snapped out of my thoughts, I turn to see my father leaning on the doorjamb, his solemn face wreathed in concern.

"Papa." The wobbled word doesn't even come out fully before I'm a blubbering mess that he swiftly gathers into his big, welcoming arms. I bury my face in his shirt, neither of us caring that I'm soaking him in the process.

"All will be well, my girl," he murmurs, rubbing my back in soothing circles.

I sob harder. "It won't. I'm a monster. Everyone saw what I *did*."

"And they also heard what the king commanded you to do," he says gently. "Besides, you handled a difficult act with so much care and grace. It was fast, finished in a blink. Even if you were watching, you wouldn't have seen any pain on their faces."

"Truly?" I sniffle.

"I promise you." He hugs me tighter. "That magic of yours is powerful. All I saw was a bright light that had me shutting my eyes and it was done. You did the best you could."

I swallow hard at his unwavering faith in me. *Did* I? Or should I have fought harder?

Breathing deeply, I stay tucked in his arms for a few more minutes before sniffing and wiping my face. My skin is hot and splotchy, and I'm sure my eyes have probably swollen to twice their size. The second I think it, a cooling sensation rolls over me and what feels like a cold compress rests against my eyelids. *Thank you, my simurgh.*

With reluctance, I step out of my father's embrace and scoop my thick hair up into a tail, finger-combing it and securing it with a tie. I'm sure my magic can fix that, too, but the familiar action helps to calm the noise in my head.

"So," he says, "how are you feeling, really?"

"Like everyone is afraid of me."

He winks. "I'm not afraid of you."

"Nor am I," a voice says at the door, and I smile at Amma, who is carrying a steaming plate of food: a large serving of her famous roasted crushed tomatoes with onion and salted fish, and fresh, flaky layers of piping-hot flatbread. My mouth instantly waters. Normally she's very strict about only allowing food downstairs, but she must be making an exception, given recent events.

"Thanks, Amma," I say, and sit at my desk to eat while she perches on the edge of my bed. I break off a piece of the flatbread and dip it in the sauce before popping it in my mouth. Maker above, there's nothing like a home-cooked meal to make a girl feel cherished, especially one from Amma. My eyes sting again.

"How are you holding up, love?" she asks.

"Better now," I say through another mouthful. I swallow. "But I wish I were staying here longer. I miss . . . home."

She frowns. "Why can't you?"

I exhale. "I promised the king that I would stand by his side, to present a clear message and ensure the peace. You saw what happened here with the assassins. He needs my help to keep the houses in line."

"Is that what you want?" my father asks, moving to sit next to Amma. "Kaldari is still a pit of vipers, and I have no trust in a system that aims to govern without counterbalances."

His opinion on the capital as well as the monarchy doesn't surprise me, considering how much persecution he and my mother faced running away with me. My father has always been a rebel. "Still riding against the monarchy, Papa?" I ask.

He shrugs. "Tyranny is born when service cedes to control and duty falls to power. There are those of us who keep a close watch on the seeds of oppression being sowed."

"Roshan isn't like that. He wants peace."

"That may be. But he is using you—and *fear*—to gain it," Papa says, face fierce with concern for me. "I ask again: Is that what you want? Because if it isn't, I will find a way to keep you here, even if it means going against the king."

"Always my greatest defender," I murmur.

I keep eating, mulling over my jumbled thoughts. I'm sick of Kaldari, of being constantly followed, of obeying all these new rules for my supposed safety, of being stared at and whispered about. Not that the latter wouldn't happen here, especially after last night, but at least I've known these people my whole life.

"I love him," I say eventually. "And he loves me. I have to believe that all of this is temporary, and the sooner it's behind us, the faster we can move on to living our lives."

I know the moment I say it that it's a naive, wishful stance. There's no way that either of us, especially a king with a kingdom to rule, will ever get to *live our lives*. As Papa alluded to before, duty will always take precedence—a good ruler is first and foremost in service to his people.

And despite recent events, Roshan needs me.

"The truth is I can't abandon him," I admit. "He's lost the only family he had, and the only one who ever protected him was his father." I glance at mine. "I suppose he has Aran, his cousin, whom you've met, Papa. I saw the two of you talking for a while."

"The Lord Chancellor seems like a man of honor," my father says. "A bit idealistic, with grandiose notions of the perfect egalitarian society, but he promises to keep an eye on things. He also promised to send me regular reports and make sure that the king treats *you* well. He told me that you've been excelling in your magical studies."

I lift one shoulder and mop up the rest of the sauce with the last piece of flatbread. "I don't know about excelling, but he's a good teacher. I'm learning more about my magic every day."

Papa wrinkles his nose and scrubs a palm over his bushy beard. "He has strong views about the gods. He insists that Saru is trapped somewhere, which was why the queen nearly succeeded at bringing Fero's return. Says he's scouring the history books for any mention of the hand of Saru. Some god-touched sword that has been missing for centuries that can be used to banish a god for good."

"A *god-touched* sword?" I echo, frowning. Saru has been in godsleep since the hundred years' war when he vanquished his twin brother, Fero.

"Indeed. There was a prophecy connected to it, too. Something about godslayers and lightbreakers and killing blades." He shrugs. "You know I don't believe in any of that soothsayer nonsense."

I let out a disbelieving huff of laughter. "Papa, I *am* one of those prophecies. I'm the Starkeeper, remember?"

My father folds his arms over his chest. "Speaking of that, he also told me how you brought the king back from the dead with your magic."

"He did?" Dread fills me at the memory. Shuddering, I bite the inside of my cheek so hard I taste blood. "I've never felt darkness like that, Papa. The queen... she nearly undid... everything Mama tried to do...." I trail off, my throat tightening at the recollection of her mottled skin and bloodred eyes, and the foul essence of the nebulous god she'd summoned. I'd come *so* close to dying.

"Sura." Amma lets out a distressed noise as if sensing my terror. Considering my mother was her sister, she would have known about Queen Morvarid's vile magic.

"I still feel like Fero is here sometimes, in the dead of night," I confess. "That I never quite got rid of him. That he's watching... and waiting... to strike when I least expect it."

"He can't hurt you, Sura," my father says.

I rub my cold arms, a rash of goose pimples appearing out of nowhere. "How do you know?"

Amma is the one to answer, her voice soft. "Because the god of death needs three things to take corporeal form," she says. "Akasha, a death magi, and an anchor."

Papa nods. "Morvarid might have her devotees, but they are not as powerful as she was. And you are protected by your magic as well as the king at your side."

I rub my arms again. "So you're saying it's safer to stay with him."

"I'm saying you should not do this alone, my brave peapod," he replies. "You need allies. You *can* protect yourself, we have all seen that, but even the best warrior has chinks in their armor, and sometimes the deadliest of enemies can strike from within."

I stare sharply at him. "Did Aran tell you that?"

"What?"

"That there's someone on the inside," I say in a low voice, "who has been feeding our enemies information. They knew we would stay here in Coban last night. Only those in Roshan's inner circle would have been privy to the king's plans."

"Vipers slither at the heart of every court," he mutters.

"Promise me you will be vigilant, Sura," Amma says, and taps her breastbone. "Trust the creature inside of you."

My simurgh unfurls and stretches, peering from my eyes at my aunt and my father, and joy radiates from her. *Kin.* The single word conveys a wealth of emotion, of connection and love, along with a deep desire to see them protected.

"She says you both must do the same. Safeguard each other." I stare at my aunt, whose face has paled. "Amma, what's the matter?"

But her eyes roll back in her head as my father releases a worried shout. The hypnotic voice that emerges from her lips isn't hers. It's Vena's, one I know well, though I haven't heard from my celestial guardian of sorts in a while.

Not since the night I died.

"Prepare, Starkeeper, for the battle of earth and sky has begun. The godslayer will rise over the embers of war."

Chapter Three

The essence of an ancient god skitters over my skin like a thousand spiders seeking entry, scuttling, burrowing, and binding me with bloodred skeins of webbing even as they crawl into my eyes, my nose, my mouth. I can't move. I can't see. I can't scream. I can only lie there in frozen horror as I feel myself being slowly devoured.

The godslayer will rise...

Magic rips through the dark in bursts of starlight.

I wheeze, fighting for breath, a phantom chokehold on my throat and air trickling into my lungs as the snare of shadow dissipates from the glow of my simurgh. Vena's words reverberate like a gong in the hollow silence. I rub my neck with numb fingers and press a fist to my too-tight chest, reaching with my free hand for the man lying asleep beside me. Deep, even breaths signal Roshan's undisturbed rest.

Heart still racing, I stare at the ceiling, the feeling of dread weighing like sludge in my veins. My palms are warm—akasha swirling through the runes patterned on my skin in an echo of battle as images from the fresh night terror linger in my mind. I shudder.

Fero's gone, I tell myself.

The god of death has been banished for good. We are safe. *I'm* safe.

It's not the first time I've had this dream, nor will it be the last. And between qualms of a resurrected Fero and the forewarning of Vena's mysterious godslayer, coupled with pervasive dread at Roshan's ruthless expectations of me, sleep is the last thing I've been getting for the past month since Coban.

Curling onto my side, I bite my lip. A sleepless night or two is a small price to pay to keep peace in the realm. At least, that's what I keep telling myself, though the mounting cost feels unforgivably hard on my soul. And each day, the king seems to slip further and further away from the prince I fell in love with. Ever since our return, he has been increasingly distant, as though something has irreparably fractured between us.

Trust, perhaps? Or maybe something even deeper.

The subsequent trips to Jaxx and Veniar had been harrowing. As he'd predicted, the story of my actions in Coban had spread far and wide, sowing seeds of fear and reverence in equal measure. The king demands obeisance and his dissenters kneel, and when they don't, I am commanded to punish.

I've turned more assassins to ash since then.

Murderers, mercenaries—evil men, certainly, but taking a life is taking a life. I fear a part of me dies each time Ris, the god of the afterlife, receives a new arrival at my hand. But the houses need to be brought to heel, at least according to the king's war council.

Maybe these constant nightmares are atonement for my sins.

With each brutal tithe on my magic, the akasha coursing through me feels different. My simurgh has been growing stronger and fiercer. There's a primal *wildness* to her that unsettles me. When I'd addressed my worry with Aran, he'd explained that in ancient times of the magi, ascending magic had to be anchored because of its potency, usually via the bonding of a soul-fated pair.

There'd been no information as far as he knew of such an anchor for the Starkeeper, but power like mine would only evolve if there was the *possibility* of a soul-fated union. It was baffling, to say the least. Because magic matching mine doesn't exist, at least not in Oryndhr.

Roshan isn't my soul-fated, that much I do know, since he possesses no magic, despite both of his parents being magi. Aran maintains that any inherited akasha might still be dormant, especially after my starlight had essentially resurrected Roshan from the brink of death.

Admittedly, I'd harbored an infinitesimal hope that he could be my not-yet-awakened soul-fated, but alas, my simurgh senses nothing but minute traces of me in his blood.

However, magic or not, I'd still *chosen* him.

My parents hadn't been soul-fated, and they'd lived happily together for years.

Roshan's father, the former king, had been soul-fated with Roshan's mother: the only soul-fated pair in centuries. As far as Aran remembers, they had never performed the bonding ritual to anchor their magic—there'd been no time to do so before Nihira had been jealously murdered by her sister, Morvarid. Soul-fated pairs are so rare, they're practically myth.

And if I had one anywhere in this realm, I'd know.

My *simurgh* would know.

There has to be a way to anchor *myself* and to stabilize whatever this latest ascendancy is. I just have to figure it out before my magic becomes more feral and puts us all in danger. Perhaps Vena will be able to shed some light on the matter . . . if she ever actually shows her face again, that is. Apart from her cryptic premonition, the Royal Star has been frustratingly absent.

Quietly, I push the covers off and ease from the bed, grabbing the dagger in its sheath on the bedside table. My mother's blade that I reforged with my own hands is a comfort more than a need. The polished golden head of the simurgh on the hilt is a reminder of where

I came from as well as what I am, and a symbol of the magical entity that lives inside of me.

I feel her ripple in response, a gentle brush along my senses.

It took weeks of training with Aran before I felt even capable of summoning the simurgh's incandescent presence—a majestic, winged spectacle that was everything the king needed me to be. And the moment I had manifested her as a demonstration of my magic in the Oryndhrian court, Roshan's closest naysayers had gone quiet. A king with the powerful Starkeeper as his right hand was invincible.

It's no wonder your keeper doesn't let you out of his sight, an inner voice taunts. *You've become the very thing you said you never wanted to be—weaponized.*

I don't know if it's my conscience or my magic speaking. My simurgh has communicated with me before, but this doesn't sound like her. No, it sounds like the lingering bitterness I've kept at bay since Coban. Exhaling harshly, I push the warning away and swallow the knot rising in my throat. I have to believe that Roshan will keep his promise that this isn't forever.

On silent feet, I pad from the bedroom to the balcony beyond that overlooks the palace courtyard. It's a moonless night, only the barest sliver of a curve visible. No stars wink through the clouds, though I know they're there. I can feel them like part of the living tapestry of my soul. Once, Vena had offered me a chance to join them in immortal rest, but I'd chosen to return to the mortal world for Roshan . . . for a chance at love and a future together.

I've never regretted it, but lately, I find myself wondering if I made the right decision.

Shivering in the cool air, I wrap my arms around myself, peering up. It's been months since Vena spoke through Amma. None of us had been able to discern what she'd truly meant.

I peer up into the sky. "Vena? Are you there? I could really use a friend."

But there's no answer. *Again.*

A sad sigh leaves me. I used to resent when she appeared on a whim in the guise of a crone with her esoteric advice on how to master my Starkeeper gifts, but now, I'd give anything to see a familiar face. Has she abandoned me? Have my actions and the abuse of my gifts sickened her? I would not be surprised: I've sickened myself. My eyes burn with unshed tears for what I've done in the name of the Starkeeper.

In the name of a man I love.

Is this how villains are born? With the best of intentions?

"Sura," a drowsy, deep voice says as two thick arms band over mine and a heavy body crowds mine from behind. "What are you doing out here?"

Desperate for any comfort, I lean back into my king's tall frame, breathing in his earthy iron-and-bergamot scent. Emotion swamps me. Stars, I've missed him. Missed *this*. Being held by him for no reason at all. One would think sleeping in the same bed would mean something, but most nights, he collapses after hours spent arguing with his council on matters of the realm, or he's gone for days to other cities to meet with the houses or the Dahaka.

"I was watching the stars," I murmur.

Roshan nuzzles my neck, and I sigh at the unexpected caress. Court life leaves little room for affection, not in public anyway, and especially not when I'm now the king's most prized weapon. Keeping up appearances as rulers to be feared is worth more than indulging ourselves in any stolen moments. "It's cold out here. Come back to bed."

Not wanting to give up whatever this tiny moment of connection is, I sketch the rune for fire in my mind, feeling my magic flare in response. Suddenly the crisp air around us heats to a balmy temperature. I've mastered most basic elemental runes working with Aran—fire, ice, air, and earth—but I'm still working on more complex magic, including wielding my own starlight.

"Better?" I ask Roshan.

"You've become adept," he says with fond amusement.

"Practice makes perfect, as Aran says." Twisting, I turn in his arms to face him, his handsome features still softened from sleep. Thick-lashed tawny eyes peer into mine, a half smile curling his full lips. A lock of inky hair falls onto his brow, and I reach up to sweep it away. "I miss you," I whisper.

"I know," he says quietly. "I'm sorry I've been gone so often. House Antares is proving to be difficult and unwilling to sign the terms of the latest tax and tithe treaties." Warm lips brush my brow. "Perhaps you can accompany me to Eloni in the coming days."

The weight of that crushes me. Most likely, I'll be joining as his weapon to hold over their heads, not as the woman he can't bear to be parted from. "I want . . . I wish . . ." I trail off and bite the inside of my cheek, but the words tumble out anyway. "I miss *us*, Ro. Sometimes I wish it could be like it was in Nyriell."

His brown eyes warm with the memory of our time in the hidden city of the Dahaka, when we'd been on the run for our lives. It had been us against the world, or so I'd thought at the time. I hadn't known then that he'd been the secret leader of the rebellion all along, and while the knowledge of his lies and the depth of his secrecy had gutted me, I'd forgiven him. He'd died to save me, after all, and everyone deserves a chance at redemption.

Roshan's arms tighten around me. "I do, too," he says. "This will be over soon, my sweet starling. Can you be patient? For me?"

Heart aching, I nod, because what else can I do? "I'd like to visit my father and Amma again. I miss them, and it's been hard to be alone when you're gone."

His breath gusts against my hair, and I feel his hesitation even before he gives voice to the denial. "It's too dangerous now," he says after a careful beat. "Too many people want to get to me and won't hesitate to hurt you to do so. I don't trust my enemies in Regulus, and I know they have many spies in the capital. We still haven't found who was behind everything in Coban. You're too vulnerable there, and I need you where I can protect you."

Led by Clem and Hamid, Roshan's kingsguard had interrogated everyone in the court, using a truth herb called Verac root from the northern lands, and no secret plot was uncovered. Which means either it had been an unlikely coincidence or our palace spy remains at large. Regardless, I don't want to be a prisoner, locked in my rooms and slowly losing touch with reality. In the king's absence, I haven't been allowed to so much as leave our quarters without an armed escort.

"You know I can protect myself, Roshan," I reply, not wanting to argue and lose the preciousness of the moment, but his refusal grates like sandpaper on my skin. "It won't be for very long, I promise. I just need . . . my family."

"It's not safe."

"For whom?" I snap.

Something like a snarl rumbles in his chest as he tips my chin up, and for a second before his lashes dip down, I glimpse whorls of violet darkening his irises, but when they reopen, his brown eyes are clear, if worried.

I blink. What *was* that? Had I imagined it?

The combination of my lingering fears about Fero and Vena's words about war and rising godslayers has me doubting my own senses. But what if I *hadn't* imagined it? Suddenly, I recall the same purple flicker in Coban, and fear blooms like acid on my tongue. A seed of darkness can take root anywhere.

I wonder . . . I've been inside his mind before, when I'd brought him back to life with my magic. I was able to sense his whole aura then. Could I do the same now?

Surreptitiously, I push out a sliver of magic toward him and brace for the worst, that somehow the king has been compromised by unnatural forces. It would explain everything: his behavior, the strange fire in his eyes, his anger.

But there's nothing there . . . nothing but *him*. No darkness. No seeded remnant of Fero. Just love and worry for me, as well as concern for the future of his kingdom.

Appeased, I pull the thread back and find him staring at me as if he'd spoken and I hadn't responded. I flush, aware that I'd entered his mind without consent, but my relief at confirming that he's wholly himself washes away any guilt. Ensuring that the king is safe from harm, even unknowingly from himself, is in the interests of the entire realm.

I clear my throat as his finger traces my jaw. "What did you say?"

"It's not safe for anyone, and I don't think it's a good idea. Not right now. Perhaps in a month when things calm down."

Resentment bleeds through me, but I hide it. "You said that weeks ago."

He drops his arms and scrubs a hand through his hair. "I didn't know Regulus was going to make a bid to unseat me with a so-called legitimate nephew." Roshan bends to rest his chin on my head. "I need you, Suraya. I need you here, or . . . we'll lose everything we've worked so hard to gain. After all the sacrifices we have made."

"Is it me you need or the Starkeeper?" I regret the clipped words as soon as they are out of my mouth.

He sucks in a breath, his voice agonized. "How can you even think such a thing? I love *you*, Sura."

Remorse immediately swamps me for voicing such an awful thought, but my inner voice perks up: *He doesn't hesitate to herd you into being his showpiece, either.* Frustration flares anew, but I tamp it down. "I'm sorry. That's not . . . what I meant."

Roshan sweeps an arm behind us. "Haven't I given you everything you could want? A palace? Your own forge? A life of luxury." I freeze, surprised at his words. When did those things become conditional? His thumb feathers over my lower lip. "You're my queen. We're a team, my precious starling," he whispers. "Us against the world, remember?"

A starling in a pretty cage...

And it's us against the world, but only as it suits him, it seems.

The simmering desolation in my heart swells. A few sweet, tender words can't erase the chasm that has been widening between us. I want to please Roshan because, yes, underneath all the umbrage, I do love him. But love also requires some measure of reciprocity. It's a give and take, not a one-way path, and I have to stand up for myself or risk being overrun at every turn.

"I love you with everything that I am, Ro, but I have to see my father and Amma," I say. "Don't you care that I am lonely and dispirited?"

A muscle in his jaw flexes, his mouth going tight. "Don't be like this."

"Like what?"

Roshan's nostrils flare. "Petulant."

The word is an arrow through my heart and I flinch. *"Petulant?"* I echo. "You think what I want is petulant?"

He rubs his brow as a divot of irritation forms between them. "There's more at stake here than your family," he replies as if chiding a child, and my spine stiffens. "Unrest in the kingdom is rampant from the capital to Nyriell, and the Scavs also have ties with this oracle threat, which changes everything. I need you to be safe, Sura. This is for your protection."

We're going around in useless circles. I beg and he denies. I'm trapped and I fucking hate it. "You can't keep me here against my will."

"I'm the king," he says evenly.

My eyes sting with a pressure I'm growing to despise. "And I'm your . . ." The words choke me. What am I? I'm his tool. Not his partner or his wife, and certainly not his queen. ". . . subject."

"You're more than that and you know it."

Clenching my jaw, I turn around and grip the balcony rails, my fingers becoming numb against the cold iron. My simurgh uncoils restlessly inside of me but waits for my lead. We have a tenuous understanding when it comes to the king . . . and his reign over us.

"Fine," I say. "Whatever pleases His Imperial Majesty."

He exhales. "Sura, enough, please." When I refuse to acknowledge him, he sighs heavily. "Don't stay out here too long in the cold." He hesitates when I remain silent. "You're the most important thing in my life."

"Am I?" I ask.

"You know you are. But I can't afford to be selfish when the people of Oryndhr need me to be the king they deserve, to keep them safe."

"The king they deserve? Or merely a slightly less tyrannical version of your brother?" I swallow hard at his sharp inhale and glance over my shoulder. His eyes have gone flinty, mouth a thin line of displeasure. I recognize the expression. This is the face the king of Oryndhr shows his enemies, not his beloved. "Ruling by oppression has never led to anything good. Your people are living in fear, under laws that you've imposed. Your army camps on their doorsteps, Roshan. That's not safety. You can't keep someone safe by locking them away!" I say furiously.

He glares, knowing I'm speaking of more than the people of Oryndhr. "When the threat is over, they will be safe. *You* will be safe."

I shake my head. "And when will that be? Six months from now? A year? Ten years?"

"When I say it is!" he shouts.

A loud rap on the bedchamber door has us both swiveling. "Your Majesty? Is all well?"

"Yes," he calls back to the guard. The king regards me once more, shoving his hands into his pockets and visibly attempting to calm himself. "I don't want to fight."

Too late for that. I pin my lips between my teeth, trying to keep my stupid tears at bay. All the power of the universe at my fingertips, and I'm on the verge of breaking down into pathetic sobs.

Roshan steps close and cradles my face in his large hands. "I didn't mean to yell. I'm on edge about other things, but that's no excuse. We'll go to Coban after Eloni, I promise. How's that?"

"Thank you," I say thickly.

"You're welcome. Remember I love you, Suraya, and anything I do is out of love and for your well-being."

My brows draw together at the somberness of his tone, but then his lips are on mine, silencing any reply. The kiss is sweet and soothing, stirring feelings inside of me to life—but the grasp of his fingers on my chin tightens ever so slightly when his mouth slants open, demanding more. It's not rough, exactly, but it makes me tense, more so when the fingers of his free hand wind into my hair and angle my head back. Usually, I enjoy his assertiveness in the bedroom, but tonight, after our exchange, it feels like he's exerting much more than that. Like this act—this *positioning*—is a punctuation of something.

His royal will.

When he breaks the strange but not wholly unwelcome kiss, his eyes are flickering with a combination of desire . . . and despair? I blink. Why would he look so torn? Perhaps he's as upset as I am about the distance between us, about the quarrels that have grown more frequent. Sands, am I the unreasonable one here? He is the king, after all, responsible for an entire kingdom.

"Truce?" I offer softly.

Roshan stares down at me, his handsome face solemn and unreadable. Usually, he wears his emotions on his sleeve with me, but lately, he has become skilled at hiding them. He lifts his hand as if to caress my face again, but it lingers in the air between us for a half second before falling away. "Promise you don't hate me for loving you too much."

"I could never hate you, Ro."

His smile is small and doesn't reach his eyes. Alarm bleeds through me and I grasp his wrist.

"We can work through this, you know that, right? All couples have disagreements. It's natural." I let out a self-deprecating laugh. "You knew who I was going into this. I've never been a passive woman."

Finally, those eyes light. "No, you're not."

"But I love you and we'll get through this," I tell him.

"I know we will," he agrees. He kisses me again, this one soft and barely a graze over my mouth. "Come back to bed soon, please?"

"I will."

When Roshan goes into the bedchamber, I stare up at the skies, willing my aching heart to calm. The clouds have thickened, and now the moon is no longer visible. I lift my palm and call the rune for fire again, watch as a dancing flame appears. It curls over and between my fingers, not hot but warm. A flicker of light across the courtyard catches my eye, on a balcony off one of the other towers. I smile. Aran holds a similar flame aloft.

I lift a hand to wave, and notice the redheaded woman emerging from his quarters to tug him back inside. Helena. My former nemesis. I say *former* because she and her father have both bent the knee to prove their loyalties to Roshan and the Imperial House, and, by default, me as the king's future betrothed. It's no shock she has now set her sights on Aran, the king's most valued adviser.

We would never be true friends—largely because she once tried to kill me in the arena—but I can applaud her ambition. In a world of men, we women have to fight for every scrap of power we can get. I'd never fault anyone for advocating for themselves via any means at their fingertips.

My lips curl into a wry smile. From how easily Aran lets himself be led back to bed, I'd say he's not complaining one bit.

Good for him.

Apart from Roshan, he and Clem are my only real friends in court, though Clem and I are nowhere as close as Laleh and I had been. Sadness wells in my heart at the thought of my best friend, who had died under Morvarid's knife. The memory of Laleh's death is gutting. Not a day goes by that I don't think of her, wishing she were here to delight in the pleasures of the palace we'd once dreamed about.

Go to bed, I imagine her saying now. *Or you'll wake up with unsightly bags under your eyes, and who wants to see that? Go spoon that tall drink of water you call a king . . . and then fork him well.*

I laugh softly. Stars, I miss her.

With one last glance to the darkened sky, I step back into the bedchamber where Roshan is already asleep. I need to be patient with him, I remind myself. We're both under immense pressure. What's a few more weeks or months when we have forever ahead of us? I slide under the covers and tuck myself into his side. He murmurs sleepily and throws a heavy arm over me.

"Forgive me, Sura," he murmurs incoherently. "Own . . . good . . ."

Heart softening, I smile at his unwitting garbled words and smooth his thick, dark hair away from his brow. The gods know the truth of the matter: I'll forgive him almost anything.

Chapter Four

One thing about a new king's coronation that I'll never get used to is the number of fancy balls and ten-course dinners I'm expected to attend. Months into Roshan's reign, and half the time is spent figuring out how to pave the way for peace while the other half is spent plying these very well-fed nobles with food, drink, and dancing to make them feel venerated and important. Being a part of the royal court is exhausting.

And, of course, the Starkeeper must always be present.

Smoothing my voluminous clothing in the Imperial House traditional purple-and-gold colors, I inhale deeply and compose my face into a neutral mask at the entrance doors before nodding at the guards on duty to open them. Their hands are shaking, I notice, and I sigh at the incongruity of my roles as weapon and consort, the former clearly gaining a lot more notoriety than the latter.

As I enter the ballroom, I can taste the collective fear of those around me on my tongue like something bitter, even as their whispers are hidden by hands. I've become an effective tool to send the message throughout the realm that no treason will be tolerated, and gossip flies faster than fire. Now the entire court no longer stares at me with barely veiled disdain as the common-born future queen; they stare at me as the king's murderous right hand. Even though I perform the execrable duty quickly, it feels as though everyone can see the blood dripping from my fingers.

Little do they know I'm drowning in blood.

"Starkeeper, how lovely you look," a low voice says, and I turn to glower at Aran. He knows how much I've come to detest the moniker that has now come to stand for death instead of hope.

"Thank you, Lord Chancellor," I reply with sweet venom, taking in his formal charcoal-gray uniform with his gold-embroidered purple sash. "As do you."

His lips quirk as he pulls a face. "Touché. I loathe that title. How are you?"

I shrug. "I've not been asked to murder anyone today, so life is good."

"Sura," he says, eyes compassionate, "you know that using your power like this is the last thing he wants, the last thing any of us wants, but if we don't put an end to brewing insurrection, more innocents will suffer. This is for the greater good of Oryndhr."

It's a miracle I keep my face from showing my contempt—I have heard those words so many times that they ring hollow to my ears. The greater good isn't always *good*, not when people die. "Have you or Clem discovered any more about who the oracle is?" I ask. "Roshan mentioned that the Scavs have ties to them now. Isn't that concerning?"

He nods. "The king has a plan for the Scavs, and as far as the mysterious oracle, we're getting closer. They can't hide forever. But in the meantime, you're the only way we can prevail."

"I know. I just . . . It's killing me, Aran." To my horror, I feel my eyes swim with unwanted tears. "I see their faces, wonder about their families. It's not right. We shouldn't be ruling by fear. We have to earn the people's trust."

"First, we have to weed out the traitors," Aran says.

I bite my lip. "You sound like him."

"Think of how many you're saving," he says. "Those mercenaries are not innocent, Sura. There are nobles who would do anything to see themselves on the throne instead of a bastard. They need to know the consequences of not offering their fealty." His mouth curls into a smile. "Together, you and Roshan are unstoppable."

"Roshan and me, or Roshan and the Starkeeper?" I murmur.

"Both, Sura. *Of course* both. He loves you."

I exhale and rub the heel of my palm over my aching chest. "He doesn't tell me anything anymore. He's started keeping me in the dark about talks with the council and his so-called plans. I have no idea what he intends to do about the Scavs or the oracle, and I have to hear about border skirmishes by accident."

"Because he's trying to protect you!" Aran says vehemently, taking me by surprise. "It's not like you've hidden your condemnation when he asks you to stand by him against his foes. He knows you hate fighting his battles, so why would he burden you with them? Think of it from his point of view, Sura. My cousin loves you and will do anything for you."

I open my mouth and close it, contradictory emotions warring inside of me. "I know he does, and I'm on his side. I had hoped to be an equal partner, to have my opinions be heard, but he refuses to listen or even confide in me. It feels like I'm nothing but his pawn." I lift my hands. "A convenient deadly weapon."

"Don't say that," Aran says, looking distraught. "Let me talk to him."

At that moment, a group of dignitaries from Veniar summons Aran. After he excuses himself to greet them, I can't help my conflicted feelings of being cherished but caged, of being treasured but not trusted. I try to distract myself by watching the couples dancing in their finery. An alderman from Regulus catches my eye. He's tall with salt-and-pepper hair, and he's dancing with a familiar face—his daughter Helena.

Both of them are masters of court intrigues, and, unlike me, she has been raised from birth to navigate these ever-eddying waters. Even now, her expression is calm but calculating as she surveys the room, missing nothing. When she whirls past, I meet those glacial, intelligent blue eyes, and they narrow slightly before she inclines her head toward me in a polite show of deference. I nod back just as graciously.

I have no doubt if things changed between Roshan and me that she would be first in line angling for a crown of her own, but again, I don't fault her for that. And although Roshan has made his intentions clear with regards to me as his future queen, he hasn't formally proposed yet, which begs the question as to where I actually stand. The plain truth is I don't wear the king's ring and I'm a fool if I don't believe anyone has noticed.

As if my thoughts have summoned him, I feel his commanding presence.

"Starling, you outshine every star in the sky."

That warm baritone makes my heart stutter as he lifts my knuckles to his lips. Stars, but he's handsome in his kingly finery, the rich purple of his ceremonial tunic edged with deep gold complementing the burnished tones of his skin. His dark hair is brushed away from his crown, and his brown eyes sparkle with a light I haven't seen in what feels like forever.

"You look well, my king," I say.

"Well?" he teases. "That's all the praise I get?"

I raise both brows, surprised to witness this playful side of him, which is normally hidden at court events. He must have received some good news to be this happy. Or perhaps he's trying to find a path forward for us, too. "Compliments have to be earned, Your Majesty."

"So what can this desperate fool do to earn sweet accolades from the most beautiful woman in the room?" he says as he draws me toward the middle of the ballroom floor. "Perhaps she will deign to grace him with a dance?"

"Only if he begs nicely."

He lowers those ridiculously long eyelashes, fingers trailing down my arm and leaving flickers of heat in their wake. "*Please*, my sweet, vicious starling, put your beloved out of his misery and dance with him." My core gives an indecent flutter even as the runes on my forearms light up with glimmering radiance. His eyes darken at the effect of his touch on me. "I take that as a yes, then."

"So cocky, my king," I murmur.

"Good thing I can read you like a book."

With a sinfully heated smirk, the king lifts me at the waist and spins me in a dramatic circle that makes my gossamer skirts float in a cloud of gold-kissed lavender to the sounds of polite applause as the musical strains of a slow court waltz begin. He leads me to the center of the room.

"His Royal Majesty, King Roshan Acharia of the Imperial House, and his starblessed chosen, Lady Suraya Saab of the House of Aldebaran," the vizier intones.

I nearly stumble, not realizing this was to be an official spectacle, but I suppose that anything with the king always is. Gone are the days of inconspicuous swaying on the periphery. The nostalgic memory of the first time we'd navigated this room together hits me like a gut punch. My gardener-prince had handed me a glass of elderflower liqueur before we'd danced to a similar song and drawn the attention of the crown prince himself.

A lifetime ago when I was an ordinary girl, and Roshan, an ill-favored son.

Being invisible was a gift we hadn't known the value of.

He bows deeply in front of me, and I perform the requisite curtsy, sinking gracefully to the floor. When I rise, he gathers me into his embrace, one arm slipping around my waist and the other weaving through my fingers. I suck in a breath as his thumb grazes the tender skin of my palm over the star symbol etched there. My runes glimmer again, and that smirk deepens with satisfaction. "Like a book," he whispers.

"Stop it," I say, but let a tendril of my magic wind around him, dancing over any bare skin I can find... at his nape, over his jawline, flicking at his earlobe. I lick my lips and let him feel it with a slick pulse of magic against his own mouth.

"That's not playing fair, my starling," he growls, but that deep brown gaze is alight with mischief and attraction. The sight of *that* look after so long does something to me.

"The rules of fair play don't factor in love and war," I say.

He drags me scandalously close so that my breasts brush his hard chest, making me quiver. "Then I suppose I'll have to change my strategy."

I gasp. "Roshan, people are staring."

"Let them."

My cheeks flame, but deep down, I want him to hold me tighter, to be the gardener I remember, the one who didn't care about propriety or royal etiquette. Conscious of the many pairs of eyes fixed on us—some filled with delight at the king's unusual whimsy, a few with evident, undisguised jealousy, and others with guarded wariness at the deadly weapon in their midst—I let our avid audience fade away until it's just the two of us in the room.

If I close my eyes, it almost feels like our first time.

Gods, I want to punch Roshan in his supercilious, controlling, kingly face. How does one go from adoration to aggravation in the space of a handful of days?

"For the love of Saru, I don't require a twelve-guard escort to go to my training with Aran!" I insist, watching as the full dozen of his kingsguard settle in place behind me. "We're in the palace, and it's your cousin." I point through the window to the second turret. "His quarters are right over there. We're supposed to meet in the arena to practice bladework and offensive runes. We aren't even leaving the grounds."

The king tilts his chin, impatience flashing in his eyes. "When I was with the Dahaka, our spies infiltrated the palace all the time. And change of plans, you're not to go to the arena. He'll meet you behind the south tower. You'll work on something else today."

His abrupt high-handedness is maddening—but I'm suddenly more curious about the arena. "Why?" I ask. "What's happening?"

If I weren't looking directly at him, I would have missed the clenching of his jaw and the dark flicker of annoyance at being questioned in his eyes. He shakes his head. "The azdaha has become increasingly violent and restless. Your magic might incite the beast."

"The . . . the azdaha is still here?" I ask, completely taken aback that he even told me the truth for once instead of his usual prevarication.

Dazedly, I recall the poor, captured creature from the arena that Javed used as a macabre sorting tool for his bride trials, culling the weak from the strong in an effort to draw out the Starkeeper. Of course, I hadn't known it was me then.

So many innocent women had died trying to escape the near-feral beast that had been starved and tortured to within an inch of its life. I remember the visceral connection I'd felt . . . when the ancient akasha flowing in its veins had sung to mine.

Pity curls within me at the thought of the poor creature that should be flying free in its own realm locked in a cell somewhere.

"I thought you had sent it back to the northern lands," I say, frowning.

"It was not possible. The terms of peace have changed and our borders with Everlea are no longer secure."

My frown deepens. This is news to me. "What does that mean? Since when?"

Stories about Everlea—the realm ruled by the purported nightmare king to the far north, the land with vast rolling plains occupied by fierce hordes, broad flowing rivers, and bottomless lakes, as well as its shining capital city of Verisia—are rampant in Oryndhr. Our borders have always been protected, if not by natural barriers like the Barrin Mountains, then by strict laws forbidding trade or travel.

A muscle leaps to life in Roshan's rigid cheek, and I wonder if he'll refuse to answer this time. But then his tight expression calms. "We are not only on the verge of a two-pronged civil war, with the nobles attacking from one side and the Scavs on the other, Suraya; we're at risk of one with the Everlean king, a war my brother started by hunting these creatures in the first place. Nightsong is adamant on the beast's safe return."

"Nightsong?"

"Their sovereign. The reports about him are fearsome. His people live under tyranny and are punished for even speaking against his reign. I'm only trying to protect us so that Oryndhrians are safe from reprisal should our lands be breached."

It's more than I expected him to say, but I am eager to continue the first open conversation we've had in weeks on anything concerning the realm. "Can't we just send the azdaha back and avoid war that way?"

"It's too late for that because the creature is dying. In its current condition, war will be declared before we can blink."

"What?" I ask. "How is it *dying*?"

He shakes his head. "We do not know."

"Roshan, you have to return it and explain your position to the king. Surely he'll listen before condemning an entire realm to death in retaliation."

He scrubs a hand over his jaw as if I hadn't spoken. "The Barrin Mountains have always been neutral territory, but Javed wanted to claim it, for his own reasons. The Everlean king refused to cede, saying it was protected land." Roshan glances at me, the lines around his eyes and mouth furrowed in thought. "I believe my brother eventually hoped to use you to take the territory by force, which is why an army of Scavs is still stationed in the northern Dustlands, near Deadman's Canyon."

"General Vogon's army," I murmur, remembering the leader of the Scavs who had been very lucid when he'd tried to take my power before Morvarid had killed him. "Why there, though? The gulch is bottomless and the mountains are impassable."

"My brother had many secrets, least of which was that cursed canyon and whatever the god he served demanded."

A shiver creeps up my spine. "God?"

"Fero." The cavalier way he says it leaves me cold. But abruptly, as if the impulsive explanation is over, Roshan turns away without another word, halting to glance over his shoulder. "Which brings me back to my original point: setting foot in the arena is forbidden for everyone, including you, for your own safety, until we understand what that thing means to Everlea and its king. Do not defy me. I forbid it, Suraya."

I forget my concerns, my anger rising at his implacable tone. He *forbids* it?

Balling my heating palms, I force my face to remain neutral as Roshan walks away, effectively ending any discussion—visible murderous thoughts might be seen as treason, after all—and count to ten in my head before peering at my silent armed contingent.

"Don't crowd me. I don't want to hurt any of you accidentally."

They won't listen. They're all following the directives of the king to the letter, and even if it means getting singed by the Starkeeper, they'll take the risk. Implicit obedience is a thing, and clearly the king expects the same from me.

Well, he can jump off the highest cliff in Oryndhr for all I care.

As we descend the staircase, I spot a familiar face marching toward us. My irritation dissipates as I wave Clem over with a smile. "Please tell me you're part of the guard I've been favored with this morning, though this is grunt work for the great General Clem Jinn."

She grins back, her face lighting up. "Hardly! And today I am."

"Truly?" I ask with delighted surprise.

"I just got back from Xersten, and I needed some down time."

My curiosity spikes, knowing that city's proximity to the canyon Roshan was just speaking about. "What's in Xersten?"

"You know I have to report to the king first," she says, and I swallow a sigh at her unyielding loyalty.

As we enter the courtyard, I can't even appreciate the lush scent of the blooming flowers or the sight of a clear blue sky or hear any birdsong. In fact, all I can hear is the rhythmic stomping of a dozen pairs of feet in my wake. I lean in toward Clem with a scowl. "Tell me you don't think all of this is ridiculous."

She doesn't even have to ask what I'm talking about, glancing at the stone-faced men and women on our heels. "He's protective, and after what has happened, don't you think he should be?"

My scowl deepens. "Obsessive is more like it. You'd think I was made of jādū or something."

Clem belts out an amused laugh. "You kind of are. The only true magical source in all of Oryndhr, and you wonder why he safeguards you like the crown jewels."

"You know what I mean." I shake my head, feeling my irritation rise, if only because she's hit the nail on the head. "And I'm not a thing to be owned or guarded. I'm someone who survived long before he came along *without* magic. He treats me like I can't make any decisions about my own bodily safety for myself." I wiggle my fingers in front of her face. "As if I can't take care of my enemies with a single thought. He's suffocating me, Clem. I'm not one of his soldiers, expected to obey his orders like gospel."

"You mean like me?" she jokes.

I falter. "No, that's not what I . . ."

"I'm only teasing, Sura. I know my place, and yes, I do follow the king's command."

I frown at her. "Even if you don't agree with it?"

"It's not my place to question what's best for the realm."

"How can you say that, Clem?" I ask, keeping my voice low in spite of my disbelief at her blasé response. "He's not infallible. He's a man who *will* make mistakes. He made them as the leader of the Dahaka, remember?" Grimacing, I shake my head. "And what's best for the realm isn't what's best for *me*."

My friend eyes me thoughtfully, gaze flicking over my clenched jaw and balled fists, and then back up to my hair, where the iridescent strands are glowing slightly in between the darker ones. "Perhaps I used the wrong words earlier. Put yourself in his shoes," she says with a sympathetic shrug. "He's lost everyone he called family, not that his stepmother and his half brother could even be considered that, and he doesn't want to lose you. You mean too much to him, Sura."

"He's going to lose me if he continues to be a controlling ass," I mutter through my teeth as the guards direct our entourage toward the third tower instead of the second, where I usually train. "He forbade me from going to the arena, can you believe that?"

"If he did, he probably has an excellent reason for it," she says, patting my arm and then narrowing her eyes at someone in the distance. "Excuse me for a second. I need to check in with Hamid."

Without waiting for my reply, she jogs away. Whatever she's imparting must be important, as her hands gesticulate wildly and her brow crinkles into a fierce frown. She points to the location of the arena, and I let out a resentful breath. Of course she's aware of far more than she lets on; unlike me, who is usually in the dark, they're both kept informed at every step.

Roshan thinks he's protecting me from unnecessary violence, but the irony is plainly lost on him when he uses *me* to eliminate threats to his crown here in Kaldari and elsewhere in the realm. When Clem turns to signal me to continue without her and yells that she'll catch up, my blood is already simmering.

Tight-lipped, I stride past the entrance to the second turret, which leads to the outer arena in the back, and then slow my steps as the path to the amphitheater beckons. What do Clem and Hamid know that I don't? What is Roshan hiding here that he doesn't want me to see? While I recognize his power as king, perversely, I want to go in there *despite* his high-handed command.

"My lady," one of the guards interjects. "The king was very firm in his orders."

I grit my teeth and send him a blank look. "I require use of a privy. Would you prefer to seek out his approval while I soil myself here in the courtyard?"

His eyes widen beneath his helm. "Of course not, my lady. Then I shall accompany you and—"

I interrupt before he can continue. "General Jinn will find me in short order. Wait here, all of you."

"My lady, the king—"

"I'm well aware of what *my betrothed* has said," I say, discomfort filling me at the lie and the unsubtle emphasis on the fact that I'll be queen someday. But the reminder does the job. "You're my escort, and I am instructing you to wait."

They look uncomfortable but, to my great relief, don't attempt to contradict me. Or perhaps it's just that I don't give them opportunity to do so when I whirl on my booted heel and leave. The corridors are cool in the shade, the pristine marble floors polished to a high shine.

Aran's quarters are in this tower, but I'm not interested in our usual meeting spot. I want to find the arena and see the azdaha. I glance over my shoulder to make sure that my overzealous guard isn't following. They will send someone to report to the king, I have no doubt of that, but I have at least a few minutes before they do. I increase my pace.

I'm panting when I exit the tower and enter the wide doors leading into the arena. The sight of the circular dome with its stone rows of seating always hits me the same way. The smell of blood and sweat is embedded in the sands, along with the memory that I almost died here not that long ago. My Starkeeper gifts hadn't yet manifested when we'd been thrown to the wolves—or to the azdaha, in this case—in a fight for our lives on the whim of a selfish crown prince.

The arena is empty now, but I'm interested in the paddock behind it, where I suspect they're keeping the dying azdaha. Not that I don't trust Roshan's word, but I want to see how bad it is for myself. I jog along the perimeter to the exit in the back, passing curious servants. No one tries to stop me, however. Instead, they give me a wide berth. Normally, I'd bemoan my feared status, but now I'm grateful for it, and the closer I get to the paddock, the more the akasha in my blood hums.

I swallow my scowl when I see the entrance to the corral blocked by two heavily armed men, and instead smile pleasantly. "I wish to see the azdaha."

One of the guards stares at me, lifting his lance to bar my path as the other follows his lead. "By order of the king, only the beast's handlers may enter."

"Do you know who I am?" I ask calmly, despite the weapons in my face. When they nod, I step closer. "Then move aside."

"We cannot, my lady."

I barely picture the rune for melting, feeling my power surge, as the two steel lances pointed at me glow white and then red hot before turning to silver liquid. The men shout and drop the ends, staring at me with fright, their wide eyes flicking to my rune-lit arms and wild, glowing hair. "I don't want to hurt you," I say, still calm. "Let me through. When the king comes, tell him I gave you no choice in the matter."

They acquiesce with shaky nods, and I enter the darkened enclosure.

It stinks of blood and excrement. Lifting my sleeve to my nose, I walk quickly past rows of empty stalls to the back where the magic signature is the strongest.

I gasp when the massive creature comes into view, my arm dropping to my side. The azdaha is seemingly bigger now than it had been when I saw it last—especially in these close quarters—and I nearly weep at its enfeebled, sickened state.

It's much worse than I ever could have imagined.

"By all the gods," I whisper. "What have they done to you?"

Chapter Five

Stars, *is* it dying?

Scuffed black and green scales absorb the light. The azdaha's pained, wheezing breaths are loud in the outwardly cramped space. Its enormous head is twenty times bigger than me, with pointed teeth as long as my arm, and its body is the size of a small house. I estimate it's about thirty to forty feet in length, though its tail seems to be curled around itself with its tattered wings folded loosely over scab-ridden flanks.

Jādū bracers are secured to its neck and legs, impairing any magic it might have, and several thick iron chains keep the creature secured to rings in the ground. Two grooms are tending to open wounds on his hindquarters, while a runecaster appears to be working on the cuffs on its limbs, the symbols glowing in the gloom. They all rear back when the beast lets out a tortured, keening whine.

"You're hurting it," I snap.

"My lady," the runecaster says, whirling around. "You can't be in here!"

I straighten my spine. "Leave, all of you."

"It's not safe," he argues. "His Majesty—"

I let my magic rise to the surface of my skin, the telltale iridescence lighting up the corral. "Get. Out."

They scurry past, but not after the runecaster gives me a sullen glare, his nervous gaze flicking to the radiance of my arms. "The king will hear about this."

"By now there's probably a line."

The azdaha's slitted golden gaze meets mine as I approach on silent feet, a warning hiss winding to the rafters. I keep my emotions calm and my intentions clear. I'm not afraid. I only feel a gut-wrenching pity for its suffering and its continued captivity. Tentatively, I open my senses, reaching my magic out for the brief connection I'd found before in the arena.

My lessons with Aran have made me more confident in wielding my power like an extension of myself. In much the same way I'd connected with the king, I delve into the azdaha's aura. But I'm not prepared when my magic links us, rage and pain slamming me in a blast, followed by so much despair that my knees nearly buckle. It's ten times worse than our last encounter—how much torture has this poor thing endured since then?

And *why*?

It keens again in a mournful whine, and I eye the jādū collar with distaste, knowing exactly what it's for. The azdaha is ancient with powerful, though clearly inhibited, magic. It's close to death—Roshan had spoken true—its withering magic evident from the dearth of akasha I can sense. It's weak, too, almost as if its life force is being leached from some fatal wound. But there's no physical injury that I can see, and apart from some scrapes, its limbs and tail are intact.

Filmy citrine eyes warily track my every step as if all it has known from anyone here has been hatred and pain.

"Calm," I whisper. "I won't hurt you."

Steam curls from its nostrils as I get closer and I take in other details. Its green scales are dull, ostensibly a mark of declining health, tarnished by burn marks and older, badly healed lacerations up its body. Twin horns spear from the top of its crown, leading to a dual row of lethal spines down its neck and over its broad back. A curled tail twitches, the deadly barb at the end enervated and still.

Even though it appears weak, I know not to underestimate the azdaha. There are two ways to approach this kind of predator: submission or dominance. Considering the ills it might have suffered at the hands of my people, I choose the former, even though my simurgh bristles at the too-close threat. I swallow. The creature didn't hurt me before in the arena . . . it won't now.

I'm hoping, anyway, even though I know that pain can make monsters of the best of us. Gathering my magic just in case—which won't save me from being bitten in half—I focus on keeping my thoughts serene and my energy nonthreatening.

When I'm standing in striking distance of the azdaha's sharp teeth and taloned forelimbs, I reach a palm out and keep my eyes to the ground. My heart feels like it's beating out of my chest, and my runes distill over my skin in a collage of light, but other than that, there's no wild protective surge in my chest from my simurgh indicating mortal peril.

Easy, Sura . . . wait for it to come to you.

I hinge closer, and after a few breathless moments, a scaly, warm snout bumps the heart of my palm. Akasha hums between us, boosted by the skin-to-skin connection. Guided by instinct to offer it some of my strength, I push my magic to flow into its body. The glow on my forearms is nearly blinding, and the azdaha rumbles softly, a thick tongue protruding to lick the center of my palm as if in gratitude. The rune there—the star symbol that maps my heart, head, life, and fate—ignites, and I gasp as silvery luminescence flickers around us.

My simurgh croons in welcome, offering its strength.

By the stars above, even weakened, the reserve of power within this beast is astounding, and I wonder why it hasn't made its escape before now. It could collapse this entire building. The palace even.

But then I remember that the azdaha's magic is constrained by the jādū collar and the bracers on its hind legs. Could I remove them?

Tentatively, I reach a thread of magic toward the collar, only to recoil at the punishing sting of the sigil-inscribed metal. The runes, now burning a molten red, are powerful. I recognize a few of them, including the ones for restriction and binding. For control and inhibition. For punishment and pain . . .

Gasping, I peer closer, but the others are not familiar to me.

Who are you, youngling?

The deep-voiced rumble that sounds low-pitched and distinctly male echoes in my head, and I blink, eyes flying upward from the glowing runes to the only other living entity in the room. That slitted, cloudy golden gaze is focused on me, and when the question—the rather *lucid* question—comes again, there is no doubt in my mind of its owner.

"Suraya Saab," I whisper in wonder. My fingers graze over the sharp-edged scales of its snout, and to my surprise, the azdaha leans into them as if finding comfort in my touch. Those long teeth are still visible, and I rest my hand far enough away to keep from slipping and unintentionally slicing myself open. "Do you have a name?"

Razulek Grayheart. A puff of steam warms my skin. *But what are you then, Suraya Saab? To wield so much akasha in a realm starved of it?*

"They call me the . . . Starkeeper."

It—*he*—exhales a gust of warm air as a scorching awareness flashes in his eyes. And then I freeze. Stars, have I taken a risk by revealing who I am? Was Roshan right about the danger after all, and I simply too stubborn to see it? Could this azdaha be one of Fero's beasts?

Bile bubbles into my throat. My simurgh would have warned me of peril, but still, questions swarm like a hive of disturbed bees in my brain.

"Whom do you serve?" I ask back, hiding my creeping fear with bravado.

The Night King.

I sigh with relief, glad it's not Fero, but worried nonetheless. Is he talking about the nightmare king? "Do you mean the one who rules Everlea?" I ask.

Yes.

The same realm that is supposedly on the brink of breaching Oryndhr's borders in search of this very creature. Perhaps I can proactively help Roshan to stave off a siege without bloodshed. I'd much rather try a peaceful way of resolution than be used as a weapon of warfare, and this animal is clearly intelligent. It's worth a shot.

The azdaha shifts, one giant wing flexing. A pained hiss escapes his mouth, and I glance up. The membranes of his wings are so tattered, webbed with blackened and cracked burn scars, that I inhale a horrified breath. I shift to skim my hands along the rough, scaleless hide of his warm underbelly. "Are you hurt?"

A constant state, I fear, Starkeeper.

"How come? Can't you heal yourself with your magic?"

My magic has become too weak. My bond with my mate is fraying, and it is taking all my might to hold on to that.

I gasp as his sorrow surges through me. "You have a mate?"

Yes.

Stars. Somehow I have to help him get back to where he belongs. But how? I don't know how to get to Everlea, and even if I attempted a portal, I wouldn't know where to anchor it. *Think, Sura!*

I glance at his wings again. If he was in better health, maybe he could use his strength to fly. That's something, at least. I'm not too adept of a healer, but Aran has taught me enough to mend small wounds for others. Healing the azdaha's colossal wings isn't a minor undertaking by any means, but I can still direct my magic to do what it can.

"Hold still, I want to try to heal you," I say, and sketch the rune for healing in my mind's eye. I imagine a conduit between us and focus on feeding my magic to him in small consistent, curative bursts.

Starlight kindles between us, and I watch in wonder as silvery ribbons seep through Razulek's veins beneath his emerald scales, making them glow chartreuse for a moment. I manage to contain my shout of triumph when the gaping lacerations start to mend. Before too long, the webbed skin is supple and unmarred.

"There, good as new," I say with a gasp as an unexpected surge of weakness makes me waver. "Keep your wings folded so they don't see."

Thank you, he says reverently, his snout bumping the crown of my head.

"You're welcome," I say, feeling the drain of what I'd given him keenly but not caring. I'd give anything to see Razulek in flight, soaring across the skies like a king of his domain. He'd be magnificent. "How did you get trapped here?"

I was tricked into a portal when my mate's eggs were nearly sto—

But his answer is interrupted by shouts and the score of heavily armed guards who march into the paddock accompanied by a half dozen runecasters, Clem, Hamid, and the king himself. A very furious king, by the look on Roshan's face. I shove my guilt away, feeling the newly healed azdaha stiffen menacingly beside me.

"Suraya, move aside!" Roshan's voice snaps like a whip, clipped and cold. His kingsguard form a half circle at his back, the runecasters already beginning to weave containment spells. The collar and bracers start to glow that ominous red from earlier, and suddenly, the azdaha's nostrils flare in distress. With the open connection between us, I feel his pain like a stinging echo, until he brutally throttles the link. I still feel it, but I know it's a hundred times worse for him.

"Call off your dogs," I shout to the king. "I'm not in danger, but I can't promise that they won't be."

Razulek whines, his barbed tail whipping out as his long neck undulates in a serpentine motion. One well-placed swipe of that thick tail or his wing, and these idiots would die.

"You're hurting him. Stop!"

The azdaha's huge head sways forward, putting me slightly behind him, and for a moment, it seems like Razulek intends to protect me, even while he's being battered by the runes on the collar. Clem lets out a loud curse, her features tight with worry. Considering the guards' reactions and their raised jādū weapons, I suspect it looks different from their perspective—like the azdaha is about to consume me as his next meal.

"Don't harm him," I yell, ducking under Razulek's head. Then I form the words in my head and push them toward him, wondering if he can receive my thoughts as I'd heard his. *Razulek, what are you doing?*

Protecting you, he replies weakly.

"They won't hurt either of us," I say aloud. My eyes flick to the runecasters and meet the king's livid face. "Roshan, please. Call them off. He's in pain, but he's defending me."

For a heartbeat, a seething penumbra slithers through his gaze, his armored fist clenching, but then he tilts his head, his voice soft and discreet. "You disobeyed me."

"You're overreacting, it's—"

He doesn't let me finish. "I forbade you, and you defied me."

His words are like blades, eviscerating me publicly. My ears burn with humiliation as I swallow and survey the guards crowding the corral. I'm not a child to be scolded, and he shouldn't treat me like one. I was never in any real danger. And if he'd trusted me in the first place with information, I wouldn't be so eager to ferret out secrets on my own and break his asinine rules in the process. My jaw sets as he shows no sign of relenting. Very well. If he wants to play this game in front of an audience, we'll play.

My chin rises. "I didn't defy you. You said not to go to the arena." With a calm I don't feel, I sweep my hand around, keeping my expression neutral. "We are not in the arena, and I wanted to assess the condition of the azdaha for myself."

He frowns at my composed reply. "And I *told* you, it is dangerous."

"Not to me," I counter. I feel my blood boil at his tone but lower my voice a smidge, though I'm sure that those closest can still hear me. "You can't control everything, Roshan. Stop thinking that you know what's best for me or that you know better. I am perfectly safe."

His eyes narrow when steam pours from Razulek's nostrils. "Are you?"

"I am safer with him than any of your militant guards." *Or with you for that matter . . .* I don't say those words, but I feel them like lead ballast tearing through my heart. When did I no longer feel safe with Roshan?

From behind his cousin, Aran steps forward, and the azdaha releases a bone-chilling growl of warning. At the king's short nod, my stomach dives. "Aran, don't hurt—"

But it's too late.

The runes on Razulek's collar and cuffs glow from red to a sickly yellow. In the same moment, a savage paroxysm rips through our muted link, making my spine bow from the agonizing force of it. I whimper, eyes darting to the azdaha, whose wings are curled down, his entire body shaking.

"Stop! Aran, stop! You're killing him. He's already weak. He won't fight back!"

Razulek whines as he cowers and finally crumples into a shuddering heap. The bracers don't only limit his magic, I realize thinly. They are designed to inflict nerve damage, packing enough of a punch to render a massive beast useless.

Belatedly, I realize that if he hadn't throttled our connection, I would likely be in a similar state. Razulek is no longer moving, his huge body twitching uncontrollably as a strangled sob bursts from me. The smell of charred flesh fills the space, the jādū collar continuing to blister the already patchy scales at his neck. He keens in agony.

Gods, why won't they *stop* hurting him? I have to do something!

My own runes burst into light, my simurgh roaring at the barbarity.

A tornado of air magic from one of the runecasters slams into me from the back, knocking me to my knees as if I'm a secondary threat, and I scramble groggily to my feet, feeling like my spine has been snapped in two. A feral growl emerges from the nearly unconscious Razulek that lifts the hairs on my neck, and his tail slashes in a burst of strength. It catches the man who struck me in his ribs with the barbed end, and within seconds, molten red boils spread over the man's skin.

"Take the beast down now!" someone commands. Hamid, I dimly recognize.

No. I feel my magic surge, snaking between the bodies before me in gleaming ribbons, on the verge of incapacitating them all.

Roshan's gaze darkens. "That is treason, my love," he whispers so softly that I almost don't catch it.

Half delirious with pain, I scoff. "What will you do, Your Majesty? Lock me in the dungeon? Put me in straps like a horse to be broken?" My throat tightens as I stare at the heaving azdaha. "Or fit me with a jādū collar like his?"

"Enough of this nonsense. Cease this ridiculous display." The king's eyes spark with anger, and I recoil at his frigid tone, my heart trembling at a stranger I suddenly don't recognize.

"Tell your guards to stand down. I don't want to hurt anyone. *Please.*"

My magic thunders in my veins and I struggle to rein it in. Razulek is near death, his pulse too faint to take much more, and with weapons pointed at us, my simurgh wants nothing more than to eliminate the obvious threat.

An imperious stare bores into me. "I said *enough*, Starkeeper."

Starkeeper. Not *Suraya,* not *Sura,* not *my starling.*

My heart fractures.

Not so long ago, my gardener-prince turned king would have dismissed everyone and taken me into his arms, no matter how upset we were. He would have kissed me, stroked my cheek with his calloused fingers, whispered words of reassurance and affection. Soothed me, trusted me, *loved* me enough to know that I could *never* hurt him.

But this king with the dead eyes doesn't move.

"Roshan." His name emerges as a faint plea.

But my gardener is gone, and the king of Oryndhr is cold, that shadowed brown gaze so devoid of empathy that it's an arrow to my chest. His answer is in his rooted stance and stony silence.

My instincts are screaming for me to leave before things get worse and before I do something I regret. I need to go home, back to Coban . . . to the last place I felt safe.

The beginnings of my portal begin to form, sparking into an oval shape. I ignore the gasps. The only reason I haven't created one before is out of deference to Roshan, as well as a lack of practical experience.

Portal magic is dangerously precise. But I'd rather risk ending up in the middle of a lava pit in Droon than stay here a second longer.

"I'm leaving," I whisper. "Don't try to stop me."

I'm so focused on anchoring the portal to Coban that I don't feel the damnable prick at my neck or hear the soft whisper of apology from Clem until it's much too late.

The portal dissolves into nothing as I surrender to the sting of betrayal and the bittersweet embrace of my most hated nemesis . . .

Jade.

Chapter Six

"Child, what have you done?"

I blink my eyes open slowly. My bleary gaze lands on the Royal Star and my favorite crone sitting on the edge of my bed. "Vena?" I croak. "Where have you been?"

"My duties have kept me away," she says. "Are you well?"

I shake my head, my mind feeling oddly fuzzy. "No. Everything is going wrong. Roshan doesn't trust me. I've become a killer. I feel lost."

"Then you must find yourself."

My head throbs. Gods, this is *not* the time to decipher Vena's ramblings. "Trust me, if it were that easy, I would have. I don't know what to do."

For a moment, she looks sad. "Perhaps I was wrong about the fluid bonds of akasha, about your destiny being chosen and not already written."

The words ring faintly familiar—she'd said something like that to me after I'd died, when she'd waxed poetic about me having a possible soul-fated. "What do you mean?"

"Your destiny lies elsewhere," she murmurs as my visions swims, and she starts to waver.

"Wait, Vena. *Where?*"

But she's gone . . . and I'm left alone and more confused than ever.

Head pounding, I stare blankly at the ceiling. My tongue sticks to the roof of my mouth, a sour taste lingering in my throat. I swallow what feels like a mouthful of sawdust and sit up, my memory patchy. Dizzily, I blink and push to my elbows. My chamber is dark with no light coming in from the windows or the balcony doors.

Breathing through my nose, I fist my aching temples. My mouth tastes suspiciously like the sour-sweet aftertaste of Jade, a dangerously addictive hallucinogenic drug made from jādū. Ashes below, have I been drugged?

A hazy feeling invades my brain on a cloud of fluffy endorphins.

Maker above, it's definitely Jade.

I let out a curse. Clearing my mind as Aran had taught me, I will my magic to heal my impaired nervous system and purge the poison from my system. It takes several tries, and when it's all gone, I should feel better, but instead, I feel curiously numb.

Blank . . . as if an integral part of me is missing.

Something's not right.

"Vena?" I call out, but there's no response. I wonder if I imagined her in the first place.

Before this, I'd been under the influence of Jade twice, each time without my consent. Once when I infiltrated a Scav den, and again when their leader, General Vogon, attempted to weaken me with a magical runic web. He'd failed. I'd been able to purge the poison both times.

But this *dearth* in the middle of my chest feels nothing like that.

This happened after I'd visited the azdaha. *Razulek*.

The thought of the poor creature is like an explosion of blinding light, piercing through my unnatural brain fog, and all the recent events rush back in horrifying clarity. The azdaha. Roshan. Aran. The standoff. The king's ruthlessness. The portal to Coban that never materialized.

An awful feeling invades my blood, paralyzing my racing thoughts. No . . . he *wouldn't* have.

But I rub my nape just below my ear, recalling Clem's remorseful words as the Jade sank its hooks into my bloodstream, and then Roshan's cold expression fills my mind. She wouldn't have done a thing without *his* order.

Hyperventilating—none of this could be real even though it clearly *is*—I take stock of myself. I'm still wearing my own clothes. But then my curious gaze hitches on the unfamiliar bracelets on my wrists, like wide molded metal cuffs. Where did those come from?

I lift one high, frowning. The steel is smelted with the memorable shimmer of jādū. I should know—I've forged enough magical weapons myself. Runic script envelops the circumference of the metal. I don't recognize all the arcane symbols and runes, but I *do* know the ones for control and submission. Because I've seen them before . . . on the azdaha.

I stare in shock at the gleaming jādū bands, remember my words to Roshan. *What will you do . . . fit me with a jādū collar like his?*

My skin starts to heat as magic fills my veins. In breathless panic, I run a finger around the edges of the cuffs, but there's no seam or lock to remove them, and they're fastened tight. The bracers glow brightly but don't crack or melt when I command them to. The magic inside of me works just fine. I can't seem to make it *do* anything.

Oh, no, no, no . . .

"Roshan!" I scream. I launch up from the bed on legs that feel like jelly and hobble to the door. But the handle doesn't release the latch. I frown and yank on it harder, belatedly noticing that there's no key in the keyhole. Is the cursed thing locked? *Why* is it locked?

I press my ear to the wood and hear noises on the other side. Someone's there. "Hello? Open this door right now! I can hear you!" I yell, banging hard for the guards I know have to be posted on the outside. "Get me the king this minute! I know you're out there. Or let me out so I can find him myself."

As I suspected, I hear more rustling and low voices. "His Majesty is attending his war council, my lady," a male voice replies uneasily.

"Then open this starsdamned door," I yell.

"We have orders not to," the voice says.

Orders, my ass.

Gathering my strength, I focus on the door and summon the rune to incinerate. My magic is slower to flare, but the scrolling runes on my skin are unmistakable. I push, forcing my starlight into the wood until the glare makes me squint. A bone-splintering shock slams into me like a lightning bolt, and I yelp in pain, bile rushing to my throat. But I grit my teeth and try again, only to be struck twice as hard.

Just like Razulek had been . . .

With a furious sob, I raise my wrists, the cuffs blurring through my tears. I scour my nails against the bracers, digging into the tender flesh of my wrists so hard that blood drips. The sharp bite of pain barely registers on top of the lingering agony of the shocks, but the sight of the blood makes me queasy and I start to feel faint.

Nauseated, I stumble back in the direction of the bed, my legs giving out as I stare at the manacles now covered in garish streaks of crimson. Panic is quick to follow as my simurgh gets wilder and angrier at being held captive. It's no secret we both hate being restrained. Short of cutting off my hands to escape, I'm trapped.

We're trapped.

Swaying on shaky feet, I crash into a small table with a vase that makes an ungodly noise as it smashes into the floor, and I drop to my knees. I don't even notice the porcelain shards from the broken vase slashing into my skin. The door cracks open and I see a face peering in at me.

"Fuck, get help!" the guard yells to someone else.

Light floods the bedchamber as lamps come to life when Aran enters, his eyes widening at the sight of the mess along with the blood spattered all over me and the floor. "Gods, Sura, what have you done?"

"Can you get these off?" I wheeze, wincing. "Hurts."

When he makes no move to approach me, I peer weakly at him through heavy eyelids. "I . . . can't," he says. "Don't use magic or you'll get hurt again."

"What do you mean?" I ask, feeling sweat start to roll down my nape. "Where's the king? Does he know I'm here? Is he safe? What's going on? Aran, I need these off!"

"You need to calm down or the suppression rune will make you lose consciousness," he says, eyes rounding with alarm when I start tearing at the stained cuffs again, my magic crashing like an angry tide within me. "Roshan is fine. He'll be here soon."

But I barely hear him as my spine bows when another violent shock blasts through my body. Shaking uncontrollably, I push my wrists toward him. "You're a magi. Take them off. *Please*."

Aran stares at me in silence, his face wreathed in guilt. Why would he be looking at me like that?

The answer is all too obvious when the guards clear a path for the king, whose face doesn't show a single ounce of surprise as he enters our chambers. That earlier fearful feeling returns as I lift my wrists. "Roshan, tell him to remove these."

"He can't take them off," he says, then glances at his guards crowding the doorway. "Wait outside." The silence is ominous after they retreat, as the king's inscrutable gaze meets mine. I pick at them again. "You can't remove them, Suraya, so stop fighting."

The panic resumes, matching my elevated pulse. "Why?"

Regret glimmers in the king's gaze for a scant second before his jaw hardens, that cold haze I've come to hate taking over his expression. "It's for your own good."

Those damning words fall like hammers on my heart, and still the meaning doesn't penetrate fully for a handful of breaths. Until it does...

He's responsible for this.

"What have you done?" I cry, lurching from my prone position on the floor toward him, but only managing a few steps before pitching unsteadily. "Tell me you didn't do this to me, please. Tell me you didn't collar me like an animal." The sobs wrench out of me, the blow of his betrayal too much to bear. "I *trusted* you!"

His mouth tightens. "This is only a means to an end, Suraya. I have to make my authority clear, or the houses will run roughshod over us."

"There is no us, there's only you." My bitter words are barely audible as I sink to the floor.

"Don't say that. All of this, everything I'm doing, is for *us*."

He swallows, his throat bobbing and those beautiful, treacherous eyes glistening with emotion that makes me sick. The cold, dead stare from earlier is gone. But which is the real version of him? I can't tell anymore.

"I don't believe you," I whisper.

He crouches down beside me. A part of me screams for me to get up and run, to lash out and immobilize him, to *fight* for my life, but another part is too heartsick to care. "I won't allow you to put yourself in danger," he says. "It's only for a short while, you'll see. I'll take you to Coban myself when things settle down. I promise."

"You're a liar," I say. "And I will never forgive you for this."

"Then that's a chance I'll have to take," he says quietly. "My duty is to my people first. To Oryndhr. The oaths of a king come before anything else."

"And what about your promises to me?" I ask, risking a glance at him. "To never hurt me or lie to me again."

"I'm not lying," he replies, his words calm, as if I'm somehow the irrational one. "That's why I'm being honest with you about what needs to be done."

I exhale a shuddery breath. "Putting me in irons?"

"Suraya—"

"Don't," I tell him. "I don't need your platitudes or creative omissions. We could have done this together instead of you shutting me out at every turn."

"You're common born, Suraya, from a remote village," he says in a cool, imperious tone that shouldn't hurt as much as it does. "How could you even understand court politics? Or how easily my enemies can snatch you and use you against me. The nobles still don't trust me. Even now, after everything, Antares is plotting to dethrone me." He clenches his jaw.

"Common born doesn't mean lacking in common sense," I reply. "You want me to blindly obey, is that it? Defer to your better judgment?"

His expression is unyielding. "In the matter of your welfare and the realm's safety, yes. I am the king."

"So you keep saying."

Sands, I didn't think my heart could crack any further, but the hits keep coming. Soon the pulverized organ in my chest will be nothing but dust. I lift an arm, watching the lamplight glint off the jādū hammered into the metal. I glance over at Aran, who has remained silent where he stands on the far side of the bedroom. It's clear now he was the magi to engineer these cuffs—he's the only one who could have.

"How did you do it?" I ask. "Control the Starkeeper magic?"

"My blood," Roshan answers.

I blink. That doesn't make sense. His blood has no magic—my simurgh would have known if any dormant power of his had awakened. Then the truth hits me like a kick to the face. Traces of *my* magic are in his veins, and somehow, he's using that against me. The sheer audacity has me vibrating with rage.

"You bastard!" I snarl, flying up at him, my fists pounding into his chest. "How could you?"

I want to carve his heart out of his body, the way mine has been. Nearly mindless with fury, I lunge for the dagger in his belt and swing wildly in his direction. My magic might be bound, but I have no intention of going down without a fight. Not like this.

The king dodges my strike and unsheathes his sword. I attack again with a violent thrust. This time he parries, avoiding my blow and catching my steel with the edge of his own blade. We've sparred like this a thousand times, though never with intent to harm. At the sound of clashing metal, his guards immediately appear, and he holds up a hand.

"Get the fuck out. You, too, Aran." Roshan doesn't look at them. He stares at me over his blade.

The guards retreat slowly, Aran last to depart with a reluctant glance.

"You don't want to do this, Sura," Roshan says when the room is empty.

I smile viciously. "Oh, but I really do. I want to make you *bleed*."

He goes preternaturally still. "That sounds like a threat, Starkeeper. Either you're with me or against me." With the ease of a born warrior, he points the tip of his weapon to me and disarms me in a single move, the dagger flying out of my grip. "I don't want to hurt you."

My stupid eyes sting again, even as my magic roils like a trapped hurricane in a bottle. Gods, how did we get here? How did I become *this*? Caught in a snare I'd waltzed into with my eyes wide open. He'd *promised* never to use me . . . and he'd broken that promise.

"Too fucking late." Unable to look at him and unable to stomach the heartache, I move toward my bed. "If you don't undo this," I say brokenly, "this will be the end of us."

"It's for the greater good," he says. "I need you, and I need you alive and whole. If you have to hate me for protecting you and keeping you safe from yourself, then that shall be a cost I'll gladly bear."

"You're not protecting me, you're protecting yourself!" I turn and cry, feeling every last remaining hope inside of me dissipate all at once. "You gave me your vow, Roshan."

"And I'll keep it, when my kingdom is at peace."

A pervasive sense of dread creeps over me at the finality in his tone. Nothing I say will change his mind. How many months—or even *years*—will I be like this? A weapon at his mercy. His to control, his to wield, in his desire for peace? Or worse, *his* version of peace, with its constantly shifting end?

"Power will destroy you," I say, the words emerging before I can curb them. "It will eat away at anything that makes you the man you used to be and turn you into a monster. Just like Javed."

"I'm nothing like him."

"Aren't you? The Roshan I knew—the man I *loved*—never would have done this," I say. "He never would have tricked or caged me."

We stare at each other, the rift between us widening with each strained breath. For a moment, a sliver of the old Roshan is there as his eyes gloss over with something like agony, but that glimmer of humanity is quickly eclipsed by that deadened stare I've come to hate.

He doesn't respond immediately. Instead, he turns and walks to the threshold. "When you've sufficiently calmed and understand what's at stake, the guards will release you."

I bare my teeth at him like a wounded animal. "Didn't you hear what I said? We're fucking finished!"

"You're overwrought and need time to think things through. We can speak later when you're not so upset." He pauses, but I can barely get past his utter dismissal, my mouth opening and closing like a fish out of water. My inability to speak must seem like some kind of passive acceptance, because he gives me a tight-lipped nod. "Whatever you may think, Suraya, you're not my prisoner."

"Then let me go," I bite out.

The king slams his hand against the doorjamb, a darkly possessive rage transforming his features. The expression on his face is bone-chilling, spectral flames exploding in his eyes. He looks like a monster from the void before he strides away, the door crashing shut. I hear the lock turning in the keyhole, the click deafening in the silence.

"Fuck!" I scream, and smash my forearms into the nearest wall. I curse as the stinging ache reverberates through my bones and then burst into unhinged laughter as I sink to my haunches and stare at the bracers. There's not even a dent in the metal.

"Vena?" I call out desperately. "Vena, are you there? I need you. Please, I need your help."

But there's no answer.

I am alone.

Chapter Seven

The Night King

My soul-fated has summoned me again.

Or at least her fear and pain have, and my ashes-cursed shadows did not relent until they'd convinced me to dreamwalk across time and realms. In truth, I feared their clamor would have triggered the curse, so I had reluctantly acquiesced.

Besides, there's no harm in giving in because my presence is not real to her. She has no idea who I am or who we are to each other, and I intend to keep it that way. In her mind, these are innocuous dreams where she seeks comfort in a world of her own making. If I can break this bond, I will not hesitate, but for now our souls and fates are tethered.

My shadows burst from me in agitation when we enter her dream space as if they can tell immediately that something is wrong. This isn't her home in the desert . . . or even her quarters in the palace. It's somewhere new. A brewing storm with violent branches of lightning splits the blackened sky overhead, illuminating a cliffside and a churning sea.

This tiny corner of her mind is shrouded in gloom, the very air seething and pulsing with a viscous anger. Unlike the last few times I've comforted her in dreams, the landscape of this night terror is bleak and barren, desolate of all life and all color. It's so unlike her that for a second I feel a pang of worry. My darkness writhes.

Calm, I tell my shadows.

We find our tiny mate sitting on the edge of a rocky outcropping, her knees pulled up to her chest, dark hair whipping in the wind. The ocean in front of us is foaming and wild, massive waves crashing into rock with destructive fury.

"You're here," she whispers bleakly as my shadows flock to her, rubbing carefully over her cold skin to warm her. She gathers them close as if they're hers to command, and I fight my rueful smile. In another lifetime, they would be—she's the other half of my soul, after all, born to command the night sky. Tightening my jaw, I steel myself, battening down my careening emotions before they spiral out of my control.

My sister has cautioned against getting too close to my soul-fated if I have any future hope of rejecting the bond. While I have played with her before, unable to resist the offer of her delectable body in her seductive dreams, I must allow myself to feel nothing. She is a beautiful inconvenience and a pleasurable distraction, no more than that.

Anything else, and the cost will be untenable.

"Why have you called me?" I growl.

"I didn't want to be alone," she replies. "I have no one. Not Roshan, not Clem. Not even Vena. But I knew you would come. You always do. You never forsake me."

I frown. "Vena?"

"The Royal Star," she says. "My guardian. She visits me sometimes, though I haven't seen her in a while, and I think I imagined the last time. Perhaps she has abandoned me, too." She drops her head onto her knees with a broken sound. "I've gotten myself into a mess. Sands, I am a *fool*. I trusted them with my magic and my heart, and they trapped me. Not they. *Him*."

She doesn't continue for a long beat, the wind howling like a dying animal between us as the tides rage in tandem with her emotions, battering the shoreline.

"I don't know who he is anymore. Or perhaps I never did." Her voice breaks on the last word, her pain so visceral that an earsplitting peal of thunder nearly drowns out her next ones. "Can you stay with me for a little while? Please."

Despite my forced ambivalence, my chest squeezes at the sound of her pain, and the beast inside of me flexes his claws in warning. It won't take much to set the curse off, not with her volatile state and her cursed connection to me. It's a risk I cannot take.

Not now.

My sister's wise counsel thrums in my head.

I grind my teeth and yank my uncooperative, protesting shadows back to me. *Enough, you've seen her. She's alive and unharmed. There's nothing we can do.* They struggle and seethe and tear against my control, even stinging me with their displeasure, but I stand firm.

"Please..." she whispers.

"I cannot," I say, watching her shoulders slump and her faint starlight dim with defeat.

It might be cruel to leave her this way, but distance is for the best.

At least, that's what I tell myself.

Chapter Eight

True to the king's word, my door is unlocked by the next morning.

Or at least I don't hear the lock click when the handmaiden leaves after delivering the silver salver with a steaming pot of tea and a basket of pastries to the table near the window. I shake myself awake, feeling oddly worn out from the dreams that had plagued me.

My skin feels numb and tight as if I'd spent much of the night shivering with cold. I remember snatches of a terrible storm over the ocean and that my dream companion had made an appearance but refused to stay.

I'd *begged* him.

Swallowing hard, I squash the instant feelings of self-contempt. It was a dream, nothing more—my own inner consciousness echoing the actions of those I trusted. But still, deep down, even his rejection leaves a bitter taste in my mouth, as if I'm not even worthy of a figment of my own pathetic imagination.

Forget him, too, then.

Stretching my sore muscles, I rise and stare at the undisturbed other side of the bed. Roshan did not sleep in the bedroom, nor was I informed where he'd spent the night. Truth be told, I was glad to be alone, because I probably would have suffocated him in his sleep. Then revived him so I could do it again.

I huff a self-deprecating bark of laughter. As angry and vengeful as I feel, I know I could never hurt him. Not as much as he's willfully hurting me. Even as I revile the unrecognizable rigid monarch he has become, my heart mourns the gentle lover I lost.

When I pad over to crack open my door, six armed guards are standing in silence in the hallway, and I sigh in defeat. I'm sure there will be six more waiting for when I step foot outside the palace. These walls that had started to feel like home now feel like a gilded cage. Despite Roshan's words, I *am* a prisoner here.

The starsdamned cuffs are a testament to that.

Betrayal surges anew. I'd felt so sorry for Razulek, seeing him restrained like a wild beast, and now, the same has been done to me. Like him, I'm unpredictable and dangerous—not just to enemies of the crown but *to* the crown. If, for some outlandish reason, I decide I want the throne myself, there's nothing any of them will be able to do about it. Roshan and Aran can claim that keeping me here is for my own safety all they want . . . but these magical shackles are for them.

Despair fills me as I pace the bedchamber. Gods, I need to get out of here, and if I can't do so with magic, I need to come up with something else. I'm strong and somewhat fit, and this bedchamber is not too far up. In fact, I'm certain I saw a trellis near my balcony. Exhaling with newfound resolve, I try those doors, half expecting them to be locked. To my surprise, they are not, though the sight of more soldiers training directly on the lawn below throws a wrench into my plans. Clem is front and center in the middle of them, running the drills.

I clench my teeth hard at the sight of her, her perfidy still fresh. I'd thought she was my friend, but at the heart of it, she'll follow the king's orders without question. She told me as much, after all. Help won't be coming from her. As if feeling the weight of my stare, Clem's eyes glance up, colliding with mine, and I see the raw guilt on her face before she shutters it, but I can't bring myself to care. I harden my gaze and turn away.

She and Roshan have both mistaken my forgiveness for weakness.

I walk back into the room to my now cold tea. My appetite has disappeared, so I head into the bathing room, where I perform my morning ablutions and reach for my forging gear. If I'm not a prisoner, I might as well try to get in some exercise and hammer the shit out of something. The sooner I get back to my usual activities, the sooner I can find a way to escape my cage.

"Lady Suraya." I turn, recognizing one of the guards. "The king commands your presence immediately in the throne room. The traitors have been found."

I peer owlishly at him, anger slivering through me at the brusque order. Can I risk ignoring an official summons? How furious would Roshan be? But then I nod. Being sullen or peevish won't prove a thing. I intend to show my warden of a king that I'm not cowed . . . that he hasn't beaten me.

When I arrive in the throne room, the silence is ominous.

Roshan is seated on his throne, his face inscrutable. My heart jumps at the sight of him before my brain can catch up, and I steel myself. Aran stands beside him. There are three men kneeling, two dressed in the house colors of Antares, one in the Imperial House colors. Sands, is that the spy? The boy looks much too young to be a palace guard. I glance around the room, noting that the aldermen of many of the houses are also here.

"Your Majesty," I greet, and bow my head. I take my usual place next to Aran, who shoots me a small smile that I ignore.

"Good, my Starkeeper is here," Roshan says. His face seems harsher and more draconian, all angles and scraped hollows, nothing like the man I know. The possessive emphasis on *my* doesn't go unnoticed, but I keep my expression blank.

His sentiment is not out of affection—it's a declaration to those in attendance that I serve at his whim. But if the king expects me to perform like a trained monkey, he's in for a rude awakening. I grind my jaw as his voice rings through the hall. "These men are convicted of treason and betraying their solemn oaths to Oryndhr by spying on the king's movements for an enemy known as the oracle, and they will die by the Imperial House's swift justice."

Every eye in the hall settles on me. I frown. We're not even offering them a chance to speak in their defense? Has Roshan even found out who the oracle is?

I lift my brows and hold up both hands. "I'm not sure what you expect me to do," I say in a low voice. "My magic is bound, remember? Remove these and I'll consider it."

The king stares at me, brown eyes baleful, and I force back a shudder at the heartless expression on his face. As long as I've known him, I've never seen such a cruel, viperous look. He reminds me so much of Javed.

Roshan nods to his cousin, who steps closer. Aran sketches the rune for incinerate and my cuffs ignite with power. I feel the magic gather inside me even though I've done nothing to summon it. Ribbons of iridescent heat curl around my fingertips beyond my own volition, and my eyes widen in shock.

It feels as though I'm watching from a distant vantage point while someone else controls my body. One of the men starts sobbing, and the stench of urine permeates the hall as a woman screams out for mercy—the boy's mother, is my guess.

"Continue," Roshan says, grim and implacable.

"Aran, what is this?" I gasp, trying to move and finding my legs glued to the floor. I'm an automaton, my will not my own, and the feeling is *terrifying*.

He doesn't answer, his face furrowed with concentration, and I watch in utter disbelief as *my* magic envelops the men, evaporating them in seconds. I slump backward, numb to the wails and cries permeating the hall, staring at Aran with horror.

It's an abomination . . . a gross perversion of my power.

"What have you done?" I whisper.

The answer comes from the king. "What needed to be done. Peace must be secured. The Starkeeper is a subject of the crown and your gifts belong to the crown."

I shake my head, unable to believe what I'm hearing. My magic is *mine*. "Roshan, what has come over you?" I ask. "I'm not a thing to be controlled."

"No? What do you think we just did?" His reply is gutting.

In shock, I lift my hands to ward him off. My throat clogs with dread as his guards all raise their weapons in unison, pointed at me. I feel so backed into a corner that I *try* to fight back, try to use my magic to incapacitate them so that I'm not in their crossfire, just long enough for me to have a window to escape.

But my magic doesn't respond.

As if he has all the time in the world, the king nods again, and Aran obediently sketches another rune. This time, however, instead of pain, it's one of torpor that sends me to my knees, curling into myself as lethargy overtakes me. Dimly, I recall Aran saying something about a suppression rune yesterday in my chambers.

It takes only a few breaths before I give in to the silken embrace of slumber.

I SLIP IN and out of consciousness, light and dark taking turns behind my eyelids.

Sitting up, I fight the onslaught of dizziness as a handmaiden presses a chalice of cool liquid to my lips. I drink thirstily, but not so fast that I expel it. "Thank you," I murmur when I've drained the glass. "How long have I been here?"

"Three days, my lady," she says.

My body feels sluggish as it recovers. The one thing I know is that my magic works fine inside my body.

Vaguely, I remember Roshan being here at one point, sitting on the bed, his beautiful eyes glossed over with regret and contrition. But I can't trust myself or my memories when it comes to him, not anymore. What if I'd imagined his presence, his tender words? Fabricated his sorrowful apologies? All out of self-preservation?

I'm so sorry, my starling . . .
It's not for too much longer . . .
Do you hate me? Please don't hate me . . .
I love you, Sura.

The last one burns like an open wound, because this *isn't* love. It's like dealing with two different entities occupying the same body: the man I chose to give my heart to and the tyrant king who stole my magic.

Easing out of bed, I hurry into the bathing room and wash the horrors of the last few days and nights from my skin. But like my invisible scars, they're imprinted on me forever. Every face, every plea, every scream, every sob. The water sluices over my hated bracers, and I curse them over and over. Even the simurgh inside of me has gone quiet, cowed into submission.

I no longer recognize myself.

When I'm dried and wrapped in a soft robe, I sit and accept the meal that has been delivered by the handmaidens. They all keep their eyes downcast and hurry out of the room.

The food smells delicious: flaky bread, creamy spinach, tender cuts of lamb. But it all tastes of dust in my mouth. Accustomed to being alone, I eat methodically, simply to fuel my body. Food is no longer a pleasure to savor; it's a necessity. If I ever get the opportunity to escape, I need to be strong to be able to take it.

A knock on the door makes me glance up.

"Enter," I say, wondering if I'm being summoned by the king for more coerced theatrics.

"Lady Suraya?" a feminine voice asks before a head of glossy auburn hair pokes around the doorjamb. It should concern me that it's relief I feel at the sight of Helena, but I'm so deprived of company that even my old nemesis is a welcome distraction. "Are you busy?"

"No, please come in. I'm nearly finished eating. And it's Suraya."

She enters slowly. She's wearing an elegant formal ensemble that fits her lean, athletic frame like a glove. The sheer emerald-green silk and jeweled stomacher complement her pale complexion, falling in delicate waves to the floor. "Supper just ended in the dining room. I escaped after the last course before the dancing begins."

My heart squeezes at the memory of the last ball and the dance Roshan and I had shared. It seems surreal, as if it had happened in a dream.

"There's a ball?" I ask, my voice emerging like gravel, though if I'm being honest I have no desire to attend any court functions.

Helena nods as she sits on the edge of the sofa and folds her hands into her lap. "The aldermen from all the houses are here to celebrate the new peace agreement."

I straighten with interest, hope blooming like a fragile flower that I might get to go home sooner rather than later. "Peace agreement?"

"One that covers local taxes, trading routes, and concessions for land, as well as how to address disputes without bloodshed," she says. "And they're discussing a courting ball."

She ducks her face as if embarrassed, which doesn't fool me in the least.

"Courting ball?" I echo, brows rising.

Helena's cheeks go a disarming shade of pink. "Potential bridal propositions for marriage to the king . . . if yours is off the table. It's political, you understand. The aldermen are insistent that the king needs to cement his position with the houses."

I want to roll my eyes. If I had a gold coin every time an alderman thought something was good for the Imperial House, I would be a very rich woman. They're all angling to get one of their own on the throne and solidify their *own* positions, not that of the king. Before I had any claim to Roshan, I'd been deeply aware of their political games. Though as the Starkeeper none of them could belittle me on the matter of nobility of birth—I outrank them all.

But now . . . I suppose things are different.

Everyone must now know that the king and I are . . . estranged. Perhaps even that I am little more than a glorified captive. Gossip is coveted currency in the capital city. Knowledge of my magical bracers and being locked in my bedchamber by the king himself would have reached every corner of Oryndhr, so no wonder the houses are scurrying to present a replacement future queen from one of their ranks.

In the past, I would have thought that Helena was telling me only to unsettle me or to drive a wedge between Roshan and me—but the king of Oryndhr has done that quite effectively on his own. I'm so numb from all the betrayals that I feel nothing at Helena's coy revelation. No sorrow, no jealousy, no bitterness. I feel strangely hollow, but the king has never owed me anything beyond reciprocation of my feelings. And the truth is, despite sharing his dreams of a future together, he'd never taken any formal steps toward a betrothal.

"That makes sense," I say eventually.

Helena frowns as if she'd almost expected me to burst into sobs or rage and make a scene. But I merely tuck my feet up on the chair under my robe and continue to finish my meal.

"You're not upset?" she asks.

"Why should I be?" I reply, chewing slowly. "Any king needs a strong queen with beneficial alliances to strengthen the realm."

"But you're the Starkeeper. You don't need alliances. You have magic."

I see Helena's very curious gaze surreptitiously flick to my jādū bracers, and I push my plate to the side, folding my hands in my lap to hide the cursed things from view.

"I'm the king's hand, that's all." I exhale and lean my head back, staring at the colorful mural painted on the ceiling. I remember when I first came here how in awe I'd been. Now I'd give anything to see the crimson-streaked desert skies of my home and the wood-beamed ceilings of my family's tavern instead. "When all the dust settles with the peace treaties between the houses, the security of the northern borders, and a queen in place to assure the succession of the royal line, I only want to return to my family."

Helena shakes her head as though she doesn't quite believe me, but then again, her ambitions are no surprise. First with Javed, and I suspect even now while she warms Aran's bed, she plots for an elevated position in court with Roshan. Honestly, she's welcome to him.

I ignore the slight pang that releases in my stomach and sigh, pressing my fingertips to my temples. Wishing for something that has been lost serves little purpose. Heartbreak is rarely survivable for extended periods, and sooner or later, time has a way of soothing all wounds, even the deepest ones.

"How have you been?" she ventures after a minute.

Her face is the picture of compassion, and I choose not to dwell on whether it's contrived or not. The conversation—even with a pretty viper—is pleasant. Still, I want to laugh. It's such an inane question, but I answer it with honesty. "I suppose I've had better days."

"How can I help?"

With a wry look, I wave my arms. "Unless you have a way to get these off, I don't think anyone can help."

Helena is quiet for a moment. She opens her mouth, then shuts it. When she does it a second and third time, I raise a brow. "What? Spit it out."

"What if I told you"—she glances at the closed door and lowers her voice—"that I could get you out of here? Out of Kaldari."

My hopes soar and crash in the same breath. "I would say that's a nice dream."

Her eyes flash with a curious blend of emotions I can't make sense of. Determination mixed with greed? Smugness with a hint of desperation? "No, it's true. I befriended a runecaster, one of Aran's trusted. He is the one who repairs any damage to the collar for the monster."

"The monster?" I frown. "Oh, you mean the azdaha?" I lean forward. "So what?"

"I think he might be able to release your cuffs as well."

I grimace at my wrists, squashing the infinitesimal flare of optimism. "Aran made these, and there's no way he'll help either of us. Trust me, no one else, not even another runecaster, will go against him or the king."

"This one would," she insists so strongly that I stare at her.

"Why are you suddenly so interested in helping me?" I ask. "My magic is bound. I can't possibly be of any service to you." My eyes narrow. "Still thinking of me as your competition to eliminate?"

"Of course not! I would never betray His Majesty like that!" she exclaims. "I suppose if you must know, I want to make amends for how I've treated you in the past."

I can't help my sarcastic laugh. Helena's cheeks redden and her gaze darkens with anger as she jolts to her feet.

Guilt swamps me, considering she took it upon herself to visit me. "I apologize for any offense, Lady Helena," I say as she reaches the door. "You're just the last person I'd ever expect to be on my side."

"Do you want to meet my friend or not?" she asks with a mollified sniff, her hand on the doorknob.

I consider my options. It's not like I have anything to lose. At the very least, an escape attempt will show the king that he hasn't broken me yet. I still have free will, even if it costs me a night or two locked in my chambers.

"Sure," I say. "Why not?"

Her satisfied stare meets mine. "Very well. I'll arrange it."

Chapter Nine

Surprisingly, Helena's a woman of her word.

A message arrives hidden on my supper tray two weeks later, catching me by surprise. I start to read it while sipping my tea and falter. *My friend has agreed to see you when the king departs this evening for Veniar to visit House Fomalhaut.*

I hadn't even known that Roshan was leaving Kaldari. I'm even more surprised that I haven't been ordered to travel with him—but then again, Fomalhaut isn't a threat to his rule. They're his allies, considering the new Order of the Magi being established as a subsidiary of that house.

When Aran isn't in court, he's in Eloni and Veniar, supervising the magi temples, particularly the new ones built to honor Saru.

Rubbing my eyes, I close the thick book on the history of runes I'd been studying from the palace library, trying to decipher the symbols etched into my bracers. But the more I read, the more I have no idea how Aran was able to do all this. The suppression, punishment, and control runes are magic that I haven't seen in *any* of the books I've studied—this book is the dozenth I've read—and I've scoured the library. So the question is *how* did *Aran* learn them?

Frowning, I stroke my temples, turning my gaze back to Helena's missive.

I still don't trust her motives, but as each day passes, I lose more hope that I'll ever get home or that I'll ever be rid of these cuffs. One of the runes carved on their surfaces is a nullifying rune, which means it consistently dampens my natural magic and my connection to my simurgh. Or at least, that's what I've been able to glean from my studies.

I suspect that Aran did that on purpose so I can't build up my magical reserves, which again strikes me as magic that seems beyond his skills. They want me powerful enough to be used, but not *too* powerful that I might be able to circumvent the bracers. For a realm that has no magic, the insight seems frightfully circumspect. Is there another magi in Kaldari or any of the other cities who is even more adept with runes than Aran?

Someone is helping him, my simurgh muses—she loathes the cuffs as much as I do.

I think so, too. But who?

In a burst of determination and perverse rebellion, I finish my meal, burn Helena's note in the hearth after memorizing the exact time and location of the rendezvous, and open the trunk at the foot of my bed. I pull out my old dark forest-green leathers emblazoned with the Aldebaran House crest. I haven't worn them since I came back to Kaldari, not since I'd become part of the Imperial House... become *Roshan's*.

A lump forms in my throat, and I scoff at my weakness. I trace the branching tree and the pair of scales on the chest plate as a jolt of sadness crashes into me.

Stars, I miss Coban. I miss my father's laughter and Amma's cooking. I miss the smell of her kitchens, and the tavern with all its varied guests. I miss spending lazy afternoons reading in my workshop. I miss being... *me*. The girl who'd run her own forge and crafted jādū daggers in secret. The girl who'd bested a *god* and lived to tell the tale. It doesn't matter that I'm the Starkeeper now. Even without magic, I'd survived.

Fucking thrived.

I fold the leathers neatly beside me and then retrieve the dagger that's resting on the bedside table. I run a finger down the flat of the blade and pause on the etchings near the hilt: the stars I'd engraved for me and the moon for my mother. The starburst is a unique rune of power I'd unintentionally created when I forged the dagger and that channeled my unique star magic.

An echo of something warms in my blood, and I feel a weak pulse as my entombed starlight responds to the rune. A faint glow illuminates the shiny blade but is gone before I can blink. This dagger has saved me in more ways than one . . . and it's a symbol of where I've come from.

Who I *am*: Suraya Saab, nobody's sandsdamned damsel.

And I *need* to remember her.

After I dress in the still-supple leathers, I comb my hair into a high bubble tail. In the old days, warriors would add a diamond-shaped blade to the end of it, the ingenious style serving as a hidden weapon. I graze a fingertip over my silver-threaded locks before I tug on my boots and reach for the dagger, tucking it into the hidden sheath inside the calfskin. The blade is too big for the braid, but at least it's some protection in case Helena shows her true colors. I can't afford to be stupid. Whatever her intentions now, she has already tried to kill me once.

As I descend to the main floor of the palace, harried servants carrying trunks and scrolls rush past me to the outer courtyard, where a dozen horses and the royal carriages are waiting to ferry the king to the nearest portal. The sun is already descending so they're cutting it close—with the threat of the Scavs, it's smarter to travel in daylight.

Especially without me.

I fold my arms over my chest and watch, until my senses suddenly go haywire. Unfortunately, they haven't gotten the message about not caring the exact second Roshan walks into a room. When the deeply familiar scent of him hits me like a blow, I try not to breathe as I strive for cool indifference.

"Were you going to leave without saying goodbye?" I ask without turning as the king comes to stand beside me.

"It's for a day, or perhaps two at most," he says.

I hate that the deep, resonant sound of his voice still affects me as much as the intoxicating scent of him does, though at least I hide that well. He stares straight ahead, hands clasped behind his back, tall and forbidding. His eyes don't meet mine. Maybe he's afraid of what I'll see there.

"You don't require my presence this time?" I ask.

"No." His answer is short and quiet. Clem and Hamid gallop into the courtyard, both dressed in full Kaldarian armor.

"They're going with you?"

At first I think he isn't going to answer, but then he nods. "The Scavs have grown bolder. A few raiding parties have been attacking portals in droves to steal the crystals used by the runecasters."

Bolder? Or more organized under a new leader? I wonder. Not that he has seen fit to inform me. I've overheard enough chatter from the soldiers to put together that this so-called oracle is more of a threat than ever and is most certainly in league with the Scavs. But I'm sure the king has his enemies well in hand.

"Will you go to Coban next?" I ask, glancing up at him.

"Soon." I didn't expect anything but a nonanswer, so I don't say anything. Eventually, Roshan turns, a keen stare scanning me from head to toe, not missing the old leathers. "Where are you off to?"

"To the palace forge," I lie, meeting a gaze that shockingly churns with conflicted emotions instead of its usual apathy. "It's been a while since I've hammered something."

Silence builds between us as he stares at me, and when his eyes soften for the first time in a long time, I feel *something*. I feel *him*.

"Sura." His voice is soft, pleading, almost desperate.

My pulse stutters. "Yes?"

Gods, that fleeting look of devotion in those beautiful brown eyes is almost my undoing. His lips part, but nothing emerges. I can see the fight in his tortured gaze, and then his jaw goes rigid, his shoulders stiffening impossibly, until that cruel, damnable, *hated* stare returns to his eyes. Refracted sunlight beams down on us from the stained-glass windows above, and for a moment, there's the slightest glimmer of purplish fire, just as there had been that night in Coban.

"The guards will accompany you," he says, signaling to a handful of soldiers behind him. "Don't be too long, it will be dark soon."

Heart sinking, I incline my head. "As you wish, Your Majesty."

A muscle tightens in his jaw at the formal address, but then he stalks away, four of his kingsguard remaining behind. At least it's not a dozen this time.

I stay there until the king and the rest of his entourage leave the courtyard. When she rides by, Clem's helmed gaze meets mine. She lifts her hand in a tentative wave, but it hangs limply in midair and then falls when I don't respond. It's clear whose side she's on, whose side she's always been on.

Despite my outward show of obedience, I have no intention of following Roshan's rules. If Helena's magi can't disable the cuffs, I've decided that I'll sever them from my body myself; I'll start with one hand and see what happens. It will be agony, but hopefully my magic will heal the worst of the wound and I'll be free to escape.

I barely notice the beauty of the setting sun as I grab a water canteen and head for the forge. The ever-obedient quartet of guards follows in silence, even entering the building to check it before allowing me through. Then three take up position outside while one remains inside.

I roll my eyes.

"Are you here to make sure I don't fling myself into the kiln?" I ask him sarcastically.

"King's orders, my lady," he says.

I snort and don a thick leather apron. "Suit yourself, but it will feel like an oven in here soon."

Sure enough, after an hour or so, the small room is sweltering.

My hammering is a rhythmic clang that I keep measured and consistent—on purpose. Out of the corner of my eye, I can see the guard's head drooping in lassitude. The hammering and the heat used to work like a charm on Laleh, always making her nod off in the corner of my forge in Coban. I'm sweating from exertion and the high temperature, which I've kept hotter than normal, but the man is nearly asleep.

Good, I think with a grin, pausing to guzzle the water I'd brought.

I keep going, gradually starting to slow my rhythm. I continue, even when I hear the first snores. Finally, after a few more minutes of work, I stop and watch him carefully. His helm hides his eyes, but his neck is lolling forward, motionless. He's out.

I don't know how much time I have, so I shuck off the protective apron quietly and head to the back of the forge. I pump my fist in triumph when I find the metal trapdoor in the floor—most bigger forges have an underground shaft in case of a fire—and I drop down as silently as I can.

Within minutes I'm out the other side and running toward the arena where Helena had told me to meet her friend. Come hell or high water, I'm leaving this place. It's not quite dark yet, so I stay out of sight as much as I can, ducking into the hedge maze whenever I see a soldier on patrol.

By now, I know the grounds like the back of my hand and manage to make it to the second tower without being seen. I hurry through the unlit passageways leading to the arena, surprised that I don't see a single servant anywhere inside. But maybe that's all Helena's doing. As I march onto the darkened sands, remembering the last time I was here, I swallow hard.

"Helena?" I call, hearing my voice echo. "Are you here?"

The steel doors clang shut ominously behind me, and I frown. The hairs on my arms rise, warning me of something that I can't see, only sense. Beneath my skin, my magic roils, but it's instantly dampened by the constricting runes on the cuffs.

"You made it," Helena's voice says from somewhere above me, and I try to place it, finally finding her in the royal box where Javed and Roshan had once stood what seems like an eternity ago.

"Where's your friend?" I ask.

She holds the railing, jubilant laughter leaving her lips. "By the maker, you are so predictable."

"Let me guess, you were lying?" I ask with a resigned chuckle of my own. "Just trying to entertain yourself at my expense?" I crouch and reach for my dagger. "Now who's predictable?"

"Oh, I plan to be entertained," she says. "Alas, I shall be the only witness to a terrible accident. A rebellious little rat defied her king to see the forbidden beast, and tragically, it escaped from its handlers and killed everyone in the arena until it was finally subdued." She sits on the seat meant for the queen. "Time to finish what I started months ago and take the place meant to be mine."

I have no time to respond before a vengeful screech pierces the silence.

Razulek. But he doesn't sound like himself.

A commotion at the gates behind me lets me know that my four guards have arrived just as a cloud of dust kicks up on the far end of the arena. "Defend the Starkeeper!" I hear one of them shout, just as Helena releases another wild cackle.

Two of my guards take up positions in front of me as a bloodthirsty monster comes barreling toward us. It's a scene straight out of my memory, only without a slew of frightened women running for cover. And the azdaha looks like a creature of nightmares, fresh blood pouring from deep wounds on its body, fueled by pain and rage.

Stars above, what have they done to him?

"Razulek!" I scream. "No!"

But either he can't hear me, or he doesn't listen, or he's too far gone to understand.

To my horror, I realize that he's not wearing a collar or bracers, which does not bode well for anyone in reach. I catch sight of the runecaster—Helena's friend, I presume—who had been tending to Razulek in the paddock many weeks ago. He's holding a jādū crossbow in his hand. Three other men have similar weapons pointed at the azdaha.

So that's their plan: watch a feral beast murder me and then subdue it.

"Razulek, stop!" I scream at the top of my lungs, trying and failing to open a magical connection between us. These fucking cuffs! I feel nothing . . . nothing but panic and impending death. My eyes flick up to Helena, who is watching the spectacle with twisted pleasure. Out of the corner of my eye, I see one of my guards drop his weapon and run, but right as he reaches the gates, he's felled by a bolt from a crossbow.

She's going to get rid of anyone in here not loyal to her . . . and spin a fabricated version of events.

Think, Sura!

Screams punctuate Razulek's rabid growls, along with the wet squelch of flesh and bone as another of my guards is devoured. The remaining two guards' weapons, forged with elemental magic, glimmer with air and ice, but they're no match for the frenzied, pain-crazed azdaha. One guard gets in a strike at Razulek's leg that makes him hiss like a cavern of snakes, but then he is crushed beneath a taloned foot, the sound of his wail cutting off abruptly.

The creature is nearly on top of us as my last remaining guard swings his sword, wind whipping around him as the jādū runes on his blade ignite. Without thinking, I dart forward, crashing into him with all my might. We roll across the sand, his disbelieving gaze meeting mine. "Why the fuck did you do that?" he cries. "It'll kill us!"

"I'm sorry," I gasp as Razulek's roar shakes the rafters right above us. "Run, if you can. I won't blame you. I just can't . . . let you hurt him."

"That thing is going to—!"

The sour stench of urine permeates the air as a mouth filled with razor-sharp teeth descends, strips of flesh and the sickening flash of armor visible in his maw. The words cut off when Razulek swallows the man in one bite.

I can smell the coppery odor of blood and, from this vantage, see the white foam—*poison?*—flecking the scales around his lips. His normally golden eyes are dull and covered with an opaque film. *Drugged?* I can't see if his wings have been hurt anew beyond the numerous slashes and lesions covering his body. They are folded and tucked into his sides.

Blood is power, my simurgh screams. *Blood is akasha.*

Stars above, what does she mean? That I need to bleed akasha? That doesn't make sense.

A deafening, maddened roar makes me cover my ears. Fuck, I have seconds, if that.

Throwing up a plea to any of the benevolent gods—Saru, Mithral, or Zora—or even Vena, if she's listening, that I'm not about to make a fatal mistake, I run as fast as I can toward Razulek's underbelly. A feral eye latches on to my position and tracks me. When I'm underneath, I slash my dagger across my palm, deep enough for my wound to not heal immediately, and press it to one of the open gashes on his hide. The cuffs don't hinder my blood.

"Target the beast!" I hear Helena scream. "After it kills her!"

Razulek roars as our blood mixes and *something* transfers between us ... or maybe that's just my very desperate imagination. I feel no telltale drain of power, no akasha, nothing but a strange surge of heat. Hysterical laughter bubbles and then dies as the hide beneath my oozing palm warms to impossible temperatures. The dark green scales surrounding all the blood and torn flesh glow a molten chartreuse color, almost bright yellow, the color of *fire*.

Oh, maker above. The collar would have prevented him, but he's rune-free, and ... he lifts his head high and an inferno erupts from his mouth, running over the sands like a deadly tsunami of flame. I hear fearful shouts and then Helena's scream as the blaze billows upward.

The entire arena is almost engulfed, but I've been around the forge my entire life, even before I was the Starkeeper. I'm not afraid of a little heat.

"Razulek! It's me, Suraya!"

Moments or an eternity passes before the bulk that was inadvertently shielding me from the flames shifts, and I brace, shoving my bleeding hand against his wound and willing my akasha into him. The azdaha's body jerks as multiple arrows collide against his hide. Pain explodes in my side and my leg, and I collapse in agony, my dagger curled to my chest. I've been shot, too. *Gods ... help me.*

"Raz ..."

Starkeeper.

Slowly, I part heavy eyelids to peer up, only to see the arrows sticking out of my torso and my thigh. Both injuries look bad and feel worse because they burn like acid before melting into euphoria. *Fucking Jade.* I can feel my magic valiantly trying to combat the wounds and the drug, but I must have given too much akasha to Razulek to clear through his fog. Everything feels rapturously sluggish. My throat is dry, my body starting to convulse, as the glorious toxin scours my insides.

Stars, is this it? Is this the end?

Suddenly, the blazing arena is covered in a swatch of darkness as something—*wings*—expands wide above us. They're the most amazing things I've ever seen. A pale green, and nearly translucent. I smile in shivering delight. They're healthy and unmarred.

"Raz . . . your wings . . . so beautiful . . ."

Stay with me, little queen.

Dimly, I see huge bloodstained claws coming toward me. Ever so gently, I feel those talons wrap around my body, and then a huge gust of wind whips around us as we are propelled upward. I'm tucked into his belly, face pressed to his heated hide. Razulek's roar thunders right as his body collides with the roof. Then there's an unholy crash and the sound of splintering wood, but I only hear them dully as if my ears are failing along with the rest of my blissed-out senses.

But those wings spread wide on the wind, and we're flying. Up and up and up.

My head lolls back as darkness dims the edges of my vision and a rhapsodic paralysis snakes through my veins. In the waning twilight, I catch a glimpse of the moon . . . and the first twinkling of my beautiful, precious stars.

Tears drip and blood bubbles from my lips, and I succumb to oblivion.

Chapter Ten

The Night King

For a moment, a blinding agony rips through me, felling me to my knees.

Frantic, I press palms to my torso and thigh, but find no indication of injury. Two tender spots sting as if they've been impaled by something sharp, and pain radiates everywhere. I can barely figure out the source before my shadows burst from me in an onyx cloud as I topple into an indecent rapture, and I gasp, fighting for control over delirium that isn't mine.

By the blood, it's fucking *hers*.

The starblessed bond I'd despaired about for years has been silent for weeks.

Until now.

At first, I had been skeptical—the magic that had dampened it for so many years had been her mother's, but this was something different. But as the days turned into weeks, the weight of the cursed tether had vanished. Either my regrettable mate had garnered enough magic to block the bond herself, perhaps after the cruel way I had left her the last time . . . or someone else had.

Either way, I was exultant. I could no longer feel my soul-fated. She was finally out of my reach. *Safe*. My mind had rejoiced while something deep inside of me mourned the loss. If I had a heart, perhaps that is where such an ache would have resided.

But hearts were for mortals.

Not gods.

Or so I'd thought...

Dimly, I hear the triumphant scream of my azdaha in my head, but I'm distracted as the delirious feelings swamping me vanish abruptly, and I feel nothing but the hollow dearth in my chest that I've become used to. My shadows flutter limply, the bond divinely silent once more.

All I can feel now is my azdaha's unbridled joy.

Indira, what is it? Are you well?

She chuffs. *He comes, Darrius. My mate!*

Recently, she'd been able to feel him weakening, and we'd prepared for war against a cowardly Oryndhrian king to take back what had been stolen from us when negotiations to retrieve Razulek had failed. I had sent my most trusted adviser—my brilliant sister—and our straightforward terms had been rejected. War, she'd proclaimed sadly, would be the only way to get Razulek back.

You're certain it's him? I ask Indira via the bond.

As sure as the stars grace the night sky. Yours comes, too.

My breath stutters to a fucking stop. *My* what *comes?*

He brings your mate.

Part II

Fear those who do not fear the gods.
—*Rothdar: A History*, vol. 1

Chapter Eleven

"Is she awake yet?" a deep, irritated voice rumbles, piercing the thickened haze in my brain like the gong of a forge hammer.

Sands, is it morning already?

I want to lift my hands, clap them to my ears, and whine for my father to give me five more minutes of peace before I'm to go work in the tavern, but my limbs won't cooperate. Frustrated, I groan and then recoil as the sound I make reverberates in my skull.

I hear the slight thud of footsteps on stone, followed by a garbled, low-toned response. I crack open eyelids that are heavier than the anvil in my workshop and wince at the blinding light. With an inaudible moan, I squeeze them shut immediately. Sands on fire, what in the pits of Droon did I do last night?

I'll bet anything it has to do with Laleh. Any time I'm in trouble, it's her fault.

As I take slow stock of my body, I feel like I've been dragged across the desert naked by a flock of wild camels, then tossed off a cliff into a mine shaft, then thrown down a sand dune inside a barrel. Everything aches. And burns. And aches some more. I have no pressing desire to open my eyes again, but I force myself to when that furious baritone that I definitely do not recognize assaults my eardrums.

By the maker, did Laleh . . . did *I* . . . bring someone back home last night?

I bolt upright and nearly vomit from the effort as flickering spots of light and dark in my vision play havoc with my disoriented brain.

"Breathe," someone cautions softly. It's not the first haughty, stern voice that had instantly raised my hackles, but a much kinder one. I blink, my speckled vision taking in a weathered face, russet skin, light brown hair.

"Here, sip some of this slowly." The cool rim of a cup presses to my lips, and I let the refreshing water slide over my swollen tongue and parched throat. I swallow with a whimper. It feels like I've consumed needles, and I nearly faint from the pain. "Easy now," the voice says gently. "A little more. It will get better, I promise. You were poisoned."

Poisoned? That doesn't sound right.

When the fog of pain finally clears, I slowly let my gaze acclimatize . . . and freeze.

I'm not in my workshop. There's no forge, no table, no cot. My mother's painting is nowhere in sight, and there's no shelf with my tools. There are other shelves, but they're cluttered with carefully labeled bottles and vials filled with liquids, powders, and various substances like an apothecary. A handful of other empty beds line the floor in a neat row.

My confused gaze flicks to the large bright window, and I squint in disbelief. Deep green foliage is visible just beyond the frame, instead of the miles and miles of desert sand that *would* be the typical view.

Sands, I'm not in Coban.

I'm in a strange room with . . . My vision wobbles between the kind healer and . . . the angry giant. *Two* strange men.

I scoot backward on the bed, my aching spine crashing into the bed frame, because I most definitely do *not* know the tall, foreboding figure on the other side of the room, seething like some kind of silver-haired eldritch creature. Something strange unfurls in the pit of my belly . . . a primal tug when that *very* unfriendly gaze crashes into mine.

"Who are you?" I ask in a shaky voice.

His cruel mouth curls into a cold smile. "I think the better question is, who are *you*? And why are you here in my kingdom?" His deep voice is like honey and burning ash, the velvet roughness of it sending a shiver dancing over my skin. It commands instant compliance and, for some reason, rings curiously familiar, though I'm certain I've never met him before in my life. I'd remember a man who looks like he could crush my bones with a flick of his little finger or eviscerate me with that cutting stare alone. "Are you a spy? An assassin? Who sent you?"

I flinch at the rapid-fire questions that make absolutely no sense. "Do I *look* like an assassin?"

"Death hides in many forms."

I suppress my shudder as he prowls closer, his fingers gripping the footrail of my bed. It takes an eternity before I drag my eyes from those lethal-looking hands up to the rest of him. From my low vantage point, he towers above me, garbed in black and with not a strand of that shiny hair daring to be out of place; everything about him is unrelentingly immaculate.

Those extraordinary locks are shaved at the sides and drape like silk across inhumanly broad shoulders. One wouldn't expect silver hair to pair so well with black eyebrows and eyelashes, but it does. The combination is . . . magnetic. Rich bronze-brown skin, an aquiline blade of a nose, stern lips, and a cleft chin come together to make my jaw sag. If only the soulless burn of those unblinking midnight eyes didn't ruin it all.

Inky markings peep from beneath his armor, twining up his corded neck and creeping down his big hands to his knuckles, wherever any skin is visible. Are those arcane symbols or runes of some kind? For a moment, I swear the ones on his neck ripple, but that could be from the irritated flexing of his throat. The stranger's face would be flawless, stunning even, if it weren't for the ferocious scowl marring it.

"Why have you come here?" he growls, black-as-pitch irises boring into the depths of my soul. "Did your cowardly king send *you* to spy on me? Do you mean my people harm?"

"No . . . what . . . wait . . . I'm not . . ." I gulp, unable to speak properly, because I have no sound recollection of anything recent. My mind is a fraught jumble of places, faces, and images that don't seem to fit anywhere, while my emotions roil like a chaotic sea, leaving me awash in confusion. Anger and pain are a lingering violent cocktail in my blood.

But *how*? And *why*?

I know that I am Suraya Saab from Coban, but I don't know *how* I came to be in this bed or *where* I've come from. It feels as though I *should* know, but when I try to remember, there's a big gaping hole in my memory. It's . . . frighteningly blank.

The last real thing I can remember clearly is receiving a fancy invitation to go to the Kaldarian palace. But there's nothing much after that.

So, is this the capital city? Had I accepted the crown prince's summons?

Frowning, I run a hand through my loosened hair and halt, pulling the shockingly lengthy ends toward me. They're much longer than I remember—but it's the color that stops my breath. Are some of the strands *silver*? How and, more important, *when* did this happen?

I press my fingers into my temples. "Why can't . . . I remember?"

He scoffs. "Can't remember? Or won't?"

"I don't know what you want from me. I don't even know where we are."

He lifts a dagger, and the sight of it is gratifyingly familiar. "Why do you have this?"

"My mother's dagger?" But even as I focus on the finely crafted weapon, I don't remember finishing it. I remember hammering the steel and cooling it, but not much more than that. It glows with an unearthly luminescence, runes carved into the blade that weren't there before. However, deep down, somehow I know it's my handiwork . . . that *I* etched that jādū-forged steel. But *when*? And *how*? My skull thumps.

"Do you intend to kill me with this?" he presses.

"No?" It emerges like a question, and I hate the fearful doubt I hear in my own voice.

"Tell me why you have come," he growls again, and I recoil.

"I can't! I don't fucking know!"

Self-preservation has frantic thoughts of escape spinning through my head.

But then I feel an odd pressure on my skull, like something is trying to peel me apart, as he continues to stare intently at me. After a few seconds, a frustrated look comes over his face and the pressure eases.

"How are you resisting me?" he spits, eyes snapping with rage. "No human can."

I frown. Resisting what? His gaze narrows in icy suspicion as if I might be a threat, but my brain is stuck on one thing: What does he mean no *human* can?

"Do you know who you are?" he demands.

"A b-bladesmith," I stammer, the answer coming to me immediately. "From Coban."

Thank the sands I'm aware of that at least. My childhood memories are crystal clear, but everything else is muddled. The more I concentrate, the more my memory feels as though it's filled with ever-widening sinkholes, but I focus on what I know.

I'm Suraya Saab.

I'm from Coban.

My father owns a tavern, which I hope to inherit and manage one day, and my aunt, Amma, works in the kitchens—she's the best cook in Coban.

My best friend's name is Laleh.

I received a coveted invitation to the palace.

With a shiver, I glance at the window again, the verdant green of the trees just as alarming as earlier. *Could* it be Kaldari? I frown. I've never been to the capital city, but my mother always said it was beautiful. Flashes of a sprawling palace appear in my head and the handsome face of a prince . . . an explosion and an underground city with striated pink-and-brown canyons . . . a tower drenched in blood.

I cringe at the last image, something in my brain recoiling like a snapping band, and I'm filled with a slew of emotions.

Fear, love, hurt, heartbreak. *Pain.*

A montage of faces, both beloved and betrayers. Shimmering runes and a giant flying serpent. A hysterical laugh bursts from my lips.

Sands, no wonder I can't remember reality properly. I clutch my aching head. "Stars above, what is happening to me?"

The healer clucks his tongue sympathetically. "You've been badly injured," he interjects after a furtive, frightened glance at the giant. "You hurt your head. Brain injuries are unpredictable, but with time and care, I think your memories will return."

I pin my lips between my teeth. That makes sense, considering how sore my body feels . . . but how did it happen? All I can see when I force myself to remember are fuzzy gray patches. My skull protests angrily, and I inhale a shallow breath and stop trying. "Where are we?" I look toward the kindly older man, feeling he is more likely to answer me.

"Where do *you* think you are?" the silver-haired man snaps as if he's nearing the end of his patience ... or annoyed that I'm talking to the healer and not to him.

I stiffen and shoot him a derisive look I know won't go over well. The sarcastic reply punches from my lips before I can stop it. "If I knew, I wouldn't be asking, would I?"

His scowl grows teeth, thick brows slamming down. Despite my brain fog, I bristle and match his hostile expression, and we glare viciously at each other. The healer at my side lets out an aggrieved gasp and takes a step toward the menace in black before stopping himself short.

"Leave us," the surly beast commands.

Much to my dismay, the healer departs—but only after a protracted moment as if worried for my safety. Shit, *should* I be worried?

Too late now.

"That was rude," I remark, clearly with no sense of survival when he glowers at me. I must be delirious if I think provoking an unhinged stranger who believes I'm here to assassinate him is wise. Not that I even know where *here* is, for maker's sake. Or *how* I got here.

Or *anything* relating to here.

I swallow past the sawdust in my mouth and catch a cloying, unfamiliar taste on my tongue. "Did you drug me?" I demand.

The man's eyebrows jump up to his hairline, that imperious stare sparking with outrage. Those big, tattooed hands of his tighten on the footrail. I bet they'll leave dents with the way his forearms and biceps are straining beneath his well-tailored tunic.

Stop ogling his arms, you ass. He's probably imagining the bedrail is your neck.

He glares down the length of his elegant nose at me. "You were found unconscious just beyond the Barrin Mountains with an azdaha that vanished some time ago. You were both badly injured. There was no drugging." His tone drips with contempt. "No one under my rule would do anything so vile."

His words sound like they should make sense, but they don't. None of that sounds in any way plausible. Everyone knows that the Barrin Mountains are impassable . . . and azdahas don't fucking exist. They're a mythical creature.

Sands on fire, what if . . . what if *none* of this is real?

Time slows to the consistency of honey.

I could be asleep and dreaming.

Or maybe this is a waking fever dream! I've had them before, the ones where I'm certain I am awake. I've even dreamed of *him* before, I think? It's all coming back in snippets: that cruel blade of a jaw, the otherworldly gleam of pewter hair, and that looming shadowy presence. I know exactly who he is . . . because he's a figment of my overly febrile imagination.

"You're not real," I crow victoriously.

A noise of pure irritation leaves him. "I assure you, I'm very real."

Forcing my weakened limbs to work, I push up on my hands and knees, and crawl gracelessly to the end of the bed. Then I heave myself up so that my nose is parallel to the stranger's armored chest. Even in my addled state, I appreciate somewhere in the back of my mind that the breastplate is of exceptional quality and has been crafted by a master blacksmith.

I poke him in the abdomen and let out a curse. "You're hard."

A deeply indrawn breath meets my ears, and I let out a deranged snort at my poorly chosen words. My fingers trail down the granite planes of his torso to his waistband and the laces tied tightly above a breath-stealing bulge. Smirking, I congratulate myself on a job well done.

"What are you doing?" my sexy hallucination snaps, his voice a rasp that sinks into my skin even as I snatch my marauding hand away.

I think back to the erotic dreams I've had over the past few years with my faceless shadow lover, the one Laleh always makes fun of me for. The proportions of my broody warden are similar enough to make all my confusion and qualms vanish. Because *of course* this is a dream... one of the ones where you think you're awake but you're not. And I *know* him.

"I should have made you more pleasant," I muse as I pull myself to standing so that I am nose to nose with my creation. "Not so much grumpy, asshole energy."

"How dare—"

I stop him with a finger smashed up against his mouth, watching his midnight gaze go wide in shock, and relish the feel of his surprisingly lush lips. A spark of desire courses through me. Maybe I can get this wild fever dream to go in a more pleasant direction. I seem to recall he's excellent at following orders... or giving them, depending on my fancy.

I trace my fingertip down and across a rigid jawline that could cut glass. "Less talking, more doing, Shadow Prince."

"King. I am a *king*."

I snicker at his boast. "Whatever you say."

My dream-lover is so tall that even while I'm standing on the cot, he still looms an inch or two above me. This close, I can see shards of refracted light in that pitch-dark stare. His hair looks so silky that I want to thread my fingers through the shiny strands to see if they're as soft as they seem. But I'm sidetracked as my gaze snags on the cuffs adorning my wrists.

My nose wrinkles. What in the pits of Droon are they?

I've never been into bondage, but maybe Dream-Suraya is? They're delicately forged metal bands with engraved runes of some kind. They'd be pretty—but something seems truly *off* about them. With a peculiar sense of doom, I twist my hands and peer at them, searching for some way to unlock them. "How in the realms do these unlatch?"

"Don't bother," Grumpy-Hole Prince of Darkness snaps. "We've already tried."

"Did you put them on me?" I accuse.

He stares, lips flattening. "*No.* We found you like this."

I shake my head, confusion flooding me anew. This doesn't feel right. None of this feels remotely right. "These aren't real," I say, shaking my head. "And you're not real, either." I tremble, a pervasive feeling of dread rising out of nowhere . . . that I am terribly, horribly wrong about everything. My voice trembles: "Are you?"

I lift my hand toward him again, but this time, he grasps below my wrist, careful not to touch the cuffs. "Oh, I promise, little infiltrator, I am most definitely real." A smirk curls those smooth lips. "And you are my prisoner, so stop testing my patience, if you value your life."

His fingers squeeze mercilessly, and I gasp as pain shoots up my arm.

Now, I definitely don't like this. I pinch my eyes shut.

Wake up, Suraya! Get up!

But when I peek through my lashes, he's still there like an ominous, unsmiling mountain of wrath. A sinking feeling ensues that perhaps this isn't a hallucination at all. "Let go of me," I snap, and shove my free arm up to push him away.

But before my fingers make contact with his chest, I am propelled forcefully but efficiently on a gust of air, falling back onto the mattress, though the man hasn't moved a muscle. Because his *tattoos* did. They are no longer on his neck or his hands, which are back on the footrail of my bed. The shadowy ribbons of darkness now tether my hands and legs, keeping them banded to the sheets beneath me. I struggle but can't move from my supine position. My eyes widen.

"What are those things? How are you doing that?"

Heavy footsteps bring him around to the side of the bed. "Magic."

"That isn't possible without a jādū crystal," I say, the hairs on my nape standing straight up.

He opens his fist, and thick black tendrils melting into liquid smoke curl over his knuckles, and my eyes bulge. "It is here," he says.

My mouth falls open in disbelief. I am utterly mesmerized by the shadow dance of the smoke that slithers up his forearm in coiling wisps. It has to be a parlor trick or an optical illusion. Even the runecasters in Oryndhr have to use crystals for any kind of magic. No one has pure akasha running through their veins. No one. At least no one . . . in Oryndhr.

A horrid sense of foreboding fills me. "Where is *here*?"

The smoky tendrils retreat, dissipating into nothing. "Everlea."

My head spins at the implication. I'm in *Everlea*? The realm ruled by a monster? The occasional traveling merchant comes through Coban claiming to have beast scales, luxurious pelts, and spelled jewelry from Everlea for sale, but the goods are almost always fake. Not much of fact is known about the reclusive kingdom—only that it has been Oryndhr's hostile neighbor since the hundred-year War of the Gods tore the realms of men apart. And its monarch is as ruthless as they come.

If what this man says is true, then how in the name of rogue sandstorms did *I* get here? Surely he has to be joking. But there's no humor on his grim face, no lighthearted delight at my expense, only a stony, arrogant antipathy as though I've personally offended him somehow with my presence. Maybe I have. He's much too arrogant to be someone unimportant.

The way the healer had scurried away at his brusque command makes me balk and swallow hard. Leaps of logic are apparently too much for my poor brain. I glance up uncertainly at him. "And that makes you . . ."

"Darrius Nightsong," he says.

"Nightso— the *king* of Everlea?" I whimper faintly and bite back my fright. Maker above, he *hadn't* been boasting before. Because *that* is definitely information recorded in the history books. Nightsong, the *nightmare* fucking king. Gods, am I going to die?

"Gold star," he says. "Now your turn. Why have you come to Everlea? Does your deceitful ruler know who you are to me? Did he send you?"

Who *I* am to *him*? What does he mean?

I don't know this man; I've never seen him before, at least not outside my dreams, which are clearly, in fact, a laughable, hideous coincidence. And I've definitely never even met the king of Oryndhr.

"I already told . . ." I begin.

His voice deepens, waves of compulsion lancing from it. "Do *not* lie."

The ferocious power emanating from him reverberates from a million directions at once, pressing down upon me and almost rattling my bones as he looms over me like a terrifying specter. The tenebrous king of Everlea. I don't have a single doubt in my mind that this man is more than capable of violence. Darkness seethes from his very pores.

Stars above, I want to obey, but my brain is still blank. "I swear, I . . . don't know."

Vengeful shadows bleed into his eyes like an ink-spill, and I stiffen at the obvious threat. Unbidden, a burst of *something* gathers in my center, like the wingbeats of some formidable creature, each powerful pulse crashing into my rib cage from *inside*.

I gasp aloud as those strange cuffs on my wrists ignite, runes lit crimson . . . and everything slams to a violent, oppressive halt.

Blood, breath, bones . . .

Sleep, something commands, and I can only obey.

Chapter Twelve

The darkened quarters I awake in are not the same as the healing wing before.

Mortified by the strange oblivion that had gripped me, I flush at the thought of whether the aptly named nightmare king had carried me here when I'd fallen unconscious, but then shake my head. He probably had one of his lackeys do it. I inhale and exhale a long, slow breath. I am alive and breathing. The pressure in my chest is gone. My head feels clear.

And said king is nowhere in sight, thank the gods.

The chamber I'm in is a bedroom fit for a princess. The enormous bed is deep and wide, with a thick mattress and soft pillows. It sits on a raised dais with filmy burgundy curtains hanging over the top. Comfortable but luxurious furniture accents the room: a pair of armchairs near the window, a mahogany dresser and vanity, and a handsome carved mantelpiece near the fireplace. The carpet is a delicate blue with intricate gold flowers.

The room is feminine and beautiful, and far more extravagant than I'm used to, but I'm more concerned with my current state and whether I can fight my way out of here if I have to. The king certainly did not leave me with a sense that I was welcome.

Slowly, I roll my neck, wincing at the sound of crackling bones, and then glance beneath the blanket to the simple shift I'm clothed in. Under the thin garment, I can see that clean bandages are wrapped around my torso as well as one of my thighs. Scrapes and faded yellow bruises cover my skin. But shockingly, most of the wounds look like they've been healed for weeks.

I haven't been here *that* long, have I?

My gaze drifts to the cuffs on my forearms, and I study the shimmering bands that are no longer glowing red. They don't hurt, and anyone would think they'd been crafted for me, fitting my wrists perfectly. I lift one, studying the plethora of runes carved into its surface. I've never seen anything like them in my life, and I've forged plenty of runic blades for Lord Vasha, a powerful Jaxxian noble.

That gives me an idea: if there's a forge here, maybe I can cut the cuffs off myself.

But first, I need to get myself out of this room, because no one's coming to rescue me. And if the king of this realm has his way, getting tortured for information I can't remember is the least of my worries—I'll likely be in an unmarked grave before day's end.

Gingerly, I sit up and swing my legs over the side of the bed and belatedly realize I'm not actually alone as I'd thought. A young woman I don't recognize is on the other side of the room, sitting at a table and hunched over a thick volume while making notes. A half-eaten sandwich rests on a plate next to her, and my stomach gives an obnoxious growl even as I yank the blanket up over my short, sheer shift.

She glances up at the noise and smiles shyly. "Oh! You're awake!"

I put her in her twenties or thereabouts, younger than me, though looks can be deceiving. I wonder if she's the older healer's apprentice or some kind of guard, though if I'm truly suspected of being an assassin or a spy sent from Oryndhr, then why aren't there more guards than just her? She's so lean, I'm sure I could overpower her if I had to.

"Who are you?" I ask.

"I'm Ani," she says, and then scrunches up her brow. "I mean, it's Anahima, if we're being formal, which I hope we're not."

I lift my brows. Anahima, as in the goddess of wisdom, fertility, and war? The only reason I recognize the name is because it was in one of my mother's old books on ancient gods and the Royal Stars. That's a substantial weight for any woman to carry. No wonder she prefers to shorten it.

"Well met, Ani. Are you a healer?"

She shakes her head, her long, dark hair swinging. "More of a scholar, but I enjoy learning about all the different magical disciplines, including the healing arts."

The casual reference to magic has me gawking, but maybe I have their supposed magic to thank for the fact that my various cuts and bruises are healing in short order. It would make sense. I still can't get my mind around it . . . and how easily the king had moved me on the bed in the blink of an eye, without lifting a finger.

"So you're not here to make sure I don't covertly murder your obnoxious monarch like the assassin he thinks I am?" I ask before I can help myself.

Blue eyes sparkle as she shoots me an amused look. "I volunteered to keep an eye on you out of curiosity. No one wants to come near the spy from Oryndhr."

"I'm not a spy." But even as I say it, I'm filled with doubt. *Am I?*

Suddenly, she lifts a finger, and the lamp on the table next to me flickers to life. Well, I suppose that answers my earlier question about guards—since she can wield magic, that probably means she can defend herself from any threats, including me.

"You can do magic like your king also?" I ask warily.

Her brows rise. "Everyone in Everlea can."

"Everyone?" How is that even possible? Magic is practically extinct in Oryndhr. It's the reason King Zarek is so overly protective of the remaining jādū mines.

Ani nods. "Yes. The numena of each magi are dependent on their level and talent, of course, but this realm is rich in akasha. Our people are born with magic."

Does that mean everyone here is a magi? Do they even use jādū? And what are numena?

The questions spawn like sandworms in my head, but I'm suddenly painfully aware of my very full bladder. I suppose that takes precedence instead of bombarding her with my curiosity. "May I use the, er, privy?" I ask. "And, um, where are my clothes?"

"Oh—of course!" A blush stains her cheeks as she hurries over and hands me a neatly folded pile. "Your clothing is being mended and cleaned. The water closet is behind that door over there."

Gratefully, I take the bundle and shuffle over to the small room she'd pointed out to take care of my needs as well as wash my hands and face. I switch out the see-through shift for the borrowed dress. It's too tight, but beggars can't be choosers.

I can't help it that I'm a healthy eater—Amma's cooking is much too delicious to resist, though my body is far more muscular than I remember it being. Like my hair, the differences are notable. Sands, how much time have I lost?

"Are you hungry?" Ani asks when I emerge, tugging on the snug bodice, as she brings over a plate holding another sandwich. I sit back down on the bed and accept the food, idly wondering if I should be eating anything, but I suppose if Ani wanted to kill me, she could have done so easily while I was sleeping.

I crane my neck to peer up at her—she's like a tall, thin reed, much lankier than me. Come to think of it, this dress, which is tight and long on me, is probably hers. "Thank you."

Suddenly too ravenous to worry about poison, I take a huge bite, the flavors of roasted meat, fresh tomatoes, greens, and dressing bursting over my tongue, but force myself to chew slowly even though I want to inhale the meal like a starving beast.

"Slowly," she cautions, and then stares curiously at me. "You don't have magi proficiencies where you come from?"

"We don't have *magi*," I say through a second mouthful. "Or magic. At least natural magic that comes from akasha, anyway."

She nods. "I read that in our history books about Oryndhr, but I didn't actually believe it was true," she says. "I can't fathom a world without magic."

"Oh, it's true." I finish the sandwich and sip the glass of water she offers, waiting for my brain to catch up with my stomach that it's no longer starving. "I suppose we stopped believing in the old gods and paid the price."

Ani lets out a cynical sniff as if what I've said is preposterous. "That's not—" she begins, and then breaks off.

"That's not what?" I ask.

"Nothing."

Clearly, it's something, because her lips are pinned tight and she won't meet my eyes. I wonder if she's been given instructions on what to share with me by the tyrant king.

"My friends call me Sura," I say, hoping that my affable tone will convince Ani that I have no ill intent toward her. Right now, I need to arm myself with as much information as possible before I take any action . . . especially before the royal *dick*-tator returns to ruin the day. "Do you know how long I have been here?"

"A few days," she replies in a slightly livelier tone. "Your wounds were extensive, but the king had the best healers in the realm trying to save you, including his own personal physician." She points to my side and my thigh. "The healer said you took two poisoned bolts and the infection had spread. You were lucky to keep your leg, but your body took care of itself."

Strange choice of words on her part. She sounds impressed for some reason. Once more, I try to remember exactly what could have happened to result in such an injury, but the gaping hole in my memory hasn't disappeared and I bite back a frustrated curse. "I don't remember any of it," I admit.

"They said when you crashed with the azdaha in that field, you shattered several ribs as well as your collarbone and arm, but those look like they've already healed."

Already? I frown—if I've been here only a few days, any kind of injury that involves broken bones would hardly be fully healed. Then I remember that I'm not in Oryndhr, where a sling and a turmeric poultice would be our best option. Here, they have magic and mystical beasts. I bite my lip. "So it's true then about the creature? Do . . . azdahas exist?"

She graces me with a quizzical look. "Yes. How else would you have gotten here?"

But for some reason, my brain cannot even begin to conceive of something so outlandish. Azdahas belong in fairy tales. Maybe if and when I see one, I'll believe it.

"Do all your healers use magic?"

"Most of the time," she says.

I take that in. Life would be so different in Oryndhr if people in poorer cities had access to magical health care. "Oryndhrian healers use compresses, wraps, and homemade remedies that take a long time to cure ills, if at all. Are your healers part of the Order of the Magi?"

"No," Ani says with a perplexed look. "We don't have anything like that."

"Political houses?"

"No." She wrinkles her nose and then brightens. "But we do have a royal court and general ranks for magic users based on their abilities. Oh, and there are the Aspačanā clans who live out in the plains, but they keep to themselves mostly. They have elemental magic."

A huff of incredulous laughter leaves my lips. I still can't conceive that magic flows so freely here that there are *ranks*. What would it be like to wield that kind of power? To have *elemental* magic?

I remember the smoky tendrils that the king had bound me with, my insides clenching at the memory of being at his mercy. I recall how they'd been an extension of his obvious power, and then my brain decides to veer down the dangerous path of wondering what else they could do, all those possibilities running wild.

My blood heats. *No, no, no.*

"What kind of ranks?" I ask Ani hastily, shutting down that train of thought with every ounce of willpower I possess. No good can come of that. *None at all.*

"I'm not really sure I'm supposed to be talking to you about all this." She stares at me and then shoots an anxious look to the door as if expecting her prick of a king to storm through any moment. "But I suppose this can't hurt since it's common knowledge. Don't tell him I told you my name, though, will you?"

Sands, this king clearly has control issues, if he'd get upset about a basic introduction . . . or that someone was being, stars forbid, *kind.* "I promise," I say, pretending to lock my lips and throw away the key. "Please tell me about the ranks. I bet you're one of the higher ones."

She flushes with pleasure and props her hip onto an ornate trunk to the left of my bed. "We have four main divisions. Basic, which is the lowest proficiency, then mestial, then dominant, and lastly sovran. I'm dominant." Her cheeks redden more. "That is, I'll be tested as dominant in a few weeks. Most children are classified as basic when they initially manifest their numena, and then they grow from there. Not all do, however. Some only have one basic numen, which means limited power over one of the magical pillars."

My mind races as I try to keep up, but forewarned is forearmed, especially with a king who wants to kill me. "Pillars?"

"Yes. Magic is classified into three affinities." She warms to her subject, her hands moving animatedly. "Aether, which includes any kinetic magic like elemental, nature, time, and weather magic. Psionic, which covers mind magic, precognition, dreams, hallucinations, illusions, and divination. And the last, corpus, relates to the body and includes animal magic, shapeshifting, and beast speech." She pauses, frowning, and taps her chin. "Oh, and enchantments to enhance or hide one's form or numena."

Shapeshifting? I try to keep my jaw from dropping open. By the maker, is that even *possible*?

"What kind of enchantments?" I ask.

An eager Ani hops up onto the trunk and settles into a more comfortable position. "A magi with a corpus designation can enchant an amulet to protect its wearer or a cloak to make someone invisible, for example. Corpus also includes healing and necromancy."

"Necromancy?" I gasp. "Like raising the dead?"

She gives me a solemn nod, face earnest. "It's forbidden, along with summoning and sanguimancy. Blood magic." From her sudden, fretful expression, Ani looks like she wants to say more about the subject, but doesn't. "So there you go. Those are the three main pillars of magic, aether, psionic, and corpus."

"That's incredible," I say, and let out a small laugh.

Why isn't any of this information in books about Everlea and the historical records of magic? Is the history I've always known incorrect or not the full picture? Though my mind is cluttered with a thousand questions, it feels good to keep it occupied with something new instead of worrying about what I can't remember.

"Do your people pull from different affinities?"

"Some do," Ani says. "But it's rare—" She breaks off, clapping a hand to her mouth as the door swings open and all the levity dies a dismal death. Ani scrambles off the trunk and drops her body into a curtsy worthy of a royal court. "Sire, your . . . guest is awake."

King Darrius's compelling presence instantly fills the room, making it seem much smaller than it is. His starkly beautiful face is as stony and uncommunicative as it had been previously, but he's no longer wearing his armor. Instead, a fawn-colored tunic sits over dark fitted breeches and worn brown boots, his imposing frame sleeker and more sinewy now without the intimidating breastplate and spined epaulets.

His wealth of silver hair has been gathered into a loose knot, drawing attention to his sweeping cheekbones and his otherworldly bone structure. Those inky tattoos thicken and wind down the column of his neck, disappearing under his neckline. I wonder how far down they go and then force myself to abandon that course of thinking immediately.

When his piercing gaze meets mine, I feel that same strange tug—much stronger now—in my center. I dismiss it as nerves . . . or pure unfiltered loathing. The man simply gets under my skin.

Displaying any weakness to him would be a mistake, so I lift my chin and opt for bravado. "Oh, it's you."

"Are you ready to talk?" he asks, that velvet and ash voice sliding over me. "Or now that you're no longer on death's doorstep, shall we see whether you choose the carrot or the stick?"

I roll my eyes. "Sands, has anyone ever told you that your charm is outstanding?"

One corner of his mouth curls, but he doesn't respond to my baiting. "Enough prevaricating. What do you remember?"

A saucer-eyed Ani lets out a squeak at the king's hard tone, but I let nothing show on my face at the threat. "I still don't know what you want me to say. I have no idea how I got here except for what you've told me. Supposedly, I crashed in a field and nearly died and have been your guest ever since. My memories are trickling back, but they're disjointed, to say the least."

As with Ani earlier, my explanation slips out readily, but this time, I frown at my willingness to oblige. Had I meant to disclose all of that? That was much too cooperative, especially in response to a person I'd rather kick in the teeth than comply with.

Frowning harder, I stare at my cup and then at a very guilty-looking Ani. "Was there something in my water?" I demand.

"Nothing life-threatening. Verac root," she admits, looking deeply apologetic. "I made the tincture myself, and it's harmless other than the effect of making you conducive to sharing information." Indignation barrels through me as she flushes slightly. "And it might affect your emotions *some*."

Isn't *that* the truth? Fury floods in the wake of the outrage, but it's not toward Ani. It's directed at the man who stands a few feet away, the pompous ass who thinks he can do anything he wants. He must have given the order for me to be dosed with a damn truth tincture.

He is a king, a tiny voice reminds me, but I'm too riled up to care.

Something visceral thunders through my veins and gathers inside of me, as if to erase the Verac root serum from my bloodstream. I know that's not possible, but I clamp my lips together and vow not to let a single compliant statement leave my mouth. By some uncanny miracle, I feel the root's unnatural compulsion dissipating and let every ounce of my small but invisible victory show on my face. My nemesis's eyes narrow at my smug expression.

"I told you what I know, Your Insufferable Majesty. But if you need to trick me to be convinced, then have at it."

Those intriguing shadows whip to life around him like chaotic vines as his lips part in shock. I stare in fascination, remembering the feel of them on my wrists. Are they prehensile? What kind of magic would those be? Aether? Corpus? Despite my contempt for *him*, I am curious about how it all works.

The king stalks forward, his long legs eating up the space between us. "Do you take me for a fool?"

I lift a cool brow. "I mean . . . if the boot fits, who am I to argue?"

He gapes. A smile touches my lips at being able to provoke him so easily. For some strange—and possibly very delusional—reason, I don't feel afraid. Instead, I feel a heady amount of exhilaration, which should be signal enough of my precarious state. Poking a man who has the power to bind and torture me isn't my wisest course.

However, if he wanted me dead, he could have left me to die. Instead, he'd told his healers to save my life.

So what *does* King Darrius want with me?

He's not going to volunteer any information, so I'll just have to irritate it out of him. I stare at him, his black eyes flashing with rancor. I try to keep my expression neutral, but I'm sure my amusement bleeds through as I lean back against the headboard. "You know, my aunt always says if you keep your mouth open too long, you'll catch flies."

"Mind your tongue, girl!" Darrius snaps, advancing on me.

Girl? My eyes burn with outrage.

Ani backs away as the tension in the room ratchets. The king's shadows whirl and snap like coiled whips, and if I wasn't so provoked, I'd be mesmerized by their sinuous dance. Every cell in me bristles. If I had magical tendrils like his, they would be flaring like vicious, vexed creatures, too, ready to take him on in a heartbeat. For a second, I imagine such a thing and feel a force in the center of my chest unspool through my veins like molten lava.

What *is* that?

The flood of power—*adrenaline?*—makes my lungs feel unnaturally tight. In fact, I might be hallucinating, but out of the corner of my eye, I notice that the cuffs on my wrists in my lap have taken on a crimson glow. Though I'm intensely curious about what made the runes come alive, I refuse to drop the king's cold stare.

"You're very angry, you know." I tap my mouth thoughtfully, easing off the bed and standing to my full height, which is not much at all, especially compared with his six and a half seething feet of intimidation. "Don't you know that anger is dreadful for your constitution? I'm willing to bet that you've been quite constipated of late. My aunt makes the most incredible carambola juice that just gets all those pesky blockages flowing. I'd be happy to whip up a batch if you direct me to the kitchens."

Those dark eyes flash, nostrils flaring, but I ignore the obvious warning that I'm treading a very fine line. King Darrius probably expects everyone around him to fawn and grovel. I might not know how I ended up here and have fuzzy gaps in my memory, but I do know that I grovel for no one. *Especially not kings.*

I blink, wondering where that thought came from.

"You insolent—"

"It's no trouble at all," I say, cutting him off with an audacious wink, ignoring Ani, whose panicky blue gaze is darting between us. "We'll get you unclogged and call it a day."

Face suddenly inscrutable, though his vengeful eyes tell a different story, the king scoffs. "Stick instead of carrot, I see. Maybe your tongue will loosen then."

I beam as if I don't have a care in the world, though my instincts are firing with warnings of imminent danger. "Mind my tongue, loosen my tongue? Which is it, Your Majesty? You seem to have quite an obsession with said appendage."

I school my features to stone as his eyes flick to my mouth, something sinfully heated flaring in them that makes my breath absolutely fizzle and syrupy heat slide through my core. For the briefest of moments, he looks at me as though I'm a treat he could quite happily and voraciously devour in the wickedest, best kind of way. I swallow a gulp.

Stars above . . .

That sensation behind my rib cage tugs and thickens, some indefinable tether reaching out and straining toward *him*. The king's eyes widen as if he feels an answering pull, too, but then he whirls on his boots and strides out of the room with a vicious curse.

Suraya Silvertongue, one. King Killjoy, zero.

Instead of examining my very confusing reaction, which includes the pounding of my heart and a very unwelcome molten sensation between my thighs, I grin at an ashen-faced Ani. "What's his problem?"

"Y-you're not afraid of him?" she stammers, still staring at the door and then focusing that chary stare at me.

Oh, I'm fucking terrified. But I shake my head. "To show fear is to give your adversary power."

The words loosen a deluge of images in my brain.

Visions of a gory battle, an altar, and an offering . . . the face of a man—*one I . . . love?*—on the cusp of death and destruction left in the wake of a gleaming, tumultuous magic . . . an arena of sand that smells like blood and a lavish room full of beautiful people dancing . . . a gorgeous palace with ornate cupolas and towering pillars, and an intricate maze that is the spitting image of my mother's painting back in Coban. It's clearly the capital city.

How do I have such a visceral memory of the *capital city*?

My head starts to pound as I try futilely to hold on to the images that disappear as fast as they have come.

"I'm sorry I dosed you with that herb on the king's orders," Ani says, but then frowns at me as I grasp my skull between my palms and sink into a crouch with a groan. "Sura, are you well? What is it? Do you remember something?"

I exhale, rubbing my temples. "Yes, but just fragments and pictures that make no sense whatsoever. And I understand about the king. It's not your fault."

"Thank you. And give yourself time," she says, leaning down to peer at my irises. "You've been through a traumatic few days, and while our healers' magic can work wonders with physical injuries, they cannot return lost memories. I pray you remember something soon, for your sake."

"You and me both."

"I'll find you some shoes," Ani says, "before the king returns to drag you away himself and march you through the entire court in bare feet."

With a sigh, I rise carefully. I wouldn't put such spite past the man. But I suppose I did bring this upon myself with my infernal taunting.

Honestly, Sura, did you have to go that far? Because gloating satisfaction aside, there's no real winner in this scenario.

As an outsider in a strange realm, it's certainly not me.

Chapter Thirteen

Turns out provoking a king with a chip on his shoulder the size of a desert isn't one of the best decisions I've made. Especially when the stick he threatened me with turns out to be starsdamned *training*. Though the gods themselves can't fathom why a man who's worried that a stranger might be an enemy spy would insist on fortifying said enemy's skills.

Dejected, I pick at the cuffs on my wrists. I'd banged them hard against the arm of a chair earlier, but all that had done was make my wrists ache. Not a single dent had formed in the metal.

When I get my memories back, I'm going to hunt down whoever put these on me and make them regret it. Partial flashes of the handsome face I'd seen before—dark hair, full lips, and warm brown eyes—hits me, but the accompanying emotions are bewildering. It feels as though I should care deeply about the person, but something inside of me recoils with echoes of betrayal and bitterness.

Who is he?

I study the bracelets. Had *he* put these on?

Repeating the question internally, I concentrate, and to my surprise, another face comes to mind, this one different with markings and . . . a name! *Aran.* Then the same oil slick of emotions assaults me: love, deceit, pain, bitterness.

Who are these two people, and more important, *how* do I know them?

The notion that I'd been in Kaldari for some time before ending up in Everlea is starting to seem real, as preposterous as it feels. But I don't remember leaving Coban, so assuming I *had* left, *when* had I done so? The black gold-dusted envelope fills that gap in my head—so clearly, I must have gone to the bridal summons despite my scornful feelings on the matter. I blink as more fragments of memories swirl: the crown prince's marriage ball . . . a ruse to find the subject of some ancient prophecy to do with the gods . . .

Now *that* sounds preposterous!

Pain stabs into my skull, and I cry out. Grasping my temples, I take controlled breaths to calm both the discomfort and my escalating panic at the new jumble of information now rattling in my brain without context.

As the pain slowly subsides, I worry my lip and scowl at the training leathers lying on the bed. I suppose I should get dressed before His Heinousness stomps up here to dress me himself. The thought that he might dare to do exactly that is enough to get me moving, as little as I feel like training right now.

I change quickly, pleased that the leathers are a decent fit. I crouch and spring upward, marveling at the suppleness.

"Good, you *can* follow instructions."

The shadow that darkens my doorway is my magnanimous host himself. He's back in his glossy black-and-gold armor, twin braids coming off his temples. The low light of the hallway makes him look even more ominous, casting shadows across the harsh planes of his face, and yet my heart gives an unsteady thump at the sight of him.

"Ready to talk?" he asks.

I smile sweetly. "Certainly, Your Majesty, but you clearly don't want to hear the only truth I have, which is that I don't remember anything." I tap my head. "Your own healers have confirmed that I'm suffering from memory loss due to a traumatic brain injury. You will be the first person to know if I am indeed here to do away with your surly self." I purse my lips. "Though let's be realistic . . . I'm probably at the back of a long line of enemies, given your shining disposition."

"Your amnesia could be fake," he says, ignoring my jabs.

I shake my head. "I wish I was that good of an actress. But by all means, keep me in this pretty room until you're satisfied of my innocence." I shrug. "Or use one of your psionic magi, one who can sense lies from truth, to see what I know. Shouldn't you have one of those? I give you permission, go on."

"I've tried," he snaps, and my brows rise in concert. "And I failed."

I blink. *He* failed? Sands, he's a mind magi, too. I should have known he would have been so invasive without my consent. How many pillars can a person be proficient in? Ani had said it was rare to possess an affinity for all three, but maybe the king does. I glare at him, grateful for whatever windfall had kept him out of my most private thoughts.

"What of your mysterious, mythical azdaha? Is the beast sentient? You could interrogate it, since it supposedly brought me here in the first place, though I'm not entirely sure I even believe that."

"Razulek has not yet awakened. Azdahas take to an intense slumber when they are gravely injured," the king says.

My heart gives an odd pang and I rub my chest, flashes of emerald-green scales, an enormous wingspan, and intelligent eyes filling my vision. Oh, *oh*. My knees nearly buckle as the memories rise. Razulek . . . Grayheart, he'd called himself. He'd even told me of a mate who was here in Everlea.

Holy *gods*. The creature *is* real . . .

I don't realize that I've uttered the words aloud until the king speaks. His voice is so cold when he replies that I swear I feel hoarfrost cover my skin. "Yes. He was weakened from severe torture, his wings frail from disuse, and some of his wounds were internal. It was a marvel either of you even made it here." The king's gaze hardens as I struggle to make sense of my utterly *impossible* memories. "Were you his prisoner, or was he yours, coerced to fly you here by your will?"

"I don't have magic," I say, "or psionic affinities."

His mouth flattens. "You blocked me, so you have some ability."

I let out a frustrated hiss through my teeth. "When will you understand that I am telling the truth? No one in Oryndhr has magic, least of all me!"

Momentary confusion glitters in his obsidian gaze before it goes blank. We glower at each other in a silent standoff, but I hold myself stiff with my head high, unwilling to give any quarter. *Show no weakness . . .*

"Follow me," he commands brusquely, and walks away.

Anger swirls through my chest, though it's frustration with myself that intensifies my feelings of utter powerlessness. I wish I hadn't lost my memories. *If* by some long stretch of the imagination I had come here to assassinate him, I'd do it with relish.

No, you wouldn't, because you're not a killer . . . though that didn't save you from committing untold horrors in the name of a man you loved.

I clutch at my temples, sinking into a crouch with a whimper of agony. Where had *that* thought come from?

Images burst into my brain: gleaming silvery ribbons of magic, fresh blood on my hands, raw pain brimming through me. I see myself on a dais, without my cuffs, standing next to a crowned but faceless monarch as he addresses his people. I dig deeper for his face, sensing that I know him, intimately in fact, and it slips away, but not before a name winks into existence.

Roshan.

Designations crash through my mind in response: *bastard, savior, lover, betrayer, foe.* But I don't recognize the name at all. Which is he? One of them or all of them?

Sands, Suraya, remember!

But the images start to bend and fold into one another until they're unrecognizable, only the faces of grotesque ghouls staring back at me, swallowing me whole with their gaping mouths. I scream until my throat burns, crumpling into myself . . . tumbling into the yawning abyss.

Eventually, a deep, commanding voice pierces the thick haze of my thoughts: "Suraya!"

How does he know my name? It's my first sluggish thought. The second is that he's touching me. The king's hands are gently gripping my face, and as I stare into his mesmerizing obsidian eyes, I see concern and what looks like fear.

But he *hates* me. Why in the realms would he look so fearful? Fear of me? *For* me? My eyes roll back as the endless void threatens to tug me back under.

"Follow my voice, Starbright. Come back to me."

Somehow in the throes of agony, I listen. I claw my way out of the suffocating, viscous pit until I'm lying shuddering on a solid polished floor, curled into a ball. "What . . . happened?" My voice is a raw whisper.

The king rolls back to his haunches, his expression still haunted. "You tell me."

"Memories," I whisper. "Nightmares."

He stares at me, but something like compassion bleeds through that glacial jet gaze. I hate the fact that he caught me in such a vulnerable position. "Painful ones?" he asks softly, surprising me.

I swallow and wrap my arms around my body, feeling the hideous sensation of being consumed from the inside out. "Horrifying. I . . . I think I might have been . . . a monster."

I feel his eyes on me, but he doesn't say anything or probe for more explanation. "We're all capable of monstrous things," he says eventually, and so gently that it makes tears spring to my eyes for no reason at all. "Some more than most. But that doesn't make us monsters."

"I am," I blurt out, and lift my arms, staring blindly at the cuffs. "There's so much blood on these, and I don't know how they even got there. I don't know what I *did* because I can't fucking remember!" The last words turn into a choked sob.

The king stands and walks a few steps. "Here," he says, returning with a filled goblet. "Drink this."

I do as he says, grateful for the coolness of the water calming my sore throat, and then give him the empty cup with a quavering hand. Those midnight eyes of his miss nothing. My skin itches with discomfort at feeling so exposed. "Why are you being so kind all of a sudden?" I blurt out.

"I can't be kind?"

I frown, abandoned walls rising with alacrity. "Let's be honest, Your Majesty. I'm your hostage. You probably didn't want me dying on your hands, causing a diplomatic incident that might start a war or something disastrous."

He stares at me in silence, then swipes a hand over his nape. "I don't want you to—" He cuts off abruptly and sighs. "You're not a hostage."

"So you'll let me leave?"

"It's not that simple," he says. "You're not safe going anywhere until you regain your memories." He points at the cuffs on my wrists. "And until we can determine what those are and what their purpose is."

"They won't come off," I remind him.

He nods. "I am aware. We tried everything to to remove them when you first arrived. The magic is . . . unlike anything I've seen, and I've seen more than you can possibly imagine."

The king extends a hand down to me. Not wanting to be churlish, I take it, blushing when my knees buckle as I rise and I slump against his big frame. He catches me easily, and we both gasp when that strange current zings between us.

For a heartbeat, every nerve in my body feels charged and alive as if I've been struck by an elemental force, and then the flow deadens and cuts off as quickly as it had come. The red glow of the runes on the bracers indicates that something had clearly happened. What *was* that?

"The cuffs did something," I whisper, pushing out of his embrace and staring at the runes that had lit up. "When we touched."

His expression is unreadable. "I saw."

The runes are arcane; there's no doubt of it in my mind. While I can't read them, I suspect the symbols etched on the bracers are powerful, inscribed by a very strong runecaster. "Do you know what any of these runes mean?" I ask the king.

He nods gravely. "Obstruction and confinement. Runes to weaken and to ensnare, runes of submission and compliance, runes of obligation, consequence, and punishment. Runes of control. Pain. Forced dormancy." He snaps the words out like they're poison in his mouth, and with each revelation, I flinch.

"Forced *dormancy*?" I whisper.

"To render you unconscious," he says.

Someone has put these on me to bind me, to *control* me to excessive extremes. But *why*? I'm nobody . . . a bladesmith from the desert. Fear snaps through my veins and I suppress a shudder. Nothing good can come from manacles like these.

"Show me your hands," he says, and I comply before I can think too hard about it.

His fingertip traces a faint five-pointed shape on each of my palms, causing me to nearly jolt out of my skin. That same deadening prickle sweeps through me, but the potency of his touch is much more carnal, as though he's stroking up the center of me. My thighs clench, face heating and breath lodging in my throat. This feels strangely intimate, his index finger softly kissing the lines along my palm. Sensation sings through my body. I gasp and snatch my hands away, miniature shock waves of pleasure detonating inside. Stars above . . . did I just . . . ?

He frowns at me. "What's the matter?"

Gods, kill me now.

"Nothing," I mumble.

Silence stretches between us as my ears grow hot with discomfort. I shuffle uneasily when his stare doesn't leave mine, his face unnaturally still like a stone gargoyle. He doesn't give away a thing, but I can tell he's thinking.

"Truce?" the king says in a gruff tone, and when I don't immediately answer, my surprise evident, he continues. "I know you have no reason to trust me. But I cannot in good conscience send you back to Oryndhr without understanding what those cuffs mean for you. If they have been placed with your consent, that is a different matter. But if they haven't, then you could be in danger."

"How do I know that I'm not in danger here?"

A strange conflict rages on his face. For an instant, his black eyes glimmer gold before returning to their usual color. "You have my word that you will be safe," he growls, as though his tongue is crowded by a mouthful of teeth. The sound of it doesn't scare me, however. Oddly, it resonates with protectiveness . . . and a hint of need, surprisingly.

Is it similar to what I'd felt earlier? He looks as though he wants to grab me, throw me over his shoulder, and do wicked things to me, but then he turns on his heel and strides out of my room, muttering under his breath. By the gods, he's so temperamental. Benign one moment, brutish the next. I frown, uncertain of whether to follow him.

"Suraya, I don't have all day."

I roll my eyes, but my feet move almost of their own volition, chasing his footsteps down the corridor. "How do you know my name?"

"I know everyone in my kingdom." He glances over his shoulder, and I inhale a sharp breath at the utter perfection of his profile. My pulse trips. Sands, if he weren't so surly, I'd be in a world of trouble.

I follow him down another hallway to a set of marble stairs that lead to a carpeted floor that feels like walking on a cloud. Another marble staircase takes us to the ground floor, more sparsely decorated but no less lavish. The furniture is polished to a shine; the mirrors lining the corridor are spotless. Golden sconces light our way, revealing massive, gilded paintings of bucolic scenes, stunning in both their size and their artistry. There are soaring azdahas and other magical creatures I've never seen depicted in them. I want to linger and study each of them, but the king keeps marching forward until we reach two massive doors leading outside.

At his punishing pace, we reach the training grounds quickly, with me practically running every few feet to keep up with him. We stop near a sweeping row of weapons racks; I'm trying to catch my breath when he throws me a sword. I fling my hand out, barely grabbing it before it impales me. I scowl at him, but he ignores it, pointing to a big man standing nearby. "This is Maxur, one of my generals. He will assess your skills."

I swing the sword around to point at him and arch my eyebrow. "Afraid to test me yourself, Your Majesty?"

He steps out of the way as another blade—presumably Maxur's—crashes down on mine, and I instantly parry as if I've known how to counter an attack all my life. I blink in shock, but am forced to defend another set of brutal thrusts in quick succession. Somehow, my body knows exactly what to do, steel meeting steel in an effortless dance.

I've known the basics of blade wielding for a long time, ever since I began making them in the forge. But I've never fought with such skill . . . or deadly precision.

Have I?

Without warning, more memories erupt. Dueling in a courtyard, a fierce grin on my opponent. *Clem*. Hours spent together, practicing with many different weapons. The man called Aran appears again, this time interspersed with more of those silvery, iridescent ribbons shooting from *my* fingers... like *magic*.

Disoriented, I falter on my feet. The distraction costs me as a searing pain runs across my hand, the tip of a very real blade catching me unawares, and I let out a choked scream. Blood wells and pools as my weapon drops to the ground from my slackened grip.

A terrifying growl rips through the air.

"It was my fault, Sire," Maxur yells out. "She stopped when I expected her to move."

Suddenly, my body goes hot all over and the runes on my cuffs burst into crimson light. Warmth floods my veins, and the throbbing pain from the cut is... gone. That's odd. Or maybe I'm in shock. From past experience of falling down a jādū mine shaft as a child, I know it can do that... make pain temporarily disappear.

"Show me," the king demands, crowding my space.

I scowl at his tone and cradle my fist to my chest. "So you can make it worse? No."

"It's already healed," he says. "Look."

"No, it's not, you fool," I snap, hearing Maxur smother a sound of amusement. "I need a healer."

"Suraya, look, please."

It's the low *please* that does me in. Gingerly, I wipe the tacky blood off on my leathers and I stare at my hand. And stare some more.

There isn't a single laceration on my skin. There's no slice, no gash, no evidence that I was injured at all. My palm is unusually warm with a faint shimmer that fades quickly... but the flesh is unbroken and perfectly healthy.

"Impossible," I whisper.

My stomach roils the more I gawk at my blood-streaked and yet completely unscarred hand. I know what I saw, the pain I felt. I send a panicked stare to the hulking men at my sides. "Why are you both staring at me? I just hallucinated this wound healing itself. I'm serious! I am sick, and I need a starsdamned healer."

The bastard of a king rolls his eyes before walking away, saying over his shoulder, "You're not sick and you don't need a healer. You've already healed yourself, because you have akasha in your blood. Now pick up your sword. Training's not over."

Mulishly, I open my mouth to retort, but then snap it shut. Is this why I healed so swiftly after the crash?

"I wonder if Ani will know anything about this," I say aloud, bending to retrieve my fallen weapon.

"Anahima?" Maxur asks.

Curious, I glance up at him as we circle each other slowly. "You know her?"

He makes a noncommittal sound with a sidelong glance to where the king is standing, arms folded over his broad chest. I follow his gaze and ignore the unwelcome leap of my pulse at his commanding form.

"She's the king's sister," Maxur says.

Sword forgotten, I blink in disbelief and think back to the kind woman I'd met, the one the king himself had chased off with his temper as if she were nothing but an inconvenience to him. He's so consumed with his own importance that he doesn't even care about his own sibling. I scowl, remembering why he'd rubbed me the wrong way from the start. Stars, the arrogance.

There's little resemblance between them. Ani is a sweet, bookish, skinny, blue-eyed brunette. The silver-haired dictatorial fiend standing a few lengths away is the size of a house with an ego to match and has soulless eyes that reflect the abyss from which he was undoubtedly born.

Maxur barks a shocked laugh. "Tell me how you really feel."

Sands, had I said that out loud? I flush and then shrug. "They don't look alike at all."

He shrugs in turn. "The king had dark hair until he ascended to his magic and the crown." He screws up his nose in thought, mischief flashing in his hazel eyes. "And maybe he's the size of a house because he likes lifting heavy things."

"Sounds like someone might be infatuated," I grunt sourly, though I'll take the small fact that I agree about the king's formidable figure to my tomb. The man's muscles have muscles. I'd felt them when I'd so brazenly poked him, seen them flex when he'd loomed over me like an unforgiving god, and practically crashed into them when I'd lost my balance. Thank the stars I'm too sweaty to blush.

But Maxur grins, seeing right through me. "You can admit it. Everyone says he's easy on the eyes."

Committed to my lie, I heft my sword and grimace. "Not to me. I don't go for the domineering, calculating, ruthless warlord who likes to order everyone around."

"I hate to break it to you, but he is the *king*. All that goes with the territory." Maxur grins, then crouches into an attack stance, coming at me in a rush that I sidestep easily. "So pray tell, my lady, what type *do* you prefer?"

"That's a hard one." I duck, slashing out, and pretend to think about my options while spinning, my steps bringing me around him to attack from the back. "Maybe a somewhat handsome, average-skilled, unwashed general with the pungent smell of overgrown onions."

His eyes sparkle with mock outrage at my teasing; he ducks, narrowly avoiding my blade. "Bite your tongue, lady! I am better than average, and I smell like roses. Glad you think I'm handsome, though."

"*Somewhat* handsome," I say with a laugh, blocking an upper swipe of his blade as I veer right to avoid his natural downswing. "Definitely courtable."

We both freeze at the low, ferocious snarl that interrupts our light banter. The sparkle vanishes from Maxur's eyes, and his entire body hunches as if he's shouldering some kind of invisible blow. I glance over my shoulder to where the king is fairly glowering at us.

Even from where I'm standing, I can see the gold shine flash in his stare.

I frown. "What's wrong with him?"

Maxur shrugs, standing straight again, though all his earlier playfulness has disappeared. "We're all fighting an animal inside. Now, attack me again."

Chapter Fourteen

The Night King

My beast is fucking feral.

All he wants to do is to rut, to breed, to claim.

But try telling a very insistent, primitive part of yourself that his soul-fated mate is off-limits, especially when he has caught the starsdamned *perfect* scent of her. A mate bond is divine, a treasure to be guarded and cherished, and in any other circumstance, it would be. Though not for me ... because of this fucking curse.

The creature will rip her delicate mortal form to shreds.

He roars his displeasure every hour of every day, nearly tearing from my skin and battering my iron sway of him, but as long as I stay in control of my emotions, I remain in control of my body. I remain in control of *him*.

And for all our sakes, if the realm is to endure, I have no choice but to resist his most primal instincts—to keep chaos deeply buried. I have been here before and know the cost.

She is our downfall.

I must reject the bond ... or one of us will die.

Chapter Fifteen

The woman at my chamber door is unfamiliar. She holds herself like someone who has power in the castle—head housekeeper, perhaps?—her eyes keen and her bearing proud. "I am Ziba, and I've been assigned as your primary lady's maid and companion. The king has sent instructions for you to join him for the evening meal."

I blink at her, bewildered. I haven't seen the king in days, not since the first training session and his bizarre reaction. I've continued practicing with Maxur, but His Majesty has been noticeably absent, and the general has been tight-lipped about his king's whereabouts, only alluding to quashing an incursion at the Oryndhrian border. When I asked whether the king was worried about war with the neighboring kingdom, Maxur's expression had gone frustratingly blank.

"A meal?" I ask, frowning at Ziba.

"That is what he said, yes," she says, walking in briskly. "But first let's get you cleaned up, my lady."

"You can call me Suraya," I say softly, when she disappears without preamble into the bathing chamber.

Collecting my scattered thoughts at the notion of a private dinner with the king, I walk to the enormous glass-paned window, which looks out onto rolling green fields as far as the eye can see. Below the ledge, brilliant, manicured plots of blooming marigolds—sunburned orange and summer yellow—catch my eye, and I sigh at the natural beauty. Marigolds were my mother's favorite flower, and the sight of them in full bloom makes my chest suddenly tight.

How had I not noticed them before?

"Lady Suraya," Ziba calls, and I obediently hurry into the next room. "Come now, before it gets cold," she says, moving to help me undress.

I shake my head. "I can do it."

She tilts her head in deference and waits quietly near the tub. When I remove the last of my grimy leathers and my underclothes, she eyes my wrists, brow scrunching. "And those?"

I shake my head. "Permanent fixtures, I'm afraid."

The layered scents of jasmine, rose, and vanilla waft into my nose when I approach the bath. Ziba offers me a hand as I step into the deliciously hot water and sink down into the velvety depths all the way to my chin.

Stars above...

It feels heavenly. In fact, I could quite happily die right here at this very moment in complete and utter bliss. I've washed in the bathing chamber before, but my cleansing routine has been quick and perfunctory, mirroring how I bathed in Coban, where water is a scarcity—a quick splash with emphasis on the important bits. Nothing like this kind of decadent luxury. *This* feels like an extravagance fit for a queen.

Ziba moves to stand behind me and undoes my sweaty braided hair over the side of the tub, where there's a convenient lip for me to comfortably rest my neck. Water from a pitcher soaks through the strands before she lathers up the tresses into a thick froth that smells divine. Strong fingers massage my scalp, and I almost moan out loud with how good it feels. Ziba rinses, then repeats the process once more before coating the locks with a softening cream.

She rinses again after a few minutes, then approaches me with a soft-bristled pad and a cloth, which I take quickly. While I enjoyed the hair wash, I don't need her tending to my body as well. With another of those benevolent smiles, she bustles away before returning with a thick, soft toweling cloth that she hangs over a nearby chair. I take my time cleansing myself from head to toe and scrub until my skin glows with radiant health.

When I'm done, I wrinkle my nose at the bathwater, which has grown tepid, but Ziba only nods as she walks by and touches her fingertip to the surface. The water clears and turns hot in seconds. I inhale sharply and grin in stupefied awe. I don't think I'll ever get used to people practicing magic so effortlessly.

She shows no surprise at my wondrous expression, so someone must have informed her about my lack of magical affinity. "Water numen," she says. "Mestial rank."

"Amazing," I say, and her cheeks pinken with pleasure.

"I'll be in the next room," she says. "We have plenty of time, so soak as long as you like. I can always make it hot and clean again."

Any elemental magic is in the aether category, I remember Ani explaining. Ziba doesn't seem disappointed that she's at one of the lower-ranking levels. Ashes, I'd be ecstatic with basic proficiency at this rate. Being able to manipulate water and ice? People in the desert back home would idolize me and crown me queen. I let out a soft snort just as a blast of homesickness hits me. I miss Coban. I miss the dry desert heat. And I miss Papa, Amma, and Laleh.

By the maker, am I ever going to get back?

Exhaling, I lay my head back and stare up at the gorgeous mural on the ceiling of peacocks with brightly colored feathers. My eyes drift closed for a handful of seconds. A vision of a white marble room with a pool at its center flashes through my brain as clear as day.

Is it another memory?

It has to be, because I can see myself immersed in bubbles, Laleh bustling around at my side, and then it hits me . . . it's for my wedding day. I nearly swallow a mouthful of soap suds and sit up so quickly that a wave of bathwater careens over the edge. I'm gasping for air like a fish out of the sea.

Betrothed to the king.

"Lady Suraya?" Ziba rushes over with a concerned look. "Are you well?"

I shudder in place, trying desperately to calm my erratic breathing. "Yes, sorry."

There's no starsdamned way I was engaged to the king of Oryndhr. But the conviction of the memory doesn't go away. So if it's real, then which king? King Zarek is already married to Queen Morvarid. Desperate for clarity but fearful to lose momentum, I don't force it. Instead, I try to relax and let myself ease into the recollection.

I feel the water in my memory. I smell the bath oils. I see Laleh's face.

A barrage of riddles, balls, and battles descends all at once, a few of the blank gaps in my brain filling in. Prince Javed, now the king of Oryndhr, had chosen me because of an Elonian prophecy and the divination of my star chart that I was a weapon of the gods. A prize with starfire in her veins. Frowning, I lift my palms and turn them over, seeing the five-pointed stars etched there and acutely remembering the warm glow saturating them.

A gift from the four Royal Stars.

My blood roars between my ears. Sands, I *do* have magic. Powerful magic. Magic anyone would kill for. I stare at the cuffs. *Coerce* me for.

The thought is inconceivable, and yet I know it to be true.

A surge of power inside of me undulates in heady confirmation, making me dizzy as the stunning vision of a gorgeous simurgh flexes her wings. The recognition is instant as I see her in my mind's eye. Stars, is she what my magic looks like? Like divinity in earthly form, all fiery energy, fierce, shimmering wings, and a proud canine face.

Hello, friend.

Her gaze is adoring, her approval flooding me in a tsunami of warmth.

Then my cuffs light up, two of the runes flaring red at the same time, and a dulling ache starts to spread. Within seconds, the bright image fades and leaves me with a bereft sensation that my beautiful creature—the very essence of my magic—has been trapped and silenced.

Heart sinking, I glare balefully at the cuffs. Someone had put the bracers on to contain my magic . . . to contain *me*. King Javed? *Why?*

To keep you leashed and in your place.

Bitterness lashes through me at the brutal honesty of my simurgh's barely audible answer. It reeks of exploitation, of manipulation.

Did I *marry* the crown prince turned king, only for him to use me?

Am I a queen? I wish I knew.

In a stupor, I lift my left hand to look for any indication of a ring imprint—even a pale strip of skin on my finger—but there's nothing there. Deep down, I know I would have fought tooth and nail against marriage, because Javed, of all people, is a self-absorbed despot who would have craved only one thing: *power*.

He would have abused any magic I had without hesitation to subjugate and rule his kingdom. Does his greed extend to conquering the other realms? Like Everlea? Is that why I'm here? To spy on his closest enemy? Destroy him from the inside? It doesn't seem like something I would do, but then again, I hardly know who I've become. Who I *am*.

When the water cools again, I step out of the tub and wrap myself in the fluffy toweling. Maker above, it feels good to be clean. Even my despicable cuffs are gleaming. They're another critical piece to the puzzle I'm trying to make sense of. If my musings are correct about my supposed magic being weaponized, then why would Javed send me here *unable* to access or use any of it? Unless he *didn't* send me, and I was escaping...

Now that sounds a lot more like me, given what I think of him.

Wrapping the towel around my torso, I shove my churning thoughts aside and go to where Ziba is waiting in my bedroom. She exits the closet with folds and folds of embroidered fabric gathered in her arms. I stare at the dark indigo ensemble that she eventually holds up for my inspection, and blanch. *That* is a bloody ball gown.

"The king had this dress made for you, my lady," Ziba says softly, noticing my expression. "You are his honored guest for tonight's dinner with the court."

There's a stubborn part of me that wants to refuse, and another, much smaller part that wants to wear the stunning gown. It would be churlish of me to not accept, so I nod.

It doesn't take Ziba much time to lace the back of the dress over undergarments that are so sheer and utterly useless that I wonder why I'm wearing any at all. The corset style of the two-piece gown is different from the loose, voluminous styles that I'm used to. The heavily pearled bodice is fitted and slightly cropped, so that a sliver of my bare stomach is visible, and the skirt is long and heavy with intricate hand-stitched embroidery and seed pearls along the hem. Similar designs adorn the fabric in a scattering of silver thread. Elegant silver slippers complete the ensemble.

When she finishes all the fastenings, Ziba directs me to a mirrored vanity where she combs my thick hair into a topknot of curls, securing it with glass-topped pins. I squint at the iridescent silver strands weaving through the inky mass. They seem more pronounced than ever. Bronze powder is lightly dusted on my cheeks, kohl applied to my eyelids, and a swipe of plum stain goes over my lips.

"There," Ziba says with a pleased expression. "Perfect, my lady."

I stare at my reflection and admit that Ziba isn't wrong. The rich color of the gown uplifts my complexion, which is flawless under the translucent powder. I reluctantly admit—on the inside—that the king has excellent taste. I spin, watching as the full skirt flares out. With a gasp, I realize that the scattered embroidery reminds me of a constellation of stars set against a backdrop of a twilight sky.

Does the symbolism have some meaning to the king, or am I reading into it? Because how would *he* know that my magic was gifted to me by the Royal Stars?

Someone knocks on the bedchamber door and Ziba goes to answer it. She glances back over her shoulder after exchanging a few short words with the visitor. "His Majesty sends his regrets that he is late," she explains to me. "Today is court day, when citizens bring their grievances before him." She pauses with a grimace. "This week there were more than usual."

"Is the dinner canceled?" I ask, feeling oddly disheartened.

She shakes her head. "No, His Majesty has suggested that you may wait here or go for a walk in the gardens. He will send for you once he's finished."

I must admit, I'm more curious to see the supposed nightmare king in action than to take a stroll in the garden. The idea of observing him, of gaining insight into how he rules his kingdom, is an intriguing one. So much can be learned about a monarch in the way that he deals with his subjects and how those under his care respond to him. Ziba's lack of fear is yet another indicator that the terrible stories I've heard about the ruler of Everlea might be exaggerated.

"Is there somewhere I can watch the proceedings at court?" I ask, keeping my expression neutral. "Unbeknownst to the people, if possible. I wouldn't want to cause distress. These sessions are public, no?"

I add the last sentence so that it doesn't come across as though I'm trying to do something underhanded that the king might not approve of. Predictably, Ziba peers at me as if to ascertain my motives, but then she nods. "There is a small balcony that used to be reserved for the Queen Mother when she was alive."

"She used to listen to civic grievances from citizens?" I ask.

Ziba nods again, a fond smile crossing her lips. "Her Majesty was very involved in the well-being of her royal subjects, but when our young king came of age, she preferred to let him handle things," she explains. "The queen was the one who opened her court to the citizens of Everlea. She always used to say that a ruler is only as good as the people he or she serves."

Wise advice. I wonder if her son had listened. I nod to Ziba. "Shall we?" She looks a bit chary, so I give her my best smile. "I promise I won't be noticed and I won't make a peep. I just want to observe."

"Very well," she says. "I suppose His Majesty won't mind."

Unfortunately, it seems that the king of Everlea very much does mind, because the minute I am ushered into the small nook with its single velvet-covered chair meant for the former queen, those pitch-dark, bottomless eyes immediately swing my way, brimming with surprise and then heated ferocity. The air is suddenly charged with an elemental tension.

I can't quite tell if he doesn't want me here or whether that smoldering gaze is a result of some other emotion. But he has me in a chokehold from that one look, a violent tingling creeping up my spine and that strange, insistent tug in my center drawing tight. My lungs feel airless, and every hair on my body stands at nervous attention.

Grinding my teeth, I steadfastly refuse to yield to his overpowering dominance. What can he do? Order me to leave in front of everyone in the middle of proceedings? Punish me for overstepping? I hardly think I'm *that* important. And yet his glare is unrelenting, urging me to flee. With a pointedly raised brow, I gather my skirts and sit. He tears his gaze from mine, that stern mouth of his twitching at my show of defiance.

While the king's attention returns to the affairs of his court, my traitorous eyes surreptitiously take notice of his commanding position on the dais. His throne is massive, the back seemingly constructed of sharp-edged scales, but his large body still dwarfs it as he sits indolently like only a sovereign can, with complete confidence in his status. Self-assurance bleeds from him.

He's dressed in black from head to toe. Charcoal epaulets adorn his shoulders and an onyx crown with spikes that look pointy enough to skewer a person sits on his head. My breath catches at how regal he looks with that bright silver hair loose and flowing to his shoulders, and his golden-brown skin glowing with an almost otherworldly luminosity. One booted foot lifts to cross over the opposite knee, and I can't help noticing how his fitted breeches pull taut against those heavily muscled tree-trunk legs.

Forcing myself to stop ogling him, I focus intently on the ongoing discussion of bride prices and dowries—is arranged marriage also practiced here?—overcrowding in the capital city and feeding the homeless, deploying the king's army, the scarcity of healers, and magical testing as each person takes their turn. The deliberation of petty crime, farming tithes and land taxes, the encroachment of the horse clans on crown lands, trade deals and treaties, and marriage proposals and alliances are fascinating.

As I listen, I parse the large hall with its marble pillars and polished floors. To the right of the king, I spot Ani furiously taking notes like a scribe. She doesn't look over to where I'm sitting, preoccupied with her duty. A handful of guards line the perimeter around the remaining crowd of Everlean subjects waiting to take up their issues with the king.

As he efficiently deals with each of them, I grudgingly concede that there's something to be said for a monarch who doesn't prioritize his time over his people's.

One small thing in his favor then . . .

It's common knowledge in Oryndhr that King Zarek has not encouraged communal sessions, at least according to my father. The monarchy has never truly cared about its citizens, and I'm certain that a tyrant like Javed won't rule differently. The king's word is law and the people simply have to deal with it. I blink. Wait, not *all* the citizens.

A sharp reminder of the rebellion—the Dahaka—hits me like a kick in the teeth.

I'd been . . . part of them? I'd fought with them against the Scavs, the bands of nameless outliers hooked on Jade, a very addictive and dangerous drug. My lungs contract as I fight for air, the pressure to remember everything making me feel lightheaded. My vision starts to tunnel as nausea pools in my unsteady belly, and I brace myself on the marble balustrade in front of me.

I feel the king's eyes crash into me again, only now his gaze is rife with concern. Because of what's happening? How can he know what I'm feeling right at this moment? Outwardly, I'm perched elegantly on the edge of my chair, a hand on the rail, sitting in privacy in the small nook and invisible to everyone but him.

But inside, I'm a roiling, chaotic mess.

Unable to breathe . . .

My skin tightens with awareness as a light sensation brushes over me, and I instantly recognize it as the same magic—the *king's* magic—I'd felt before pressing against my mind that first day in the healing wing. Only now, it's softer . . . concerned, like a soothing balm over my scattered, rioting senses.

All my senses.

Magic strokes over my shoulders and down my spine like butterfly wings, making the throttled air hiss out of me on a protracted sigh, and suddenly I can breathe again. I preen like a pet being stroked, wanting to arch my back and lean into the exquisite sensuality of it. Who knew magic could feel so... *decadent*? To my mortification, my nipples tighten in my bodice, warmth pooling between my thighs. I cross my legs and gasp with alarm as the king's eyes widen, the ephemeral touch retreating as fast as it had come.

Sands, please tell me he hadn't sensed that!

But from the slightly shell-shocked look on his face, I know he has. A muscle comes to life in that uncompromising jaw, long fingers tightening on the arms of his throne, as the faintest flush settles upon his cheekbones. Oh, the ignominy. I swallow my embarrassment and chase away the fledgling wingbeats of arousal. It's a biological reaction, nothing more, and absolutely *nothing* to be ashamed of.

Besides, what in the realms was he doing, caressing me with his magic like that? Shouldn't that be forbidden? Or at least considered an intimate exchange between husbands and wives or lovers... which we most definitely aren't. And yet, something inside of me still yearns for that lush caress. Yearns for *him* and more of that pleasurable touch.

Sands, what is *wrong* with me?

I shift my attention to the Everlean people, *not* my private and exceedingly dangerous longings.

The next grievance is from a farmer who wears a distraught expression when he falls to his knees. "My king, I've come to plead for assistance. A terrible monster has been terrorizing my cattle. I have lost half my herd already and I'm at my wit's end." He exhales a heavy breath. "The men in my village have tried everything to hunt the beast, but I suspect it's feral."

The king leans forward on his throne. "Feral? What kind of creature?"

"A b-basilisk, Sire."

My interest spikes. Like azdahas, basilisks are creatures of legend, famed for their ability to kill a man with one look of their eyes. How dangerous would a feral basilisk be? From the king's intense expression, the threat level is high. "Are you certain?" he asks.

"We found a . . . skin, Sire," the farmer says.

"It must be a juvenile," the king says. "They don't shed as adults unless they're ill. How large is the skin you saw?"

"More than thirty feet, Sire, and mottled yellow."

The king swears softly. "Unquestionably a sickened adult then, which means your families are in danger, not just your cattle. I will find the beast, you have my word."

"Thank you, Sire." The man bows, looking relieved as though he has no doubt that the king will prevail, and it makes me wonder just how powerful he is to take on a full-grown *feral* basilisk that can kill a man with a stare.

I'm still pondering basilisks as the next man steps forward, so I completely miss his words. I only snap to attention when I feel a shift in the energy of the room.

"What do you mean you cannot pay the quarterly taxes *again*, Lord Donnan? All noble estates are beholden to the crown and my protections." The king's voice is a growl, menace rising from him in waves. The hairs on my nape spike.

The man—Lord Donnan—is short with light hair and clad in fancy robes, standing puffed up and red before the king. "Because they are exorbitant . . . Your Majesty." The lord's tone is scathing, and it's more than obvious he's not an advocate of the king. Still, to be so bold to the king's face takes audacity. "Our yield is small this year."

Face carved from stone, the king cants his head. "Or is it because you're lining your own pockets, Donnan, to pay for your gambling habits, while the people on your estate and in your care starve," he says in a silky voice. The room grows unnaturally silent, and my magic sparks, warning me of danger.

The man pales. "No, Your Majesty."

"And now you're lying to me." The king glances at Ani, who promptly holds up a ledger. The nobleman's eyes grow so wide that they seem to bulge from his face. "We have evidence of your unpaid accounts. Your debt—a *life* debt—is now mine to recoup. And you have the money, don't you, Lord Donnan?"

"Wait . . . that is . . . wait . . . I was . . ." he splutters, going puce. Suddenly, the man is unnaturally silent as if something is preventing him from speaking. I squint, watching his color heighten and his eyes redden as he claws at his throat.

"No excuses. The proof is there." The king's voice goes multilayered with a powerful burst of compulsion that even I can feel. "Now tell me how you got such an influx of coin."

By now the lord, so cocky before, is shaking in his expensive, polished boots. His stare swings between the ledger and the king, and grows panicked. His face turns purple. Equally horrified and mesmerized to see the king's psionic gifts in action, I lean forward. Everything about his seated stance is nonthreatening, except for the coiling dark smoke that expands and retreats like living breath around him as if waiting for permission.

Can everyone see those shadows?

"Wait!" Donnan begs openly now, able to speak again, his eyes on that coiling vortex. Well, that answers my question. "Your Majesty! I can pay!"

The king tilts his head. "How?"

The power in that single word makes every bone in my spine snap tight. *Sands.*

"I have money! I don't compensate my workers fairly. I am a liar and a cheat," the man cries out, sobbing as the truth is yanked from him. He closes his mouth, but he has one more confession. "My men hunt azdaha eggs!"

The revelation bursts through the throne room, leaving whispers in its wake, and I swear the king starts to vibrate with rage.

"You *what*?" King Darrius thunders. *"Explain."*

But the man tears futilely at his throat once more, mouth opening and closing like a fish out of water. His terrified gaze swings to Ani's ledger again as if it contains all his secrets. "I . . . I . . . I . . ."

Something else is clearly stopping him from obeying the king's compulsion and revealing more. An enchantment? It must be, as my stare swings to the king, who looks like he has come to the same conclusion when his face hardens.

"You know the law," he says softly.

"Spare me, Sire." Lord Donnan whimpers, reaching toward the ledger. "I . . . I . . . right there . . . paid . . . please . . ."

Shadowy smoke bleeds down the stairs of the dais, the man's eyes widening in fear as he takes several steps back, but the guards who are suddenly behind him prevent him from fleeing. I watch in mute horror as those spectral, inky ropes—the same ones that had held me down in the healing wing—twine up the man's legs like serpents, banding around his torso and thickening over his neck . . . slowly tightening. A smothered scream leaves his throat, and the king only stares in sinister silence.

He does not relent, his magic so powerful that there's not even a twitch of effort from his facial muscles. His shadows swarm like agitated wasps, and then suddenly the only noise in the hall is the nauseating snap of bones as the man's neck shatters.

He slumps to the floor, lifeless.

"Remove this filth from my presence," the king commands to the waiting guards.

Those fathomless dark eyes meet mine, and I shiver.

Chapter Sixteen

The hall empties, and I stand to make my escape, only to find my way blocked by a maelstrom of shadows. I shudder, the ruthless killing power of all those tendrils front and center in my brain. If they meant me harm, I'd already be dead, so I reach for calm and stay still.

In the next heartbeat, the king appears in the middle of the mass, the whorls of shadow sinking into his luminous brown skin, climbing his throat and settling into place. *Aether pillar,* I think—moving through darkness has to be kinetic—and the ease with which he does it proves that he's undoubtedly of sovran rank, which I suspected already.

Ashes below, the man is scarily large. Those epaulets make his shoulders seem even broader, the spiked edges adding a ferocity that makes my pulse skip. Or perhaps that's just his looming presence, the magic within him barely contained by that powerful, lethal body.

I force myself not to notice the sharpness of his jaw as he towers over me, the harsh mouth that isn't overtly full but sensual nonetheless, and the darkly possessive look in those eyes as they roam over me from head to toe.

Though what he's possessive about, I have no idea.

Shutters slam down over his gaze when he notices me staring

back, his gaze going purposefully blank as if he hadn't meant to be so transparent.

I attempt a curtsy and break the fraught silence that throbs between us. "Your Majesty."

"I knew you would shine more than the brightest star in the sky," he rasps. "That suits you well."

Oh. The gown. I'd forgotten I was wearing what he had chosen.

"I'm not a doll you can dress to your specifications, you know," I tell him, despite the indecent—and categorically unwanted—rush of pleasure at his words.

One of those dark eyebrows vaults, his lips curling into the tiniest smirk. "I don't make it a habit of playing with dolls, my lady. At least not until I'm behind closed doors."

The underlying gravel in his words makes that reply far more provocative than it should be . . . and has me unsettled. "By the maker, is that a *joke* from the cruel nightmare king?" I shoot back, his nearness and his smoke and rich oud scent clouding my good sense.

"Cruel nightmare king?" he echoes. "I suppose I've been called worse."

"It's not a compliment."

Instead of responding, he runs a hand through his hair, his fingers making the silken silver strands catch the light of the nearby sconce. "I wager you're as stingy with those as you are with your truths."

I sniff. "I do not offer praises lightly. Like many things in life, they have to be earned. And I've told you the truth as I know it."

"Though not as it may be," he replies cryptically.

Why does it feel like every time I speak to this man he knows far more than he is saying? A *lot* more, from the riot of emotions burning in that midnight gaze, the least provocative of which is that strange undercurrent of possessiveness.

And worse, why do I feel so drawn to him?

"Are you compelling me with your magic?" I ask softly.

His dark gaze drops to the cuffs at my wrist. "I could not even if I tried. There are runes on those that prevent another's influence. Even mine." I blink in surprise. "The binding runes on those cuffs are spelled to not only reduce your magic but to inhibit it. And whenever your magic threatens the integrity of the cuffs, the dormancy runes force you to sleep." He exhales. "In truth, I suspect there are runes that tampered with your memory as well, in case you fell into the wrong hands."

"So it's *not* a brain injury?" I ask, frowning.

He shakes his head. "Your magic would have healed you by now. That's what it has been doing all along, slowly but surely."

Once more, I want to tear the cursed bracers from my body and lay waste to them with every ounce of my being. Powerless anger blooms. My magic, like my body and my mind, is *mine*, no one else's.

"We will find a way to get them off," the king promises, and I startle at the viciousness of his tone as if he'd heard me.

My eyes narrow on him, face heating. "Can you read my thoughts?"

The slow, sexy smirk that curls one side of his mouth shouldn't be that devastating. Or so mesmerizing. Stars above, what would a full smile look like on him? It would be a weapon of unmitigated destruction, leaving a slew of broken hearts—and ruined undergarments—in its wake.

"Why, Starbright? Afraid?"

"My name is Suraya," I snap, peeved at myself for feeling so much as a whisper of delight at the nickname. "No, I'm not afraid. I have nothing to hide from you or anyone."

"Noted," he says, and then cants his head. "I can hear thoughts if they are not properly guarded, or if they are projected specifically to me. Intrusion into the mind is an indelicate, invasive thing, requiring an obscene amount of magic. I am capable of it, of course, but without consent, it is unforgivable. A crime worthy of severe punishment."

I suppress a shudder. Power of that magnitude, being able to breach someone's mind, is inconceivable to me. "If you believe I am such a threat, then what's stopping you from finding out once and for all why I'm here?"

"Because as much as I don't trust you, that is a path that leads to a place of darkness I don't wish to traverse."

Curious, I peer up at him. "Darkness?"

"Fero's domain," he says tightly.

The hairs on my nape stand to attention. Thanks to my mother's books, I'm familiar with the pantheon of gods and goddesses. Saru, the god of creation, and Fero, his twin brother and eternal opposite, the god of death, are at the top. Do the Everleans serve the old gods? No one believes in them in Oryndhr, except for a few arcane heretics. When magic died, so did any devotion to the gods. But here, magic is thriving, so the gods must be, too.

An oily feeling kisses my skin—a sensation I have felt before—and I cringe. My head throbs as the fog in my brain convulses. The thought of Fero evokes something visceral . . . the memory of the dark god's foul touch. Images burst into light in my mind: an altar and a sacrifice, the chanting of death magi summoning their master to devour my soul . . .

Something instinctive detonates inside of me—an explosion of heat—and the thick fog that has kept me prisoner clears for a few extended heartbeats.

But then my cuffs flare red, knees buckling as my eyes roll back in my skull from the instant compulsion of the runes. Quick arms catch me before I hit the ground, and I am swept up into a strong embrace. I close my eyes and cling to the king for dear life as his magic lifts us into fluid darkness.

When it clears, I'm horizontal and on the softest surface imaginable.

My eyes flutter slowly open. I don't recognize the room, but opulence is in every detail—in the enormous mahogany pillars at each corner of the bed, the lavish furniture and ornate golden sconces, the rich carpeting and intricate tapestries from ceiling to floor.

"Where am I?" I mumble.

"My chambers," a deep voice answers, and I feel the caress of it all over me.

As a result, my brain is slower than usual to catch up, but when it does, I balk. Sands, the *king's* chambers? His *bed*? I sit up and instantly blink at the dizziness assaulting me.

The memories I'd regained from the fog hit me next.

How could a queen turned death magi reincarnate a dead god... and use *me* as a receptacle to do it? *And* nearly succeed? Even now I can still sense the chilling grasp of the god of death reaching for my soul, and it feels like a thousand graveworms slithering across my skin, searching for the tenderest parts of me to consume. That cannot possibly be real!

I rub my arms hard, recalling the heated burst inside that had sent me spiraling into oblivion.

"What happened back there?" the king asks. "Why did you react so poorly when I mentioned Fero?"

"You worship the old gods?" I counter. I don't know the full context of what I've remembered, no matter how impossible it is, and I'm not sure I want to share the pieces with him when I don't understand or believe them myself.

He eyes me, his handsome face vexingly unreadable, as usual. "Don't you?"

"No. In Oryndhr, it's heresy."

A grim laugh leaves him. "That's rich, considering you are—" His words cut off as he blinks, stopping himself and looking away.

"I'm what?" *An abomination? Unnatural?*

"Nothing." He turns and stalks to the window, his fists balling and releasing, standing there with his shadows swirling about him, as if they, too, are agitated by his state of mind. "Magic didn't vanish from your realm. You were cursed and stripped of akasha by Saru himself."

My jaw sags in surprise. I remember Ani alluding to a different explanation when I'd said Oryndhrians stopped believing in the old gods and that's why we lost our magic, but she'd cut herself off before explaining. "What do you mean?" I ask the king now.

"The War of the Gods decimated nearly all of Endara," he says. "Mountains turned to dust, cities were broken, and lands were swallowed by the seas. Whole realms were shattered and picked apart by monstrous things, because when gods go to war, everyone suffers. The three realms descended into chaos."

I frown. "What do you mean three realms? There are only two."

He shakes his head. "No. There were three: Everlea, Oryndhr, and Rothdar. When those who served Fero in Oryndhr and Rothdar leaned toward arcane arts for their master, corpus magi used necromancy to reanimate soldiers with death magic, to summon souleaters. The rot was rapacious and everywhere." Wide-eyed, I stare as he goes on. "Necromancy is forbidden because of the cost to a magi's soul, but they did not care. Fero promised them amr'ita. Immortality. When Fero was finally beaten and banished by his brother, Saru used enormous power to rid Rothdar and Oryndhr of the rot, which put him into god-sleep. He could not save Rothdar."

I exhale. "And the curse on Oryndhr?"

"Before he slept, he stripped the magi of your realm of magic and ever having akasha. Your people were simply not responsible enough to wield the gods' power. Since then, instead of begging forgiveness and proving themselves worthy, your sovereigns have chosen to serve the idols of men: wealth and power." He prowls toward me, those surging ribbons of shadow surrounding him growing wilder with each step. "Tell me, Suraya, are you here to unearth my weaknesses? To unleash my curse?"

I frown. What curse?

I open my mouth, but the king is almost on top of me... a seething, powerful beast of a man, intimidating me with his size alone. Caging me between his arms on either side of my head, he bends to my neck, his eyes flashing to gold. He inhales deeply. To my horror, my skin shivers, and something dark clenches in my core. "I smell him on you, you know," he whispers.

I dare not breathe, his tantalizing smoke-and-oud scent all around me and toying with my senses. "W-who?"

"The god of death," he murmurs. "His essence." His voice lowers to an inaudible tenor that I barely hear as a gloved palm snakes up my arm to encircle my throat. "He tried to steal what's mine."

The air in my lungs hitches as I go still. All I'd caught was the possessive growl on the last word that sounded like *mine,* but I can't even begin to decipher if I've even heard him correctly, as the sheer impossibility of being possessed by a dead god returns with a vengeance. Stars above, was that *real*? My breath shortens to panicked pants as I clumsily try to cobble together an explanation that makes rational sense.

Gods don't try to occupy human bodies, do they?

"But you're not human, are you?" the king murmurs, his fingers like manacles around my neck, not squeezing but inescapable.

"I thought you said you wouldn't go in my head." My skin feels like it's on fire from where he's touching me, long fingers collaring my throat, conflicting feelings flooding my body... desire, disgust, need, horror. I keep my hands fisted firmly in the sheets lest they rise up and wind in his shirt.

"You're shouting your thoughts, Starbright."

My lungs tighten and tighten with unbearable pressure as he hovers over me. His long silver hair falls in a shimmering curtain on either side of us, his scent and shadows everywhere. My core goes molten when he lodges a thick thigh between my parted knees and spreads them, my skirts accommodating him all too easily while he shifts closer. The position is highly erotic, and I can't begin to imagine the picture we make. The huge, commanding king looming over his captive, wedged in between her legs, one hand at her throat, the other kneading her hip.

Senses overcome, I want to writhe, to hook my ankles over his legs and drag him down to the heart of me. His eyes rake mine, and they're not so cold now. No, they're burning with pure want and possession that should make me want to run for my life, but all I want to do is submit. I *want* to drown in him, lose myself in the wild current of lust raging between us.

The trapped magic inside of me sings as if it can feel his shadows sifting through my hair and caressing swaths of my bare skin. His lips are inches away. If I push up, I could meet them. But I don't have to. Ever so slowly, he lowers his torso and slides the tip of his nose against mine. The touch is so tender and unexpected I can't even frame a coherent thought. We share breaths, the moment so intimate, so intense, that we're both trembling.

"Pátnī," he says softly, reverently.

"What does that mean?" I exhale and lift a hand to touch his jaw when he doesn't answer me, only holds his forehead to mine. "Darrius?"

It's the first time I've ever used his name. His gaze goes wide, colliding with mine in shock as if the sound of it is something he never thought he'd hear, and then his eyelids slam tightly closed. When they reopen, it's like watching the spirit leave someone.

His irises are an endless black, reflecting the abyss I'd only had glimpses of before—a swirling darkness that rises with predatory interest. His lips part. My heart flinches, bracing for something awful, because I know deep down that whatever he says next will be lethal. I *feel* it like a change in the wind.

"It means you make me fucking weak."

The snarled words punch through my soul. I freeze, my longing forgotten. And yet, his eyes betray his mouth, torment in them as if he's torn between two separate beings, ever the dichotomy of heat and ice, softness and stone.

Man and monster.

I reach up to grasp his wrist at my neck, my eyes stinging with hurt and blazing, mostly with fury at myself for being sucked into whatever *this* is.

"Then release me," I bite out.

"By the gods' mercy, I *cannot*."

The king shoves himself off me so forcefully, I feel the wind against my skin as his shadows coalesce, and then he's standing near the window again, shoulders heaving. I'm cold without the heat of him above me, my thoughts whirling with confusion, but I refuse to be a victim or a pawn in some game I cannot understand.

"Can't or won't?" I ask.

A muscle flexes in his cheek. "I'm already damned," he mutters, scrubbing a palm over his face. Bracing against the windowsill with one hand, he hangs his head and hits his chest. "Because he won't let me do what I need to do."

He? I frown, watching him as he scours harder at his ribs as if there's something there he can't vanquish. Sands, is the king well?

"He won't let you do what?" I press carefully.

The growl that leaves him is inhuman. "End you. Do what must be done to sever this godscursed—"

He cuts off abruptly, breathing harshly and counting audibly as if those breaths are the only things holding him together, but all I hear on repeat are the first two words—everything else is noise.

End. You. End. You. End. You.

Thunder rushes between my ears, my magic crashing violently against a castle of bone and blood, the bracers flaring in response. Sands, I want them to break. I need this raging wildfire to demolish its target—*him*—the biggest threat in the room. Runic patterns scroll to my elbow, but eventually the glow wanes and dims as my magic is forcibly restrained. For once, I'm grateful for the cursed cuffs. I never would have been able to control this much power.

When the king stays put and doesn't explain himself further, I gather myself and gingerly stand, smoothing the wrinkled skirts of my gown. I hold my head high with as much dignity as I can muster as I cross the room to the doors, hoping he'll keep whatever is tearing him up inside at bay, at least long enough for me to leave.

I push one open and tense, but all he does is breathe and count.

Chapter Seventeen

"The king has a job for you," Ziba announces, bustling into my chamber. She opens the drapes wide, and I whine at the onslaught of sunlight, throwing an arm over my eyes. I flop back down onto my pillows and mutter a curse at the throbbing of my head. I've barely slept. And on top of that, my restlessness veered between dreaming about the king's heated touch and wondering if that darkness seething within him would eventually snap.

I've witnessed those shadows kill a grown man.

But the memory of them caressing my body in the heat of the moment is searing. A vision of those night-dark eyes filled with the flames of passion flashes through my brain. Stars, I'd been so close to doing something utterly unforgivable, and from his reaction, he'd been just as close, too. Until he'd torn himself away, visibly striving for control.

And then said he wanted to end me.

With effort, given my sleepless night, I rise from the bed and perform my morning ablutions. Ziba has put out a fresh set of leathers for me. No dresses then. What kind of labor am I meant to be doing? If I'm lucky, it will be in the castle forge.

"What is this job?" I ask, after Ziba sets a tray down with fresh, warm buttered bread, along with a pot of tea.

"You're to head to the stables," she replies. "Princess Anahima will accompany you."

"*Princess?*" I echo. I suppose if she's the king's sister, as Maxur had told me, she'd be Everlean royalty. "She told me to call her Ani. Is that allowed?"

Ziba moves to the bed and begins to refresh the bedding while I eat. "I suppose so, if she gave you leave."

"She seems kind," I say. *Unlike her volatile brother.*

"She's an eccentric one," Ziba says, her face ruddy with exertion. "Always studying and reading. I honestly don't know where she puts all that knowledge. You can ask her anything about Everlea, and she will know the answer. I believe she has read almost every single textbook in the royal library."

I'm assuming the library is large since this is a palace, after all—which means my friend has read an impressive amount of books. I smile. Somehow, Ani's thirst for knowledge doesn't surprise me one bit. I finish my breakfast and drain the last of my tea, wondering if I can plead my case to her to go to the forge instead. It's worth a shot.

"Sura!" Ani greets me warmly from the bottom of the steps in the luxurious entrance hall. With her loose black hair and twinkling, intelligent blue eyes, once more I note the obvious differences between the siblings, but I can see the resemblance now. They have the same strong nose and high cheekbones, but Ani's mouth is fuller and her jawline much softer.

"Hello, Ani," I say.

"Good to see you up and about. I'm sorry I haven't visited you. I've been busy with urgent court business. How are you feeling?"

I stop beside her. "I understand. I'm much better now, thank you for asking. Everything's on the mend."

"And your memories?" she asks.

"Getting there."

We walk in companionable silence through some manicured gardens blooming with multicolored rosebushes that smell divine. As we start to descend a hill beyond the gardens, noises of clashing steel and loud grunts pierce the air.

Across the grounds below us, multiple warriors are dueling, using swords, axes, spears, and bare hands. An obstacle course takes up nearly half the space, and soldiers run through the hurdles with stunning grace and agility. I stare in fascination as two opponents battle with magical strikes of fire and ice, while another pair fights using lightning and metal manipulation.

"Those two are incredible," I murmur. "He created a blade in midair!"

Ani follows the direction of my gaze. "She's a mestial electrokinetic and he's a dominant ferrokinetic."

That kind of talent would be so useful in a forge!

I catch up with Ani, who is standing at another fighting ring. I recognize Maxur, who is facing off against another man, and half lift my hand in a wave. But my eyes round with complete shock when both fighters start to shift from their human forms. In a blink, their bodies crack and snap, bones moving, flesh bulging, and hair sprouting. Almost double in size, one is a wolven creature and the other resembles a bear. They exchange lethal swipes of claws and teeth, their snarls echoing into the air.

"Mother of sandstorms," I whisper, stunned that the man I'd trained with is hiding an actual monster beneath his skin, and I hadn't even known. "What are they?"

"Corpus magi," Ani says. "Shapeshifters."

The wolven beast whines as the bear takes a chunk out of its shoulder, but then it crunches its enormous jaws around the bear's hind leg. Blood spurts to the ground as the bear howls and bares its neck in submission. And just like that, the fight is over. I watch, mesmerized, as the two beasts shift back to fully human, and the bear-man limps to the side.

The older healer who had attended me the first day runs a hand that glows with gleaming magic over the man's leg when he lowers himself to a bench. I'm not close enough to see it heal, but after a moment, the fighter drags on a pair of trousers and walks away without injury.

I shake my head and laugh. "If I hadn't just seen that with my own eyes, I don't know if I ever would have believed it to be possible. And the way the first warrior only partially shifted, is that normal?"

"For some, it is," Ani says in an odd, choked voice. "General Maxur is particularly skilled." I glance up to see a deep flush spreading over Ani's high cheekbones before she ducks her head away from where Maxur is celebrating his victory.

As if he heard Ani's remarks, Maxur glances up, his eyes fastening to her. The moment is so intimate that, after a handful of seconds, it feels like I'm intruding on something private. With a distressed sound, Ani hurries away, and I hasten to follow her.

"Are you two together?"

"No," she says. "It's not like that." She sighs. "It doesn't matter anyway. My brother does not approve of fraternization with his generals."

Irritated on Ani's behalf, I scowl. "That's because your brother has a great big stick up his ass and wouldn't know how to have fun if it hit him in the face."

Ani snorts. "You're not wrong, but when you're king and constantly trying to keep the peace, manage a kingdom, and deal with external threats, sometimes you don't have time for relationships. And, well, when soul-fated mates are involved, it doesn't make sense to pursue other affairs."

I blink, a cold sensation gripping my insides. "The king has a soul-fated?"

Immediate shutters crash down on her face, and I realize that I've stumbled onto something I'm not supposed to know.

I poke her in the side. "Ani?"

She grits her teeth. "Yes, but it's not my place to talk about it. Forget I said anything." She glances down at me with a resigned smile. "Gods, why is it so easy to talk to you? I feel like I've known you forever, and we only just met, and here I am spilling precious secrets. You're not a spy, are you?"

"I'm not. I wouldn't even know how to be a spy." I reach for her arm and loop mine around hers. "Well, a soul-fated is good, right?"

"Not if he rejects her," she says, and then claps the heel of her palm to her forehead. "Damn it."

Well, this just got juicier than a golden pear in the high season. "Why would he reject the match that the fates made for him?" I ask. "Is he *that* arrogant? I thought soul-fated mates were a bond blessed by the gods themselves. That even a king would be bound to their will."

"Not *this* king," Ani murmurs.

But I forget all thoughts and replies when Ani comes to a stop, and I see the bond-breaker himself, sparring bare-knuckled with a man who looks twice his size. A crowd surrounds the ring, cheering the combatants on. The king is shirtless, with his silver hair in a high warbraid, all those striking tattoos and flexing, sweat-covered muscles on bold display.

My mouth goes as dry as the desert.

Darrius Nightsong must have been sculpted by the gods themselves. Sinewy arms and broad shoulders flow into prominent pectorals and ridged abdominals, every single muscle a testament to his strength as he weaves and ducks, then throws a powerful series of punches into his opponent's torso.

Scars pepper his inked torso and flanks, some faded and others raised and visible. There are slashes and gouges from weapons, but others look like they're from claw and teeth marks. I swallow at the four vicious scars cutting across the tattooed azdaha on his chest. I wonder why he hasn't healed any of them, but maybe they're a matter of pride and battle proficiency. It's obvious his body has seen more than its fair share of war, because those marks tell a violent tale.

His brutal reputation is earned.

I let my gaze drift down, following the trail of one particularly vicious cicatrix over his side and hip to where it disappears down the front of his low-slung waistband. My neck heats. *Everything* heats.

"Drool much?" Ani teases.

"Hardly," I lie through my teeth, when the truth of it is, all I can think of is that sweaty, scarred, tattooed body pressed over mine. And by every star in the sky, the fantasy of a fully nude Darrius makes me nearly whimper with need. A spike of arousal hits me so hard that my knees shake.

His obsidian gaze snaps up to mine, nostrils flaring as he inhales deeply, and I stiffen. There's no way he knows about the storm raging through my body right now and no godsdamned way he can scent me from so far away. But when his irises ignite with that bright gold luster, the sheen of a predator with prey in its sights, my heart starts to gallop.

Stars, what in the pits of Droon is wrong with me?

My lips part, and his stare doesn't waver from me until three hundred pounds of muscle collide into his side and take them both to the ground. An involuntary noise of alarm leaves my mouth, but Darrius is quick to vault to his feet, his lithe body moving like liquid, and he returns the attack, despite the fact that that blow would have killed a lesser man.

The onlookers go wild, money changing hands as more wagers are made. The king swipes his opponent's feet from under him, and the crowd cheers as he follows up with a slew of vicious strikes. For such a big man, his body is poetry in motion, moving with such sublime grace that he could be dancing in a ballroom.

Darrius doesn't look at me, though I sense that the connection between us is as intense and visceral as ever. I can't explain how he can feel me, only that I know if I were to move an inch, he'd be aware of it in seconds. How is he doing that? Focusing on the fight *and* me at the same time? I can barely control my own traitorous body.

You were given orders to go to the stables.

I startle at his deep voice resounding in my head. Somewhat awed but hiding it, I send my thoughts back. *Don't blame me. It's your sister's fault we took this detour.*

He doesn't reply—perhaps because he's fending off his enemy with a series of spinning kicks that makes my breath catch. The expression on his face shows nothing—no pain, no anger, no triumph. In fact, the only spark of emotion I'd seen was when he'd noticed me. He fights with a cold, unearthly precision, every attack perfectly timed and executed.

Suddenly, the man he's sparring with transforms into a snake and wraps his sinuous body around him in heavy green coils. I hiss out a sharp breath, but Darrius doesn't even appear to be worried. I shouldn't have been alarmed, either, because in the next second, his entire body dissolves into a vortex of shadows that swallows the snake entirely for a handful of heartbeats.

Sands, will the shadows eviscerate the snake? But in a blink of an eye, they release their prey and dissipate, and the two men face off once more.

Slightly traumatized, I glance at Ani. "That was . . . unusual."

She grins at my pale face. "Magic is a weapon like any other here and meant to be used. It's a gift on and off the battlefield."

"I bet."

I'll deal with my sister later. You should not be here.

Stars, even his inner voice is domineering. *Why? Are you worried that I'll use your distraction to subvert your precious kingdom?*

I sense the burst of irritation, barely visible in the tightening of his facial muscles, and I revel for a foolish second in the fact that I alone can disrupt that stony, impenetrable exterior.

Careful, Starbright.

I lift a brow when his eyes catch mine for a split second. *I thought "intrusion into the mind is an indelicate, invasive thing" and that you require consent?*

I am projecting my own thoughts. You are choosing to receive them and reply, which in its own way implies tacit permission.

Very well, then I choose to send this.

I envision the clearest picture of a middle finger I can manage.

He must have decided he's done with sparring, because he lets out a growl that I can feel to my toes and takes his adversary to the ground with one knee to the back and an arm around his neck. The man yields with a shout, and a chorus of cheers and groans ensues as wagers are concluded with coin changing hands. The end of the match is so fast and so easy that I wonder why the king wasn't fighting with all of his skill before.

And then the answer is obvious when he vaults the fence and comes striding up the small hill toward Ani and me. *Shit.* I straighten as he closes the distance, ready to do some verbal sparring of my own, but then his delicious scent surrounds me, and I can barely put up any kind of valiant offense. My senses scatter like dandelion seeds in the wind.

Gods, it isn't fair for a man to smell so *good*.

I swallow my groan. When did I develop some kind of peculiar olfactory obsession? My eyes rove over his exposed skin. Or a tattoo and glistening muscles obsession? Those inky designs curl lovingly over his defined body in intricate swirls, arrowing down his torso to those dangerously low pants. Do the markings go *all* the way down? I feel my core clench even as I yank my gaze back to a respectable level.

Down, girl.

"This isn't the stables, sister dear," he says to Ani. He slings an arm over her shoulders, dragging her close, and she squeals.

"You're sweaty and disgusting. Get off!" She shoves him away, and he laughs. *Laughs!* "And we *were* on the way to the stables. I opted for the scenic route."

I'm picking my jaw up off the ground as I watch the interaction in surprise—a far cry from the stilted, rude ones I'd seen before. But I suppose the first time in my room, he'd been more concerned with guarding his precious secrets from an interloper, and in the throne room, Ani had been his scribe.

"You should spar more," he tells her. "We miss your skills in the ring."

My brows shoot up. Ani looks like a strong wind could blow her over.

"I've been busy with my duties, Dare," she says, eyes flicking to me before she shrugs. "The king of Oryndhr has been difficult, insisting we've committed an act of war. He refuses to be civil or reasonable. And the horde clans are refusing to agree on anything, as usual."

Surprise makes me falter again. Darrius must trust her implicitly to let her speak on his behalf to another king or be a representative to his subjects. I love that, especially because she's a woman. In Oryndhr, women are valued only for breeding and marriage. It's inspiring to see one in a position of influence.

"War serves no one," he says, and I feel his gaze brush over me. "Stall Acharia if you can. Until we have all the information about the matter in question, I refuse to concede to his demands. What of the basilisk attack?" he asks her.

I perk up with interest, recalling the farmer who had asked for help. "It's gone," Ani says. "The men hunted for hours. No sign of it."

Darrius scrubs his jaw. "I'm not convinced it's gone for good."

She nods. "Me, either. They're territorial and don't give up that easily, even if they're sick. Maybe we're lucky and it's dead somewhere, but we can't take that chance."

"Agree. Set up a patrol."

With a wink, Ani cants her head in automatic deference. "One step ahead of you, brother."

His smile is fond . . . and genuine. Sands on fire, I nearly swoon at the unexpected sight and what it does to that austere face. "You always are. Very well, keep me informed of any developments."

"Of course, Dare."

The entire conversation and the obvious use of a nickname imply that they're closer than I realized. If I had to guess, I would say that Ani is the official hand of the king, and who better to act in his stead than his own sister? It makes me grudgingly admire him more. Some men are threatened by women in power, but clearly not this monarch.

As if feeling my shifting esteem, the king turns and glances in my direction. "Change of plans then, since you and my marauding sister don't take orders from your sovereign seriously."

Faced with a full-frontal view of that rock-hard abdomen, I can't even pretend to have a snappy comeback. I'm too busy keeping my fingers from reaching out to touch every ridge. "Don't you have a shirt?" I mumble.

A corner of his lips curls. "Too much to handle?"

"Hardly," I manage, but my ears feel like they're melting off the sides of my head.

With a low chuckle, the king waves his hand and a portal forms. I still can't get over how easily magic is wielded here. *His* magic in particular. "Where are we going?" I ask.

"Razulek has recovered."

My heart races at the thought of seeing the mystical creature from my memories in actuality, and I very eagerly follow the king through the portal. Swiveling, I roll my eyes at a smirking Ani, who pretends to be wiping her chin of drool behind her brother's back. What an imp!

We emerge on the cliffside of a mountain, and I can see the rise of higher crests beyond. The portal winks out of existence. "Are these the Barrin Mountains?"

"Yes. We're in the Bone Forest, the hunting grounds of oviparous azdahas," he says. "Their main colony is to the northwest." I swallow as I glance around nervously, half expecting one of the enormous creatures to fly at me out of nowhere in a protective rage over its eggs. A few graceful shadows that look like specks, though I know they are massive, soar high in the sky. I wonder how fast they can fly—they'd be lethal in battle. Or while hunting.

The king snorts when I unconsciously take a step closer to him. "Don't worry. They lay eggs in the depths of Deadman's Canyon at the hottest part of the realm's core. That's where their younglings hatch and where they're the most territorial."

"That man from the throne room. Lord Donnan. He said he was hunting the eggs?"

The king's stern face tightens. "They're very valuable. They're rare and getting rarer. Azdahas live long lives, but their fertility rates are low. It's against our laws to steal the eggs."

"Razulek told me he has a mate," I murmur without thinking.

The king inhales sharply. "He did, did he?"

"Why? Was that wrong?"

He shakes his head. "Azdahas rarely speak to others unless they're bonded via akasha."

"Well, he spoke to me." I worry my lip with my teeth. "He knew I was no danger to him."

King Darrius doesn't answer, both of us distracted by the thunderous whoosh of incoming massive wings. I let out a small shriek when a huge shape sucks up the remaining light and thumps to the ground in front of me, sending a small landslide of rocks cascading down the cliff.

It's an azdaha, one even bigger than Razulek, with deep bloodred scales. It looks monstrous but regal with a crown of enormous pointed horns and fangs as long as my forearm. A huge crimson-scaled chest rises and falls with its breaths, deadly talons dig into the earth at the end of thick hindquarters, and a long, spined tail with a plume at the end curls lazily behind its immense body. Massive wings flare when its forelimbs crash down.

With an involuntary scream, I fall onto my ass and scuttle backward like a crab, wanting to search for the king but afraid to tear my gaze away from the very large predator in front of me.

"Calm, Starbright," Darrius says from somewhere behind me. "You will not be harmed."

Says him. Has he seen the size of those *teeth*?

I gulp and try to reason with my palpitating heart, but no amount of soothing will quell the hammering drumbeat of my pulse. From its towering height, the azdaha watches me like a cat with a mouse. It leans its great head down toward me, and I'm sure I'm going to be gobbled up, but a slitted scarlet eyeball merely studies me. That barbed tail flicks around, and I freeze, watching those deadly yellow-tipped spikes get too close for comfort.

I swallow past the oversized knot in my throat. "Please don't kill me."

It chuffs, a sound like amusement puffing through its lips. An echinated snout bends to touch my head, and I feel a well of connection open up, just as it had with Razulek back in Kaldari. The cuffs don't seem to diminish the mental link. I sense its power acknowledge my magic and the slumbering simurgh inside of me, its sinuous neck canting in a sort of graceful bow as it bares the underside of its throat to me.

I frown at the seeming show of submission. Why would this azdaha bow to *me*?

All dragonkin are born of stardust, Starkeeper. A female, I realize, as her elegant, smoky voice resonates through my mind. *I could never kill the one responsible for bringing my mate home. I am Indira.*

I blink up at her, my brain stuttering. "You're Razulek's mate?"

Yes.

A rush of unexpected joy fills me. "How is he? He saved me, too, I think. I don't have all of my memories yet, but I know he rescued me from something deadly. Is he with you?"

Yes, Starkeeper. He comes from our nest. I was already in the Bone Forest hunting. She fixes me with an assessing look. *How does your sidereal magic fare?*

Hadn't Ani called the highest rank something else, or had I heard it wrong? "Do you mean sovran?"

That jeweled red eye fastens to me. *Sidereal rank supersedes all, including sovran. A Starkeeper is matchless in power.*

Twisting my lips, I hold up my cuffs. "Not while these are on."

She snarls loudly as if taking personal affront to the bracers, chest engorging and something like acid bubbling up on her tongue that makes my eyes smart and my nose sting. I take a hasty step back.

"What is that?" I ask.

Darrius comes to stand at my side, one hand rising to give Indira's snout a fond pat. "She's a poison azdaha. She's displeased by the cuffs."

The acid dissipates. *Razulek told me about those and how they were used to trap him for so long.* She stares at me. *I will use any power I have to honor my life debt to you.*

"You don't owe me anything."

He would have died without you, she says solemnly. *I felt death coming for him, the mate bond stretching to its limits, and I thought all was lost. I would have died with him, so you have saved me as well.*

I feel the warm touch of her snout on my head that feels oddly like a kiss. *But now, thanks to you, we have two eggs to hatch and a future to live for.*

Oh, my heart. *Two.* My chest swells and my eyes burn with unshed tears at the thought of Razulek having a family. As if my happiness has summoned him, I hear the whooshing sound of approaching wings again, and I recognize his emerald scales sparkling in the sunlight when a soaring figure dives toward us. Razulek lands on the cliffside beside his mate, folding his wings to his sides. Smoke curls from his nostrils.

Glimpses of him from the arena pop into my brain, and a horrified gasp leaves my lips at how unhealthy and sickly he'd been. Now, he glows. Stars, he looks so *good*. Healthy and powerful.

"Razulek," I say, choking up. "Thank you. I don't remember everything yet, but I know you saved us. Saved me."

He cocks his beautiful horned head, a single golden eye examining me. *What do you mean, little queen?*

"Your king thinks the cuffs might have done something to my memories," I say, lifting them to show him. His reaction is as violent as Indira's, a deep growl rumbling from him. "They inhibit my magic, too."

Like the collar they forced upon me, he snarls.

I nod, powerless fury rising in my veins again, while the simurgh inside of me awakens. She's more alive than I've seen her in weeks, even with the dampening effect of the bracers. She rises within, and I let the magic show in my eyes as the runes on my arms light up in welcome to the two azdahas. To my surprise, they bow in unison as if paying homage to something greater than themselves.

My lips part in awe at their deference, and I feel my simurgh's gratitude. "She says thank you," I whisper to them.

Darrius smiles at Razulek. "Good to see you well recovered, old friend."

Razulek inclines his head, and I wonder if the king can hear him in his head as well.

"Of course she is," the king says aloud as if in answer to an unspoken question, and then grins. "You're ready, aren't you?" he asks me.

"Ready for what?" I ask doubtfully.

"To fly," he says.

I balk as his meaning sinks in. "On *them*?"

Razulek and Indira both chuff at my screeched words, and I watch, mesmerized, as Darrius easily scales one of Indira's extended wings and settles himself in place behind a ridge on her sinuous neck. He looks so small up there, and I let out a stunned laugh.

He waves. "Your turn, Starbright."

"I'm not doing that," I say. "No."

He doesn't try to convince me. Instead he shrugs. "Your loss. Razulek's, too, as he has chosen you as his bonded rider." With that, he gives some signal to Indira, and she dives off the edge of the cliff, taking him with her and making my heart lurch. It's only when her crimson wings spread wide that I am able to breathe. Together, they climb the winds.

"What did he mean that you chose me?" I ask Razulek.

Azdahas can only have one bonded rider at a time. You are mine.

I exhale and bite my lip. "What if I fall off?"

His snout brushes my side. *I would sooner die than let you fall, little queen.*

I watch as he extends a wing, similar to Indira, and the slant of it doesn't look that hard to climb. Without letting myself think too much about my fear, I start the ascent, using the bony protrusions as makeshift steps, until I am nearly at the apex where the wing bones meld into huge overlapped scales. I touch them and gasp—they're hot under my fingers.

Careful on the scales, he cautions. *They are sharp and slippery.*

Using the small groupings of spines that dot his powerful flanks,

I gingerly maneuver my way to a similar ridge on his neck where Darrius had positioned himself. The hide there is more reptilian than scaly, and I wedge myself in place in front of the thick, ropy muscles of his wings, keeping an eye on the rows of long, frilled spines that look viciously sharp in front of me.

Grip the spines atop the ridge, he instructs, and I do as he says. *Now tighten your legs and hold on.*

"Wait, Razul—" But his name cuts sharply into a shrill scream as we leap from the cliff's edge and my soul practically stays behind. Shrieking, I clutch the spines in a death grip, my thigh muscles shaking as I dig my heels into his leathery sides, feeling the pressure of his formidable wings as they flare and widen, keeping us aloft.

His huge body ripples beneath me, the connection between us pulsing with magic. With pure akasha. The bracers on my wrists don't even brighten—nothing of the earthly world, no human-wrought magic, can suppress this. Air rushes into my face as we soar upward to where Darrius and Indira are but a speck, the mountain range dropping away and becoming smaller and smaller.

As I suspected, you were born for this. Razulek's voice is more than a little smug, but I can only grin so hard that my cheeks ache. By the gods, we're fucking flying!

This is amazing, I think back to him, our bond humming. *Faster, Raz.*

He roars victoriously, and those great wings pump, propelling us through the sky like a shooting star splitting the heavens.

Chapter Eighteen

The Night King

Gods, she's so fucking beautiful upon the azdaha—a queen in her own right—that I can hardly think as all the blood in my body rushes south in a frenzy of need. I want her. I need her. My curse rattles its cage, and the reminder of the fact that I can so easily condemn her to a monstrous fate is sobering.

For all my posturing about wanting to end her to break our soul-fated link, I can no sooner harm a single hair on her head than I can wound myself. Keeping her at arm's length, and safe, is the only way I can survive her presence. *Not* coveting her like this. *Not* wanting to spend hours in the blissful wake of her joy. *Not* craving her like my next breath.

And while the smartest path of least resistance is to return her to Oryndhr—and her king there, as he has demanded or he will bring war to my doorstep—I cannot bring myself to do so, not with what Razulek has now shared with Indira.

They treated her like a thing to be controlled, chaining her will and binding her magic to those godscursed cuffs. I have tried everything to remove them, but not even the sovran strength of my magic can break the hold, not when it's her own divine blood being harnessed against her. She is both lock and key.

I watch her fly for hours, long after Indira leaves to tend to her nest, feeling the chaos bleed into my veins as the curse takes root.

I'm a king chained to a soul-fated bond and damned by a devious god . . . a man doomed to tear apart the one he loves if he embraces the union. It's only by rigid self-control I've resisted chaos, eschewed passion, forgone feeling.

Until now. Until my entombed heart felt her starlight.

But I must be heartless if she is to live. I reach for the discipline that has sustained me since her soul summoned mine, but all I feel is infatuation and glorious arousal, followed by bitterness and rage for what I cannot have.

For what has been *stolen* from me.

Anger roils as I try to breathe and count in order to stave off the shift, but it's much too late. Beneath my skin, my bones begin to thicken. I distill to shadow to seek out the cover of the forest and re-form into a grotesque, excruciating half shift as the god curse erupts.

Mindless, I open my mouth and roar.

Chapter Nineteen

The king is missing.

He has been absent for over two weeks now and no one, not even Ani or Ziba, or even Razulek and Indira, seems to know where he has vanished to. Or, at least, they're not confiding in me. Then again, everyone here has so many secrets, what's one more? I have my own problems to worry about, namely the last pieces of my memory, which I suspect are the most critical ones.

I know by now who I am and why I escaped, that people who I thought were my friends are my enemies, and that my magic has been weaponized. By the king of Oryndhr. *Javed.*

When I push, I see vague snatches of another royal, but my emotions are so conflicted about him for some as yet unknown reason, warring with some deeper instinct that I can't pinpoint. Gods, why can't I just *remember*?

The cursed cuffs heat, and I know exactly why I cannot. My blood simmers, magic coiling in my veins with nowhere to go—the despicable runes on the bracers flaring to suppress it.

Sands, I need to get some of this frustration out! Get some answers! Do something!

I reach through the bond. *Razulek.*

Miss me already, little queen? he answers immediately, and though our connection is not limited by distance, I am guessing he's not near the castle. Fond affection rolls through the bond and my breathing eases.

I need to see you. Please.

He pauses, and I feel guilty for pulling him away from his paternal duties. I'm about to tell him to ignore my request when I sense him again. *Meet me in the meadow beside the castle.*

Hurriedly, I dress in a fresh set of leathers and run out of the fortress as fast as my feet can carry me. It doesn't take me long to jog through the gardens with the marigolds and a thicket of trees to reach the wide expanse of field beyond. I wait impatiently there, staring into the sky. Eventually, a small speck grows larger and larger, blotting out the sun as my azdaha gracefully lands, the gusts from his wings nearly toppling me over.

Wondrous awe fills me as I take him in, marveling at the shiny emerald scales that glint with shades of chartreuse and teal in the sunlight and the long, elegantly frilled spines from his crown to the tip of his barbed tail. I wonder idly if his hatchlings will look like him or Indira, or be a combination of both. Or even another color altogether.

His snout nudges my head as he lowers to a crouching position, one wing splayed downward toward me. *Let's fly, and then you can unburden your thoughts.*

The notion of riding him so soon fills me with joy, and as I scramble up his extended wing to the pebbled divot at his neck, a sense of rightness settles inside of me. Akasha ripples between us, weaving our auras together, and I marvel at the instant connection that holds me in place. The magical tether with this mystical creature is still astounding to me.

Grasping his spines, I tighten my thighs and brace as Razulek launches off his hind legs with a massive pump of his wings, taking us high into the sun-drenched sky in a matter of seconds. My stomach feels weightless, but I'm not afraid. I know he'll never let me fall. We climb steadily for a bit and then he spreads his wings wide, coasting on the winds above the clouds. I tip my face to the warmth of the sun, but my heart still weighs too heavy for me to truly enjoy it.

What's troubling you, little queen? Razulek rumbles.

"I feel lost . . . and afraid," I say aloud, knowing he can hear me—speaking the words helps me to parse my chaotic feelings. "My memories are inconsistent, but the terror I feel is real. Like something is brewing and I have no idea what it is. I need to know what's happening. Is there anything more you can share about your time in Oryndhr that might jog my memory?" I stare balefully at my wrists. "Or even how we can get these starscursed cuffs off?"

His big body heaves with a few flaps of his wings as he thinks, his head curving back with a slitted, jeweled gaze narrowing on my cuffed wrists and flashing with rancor. *Much of what I remember is pain. The collar they shackled me with had their symbols that repressed my magic. I tried everything to remove them, even my fires, but nothing worked.* One eye swivels to mine. *And until you, I despaired of ever feeling the blissful touch of akasha again. What does your simurgh say?*

"She's a captive as well," I admit. "Our magic is bound." I inhale a ragged breath, fingers tightening on his spines. "What do you know of the rulers there?"

There was an older king, but I saw him only once. The queen reeked of darkness, and her son, who eventually became king, was worse.

"Javed."

Razulek huffs. *I know not any names, but he was cruel. He wanted me to bare my neck and submit, but I never did. No azdaha has ever been forced to serve the sons of man. I was glad when I heard of his death.*

"Wait," I say, frowning at the revelation, which throws my theories to the wind. "He died? Do you know this for sure?"

The magi who drew the runes on my collar spoke often among themselves when they thought I was asleep. He looks back to me again and his lip curls up, baring his teeth in what I expect is a savage grin. *And how proud I was, little queen, when I heard you had slain his mother, the foul death magi. I praised the gods for the blessed hand of their vengeance.*

I stare at him in shock. "*I* slayed the queen?"

But as I voice the preposterous question, images flicker to life in my brain. Morvarid's bloody smile . . . my dagger sliding in between her ribs. But no celebration, only sorrow, because someone dear to me had died. A man . . . a prince who'd loved me. The memories dissipate before I can grasp them or see his face or know his name. *No!*

"Raz? Was there another prince?" I ask desperately.

No. There was a . . . king.

If there is another king besides Javed, I have no recollection of him. My confusion must show on my face, because I feel the press of akasha in the bond between us, and suddenly, I can see into Razulek's memories. A tall, dark-haired man, resplendent in purple-and-gold clothing, stalks across Raz's gaze. I don't recognize his profile.

"Are you certain this will work?" the man demands of a runecaster I *do* recognize from my scattered memories: Aran, who holds a pair of familiar bracers in his hands. Maker above, those are the exact ones I wear now.

"Yes, Your Majesty," Aran says, though the anguish on his face strikes me as odd. "With the changes we discussed, you will have complete control. Are you certain—"

"If I wanted your opinion, I'd give it to you," he snaps. The king turns to face me—Razulek—and I gasp. He looks familiar, but also *not*. His eyes are filigreed with purplish smoke, a cruel smile twisting his full lips. "Proceed. And bleed the beast for touching my property."

I'm thrust from Razulek's mind just before the memory of his suffering hits.

"Who was that?" I wheeze, coming back into my own head.

He came before with his guards when you healed my wings. I tried to protect you, but the pain was too much to bear. They took you from me. I am so sorry that I failed you then.

I remember the taste of Jade in my mouth, the prick of the needle into my nape. The betrayal. I reach forward to stroke the side of his neck, pressing my palm into his warm, rough hide. "No, Raz. You didn't. They did that to us. *They* hurt us. But we're here now, and we're safe."

For now, he says. *He will come for you.*

"Did Darrius tell you that?" I ask.

I have seen the army that camps on the other side of the mountains myself. The Night King fears that war is imminent. He has tried to negotiate with the Oryndhrian king, but to no avail.

I remember what Ani had told her brother about the king being difficult.

"Do you know where Darrius has gone?" I ask, dread pooling anew. "If they mount an attack, Everlea will be vulnerable without its leader. Ani is in line for the throne, and if her brother doesn't return, the responsibility will fall to her. I know he thinks she's capable, I can tell how much he esteems her, but what if she can't?"

The curse the king bears will be his ruin.

Blinking, I frown. "Curse?"

I have shared too much already, and it is not my story to tell.

Despite my intense curiosity, I don't press, knowing he won't betray his king's confidence. I'll ask Darrius about the curse and the army at the border when he returns.

If all else fails, I will offer myself up to the Oryndhrian king, if only to save Everlea and its people and prevent war. They should not have to suffer for harboring me. And then I have to get back to Coban and my family.

"How did I come to be with you when we escaped?" I ask Raz as he makes a wide bank after passing the mountain peaks of Lora, out over the Glacier Ocean to head west back toward the castle, and the sight of the open expanse of blue below us makes me instinctively tighten my grip.

A noblewoman summoned you to the arena. It was a trick. I frown at his words, a woman's treacherous face winking in my vision. She had hoped to kill me. *I had been punished, poisoned, and starved until all I knew was pain and rage and hunger. Your blood healed me, helped me see through the darkness of the lie.*

"I healed you with my blood, not magic?" I ask.

Akasha flows freely in our veins.

I exhale. "What happened after that?"

You gave me your light, little queen, and together we burned through the heavens.

"Darrius says there are wards between the realms. How did we get through them?"

My mate informed the king of my return. Raz chuffs, and I can feel the devotion in his heart to Indira through our connection. *Now what do you say we do a few flying drills?*

I let out an unhinged scream when he does a barrel roll to flip us upside down, but the bonds of akasha keep me firmly in place after he rights us once more. I've barely had time to catch my breath as he folds his wings tight to his sides and plummets toward the ocean. The onslaught of wind makes my eyes stream, and I blink wildly, desperate to see what's ahead, but there's only a deep, dark blue.

Gods, are we going to go under?

But my devious azdaha levels out just above the surface of the waves, those powerful wings flaring wide and making my stomach swoop as we glide gracefully a few feet above the crystalline water. Raz drops one clawed hind leg into the sea, creating a wake of white foam behind us.

I'm so mesmerized by the glittering stream that I don't spot the movement until some kind of spinning sea serpent with an open maw full of fangs launches itself from the indigo depths right at me.

At the last second, Raz veers upward, his huge body shuddering with fright as the monster narrowly misses us and dives back down.

"What in Droon was that?" I yelp, watching it arrow through the water beneath us.

Oh, Starkeeper, you should have seen your face. Raz shudders again, and I realize that it's with *laughter*, not fear.

I scowl and yank on one of his chartreuse frills. "You did that on purpose, you overgrown lizard!"

That is a razortooth eel. It's mating season so they're extra vicious. He flashes me a hint of fang in amusement. *They're good eating.*

I sigh theatrically at the hopeful note in his mental voice. "Fine. I suppose I should thank Indira letting me steal you away from your duties yet again. Let's go catch some eels for your fierce mate. Just don't drop me."

Not on my watch, Starkeeper.

Today is day fifteen, and still no Darrius Nightsong.

In his absence, Ani has been a stalwart companion whose company I value greatly, even if she's infuriatingly tight-lipped about her brother's whereabouts. Our routine since Darrius vanished has been consistent, spending most of our days and meals together.

"Is the king well?" I ask Ani while we get our lunch from the cook and carry it to the library. My mouth waters at the smell of the savory lamb, eggplant, and tomato stew, served with piping-hot rice, that the king's thoughtful cook prepared as a treat for me. I suspect, however, that the kind gesture is because of *him*. The missing monarch himself. And I don't want to like that at all.

"Yes," Ani says.

"He's not in any danger, is he?"

Ani lifts a brow as we enter the library, but she doesn't tease me about my concern. "No."

"Does he do this often?" I venture. "Disappear?"

"On occasion."

"Why?" I ask.

Ani shrugs. "His story to tell."

I groan inwardly: that was the same thing Razulek had said when we'd flown together. Gods, it's like pulling teeth to get anything but noncommittal answers from anyone. So, I ask the question that is really troubling me. "Does he usually return unscathed?"

To my surprise, Ani lets out a snort. "I wouldn't say unscathed, but he's usually in better spirits when he does. He hasn't been gone this long for some time, however. Not since . . ." Her face clouds slightly. "Well, it was a while ago, perhaps half a year or so. Something terrible happened, I believe, and he disappeared for weeks."

"Where does he go?" I prod, encouraged by full sentences for once.

"Why so curious?" Ani returns. I feel my cheeks heat at her scrutiny.

"I'm not," I say. "I just want to go home, that's all."

I rub my eyes. My desire to return to Coban is no secret, but the only person powerful enough to open a portal to another realm is the missing Darrius.

"Is portal creation another of your brother's numena?" I ask Ani.

"Yes, there's a reason he's the only sovran in Everlea," she says. "He has master rank over kinetic magic as well. To open a portal across the realms, one would have to be an ergokinesis master with the ability to manipulate raw energy."

"And no one else can?" I ask.

Ani's face is solemn. "No, and even if they were powerful enough, it's forbidden for anyone else but the king to do so." She shoves the pile of books I'd saved from our last library visit toward me. "Don't worry, he'll be back soon. Catch up, you're behind."

Given the size of the library, I've been diligent about learning runes as well as researching what I am, but most of the history is different here. There are few tales about the legendary Starkeeper and his role in ending the war. The prophecies are different, though they seem to be pulled from similar places—each of them that I've read speaks of a celestial being blessed by the four Royal Stars whose star magic is reborn in times of dire need.

I sigh and start to eat while perusing the book on the magic systems of Endara, divided by realm. True to what Darrius had imparted, there were three realms once: Everlea, Oryndhr, and Rothdar. The little I can find on Rothdar also supports what he'd told me—it's a dead realm of graves, ghosts, and bones.

Curious, I stare at the enormous map on the far wall, and I make my way over to it. I recognize the major cities in Oryndhr, including Kaldari and Eloni, as well as my desert home of Coban. The Dustlands, the home of the Jade-addicted Scavs, take up most of the middle.

With a fingertip, I trace the Barrin Mountains that divide the continent into two, with Oryndhr at the bottom and Everlea at the top. I tap the spot near Deadman's Canyon where I'd flown with Razulek. Half of Everlea is steppe, I notice, the area divided among four names according to the drawn borders.

"Are these steppes home to the horde clans you mentioned? The ones with elemental magic?" I ask Ani.

"Yes, the Aspačanā," she replies, coming to my side and pointing each of them out. "Rakh, Karkad, Chamros, and Shabra are horse-riding nomadic warriors. Each of them is gifted in akasha. Rakh are fire wielders; Karkad is water; Chamros, air; and Shabra, earth." She eyes me. "You should meet their leaders."

My brows rise. "Why?"

She gives a nonchalant shrug. "The Aspačanā clans are interesting and have their own magic. Perhaps they might have insight into your cuffs."

"Would they really?" Hope rises in me.

"It doesn't hurt to try," she says. "When my brother returns, you can get his opinion, if you need it to decide."

I bristle at the not-so-subtle insinuation that I need Darrius's permission to make up my own mind. "Tell me more about them. What are their leaders like?"

"In each clan, there is a warrior queen or warrior king. At the moment, there are two male rais and two female raissas, but that changes frequently."

"They're not a patriarchal society?" I ask in surprise.

She shakes her head. "Gender independent."

The idea of a society where women are equally valued as men is deeply fascinating, but their whole culture sounds very different from what I am used to.

"You truly think they can help?" I say, lifting the cuffs, and Ani gives an uncertain nod. The truth is, though, it's the only new lead I have—I've found no other answers in this library. "Well, let's hope that your brother comes back and can arrange a meeting."

"I can take you," Ani offers.

I want to blurt out a yes, but something stops me from accepting. I want to be rid of these bracers, but this is still Darrius's realm, and I'm unfamiliar with the territory and the people. It's best to tread cautiously. With my luck, I'd end up causing a diplomatic incident.

I wrinkle my nose and walk back to the table. "Best to wait for the king."

THE NEXT AFTERNOON, on Ani's suggestion, I go to the stables. All she had to do was mention something about newborn foals and I was out the door. Who doesn't love baby animals?

But all the buildings are strangely quiet.

"Nuadar?" I call out. Ani told me he is the grouchy beastmaster and gamekeeper. He pops out of a stall, offering a surly grunt for a greeting. "I've come to see the foals."

He frowns. "Foals?"

"Ani said there were babies."

His brows lower even more. "The princess must be mistaken."

"Are there any other types of animals besides horses here?" I ask, disappointed but determined to not have the time be a waste.

"Some," he says brusquely.

"What kind?" I press, but he glares at me, muttering about how he is too busy to trifle with silly Oryndhrian interlopers, before spinning on his heel and walking away. I stare and shake my head. *Rude!*

With a sigh, I cross the exercise yard, where a handful of grooms are training sleek-looking, enormous warhorses, and then march toward a set of joined towers I haven't seen before. I have no idea where I'm going, but it feels good to be out on the grounds.

Out of the corner of my eye, I notice Nuadar keeping pace a few lengths behind me and trying to stay out of sight. I grin. Good, at least I won't get lost or stumble somewhere I'm not supposed to be.

After walking down a narrow path, I notice a much larger, fully enclosed paddock that stands on its own near the forest behind it. I feel an odd pulse of magic, which makes me slow with curiosity—and then a massive howl pierces the air. Chain links rattle and then snap as another guttural, inhuman roar nearly makes me leap out of my skin. I rear back at the sound of something huge trying to escape its cage and crashing over and over into the gates of the paddock enclosure.

"What's in there?" I shout to the gamekeeper lurking behind me. My heart is in my throat as we both watch the reinforced gates nearly buckle beneath the force of whatever's attacking it.

Nuadar, usually so dour, has an *awful* look on his face as he beckons me toward him. "Nothing to concern you. Quickly. He's probably scented you already."

"What has scented me?" I whisper, as the banging grows more frenzied.

But before either of us can move, the gates buckle, one flying off its hinges, and the biggest beast I've ever seen prowls toward us. Toward *me*.

The air punches from my lungs, blood draining from my body in a rush and leaving me in a shivering, utterly useless heap. I am frozen in terror, unable to draw a single breath. *Gods,* what *is* that? A lion? But then my eyes see wings and a bulb-tipped tail that looks like it belongs to a scorpion. My brain stutters as I realize what it is with a strangled, petrified gasp: *manticore.*

A man-eater.

The monstrous beast sets me in its voracious, glowing golden sights as my legs soften to the consistency of jelly, and my trapped magic is crashing through me, trying to handle the flight-or-fight response taking over.

Stay calm, stay calm, stay calm.

Nearly the size of a warhorse but far more muscular, the creature has a wild golden mane, a lion's face, and fangs as long as my forearms. Ropy muscles shift and contract beneath sleek reddish-gold fur with every soundless step it takes. It could be right behind me and I wouldn't even hear it. My eyes return to the pair of gold-veined scarlet wings flaring out over its back, then move down to the wicked talons of its feet, which tap the ground with ominous clicks. What's most mesmerizing is the scorpion's tail flicking warningly over its hindquarters.

If my heart wasn't trying to dive out of my body, I'd be fascinated by how chillingly beautiful the creature is.

A beautiful monster.

One that looks like it wants you for dinner.

"Nuadar? What happens now?" I whisper over my shoulder, where the gamekeeper is standing utterly still with petrified eyes. Fuck, this is bad.

"Whatever you do, do *not* run, my lady."

The formal address makes me panic. He was grumpy before, which means I'm definitely about to die. Without magic, no amount of training will save me from this thing.

It roars again, and I swear I can smell death on its breath. Fuck this. I'm not standing here like some kind of sacrificial offering.

Ignoring Nuadar's frenzied shout, I turn and bolt.

Chapter Twenty

Running into a wide-open forest I have no familiarity with is a disastrous idea, but going back inside where other injured animals are being kept isn't an option, either. I thank the stars that my body is in better shape than it has been from my grueling physical training with Maxur. I have no doubts that I am absolutely incapable of outrunning a manticore, but with luck, I can at least climb a tree.

It has wings, you fool.

Hide, then.

My toe catches on a root and I flail wildly, finally losing my balance and falling hard to the ground. As I scramble to my feet, I smell the blood from my scraped-open palms and stinging knees. I wince but push myself forward—my magic will heal the wounds eventually.

I hear the beast crashing through the foliage behind me, and I put on a burst of speed. I have no idea where I'm going. The canopy is thick and dense, and the smell of moist earth and decomposing vegetation is pungent. I can barely get air into my lungs, my gasps ringing too loud in my ears.

In my wake, a huge crash echoes through the undergrowth, and the new sound of *two* creatures roaring nearly makes me stumble.

Good, if something else distracts the manticore, that's better odds for my survival. Well, except if that *something else* decides to come for me . . .

Frantic, I look for somewhere to hide. Just ahead in the distance, I spot what looks like the gnarled roots of a tree with a small gap that I can squeeze through. Relief is sweet, but much too long in coming. I'm nearly there when a darkness devours every bit of light around me, and I nearly scream in horror, only to recognize Indira's red scales at the very last second.

She lands in front of me, making the ground tremble.

"There's a thing," I babble, pointing over my shoulder. "A monster. Is Raz with you?"

Yes. He's here. Her mental tone sounds resigned but not afraid. She glances up over my head to where the commotion is coming from and makes that chuffing amused sound again. *He's having his fun.*

My brows collide. "Fun? There's a rabid manticore back there! We have to help him." The sound of a large tree snapping in half makes us both glance in the direction of where her mate is. "Shit, Raz!" I shout.

Your concern is touching, dear one. Indira bends her long neck so her huge spined head is once more at my level. *They have likely moved a fair distance in flight, but I can carry you, if you wish it.*

I glance at her with trepidation. She is Raz's mate, but Darrius is her rider. Wouldn't there be rules about who can mount the king's bonded azdaha? But I can't let Raz face that monster alone, not when this is my fault to begin with. I inhale a gulp of air and nod. But instead of extending a wing for me to climb on her back, her massive hind foot stretches in my direction, scooping me up gently before she takes to the skies in a huge whoosh of air. My stomach bottoms out as we soar upward.

We don't fly far enough for me to get used to being carried in her claws—perhaps four or five gigantic wingbeats—before she descends into another clearing. The place is utterly destroyed, trees ripped from the roots, branches shattered, and an enraged manticore and a smoking azdaha circling each other.

Indira releases me, though she settles her bulk defensively in front of me.

I peek around her huge hind leg. Despite the destruction and the superficial scratches on his hide, Raz's tongue is lolling out of his mouth like a giant puppy. He doesn't seem like he's fighting for his life at all. Perhaps I should've taken Indira at her word. She must've known her mate wasn't in any real danger via their bond.

Or . . .

Do they *know* the manticore? Is it sentient like them?

Singe marks from Raz's fire cover the manticore's side and a bit of its thick golden mane is missing, but it no longer seems feral, the way it had earlier. I can't help staring at how regal the creature is. It's gorgeous in the way that wolves are—mesmerizing but undeniably deadly.

Come to see the show, little queen? Raz greets me when he sees me peering out from behind his mate's leg. His usual affectionate salutation is met by a vicious roar from the manticore as if it had somehow heard Raz's mental address and didn't like it in the least. I nearly leap a foot into the air when that golden gaze locks in my direction.

"Mine."

That growl makes my hair stand on end. It can *speak*? Blinking, I shake my head. Does it still think I'm its prey?

"I'm very bony," I call out. "And I have a sour disposition that might not suit your palate."

Indira chuffs above me, earning herself a nuzzle from her adoring mate. The manticore lets out a noise between a whine and a growl, that very lucid, very covetous glowing gaze trained on me, its deadly tail swishing like a feline's. That means aggression, no? I hiss out a breath as it runs a forked tongue over its sharp canines, studying me, the intensity unsettling. Sands, why does it look so *ravenous*?

My father used to say back in Coban that the only way to stand up to certain predators is to make yourself as large as possible. Knowing that Indira and Raz won't let anything happen to me, I straighten my spine and stare the manticore right in the eyes. Instantly, the beast goes preternaturally still, its amber irises glowing with brighter gold filaments. Its nostrils flare at my overt challenge, and a low, dangerous-sounding growl leaves its maw.

Oh, *shit*.

Don't mind him; he's in a bad mood because I trounced him, Raz taunts. Too fast to track, the manticore fires one of its poison barbs from its tail toward my azdaha—one Raz easily dodges with more chuffing noises.

"Do you know who he is?" I ask, mind racing with possible explanations at Raz's familiar tone and the fact that the monster is male. "Is he a corpus magi?"

Raz takes much too long to answer, and I have a feeling that the manticore is following the conversation, because those gorgeous, flared wine-red wings fold inward and his aggressive stance relaxes slightly. It's probably just for show—a beast of prey like that never actually lets his guard down.

Raz billows a stream of smoke. *Not exactly, no*.

My gaze shifts to him. "What does that mean?"

It means that he's not a shapeshifter, little queen.

The manticore roars even louder than the last time and bares his razor-sharp fangs at the azdaha. That can't be a coincidence. He clearly doesn't like Raz calling me that name.

"Go, R'zlek."

They're mostly gravelly, growled sounds, but Razulek crooks his neck and glances at Indira at the manticore's clear command. I blink as they bend their powerful hind legs and spread their wings. Wait, what are they doing? Are they *listening* to the beast?

"Where are you going?" I shout, starting to hyperventilate. "You can't just leave me here!"

Raz nuzzles my head fondly, a blast of his azdaha heat surrounding me. *Farewell, Starkeeper. Tell the king to bring you to visit our nest sometime.*

"I won't be able to visit if I'm dead, now, will I?"

Both azdahas chuff, Indira's crimson eye meeting mine. *A manticore will never harm his mate.*

My mouth falls open in shock, but no sound emerges for several fraught heartbeats. "Are you saying *I'm* his mate?"

Trust your simurgh, Raz adds unhelpfully.

Two powerful gusts of wind nearly sweep me off my feet as they take to the skies.

On a conscious level, I know that Razulek would never leave me in danger. But every nerve ending in my body is on high alert as the wind settles and silence descends on the clearing.

Taking Raz's advice, I reach for my simurgh . . . but she doesn't budge from her slumber, as if she can't be bothered to protect us. Or doesn't need to . . . because we're not in any true mortal danger, even if that thing thinks we're his mate. Maybe I can use that to help me get out of here.

"Good kitty." I ease out a breath, facing him but backing away ever so slowly.

I let out a squeak as the manticore crowds my space with three bounds. Huffing a strangled breath, I brace—for what, I don't know—but as the creature pads around me with his leathery wings tight against his sides, his elegant leonine muzzle snuffling my torso, my hair, and my back, fear is not the first emotion I'm feeling.

It's *wonder*.

My fingers itch. Would that velvety red-gold fur feel as soft as it looks?

His scent of woodsy earth, petrichor, and smoldering hearths fills my nose. He makes a low, whining noise and bends his nose to my knee. That pink two-pronged tongue slicks over the dried blood on my shin from my earlier fall, and a shiver runs through me as he repeats the soft swipe on my other shin. It feels . . . affectionate.

You are delusional, Suraya.

Maybe I am.

But when his muzzle traces the outer curve of my thigh to land squarely between my legs, my thoughts scatter as he presses deeper and inhales, his big body rumbling with . . . pleasure.

What the *fuck*?

His scent deepens and sharpens, curling into my nostrils like a drug. To my horror, I feel myself respond. Oh, gods, no. What is that? Pheromones? Without thinking of the repercussions, I shove wildly at his big head, subconsciously noting that his sleek hide feels like the softest velvet, and clamp my legs together.

"Oh, no, you don't, you furry pervert!"

But he lets out a noise that sounds bizarrely like an amused purr and rubs his giant lion's head against my stomach. Intense, intelligent amber eyes meet and hold mine as if daring me to push him away again, but for some reason I don't. Instead, I let my hands float to his mane to tangle in the soft golden mass.

As I sift my fingers through, I can feel the strength of the muscles beneath, the heat of his lion's body like a furnace. That purring sound grows louder, rumbling through me like a soothing balm. My simurgh stretches lazily and undulates as though she, too, enjoys the strange connection. I almost laugh at the incongruity of a man-eating monster making us both feel calm.

Or the fact that I'm petting it like a giant cat.

"Where do you belong?" I whisper. "If you let me go, I promise to find someone who can help you get home."

"No," he growls viciously, making the air shrivel in my lungs.

"Fine, you win. We'll both stay here forever."

My eyes flutter shut, and I force myself to think. There has to be a way out of this. But before I can come up with a plan, there's a new presence in the glade.

Nuadar stands there with a handful of guards, including Ani, and they're all armed.

Sensing the threat, the manticore lets out a chilling howl that shakes the ground just as a river of flame blisters his hide. He jumps away from me, wings flaring with aggression when a spear of lightning comes at him, hitting his right side. The scorpion barb swells and fires a dart, but a wall of ice shields the guards as they move into a defensive formation.

"Ani," I call out in relief.

"Stay calm, Sura," she says in a low, monotone voice. "Don't move."

This time, I listen. Scanning their faces, I recognize the snake shapeshifter as well as the ice and flame wielders. Lightning dances over another guard's hands. A flicker of worry spills through me. Do they mean to kill the manticore? I want to be safe, but I also don't want him to be harmed because of me.

"*Mine,*" the creature growls.

Ani's blue eyes fly wide in shock as if she hadn't expected the monster to speak. "Ashes, that's new," she mutters. "Nuadar, I'll blind him temporarily. Get the bow ready. The rest of you, in position. Remember, do not use lethal force. Incapacitate only."

I dimly register the crossbow that Nuadar is holding, which has an arrow that is glowing green, but then four things happen in succession. Slithery coils snake around me from behind while sunlight flares from Ani just as the beast roars in rage and attacks the serpent shapeshifter who has me in his grasp.

The manticore doesn't even register the arrow piercing his flank. We go tumbling to the ground, the huge snake hissing in pain when the manticore's jaws snap tight over his scales, and I'm released from his coiled grasp. Out of the corner of my eye, I see the shapeshifter crawl away and transform to human form, clutching his mangled, bloody arm. His left leg hangs by a tendon. Gods, the manticore nearly bit him in half.

Three others are felled by poison darts from the scorpion tail, dropping like flies, and Nuadar looks wild-eyed with fear when the beast crunches the head off the fire-wielding guard, flames and all, and finishes a sixth with a lethal swipe of his claws. He stalks Ani with a vicious snarl as Nuadar loads another crossbow with shaking hands, but even I can see that the manticore is too powerful.

Stars above, where is the king when his men and sister need him?

To my horror, Ani drops her hands and approaches the beast, putting herself directly in his path, voice low but audible enough to me. "*Brother.* Stop this."

The earth spins beneath my feet as my brain stutters. *What* did she say?

"You know you'll regret it if you kill me," Ani goes on, her voice monotone and unthreatening.

The manticore stumbles, shaking his mane, and then roars. His front leg wobbles and then buckles, and then before my eyes, he slumps down to his side as whatever sedative Nuadar had shot into him finally takes effect.

"Sura!" Ani cries, running to my side. "Did he hurt you?"

But my mind is spinning, my gaze stuck on the enormous, unconscious form of the manticore. I half sob out a wheezing breath. "What you said . . . what you called it. Is that thing . . . the fucking *king*?"

She stares at me sadly, blue eyes somber. "It's his curse."

Chapter Twenty-One

Nearly a fortnight later, I've summoned enough courage to stand in front of the manticore's enclosure, staring at the new reinforced magical doors that house the cursed form of the Everlean king. I swallow past the knot in my throat and tug on the collar of my tunic.

I don't know what I'm doing here, or what kind of answers I'm seeking.

According to Ani, this is the longest—over a month—that the king has gone without shifting back to human form. Not many people know of the curse, only her, Nuadar, a handful of trusted guards, and now me. She'd also confided that the manticore had never uttered a single word before, so his speaking had shocked them. I hadn't told her that in addition to that, Razulek and Indira had also called me his mate. I'm sure *that* would have gone over well.

"Oryndhrian," Nuadar growls rudely from behind me, "you're looking for trouble. You don't belong here. You should not be going in there!"

I bristle at his antagonistic tone and derisive address. "Open the door."

Scowling, he waves a hand toward the door and the locks disengage. I've since learned that Nuadar is a dominant corpus magi with a near sovran numen for toxins, which explains the tranquilizing serum he made to weaken the manticore.

"Thank you," I tell him, but he only grunts with a curse.

Breathing calm into my body, I walk inside and hear the locks reengage behind me. I try not to let the fact that I'm locked in with a bloodthirsty, inhuman monster affect me, but there's no hiding the uptick of my pulse. The space is shadowy, and there's no sound except for the slight scuff of my feet as I head deeper into the darkness.

With each step, my heart races more, but I won't allow my fear to stop me. Lamps ignite on the walls—more magic, I realize—and I see a huge, shadowy form held in place by thick golden chains. They're connected to massive rings in the walls and the ground. Slitted amber eyes track my progress, but the manticore doesn't raise itself from its prone position.

About six feet away, I crouch, studying it. When it doesn't move, I hesitate only for a moment before sitting down. I have no idea what the reach of those chains is and whether I'm playing with fire, but I make myself comfortable.

"Darrius?" I whisper.

There's no reaction, not even a blink, but those sharp predator's eyes don't waver from my person. Other than the rise and fall of his chest, he doesn't move, just stares. I sit there for an hour before my leg starts to cramp, and when I eventually stand to leave, the only sign that he notices is a barely audible sigh. Does it sound like disappointment, or is that just what I imagine it to be?

He could be relieved I'm leaving for all I know.

Despite that, I return the next day and settle myself a foot away from the manticore. This time he moves, but only to settle his head closer to my knee. His eyes close with a sound like a contented purr. I must let out a noise of surprise, because he glances up, his tongue emerging to place the smallest lick—*of reassurance?*—on my bare elbow before he settles back down.

My adrenaline spikes, my magic surging in my veins, though not with alarm... but with an odd kind of exhilaration, as though my simurgh *enjoys* the company of the monster. She hadn't been worried in the forest weeks ago, and now, all I can sense is intrigue. I wonder if it's because like recognizes like—my simurgh, though not a corporeal incarnation like the manticore, is a similar mythical being. A creature that gives life thoroughly fascinated by one that takes it. I don't miss the incongruity of such a pairing.

"Hello, Darrius." I wrinkle my nose when it sounds strange to my ears. "Though is that even your name? Are you him? Or are you your own furry, feline self? Shall I call you Dare, then, like your sister does?"

Feeling a bit ridiculous with my one-sided conversation, I proceed to recount all the facts that I remember about myself—from my birthday to my childhood in Coban to what I can recall of my lost memories—all the while with his nose pressed into my knee, his warm breaths feathering out over my skin.

It's shocking how natural it all feels.

And that he might even understand what I'm telling him. But he's intelligent—he'd communicated with Razulek—so I believe he does.

The following afternoon, though a little later than I usually visit, I approach the enclosure. By now, Nuadar's face is a permanent scowl, but I ignore him. He's convinced that one day he'll have to drag out my remnants piece by piece because of my own folly.

"You're playing with death, Oryndhrian," he snaps. "That thing is *not* human."

I pause, bristling at his rudeness. "I know he's not, but that doesn't mean he's undeserving of care. And he's your king, in case you've forgotten."

His eyes slit at the reminder. "In that skin, it is a monstrosity."

The laugh that emerges from my lips is cold. "We're all monsters in some shape or form. Open the door, Nuadar, please."

He does, though his expression is openly hostile as he stares at me. I don't know how we got off on the wrong foot, but it's clear he doesn't care for me very much. However, if I remember one lesson from my childhood, it's that I can't take responsibility for his bad feelings.

Entering the enclosure, I let the coolness of the dark interior and the rich hearth scent of the manticore that has penetrated the space flow over me. Sighing, I shut my eyes and inhale deeply, everything inside of me settling in a peculiar way that astonishes me every time.

"Good afternoon, Dare," I say, closing the distance to find him lying in the same place as yesterday and the day before. I have a feeling he situates himself in exactly the same position on purpose, as if he's conscious of my sense of safety and comfort. While he may be a monstrosity according to Nuadar, the small act leaves me reeling with a peculiar feeling of gratitude.

I plop down right next to him and breathe in his warm, earthen scent as I reach out a hand to stroke the very edges of his mane. He doesn't react, those golden eyes remaining ever vigilant. I'm under no illusion that this beast has been tamed by my peaceful visits, but I trust my magic, and my simurgh maintains that he won't hurt me. Raz had said to trust her, and I do. Implicitly.

I stroke through the strands of his mane again and, as I grow braver, lean over to run my fingers down his muscled side. The shorter fur there feels like the sleekest velvet. The ground-shaking rumble of his purr makes me even bolder, and I venture to run the tip of my finger over the leathery curve of his folded wing. He quivers with pleasure, his purr growing louder.

Intrigued, I let out a small laugh and continue my gentle ministrations, exploring the delicate bones that run the length of the wingspan, then return to his fluffy mane. "I like you like this, my king. Quiet and unable to annoy me." For a second, I think humor glints in those bright, golden eyes, but then they shut on a lazy blink as he sets his huge head upon his paws. "How long will you stay this way?" I muse. "And why now?"

As the minutes pass, I keep talking, unsure about what's compelling me to do so. But being here brings me a sense of peace I haven't had in what feels like a lifetime. I tell him more about Coban and my childhood, about my family, about Laleh and our adventures. And when I'm done with those, I confide things that I've never told anyone: that I'm afraid I'll never get all of my memories back, that I'm scared of what awaits me back home.

That deep down, I might not want to leave.

The manticore doesn't respond, but I know he's listening to the sound of my voice because his soothing, rhythmic purr never stops. The more I talk, the more relaxed I feel, until my eyelids start to droop and then slowly flutter closed.

I WAKE TO intense agony.

Groaning at the sharp, excruciating ache in my bones—the obvious consequence of falling asleep on a very hard floor—I stare up at the cavernous ceiling with the first touches of dawn creeping through a large skylight. My brow wrinkles.

Where am I?

The answer hits like a jolt, and my entire body goes stiff when I realize that my head is lying cradled on a very warm chest that is rising and falling with deep, even breaths from underneath me. Dear heavens, did I truly fall asleep? I blame the somnolent purring, though I'm not going to complain.

One, I'm alive, and two, despite my unhappy joints, that was the best night of sleep I've had in a while. I sigh as my simurgh stirs, magic rippling through me in a restorative wave.

My makeshift pillow is still asleep, thank the stars. Gingerly, I inch my head up and peer to the side, catching sight of skeins of silvery hair and tawny skin. Then I blink. Wait, that's not right. The manticore is reddish gold ... and furry. *Not* brown and mouthwateringly lustrous.

I scramble off him and turn, only to feel my face light on fire.

The king is naked. Very, very, very naked.

And human.

And *naked*.

Swallowing past my dry throat, I stumble backward, feeling like every nerve in my body is in a state of acute awareness, but I can't stop gaping. I'd seen Darrius shirtless in the ring and know he's nauseatingly fit, but this is beyond any of my wildest imaginings. From his well-shaped bare feet and the bulging calves dusted in dark hair, to his even heavier, ropier thighs and the thick half-hard manhood, the man is sculpted like a scarred, battle-hardened warrior god.

And yes, those tattoos *do* go everywhere. I hadn't had a chance to study them in depth before, at least not the endlessly complex swirling lines on his biceps and chest that never seem to remain the same. Interspersed between those on his paler brown hip bones and thighs are twining roses and vines, the head of an elegant azdaha rippling over the corded muscles of his torso, its body disappearing to his back, and several different kinds of weapons, as well as gorgeous lines of a runic script I don't recognize along his muscular thighs.

The shadow tattoos—the ones made of magic—swirl and dance with the litany of scars and art that cover him over and down what Laleh calls the pin-me-to-the-wall muscles, right to the base of that long, impressive ...

Stop ogling the king.

I compose myself like the civilized lady I am, swallow my drool, and clear my throat.

"Your Majesty?" I say quietly, not wanting to startle him. When he only lets out a soft but slightly adorable snore, I try again, this time a little louder. Slowly, his pitch-dark eyes open and find me where I'm standing. It takes a second or two for him to realize whom he's looking at, but eventually, that soft, sleepy gaze narrows and frosts over with stony coldness. I remember what Ani had told me about him keeping a relentless grip on his emotions, and I bite my lip.

So many secrets abound in this realm . . .

Who is this king, really? Had I been the cause of his most recent shift? Why do I feel warmer toward him when it's abundantly clear from the cool expression in his stare that I am someone he keeps at a distance? Strange that I felt more at ease with the manticore than I do right at this moment.

With a shiver, I take a small step back. I see the moment his onyx gaze leaves mine to flick around the space and then go wide with realization that we're not in the castle and he's not in his bedchamber. Or mine.

He glances down to the manacles around his wrists, ankles, and neck, which have magically reduced to fit his human frame. With a single command from his lips, the shackles fall loose and clatter to the stone floor. They must have been spelled to change with his size and restrain him only while in his manticore form.

The king rolls easily to his feet, but I avert my eyes, forcing myself not to gawk at what six and a half feet of a naked Darrius Nightsong looks like upright. Vertical, horizontal, upside down—the man is stupidly attractive.

He walks over to a corner of the room and pulls on a pair of trousers.

His jaw tics when he turns back to me, looking deadly, disheveled, and too delicious for words. A distracting hint of dark scruff covers that angular jawline, giving him a rakish look and an uncivilized hint of the beast he'd embodied that shouldn't be so appealing. I like it far more than I should.

"What are you doing here?" he demands in a raspy, unused voice.

"Don't you remember?" I ask.

Shadows slink over his eyes, and then his brow wrinkles. "Did I . . . did he . . . bring you here? Forcefully?"

I blink. "What? No." I hesitate. "I was exploring and he chased me, and I fell, but that wasn't his fault. My magic healed me instantly."

That midnight gaze sharpens and instantly scans me for injury. His fingers ball at his sides as if they want to examine every part of me as well, but after a minute of intense scrutiny, his stare falls away. His throat works. "So, he didn't . . . hurt you?"

It's my turn to stare quizzically at him. "You truly don't know what happened?"

With a frustrated sound, the king runs a hand through his silver hair, which falls in a tousled waterfall over his chest. His lips tighten in obvious displeasure. For a moment, it looks like he isn't going to deign to explain, but then he sighs. "No, only flashes."

"So you're . . . different entities. Not like a shapeshifter."

He nods curtly. "It's not a true shift. It feels like an alternate identity in physical and mental form. I retain little to no humanity as the manticore."

"You do," I venture, and his attention snaps to me. My spine stiffens at the look of disbelief and suspicion warring in his eyes. "I came here for several days. Each time, you . . . *he* waited in the same spot. That's not something a mindless, inhuman beast would do."

"It's training. Any animal can be taught."

I give a placating shrug. "I suppose you know best, but I know what I saw and felt. Do you retain any emotions from your time as him at all?"

He exhales, a muscle jerking in his jaw as if confiding in me of all people is too awful to contemplate. "There are ephemeral sensations at best. Mostly hunger and rage." He pauses, his eyes not meeting mine as he palms his nape, unrest evident in every rigid line of him. "This time was the same, but I also felt . . . peace."

Oh. Warmth sluices through me.

"Nuadar must have increased the magical sedation," he says, and my burgeoning warm feelings instantly wither.

He strides to the exit, where both the beastmaster and his sister are waiting. Ani's blue eyes are shadowed, mouth tight as her gaze settles on me behind the king. The princess exchanges a look with Nuadar, both of them wincing at the same time when they take in the king's now livid expression.

"Next time, keep her away from here, if you know what's good for you," he growls, stalking past them. The shards of gold in that obsidian gaze glitter mockingly as he turns back to me. "You were lucky you were an intriguing diversion to the manticore. Next time, I can't promise he won't kill you."

I want to shout that he's wrong, but I know he's too incensed to listen. Staring after him, I grind my teeth and stand in silence, mourning the loss of the gentle, stoic monster he'd been.

In truth, I'd take the manticore over the man in a heartbeat. *Gladly.*

Chapter Twenty-Two

The Night King

For the first time in the years of living with my curse, after this shift, I recollect more than just residual feelings of bloodlust and fury, or the lingering human disgust and remorse at how many I've harmed in my rampage before I'm forcibly restrained and caged. This time, I recall images and snatches of conversation.

Is it *her* doing?

After a much-needed hot bath and a meal, I push my mind out, connecting to the bond I have with Indira. She's warming her clutch but greets me fondly through the link. *I was hoping you would return to us soon. Your soul-fated is strong. Razulek was right about her being a good match for you.*

Scowling, I shove down the urge to snarl. I've learned the hard way that I can never win a snarling match with a full-grown female azdaha, much less one who is the queen of her kind. *I saw you both with her,* I say. *In the woods.*

There's a protracted beat of silence. Indira knows what this means.

As your beast? she asks with interest. *You* see *his memories?*

I exhale. *Images, feelings, nothing more.*

That's encouraging, she says. *It means the curse is evolving. How was he with her? Did he rut her? Claim her? Mark her with his bite? In the forest, he was territorial: typical unclaimed mate behavior. Razulek did not want to be faced with a formal challenge, so we had to leave. We knew he would not harm her.* She chuffs. *At least not fatally.*

Azdaha matings are notoriously violent. Razulek had a chunk missing out of his hindquarters for weeks, and Indira's wings had torn from the force of his talons ripping through them in a display of dominance. I don't want to think of what my beast's claws would do to Suraya's soft skin, though a deeply carnal thrill sweeps through me at the idea of marking that pretty brown flesh. On the heels of such visceral arousal, I feel my body start to convulse with magic as my thoughts veer toward the chaos of lust, and as always, the curse rears its head.

By the fucking blood, control yourself, Dare.

Gods, I can't change back into the manticore so soon after only just having shifted back. Reaching for equanimity, I take the time to breathe and gather my thoughts, despite the fact that they are much too heated and tumultuous at the idea of finally claiming my soul-fated. That's the primal allure of the bond, nearly impossible to resist. Clenching my fists, I shove open the windows and suck in the cool air, locking down my desires behind my iron will.

The manticore's needs have grown louder than ever in my human consciousness, which makes me also believe, like Indira, that the curse is evolving. I've never heard him so clearly before.

I have to understand what that means for all of us. For me. For Everlea.

There was no claiming, I say to Indira, and then pause. *But he's fascinated by her. She stayed with him for days in the paddock. She fell asleep on him!* That recollection alone had shocked me. How she survived remains a mystery, one that slowly becomes clear as I try to understand more of the creature that takes over my body and my mind. He sees her as his to protect. Which is a fucking calamity.

Indira's surprise radiates down the bond. *For a beast governed by his most primitive instincts, that is interesting.*

Interesting how?

Perhaps these changes are not one way, she says. *Perhaps he can hear and feel you, too.*

I rub at my chest. That's what I'm afraid of.

With grateful fondness, I thank my bonded azdaha and release the link, and then I do what I swore I'd never do in a million years: I send out a summons for Venant, or Vena, or whatever the Royal Star now calls herself. She's the Starkeeper's guardian. Perhaps she will have some insight.

I don't have to wait long.

Within seconds, a figure shimmers into being. It's not the face of the deity I have seen before, nor is it the crone she's favored more recently. Instead, it's an androgynous face with dark blue skin and pure white eyes. The latter takes some getting used to, but who am I to judge? I turn red with a mane and grow a scorpion for a tail. Short bluish hair graces her head, and she's a few inches taller than she was last, but her divine energy is still the same. "Your Majesty."

"How shall I address you?" I ask, after a familiar smugness settles on the Royal Star's lips. I suppose her shape changing doesn't alter the innate arrogance that most seers have. "Venant? Vena?"

"Ve is apropos, though I cede to no gender."

I nod in affirmation as that eerie white gaze scans me from top to bottom.

"Something has changed about you, Your Majesty." They blink and tap a blunt fingernail to their chest, eyes fluttering shut. "Your soul-fated is here."

"Yes," I say.

"So you've changed your mind about completing the bond?" Ve asks.

I shake my head, registering their disappointment, but maybe once they understand what's at stake, they will support the only viable strategy to stave off another realm-decimating war. "We can never complete the bond because I am cursed."

Ve stares with those unsettling white eyes for a long moment. "What do you mean?" they finally say.

"The moment I feel any emotion, I transform. I lose myself in the form of a manticore that goes on a killing spree, until all the emotion and madness is bled out of my system."

They stare at me in utter horror. "How?"

"I don't know. Thankfully, the curse has taken hold only a handful of times, mostly related to my soul-fated, but each time—especially recently—my interval as the beast has grown successively longer." I shudder out a breath and continue. "The longest period was the most recent, and prior to that, when she gave herself to the king of Oryndhr. So if I ever truly, *fully* bond with my soul-fated, or fall in love with her, there's a chance that the change..."

"Will be permanent." Ve stares at me, an aghast expression on their flawless face. "You can't feel *any* emotion at all?"

"Nothing extreme. I can find some mild pleasure in conversation, food, sparring, and other innocuous activities without change, but anything chaotic, any intense emotion, and I'm lost for days and now for weeks at a time." I pause. "There's another thing. Previously, my consciousness remained entirely separate. Now, there are tethers."

"Tethers?"

"I see and hear the manticore. Almost like a spectator."

They tilt their head thoughtfully, a myriad of feelings crossing their face as they consider what I've shared. "I suspect your beast has no familiarity with your human side, which translates to no real power over your magic in that form?" They scowl when I nod. "Does the Starkeeper know all this?"

"About the curse, not about the soul-fated bond," I say, "or about the possible evolution of our magic once bonded."

Ve approaches, their eyes boring through my soul. "Why tell me now?"

Clenching my jaw, I wave my arm. "I know you and the other Royal Stars are aware something is coming. The rot that Saru chose eternal sleep to eradicate centuries ago is rearing its ugly head. My advisors speak of necromancers in the southern realm, the secret plot to return my father to his throne, and those very men who want to use my soul-fated to bolster their power." I exhale a troubled breath. "Fero lingers. I can feel him infecting the realms. Maybe not all of him, but enough to disrupt the flow of akasha. His power is growing while Saru remains in god-sleep." I meet the Royal Star's gaze. "We need to be ready for whatever comes *without* anchoring the Starkeeper's magic."

"Is there any way to break this curse?" Ve asks, an uncharacteristic waver to their voice.

Powerlessness fills me. "No. I must reject my soul-fated and the most precious, divine gift of the bond, because if I succumb, the price could mean her death. I cannot anchor her magic in that form. The simurgh will eventually consume her."

"You need to tell her," Ve says softly. "She deserves to know the truth, Darrius. All of it."

Though I don't want to admit it, deep down I know they're right.

Chapter Twenty-Three

Ani is angry, and rightly so, that I deceived her. After several days of giving me the silent treatment, she relents only when I corner her in the library. "Are you going to avoid me forever?" I ask.

"I thought we were friends."

The guilt weighs heavy in my heart. "We *are*. I needed to see him, Ani, and I wasn't sure you would let me."

"He could have killed you!" she snaps. "Gods, don't you know what could have happened? The curse . . . the bond . . . you have no idea what you—" She breaks off with a strange half sob, leaving me desperate for her forgiveness, but eventually my softhearted friend takes pity on me. "Promise me you won't risk yourself like that again."

"I promise."

When she indicates with a sigh that I should occupy my usual chair across from her, I gather the books I've been studying and sit gratefully. We read in silence. I vacillate on confessing what had happened with the manticore, but I don't want to get the same reaction I'd received from her brother. It's all too clear the king does not believe me, though I know in the depths of my soul that the manticore would *never* harm me. He might be monstrous to everyone else, but he's not to me. How I know this, I have no idea.

"May I join you?" a deep voice asks, making both Ani and me glance up from our texts.

The king of Everlea stands beside the table, looking tall, windblown, and annoyingly handsome. Silver hair loose over his broad shoulders, he is dressed simply in a black tunic and pants, sans his usual armor, with his tattoos peeking out at his collar and winding over his arms. His expression is not as cold as it usually is, though I don't pretend to know what each degree of coldness means when it comes to this mercurial man.

There's no doubt, however, that my ill-advised attraction hasn't waned. I try to hide the feelings that the king evokes in me, but his presence is impossible to resist. I feel Ani's notice turn my way, but I keep my face neutral despite the wild flurry in my body. "Fine by me," I say casually.

Ani points to the empty seat, and her brother sprawls in the chair. "To what do we owe your visit, Dare?" she asks, her surprise evident, considering he has been avoiding us both.

"Can't a man visit his own library?"

"You haven't before, so what do you want?" she asks. "We're busy."

"What are you researching?" he asks, staring at the books scattered on the table.

Ani shoves a tome from her pile of books over. "Runes, specifically Oryndhrian runes. We need to get those cuffs off of her, if she will be expected to protect herself here." She shoots her brother a pointed glance, and the king winces before his usual frigid expression slides into place.

"I might have an answer," Darrius says, and waves an arm, beckoning someone over.

A person saunters over, and my jaw hangs open. Memories crash into my brain, not that the new arrival is recognizable, but I *know* her. I know those brilliant starlit eyes that hold galaxies within them. She'd come to me as a crone, showing me how to use my Starkeeper gifts, teaching me, and guiding me. More gaps fuse in my mind as my history fills in like the colors in a mural finally exposed to light.

"Vena?" I whisper.

"Child. Setareh Framātāram." Long arms engulf me, and though they don't feel the same as the ones in my memory, the energy is exactly the same. My magic warms and surges in response as though greeting an old friend.

"Not much of a master of anything these days," I mutter, but only the king's gaze flicks to me.

Vena turns to Ani. "Princess Anahima, I don't believe we have formally met."

To my surprise, something like distaste passes over Ani's face before it's hidden. I get it. Vena can be quite over-the-top and off-putting for some. When I first met her, I thought she was a creepy fortune teller. Plus, this new six-foot-tall *blue* form of hers is rather intimidating.

"Eminence," Ani greets with an elegant cant of her head, and I wonder at her formality. Does she know she's a Royal Star? Does *Darrius*?

"I like this new look," I say, admiring the glow of her navy skin and her strange glimmering pale eyes. "Decided to age down a little, Vena?" I ask cheekily, and earn myself a fond swat.

"The Royal Star is gender nonconforming and goes by Ve now," the king says to me, inadvertently answering my earlier unvoiced question. "Show them the cuffs."

I bristle at the terse command, but I raise my wrists. Of course Darrius knows who she—*they* are. He's the ruler of a realm that's rich in akasha.

Ve studies the cuffs, their fingertip tracing the runes, and when they look up, their face is wreathed with rage. "He dared?"

I open my mouth and close it. "You know who did this?"

Shutters slam down over their face as they study me for a protracted moment. "The cuffs impair your memories," they say eventually.

"*Who* did this, Ve?"

"I cannot interfere with what has been written," they say, exchanging a dark look with Darrius. "The fates declare that you must recall what you've lost on your own."

"But you *know*, don't you?" I press.

"Ve, the cuffs," Darrius says, interrupting me. "Can you remove them?"

Ve shakes their head, eyes glowing slightly. "The magic in the bracers are tied to the Starkeeper herself. This lock only she can undo."

"I've tried!" I cry, and then frown as Ve's corporeal form starts to shimmer. "Where are you going?"

They heave a heavy sigh. "To prepare."

Another dark, weighted look is exchanged with Darrius, and then Ve vanishes from sight.

Ani immediately rounds on her brother. "What the fuck was a Royal Star doing here, Dare?"

My jaw drops to the floor in shock. That's the first time I've heard Ani curse. The king opens his mouth to respond, but a commotion at the library entrance has us all rising. One of the kingsguard crashes through and falls to one knee in front of the king.

"Your Majesty, the basilisk is loose near Shabra," he says breathlessly. "The Aspačanā are calling for aid."

My stomach drops at that. I'd forgotten about the farmer's plea, and with Darrius gone in manticore form for so long, that thing must be on a rampage.

The king glances at his sister. "I thought you said it was gone."

A still furious Ani shrugs. "It was, but I also said that those creatures are territorial."

"Is my horse ready?" the king asks his kingsguard, expression troubled.

"Yes. Outside, Sire."

Darrius leaves the table, Ani at his heels. And I find myself hurrying after them. "I'm going with you," I say, surprising myself.

"No," the king and Ani say at the same time.

Glaring at them in turn, I set my jaw. "Either you let me go with you or I follow on my own. Even if you lock me in my chambers, I'll find a way."

"The creature's gaze can kill, its bite is venomous, and it spits acidic venom."

Fear skitters up my spine, but I jerk my chin. "I'm aware."

His dark eyes flash with irritation, but time is ticking. "Can you ride?" he asks me, and I nod eagerly, not trusting my mouth to blurt out the truth that when it comes to horses, I am extremely adept at bouncing around like a sack of potatoes. Something about the different gaits just throws me. Besides, I'm almost certain there won't be akasha binding me to the saddle like there is with Razulek. But I won't let that stop me.

"Get her a godsdamned horse," the king says to his guard.

"I'm coming, too," Ani says, and then glowers at me. "To keep you out of trouble."

"Fine, tell the whole fucking castle to come," the king mutters. "Get my sister and my"—he cuts off abruptly and curses—"*her* some damned armor."

I don't even care about whatever he meant to call me; I race to my chambers, and Ziba helps dress me in fresh leathers and a protective scale mail vest. Once I'm back down in the courtyard, a mare is provided for me by the small army waiting there. The king comes out a moment later, dressed in his own silver armor, a massive sword on his back. Ani is already mounted, her face unhappy.

"You don't have to come," I tell her, and her only answer is an eye roll.

I hike myself gracelessly into my saddle and settle in place when the king guides his stallion over. His tattoos peek out from the chest plate, twining up the strong bronze column of his throat, and a thin obsidian circlet holds the long silver strands of hair off his brow. "Here," he says, and hands me a leather-wrapped harness.

"My dagger!" I cry, hefting the familiar weight in my palm, and though my magic doesn't flow through the steel, it still feels right. "Thank you, Darrius."

Do the king's eyes warm slightly? "Just don't stab me with it."

"I make no such promises." The involuntary half curl of his lips that barely qualifies as a smile makes my breath hitch, and I wonder what the man would look like if he ever deigned to smile at me for real. I imagine it would be like seeing lightning strike. I drag my gaze away before it becomes too obvious that I'm staring at his too-beautiful mouth.

Strapping the harness around my hips, I exhale. I'm grateful that the horse is placid and starts to move only when the company does. However, my feeble ability to go from a trot to a canter becomes abundantly clear as we leave Verisia and reach the open plains. Cursing my recent choices when the mare starts to gallop, I hang on with my knees, hands white-knuckling the reins, and try to keep my teeth from cracking or the tip of my tongue from being bitten off.

"You're ghastly at this," Ani says, pulling alongside my horse. "Haven't you flown on an azdaha? It's the same. You move with the mare."

I glare at her while trying not to fall off. "Thank you for your expert opinion, *Princess*. And it's *not* the same with horses at all. This is *diabolical*."

Lips twitching at my disgruntled expression, she reaches over for the reins, slowing both mounts and patting the back of her saddle. "Here, you're better off behind me."

But before I can shift over to Ani's horse, the sound of some command being given reaches my ears, and the king splits off from the lead to gallop back to us. I only belatedly register being scooped up and deposited onto another mount. The *king's* mount. The siblings share a look before I'm plastered back against an armored chest with a gasp.

"She rides with me."

The dominant rasp makes the hairs on my nape rise. Ani says nothing, though her eyebrows raise at the overt display of whatever this is, but then she urges her horse into motion to join the contingent of guards ahead.

One of Darrius's arms bands about my waist, and I swallow.

"I can manage on my own, you know," I say primly.

"Can you?" he replies, his warm breath skating over my ear. "I don't need you falling and snapping your pretty neck."

I tilt my chin up, catching sight of his sharp jaw and very grim mouth. I look away as my pulse doubles, his scent surrounding me. "As opposed to you having the honor?"

"Exactly. The pleasure of your death is mine and mine alone."

I blink. Was the king being . . . *witty*? And why does his husky tone sound like he's not talking about death at all? I suppress a shiver.

The horse speeds to a gallop, and I brace myself to flop around as I'd been doing so ungracefully before, but between his mastery of the enormous stallion, his firm grasp around me, and his own fluid gait, it's like night and day. My hips and bottom are plastered to him, and while his armor keeps us from actually touching, that doesn't stop my brain from venturing into places it shouldn't.

His gloved thumb skates over my mail-covered ribs, dangerously close to the underside of my breast, and I suck in a breath, torn between wanting him to go higher and throwing myself bodily off the horse. "What's the matter?" he asks.

"Nothing," I choke out. "What will happen to my mare?"

He pauses as if he knows I'm deflecting. "She'll find her way back.

One of the grooms will retrieve her. Is that what you're thinking about?"

When I don't answer immediately, his arm tightens slightly, that maddening thumb stroking my oversensitive skin in a much-too-distracting manner.

I clear my dry throat. "Ani mentioned the Aspačanā clans. Will they be there?"

His thumbs stills. "Yes. We are going to the edge of Shabra territory, which means the current raissa will be there, and the rais of Chamros likely won't be far behind."

"Ani said they might know a way to help with my cuffs." I shift around, trying to get comfortable and failing. He's so hard it's like sitting on a slab of unyielding granite.

"Did she?" he says, his voice like gravel. "Stop wriggling."

"Are they dangerous?" I ask, muscles locking up in an attempt to stay still.

Something cool glides over me in an inky blanket, practically gluing me to him, and though I can't see them, I know they're his shadows. They're meant to be comforting, but when I feel one snaking across my bare skin over my collar to wrap around my throat, my breath fizzles even as heat tracks like wildfire through me.

"I won't let anything happen to you. They know you're mine." The stark possessiveness in the last sentence should aggravate me because I belong to no one but myself—but it only makes me feel stupidly warm. This ride must truly be knocking my good sense out of me.

The tendril caresses my jaw and feathers over my bottom lip. His breathing quickens behind me. I wish I could see his face, but it's impossible at the speed at which we're charging forward. I don't want him to stop whatever this is, though sometimes it seems as though his magic has a mind of its own. When the silken tip eases inside my mouth, I nearly combust. "Darrius."

"Weapons!" Shouts up ahead followed by screaming have me jolting out of my lust stupor.

Gods! We're here already!

The king pulls up alongside his sister, who has halted near a small copse of trees, and deposits me unceremoniously in front of Ani. "Don't let her out of your sight."

"I can help!" I protest. "I can fight, remember?"

Stony, obsidian eyes meet mine. "No. The creature is sickened, and I need you out of its line of sight for your own safety. One glimpse and you're dead. Stay here." That stare softens slightly when he directs it to his sister. "Keep her out of harm's way, please. By magical force, if you have to."

"I will," Ani says as I splutter in outrage.

I struggle against Ani's unexpectedly strong grip, but her hold is relentless. I glance down, but her arms aren't even around me, and yet, I cannot move. Stars, is she actually using her magic to restrain me? I push forward, and the loose scale mail of my vest tightens against my chest. Of course, she's a ferrokinetic who controls metal.

The clash of steel echoes up to us, and the despondent cries of the soldiers. I lose sight of the king in the chaos of the battle unfolding, a mix of men on foot and those riding, the horses kicking up dust amid the waving grass. But then I see him again, wielding that huge onyx sword of his with unfailing precision. Sands, his eyes are closed, and yet he moves with such confidence.

His shadows must be guiding him, I realize.

Curious, I study the first Aspačanā horde I've seen in person. They have to be Shabra, considering we're on their territory. Ani had said their power was earth-based. That makes sense with the rising dust cloud and rumbling earthquakes. Even from a distance, they're huge and their horses even bigger. Covered in brown-plumed helms and scratched bronze armor, a dozen of them form a loose circle where

Darrius disappeared over the knoll, their battle-axes and enormous bows at the ready.

The basilisk roars and rears up as Darrius continues to wound it, using strikes of magic in tandem with his blade. Huge ice spikes pin its tail even as flames surround its torso. His kingsguard lose no time in protecting his flanks while launching their own magical blows. It seems for a moment like they have the upper hand until a burst of venom sprays from the serpent's mouth, taking out nearly a dozen men when their armor and flesh starts to dissolve.

"Can you see what's happening?" I ask, heart pounding when Darrius disappears from view.

Ani squints. "No. Don't worry. My brother's magic is powerful. It won't be long."

"I'm not worried about *him*," I lie, and hear Ani scoff from behind me. Glad to know that I'm so transparent.

Another fierce horde on horses arrives from the south, kicking up a cloud of dirt behind them. The plumes of their helms are bone white, and their armor glints silver. Their horses seem leaner than the ones from Shabra, though they're just as menacing. As one, I see them rise up and loosen arrows from their bows toward the center of the battle, causing a magical cyclone to whip the basilisk into the air for a second.

"Guard your eyes!" someone roars, but the warning must come too late as three warriors topple from their horses, struck dead by accidentally meeting the lethal stare of the monster.

"Gods," Ani mutters. "Chamros. Their rais, Azes, is an arrogant prick."

"Let's get closer," I say, adrenaline humming through my veins.

"No, we stay here, out of sight. It's too dangerous."

I still can't locate Darrius. Did the venom get him? I might not have offensive magic, but I know my blood can heal. It had healed Razulek. And I need the king alive to get me back to Oryndhr. That's what I tell myself anyway. That's the *only* reason I care. And besides, my dagger has magic—the runes and jādū smelted onto the blade mean I won't be completely vulnerable.

"Well, at least let me up so I can see then," I say.

Her magic relents, and I'm able to push myself up to balance precariously on the saddle. It doesn't help—I'm much too short for it to make much of a difference—but her horse decides at that moment to rear. With a screech, we both go tumbling to the ground. I brace for impact, taking the fall on my back and rolling out of the way of the horse's hooves. My magic assuages the bruised area immediately, and then I am up and running before I can think twice.

"Sura! Wait!"

Just in case she decides to reel me back in with her magic, I throw off the metal vest and keep running. Admittedly, getting rid of my protective armor isn't the best course, but that's a problem for future me, because current me clearly didn't anticipate a giant serpentine body tumbling from the sky in my direction. I whirl to evade it, but it's much too late. I lift my dagger and send out a desperate plea to the goddess of time or the wind gods, only to feel nothing as everything goes preternaturally still.

The wind, the sounds of battle . . . the world halts.

And then restarts.

Holy shooting stars, did *time* just stop?

Thank Zora! And the twins of wind, Vara and Vati!

Shadows writhe around me as the body of the king coalesces between the beast and me. His magic is terrifying to behold as it surrounds the creature in a maelstrom of onyx flames. The basilisk screams, its rooster-like features and feathered plumage melting into its multihued gray and green scales. Gods, I've never seen anything so beautiful and so devastatingly macabre in my life.

Look away, Suraya! the king roars in my head.

But I'm utterly frozen as a jeweled, kaleidoscopic stare wreathed in violet flames slams into my eyes. In a single heartbeat, I face death. I can taste it on my tongue: the vicissitude of the grave. The emptiness of the void reaches for my soul to pluck it like a flower as Ris croons his welcome in the space where time ends. Magic rears up inside of me in a tsunami of rage, my cuffs glowing in instant response. But nothing—not even the dark power suppressing me—can hold the tide back. My simurgh screams, the edges of my skin glowing with power as my runes ignite, rolling over my skin in an undulating wave.

My magic becomes a mirror, a shimmering surface.

In my mind's eye I see the basilisk catch sight of itself and give a massive shudder. It feels like peace . . . like relief. *Thank you, Starkeeper.* The whisper comes on the wind like a measure of song. Otherworldly power yields to my simurgh, who tilts her head in regal salutation as the basilisk curls into itself and exhales a death rattle.

May Ris bless you in the next life, she tells it.

Those purple flames in its eyes dim as it dies with a sigh.

The glow of my runes fades as my magic is absorbed back into my body, and Darrius's unreadable face comes into view. I can see him fighting for calm, sensing how close his manticore is to the surface. Is it because I was in danger? Lines of tension gather around his gold-sheened eyes and flattened mouth, as we're interrupted by a slew of cheers and hollers. Ani rides up, but the irritation in her eyes tells me I'll get an earful from her later.

A handsome and very large tattooed man with red hair and pale skin descends a horse and walks toward us. He stops briefly to greet Ani, and their exchange is quick before he halts in front of me. His tattoos are of animals in battle and strange alchemical symbols, and gold torcs at his collarbones are inlaid with turquoise gems. His curved pickax is wet with blood as he arrogantly studies me from head to toe. "I am Rais Azes. You will come to Chamros."

I stare back at him, refusing to be intimidated by him or his demands. "Are you telling me or asking me?"

Blue eyes gleam with interest as he reaches for my hand. "Your Starkeeper magic is needed to save our herds from the rot."

Frowning, I step backward, out of his reach, but it doesn't deter him as he presses forward.

A second horde warrior, this one female with similar tattoos and thick blond hair that glows against her light skin, approaches on horseback and leaps off her horse before it comes to a full stop. Like the man, she's tall and splattered in blood, and scrutinizes me with curiosity. "I am Raissa Karânî. He's right. You must help us—" She reaches out toward me, and I flinch, my simurgh swelling with aggression beneath my skin. In warning?

"Don't touch her." The growl comes from the king, who looks like he's going to go on a slaughtering spree. He glowers at both Aspačanā horde leaders with the terror of death in his pitch-black eyes.

The beautiful raissa doesn't bend, only stiffens and then smiles. "Then I invoke the Gauntlet of Mithral and exhibition tournament to honor the esteemed Starkeeper on our lands."

"A wonderful idea," Azes exclaims immediately.

My stomach swirls with confusion. I glance over at Ani, considering she knows so much about the clans and their cultural traditions, but her expression is blank. What is this Gauntlet? I only know that Mithral is the god of the sun and spiritual fire. Perhaps this is some celebratory custom? I wait for Darrius's reply, but before the king can speak, a shout goes up.

A rider races toward us, an unconscious body draped across the saddle in front of him. He dismounts, and I catch sight of spiky green hair before her beloved face comes into view. I slump to my knees in complete and utter shock. Sands on fire, it can't be.

But it is . . .

Laleh.

Chapter Twenty-Four

My best friend is sitting up and eating soup when I burst into her room two days later, having just received word from the healer that she is finally awake. For a moment, a faintly putrid smell greets me, like something is rotting in the room, but it disappears as soon as it had come.

"Laleh!"

"Sura," she whispers as I reach down to hug her.

Thankfully, she smells more of floral shampoo and the ozone scent of magic, an odd combination, but I suppose she would, given the Everlean healers tending to all her injuries. Laleh makes space for me on the bed, and I look her over. Indeed, she's no worse for wear, though her eyes still show signs of weariness and . . . worry.

"You're safe," I tell her. "I've been treated well here. You have nothing to fear." Except for the volatile, much-too-handsome king who despises me for no logical reason and changes into a feral manticore when he gets overwrought, though I keep that information to myself. "How did you get here? How are Papa and Amma? And the inn?"

"I was looking for you. I paid a runecaster from Veniar to make a portal . . . and of course it dumped me into a fucking basilisk lair." She swallows, revulsion crawling over her features for a second before her eyes brighten. "If those smoking hot, bend-me-over-a-windowsill horse people hadn't come along, I'd have been that thing's dinner."

"It's dead," I say with a snort. I've missed her ribald humor. "Why were you looking for me?"

She cocks her head. "So it is true then. You've lost your memory? One of the healers mentioned it," she explains at my look of confusion. "The pretty, dark-haired woman who asked me a million questions with a sandsdamned truth root."

Oh, she must mean Ani.

"She did the same to me. And I haven't lost all of my memories. I remember you and my life in Coban. Everything else from later on is . . . scattered. Kaldari. The prince's selection. The wedding to Javed. You were there, I know that." I pause. "But there are also big gaps, and when I try to remember, it hurts." I don't tell her that filling in some of those gaps leaves me with an awful feeling that my brain is trying to protect me from something terrible. Something *excruciating*. I think of my family and my heart free-falls. Is that why she didn't answer my earlier question? "Laleh, are my aunt and my father . . . well?"

She nods fervently. "They're fine." She pinches the side of her belly between her thumb and forefinger. "Amma makes sure I'm being fed your portions of food, which is probably why that basilisk wanted me in the first place. I'm excellent eating." We share a laugh that makes my chest squeeze with joy. "They want you to come home, Sura. We all do."

"I want that, too," I say, lowering my voice, though the healer on the other side of the room can't possibly hear us. "But only the king can open a portal because of the magical wards here. In fact, I don't even know how you managed to get past them."

She shrugs. "Me, either. But I found you . . . so, win?" Laleh grins, and I feel my eyes smart with tears at the familiar sight. "So what happened? We heard so many conflicting things. Some snooty noblewoman from Regulus said you'd been eaten by the king's pet monster. The rumors were wild."

Sands, how do I explain what happened? And why am I strangely reluctant to do so? Laleh is my best friend... I *should* want to tell her everything. But many of the secrets I now know aren't mine to tell. They belong to Everlea and to its king. Where has that strange sense of loyalty come from? An odd tug in my center is my only answer.

As if my thoughts have summoned him, the door opens as Ani and the king of Everlea walk in, instantly crowding the small room. My breath catches in my throat at the sight of Darrius. Tattoos peek from his polished armor and writhe slightly as if to remind me of what they can do. A shiver winds over my skin, pebbling my nipples in an inconvenient burst of arousal, and I cross my arms over my chest. Cheeks heating, I drag my eyes away, back to Laleh.

I notice her tense, but I remember doing the same thing. Darrius is intimidating at the best of times. I risk a glance back at him. His eyes are fastened on me, but they immediately flick to my best friend and cool a few degrees. Her eyebrows arch as she sends me an intrigued look that means I have to spill *those* secrets the minute they leave. My cheeks flame hotter.

Stars... pull yourself together, Sura!

"My sister has explained everything you told her under the Verac root," the king says to my friend in a measured voice, though I can sense his unease. "How did you circumvent my wards? No one can portal into this realm."

"I paid a runecaster," Laleh says. "Maybe there's a flaw in your wards."

"Or maybe you have a spy on the inside," he says. It's a miracle he doesn't look at me, considering how many times he has accused me of being one. But I have no functional magic, so no viable way to weaken his wards. And I arrived here with the mate of his bonded azdaha.

Laleh lifts one shoulder. "Sounds like a *you* problem."

I stifle a giggle as that incredulous obsidian gaze widens in affront and then lands on me when I pin my lips together to keep from bursting into laughter.

"I can see why you're friends," he remarks humorlessly.

"*Best* friends," Laleh says, and my eyes well up with joyous tears again. I reach for her hand and grip it tightly. It's good to have someone I know and trust with me. A small smile touches Ani's lips as if she knows exactly what I'm feeling and is simply glad to see me happy. *Two* people, then. I catch sight of Darrius's glower and sigh.

"There is a feast tonight in honor of the Gauntlet of Mithral," the king says, his mouth thinning as he peers down the length of his nose at me. "With the Aspačanā. We cannot refuse them our presence or it will be taken as an insult. They seek to honor the slayer of the basilisk."

"I didn't actually kill it," I point out. "It was already dying."

His mouth flattens even more. "Nonetheless, yours was the final stroke. The feast and tournament will move forward for now."

"Can't we politely decline?" I ask.

His jaw flexes. "Not without repercussions. They take the gods very seriously. For the harvest ritual in autumn, the clans honor Huma, the god of harvest and rain, for a full month." He shakes his head with a thoughtful frown. "But the Gauntlet of Mithral hasn't been celebrated in years. It's odd they would choose to do so now."

"You can claim—" Ani begins, and is immediately silenced by a fulminating glare from the king. I frown, staring at the siblings. What had Ani been about to say? Claim what?

A muscle throbs in the king's cheek. "This couldn't have come at a worse time, when our borders are being threatened, but I will be expected to participate in the tournament," Darrius says, and my brows jump to my hairline.

"You will? Why?" I ask.

"It is tradition. As king, I must. But this celebration in your honor means you will be exposed. Our enemies will not announce before they strike."

"You think the leaders of the horde clans mean me harm?" I ask.

A low growl makes the hairs on my nape lift. "Not if they wish to die."

I frown at the faintest crack of bones and the ripple of fur as his eyes lighten to gold and flash back to onyx. His fingers clench and unclench.

"I have an idea," Laleh pipes up. "Open a portal and send us home. Problem solved."

If looks could kill, my friend would be ash when Darrius swivels in her direction, nostrils flaring. "She. Stays."

The king speaks as though it's through a mouthful of fangs, his gaze glinting the gold of the manticore and turning utterly feral.

Without another word or heated glance in my direction, Darrius turns and leaves. I blink, shocked at his brusque manner, though by now I should not be. I fight the urge to run after him and keep myself firmly planted at Laleh's side. The king can manage his own curse.

Ani clears her throat and bows slightly. "Forgive my brother. He's . . . worried."

"What were you going to say before?" I ask. "He can claim what?"

Her cheeks redden. "Never mind."

"*Ani.*"

"You should let your friend rest," the princess says. She looks at Laleh. "Your presence is not required at the feast, but you are welcome if you feel well enough."

Laleh lets out a cackle. "Oh, I would not miss that for the world."

Ani takes her leave after speaking quietly to the healer. As I rise from the bed, Laleh grips my fingers as though she doesn't want me to go. "Promise me we will get a chance to really talk later."

"We will." I peer at her, a belated thought occurring to me. "Laleh, was I romantically involved with the new king of Oryndhr?" I pause, the words tying up my tongue. "I'm not engaged or married to him or anything, am I?"

Her brow furrows, a peculiar, confused look passing over her face. "No, you're not." She shakes her head, but then, it's as if a dark cloud lifts because she grins and winks. "Don't think you and I won't have a nice long chat about all that *throbbing* sexual tension earlier, so save me a dance tonight," she warns, waggling her eyebrows.

I shake my head and release a breathless laugh at her glee.

Good to know that in all of this chaos some things never change.

THE FEAST TAKES place in the massive open meadow behind the castle. The expansive grounds are covered with colorful tents, and music spills from the biggest one at the center, while the smaller ones appear to house foods, curiosities, and various performers, including magical fire eaters, ice wielders, and earth carvers.

Multicolored lanterns dance over the whole space, held aloft and in place by air magic, and cast rainbow prisms over everything.

Despite the reason for the feast, I can't help feeling a small thrill of excitement.

"Come, Lady Suraya," Ziba calls, tugging me away from my window. "Let's get you ready."

Two handmaidens enter my chambers, holding a gold-spangled black gown threaded with crimson. Red, gold, and black, the royal colors of Everlea. *His* colors. I open my mouth to protest, but Ziba shoots me a quelling look. "The dress is Everlean. You will cause great offense if you refuse to wear it."

I press my lips together. She's laying it on rather thickly. "Fine," I mutter.

The gown is gorgeous, the gossamer fabric sparkling ethereally. The women carefully pull the voluminous folds over my head, letting the tiny cap sleeves fall into place over my shoulders and lacing the bodice at the back. The skirts tumble down in panels of luminous midnight silk—and it feels like I'm wearing nothing.

"It's spelled," Ziba whispers. "The fabric is as impenetrable as armor."

My eyes widen in disbelief, and she flicks my dagger, point first, across the edge of the skirt. I gasp, already mourning the ruin of the dress, but nothing tears or even wrinkles. "Incredible," I say. She smiles and bends to lift the hem and fasten the thigh harness in place.

"There are usually no weapons allowed at the feast, as all acts of war are forbidden," Ziba says, standing to smooth my curls over my bare collarbones. "However, the king insists that you have your blade. Things can get rowdy with the Aspačanā. They can be very enthusiastic with their celebrations."

How does he know I'd feel naked without it? His thoughtfulness is unexpected. "Tell him thank you for me."

Ziba hides her smile. "Tell him yourself. His Majesty is outside, waiting to escort you down."

"Oh." Suddenly, I'm breathless with anticipation. I don't know if it's vanity that makes me check my reflection in the mirror, but I do it anyway.

I let out a gasp. The women have outdone themselves. The bold hues of the gown complement my complexion perfectly, making my skin glow with health and radiance. My thick-lashed gray eyes look huge in my face, cheekbones rouged and my lips glistening a shiny plum. My dark curls have been brushed to a glossy sheen, the iridescent strands braided across the top into a crown of sorts and interwoven with a strand of glimmering opals. Stars above, I look like a princess... no, a *queen*.

Nerves assault me as the door swings open and the king of Everlea enters.

Slowly, I turn to face him. I should notice the rich crimson velvet of his formal jacket with the touches of gold, and the way his charcoal tunic and trousers hug his towering form. I should notice the gleaming waterfall of silver hair beneath the sleek onyx crown and the compelling, arresting face that steals my breath away. I should notice the utter stillness of his shadows as if they, too, are somehow transfixed.

But all I can see is the way he looks at me and the unguarded desire *burning* in those midnight eyes, threatening to incinerate everything in this room.

"Gods, pátnī, you undo me."

A gasp from Ziba has my eyes darting toward her, but her head is bowed. The king's shadows burst into frenetic motion after his whispered words, whirling around him as if barely contained. The last time he'd called me that, he had said it meant he should stay away from me.

"Leave us," Darrius says, and the room clears.

"Does that mean you don't actually hate me?" I tease for lack of anything cleverer to say when we stand alone.

"I could never—" He chokes on his words, his throat working. "Hate you." Sands, is the cold, impervious king actually tongue-tied? Clearly fighting something inside—*is it the curse?*—he lifts his hand to rub at the center of his chest as he inhales and exhales deeply. "What I feel right now is, in fact, the opposite of that."

I blink at the measured choice of words, refusing to read more into it. It's a compliment, that's all. He approaches, and his rich scent envelops me. I feel the devoted touch of his shadows, too, but I welcome their adoring, worshipful energy. My simurgh preens in response to their obvious reverence, making the runes on my arms brighten.

I wonder at their unusual connection—our magic always feels so familiar—but the thought flies from my head when the king stands at my back and turns us to the mirror. Pulse racing, I stare at his reflection, his immense frame looming over me as he wraps a gold necklace with a black pendant the size of a quail egg around my throat.

"This opal will protect you against anyone who might wish to do you harm," he says, his fingers inordinately gentle against my skin. Tingles race at the points of contact.

I swallow and lick my lips, reaching up to touch the inky orb, seeing the light refract off the gem's surface. "It's beautiful."

"It belonged to my mother," he says softly.

"Thank you, Darrius."

When we arrive at the main tent, where the music and dancing are already in fine form, the king's presence is heralded. Everyone drops to one knee and bows before he gives them leave to rise. I immediately want to make myself scarce, though I can see that it will be impossible to hide in this dress. No wonder he wanted me to wear it.

Wearing his royal colors makes a statement, one that I can see does not go unnoticed, particularly by those from the Aspačanā delegations. As we sweep by, I groan at the sight of two thrones on the dais. Surely Darrius doesn't expect me to sit up there!

But of course he does.

"A throne is for your queen," I say through my teeth when he directs me toward the dais.

He stubbornly refuses to respond and welcomes everyone, including the citizens from Verisia as well as other outlying cities, and finally, the Aspačanā.

I recognize the redheaded Azes and the blond Karânî, standing with their warriors. There's no blood on them today, but they are no less fearsome for it, even garbed in their fine clothing. Heavy gold jewelry adorns their necks and wrists, and they are dressed in their respective colors: bronze for Shabra, bone white for Chamros. I instantly catch sight of the giant in dark blue, who must be from

Karkad, the water clan. The last in red, approaching the dais, is a diminutive woman who must be from Rakh.

"My king," she says, "I see word of the guest of honor is not unwarranted in this case."

Darrius lets out a noncommittal grunt. "Raissa Tabiti, you look well. May I introduce you to Lady Suraya."

"It's my pleasure," I say politely, and study the tiny brunette dressed in a stunning crimson cropped tunic and snug trousers. It's meant to showcase the jewel glinting in her pierced belly button and the chain that winds around her trim waist. Her features are too sharp to be beautiful, but she is certainly striking... and not someone I'd want to cross on a battlefield.

Penetrating green eyes meet mine. "Word of your skill with the basilisk has already spread far and wide. You saved many."

The king tenses beside me, but I keep my expression neutral. "Thank you, but I did not do it alone."

"May I present the rais of Karkad," Darrius says, the slightest growl in his voice letting me know his feelings on this particular leader. I look up and up and up. The dark-haired man had seemed like a giant from afar earlier, but he is truly huge at nearly seven feet. He's also older than he first appeared.

He bows. "I am Masišta. I look forward to winning the tournament." Before I can respond, he signals to a woman behind him and ushers her in front of the king. "You know my daughter, Sire, Zahre."

If I thought that the fire raissa was unclothed before, this woman makes her look like she's overdressed. Unlike her father's blue garb, Zahre is boldly dressed in red and black—the king's colors, which irritates me for no good reason—the ribbons of scarlet silk clinging lovingly to her curves in crisscross patterns before falling to a sheer skirt that leaves little to the imagination. Her hair is a reddish blond, her skin the color of fresh cream. Sparkling blue eyes hold the king's boldly, a hint of a smile playing about her lush mouth.

Sands, I despise her already.

As the king is engaged in conversation by the two, I search the room for Laleh and see her standing next to Ani, in deep discussion.

I make my escape. I feel Darrius's stare on my back, but I don't look at him. I don't even look at how well suited he and Zahre seem to be. She can be his pretend queen for all I care. And I *don't* care, not one bit. I thread through the crowd to where Ani and Laleh are talking, but they stop when I reach them.

"You look gorgeous," Laleh says.

I scan my friend's bright orange dress with its gauzy skirt and notice she has somehow dyed her hair to match. "So do you!" I turn to Ani, who is in a snow-white gown edged with scarlet embroidery that looks very regal on her. "You're beautiful, Ani."

"Thank you." She ducks her head and blushes, and I want to grin at how adorably awkward she is.

I fully expect to be immediately interrogated by Laleh, considering my arrival on the king's arm, but she is whisked away to dance by one of the Verisian nobles, leaving Ani and me alone. She hands me a tumbler, and I take a cautious sip, eyes wide at the rich, lemony taste.

"Careful, it's strong."

"What is it?" I ask.

"Dandelion and steppe grass cider." She wrinkles her nose. "Has an effect on the libido. The Aspačanā make it. Their festivities can get very raunchy very quickly. They climb each other like trees."

I snort at her quip; Laleh's influence no doubt. Best I drink very sparingly, then. Even though there's only one tree I wish to climb, and said tree is being commandeered by a very beautiful woman who makes me look like a sad, invasive weed. Unable to curb my jealousy, I stare at them as the king escorts Zahre to dance.

They seem to touch each other quite familiarly, and there's no doubt that they are a stunning couple. His silver hair and dark good looks are offset by her flame-red locks and creamy complexion.

"Who is she to him?" I ask Ani.

"Uh . . ." Her hesitation makes me glance at her. "No one?"

"She doesn't look like no one."

Ani sighs, dropping her eyes. "A past dalliance, if you can call it that. There was a time when everyone in Everlea expected them to wed. At least, there were negotiations in progress, which I was instructed to pursue on his behalf."

"And then?" I prod, drowning in despair, knowing that Darrius would have trusted no one else but his sister for something so important.

"You arrived with Razulek."

By the maker, that wasn't too long ago. Have I imagined all the moments between the king and me? The way he looked at me in my chambers? The territorial touch of his shadows? His words and letting me wear his mother's necklace? Gods, I am the queen of fools.

My lungs feel as though they can't fill with air. "Is she his . . . soul-fated?"

Ani's eyes widen. "No. He rejected that bond years ago. This was to be a political alliance. He doesn't love her, Sura. He *can't* love, not while he's cursed."

But the way Zahre is looking at him—it's not only political to her. And why should it be? Torturous visions of them lying tangled together as the king unwraps that red and black fabric from her voluptuous body invade my brain out of nowhere. I claw at my bodice that's suddenly too tight and constricting. Sands, I need air.

Gasping for breath, I gather my skirts and leave.

Chapter Twenty-Five

Bitterness and mortification have me in a dual chokehold.

There are only two things that can get me out of my own head: magic or the forge. And since I don't have use of the former, the latter will have to do. But I can't hammer steel in a gown, so I stomp into the castle to my quarters, trying to ignore the strains of music and the accompanying images of Darrius and Zahre wrapped together in a sultry dance.

Where did you go? The thought blasts into my head. Of course it's the king, undoubtedly wondering why I'm ruining the important feast with my disappearing act.

Shouldn't you be busy dancing with your almost betrothed? I shoot back waspishly.

She's not my . . . Where are you?

None of your business.

He growls. *It is my business when Masišta is no longer here. I told you that you could be in danger. Don't be reckless, Suraya.*

I hiss out a tight breath, unnatural jealousy riding me. *Why don't you ask your fiancée? It's her father, after all. Perhaps this is all part of some great plot I contrived to assassinate you.*

Then I fling up my walls and block any further connection.

Sands, I hate that I'm so pathetic. *Why* am I feeling this unhinged?

My eyes sting as I hasten up the stone steps. When I reach my quarters, I dismiss Ziba and the handmaidens with a forced smile. I don't want anyone to witness whatever this is. Chest aching, I remove the king's necklace, wanting to fling it away. Instead, I clutch the opal in my fist and feel the hopeless tears streak down my cheeks. Gods, what did I think? That the precious gift had meant something? That *I* meant something? A sob catches in my throat as I set the necklace carefully on the dresser.

I kick away my slippers and tear off my stockings before dragging the pins out of my hair, feeling the heavy curls loosen to fall down my shoulders. Then I curse because I've sent everyone away and the stupid fastenings for the dress are on my back, which means I'm stuck. Unless . . . I reach for my dagger and prepare to cut the bodice, when I'm reminded that the material is impenetrable. Damn every spelled thing in this wretched place!

Suddenly, the bedchamber door flies open and crashes into the wall.

"What are you doing?" I shriek, as a wild-eyed Darrius peers around the room, onyx sword drawn. His gaze snags on the dagger in my hand, and he lets out a savage growl. His eyes flash gold.

"Why the dagger? Is there someone here?" he demands, his stare scouring me from head to toe. "Where's your necklace?"

I narrow my eyes at his tone but stay calm, not wanting to bait his temper more and incite a shift—especially not when the tournament is imminent. Surreptitiously, I wipe my face, hoping he doesn't notice my reddened eyes. "No one is here. And the necklace is over there."

He doesn't look happy about that when he spots it. "You're certain no one followed you?"

"I'm fine. There's no one else here, Darrius. I dismissed the handmaidens." I wasn't paying attention as to being followed, but there are guards posted everywhere. "Are you expecting an attack?"

"I'm always prepared for that." He breathes in deeply, expression troubled. "What you did with the basilisk, even with your magic contained, heightens the threat. I don't trust anyone not to abduct you for their own ends. With your magic restricted by those cuffs, you'll be defenseless."

I lift my dagger. "Not entirely defenseless. And why would they do that?"

"Anahima says that for some reason the Aspačanā believe you can cure this *rot* that has been plaguing the steppes."

I frown. They do? "Why would they think that?"

"Your magic cured the basilisk before its death. Word of that has spread." Finally convinced that I'm not overlooking assassins under the bed, he lowers his sword and sheathes it into his scabbard with a deep sigh. "I am sorry to have barged in here, but I was worried. Masišta and Azes both vanished when you left the feast. And I know you're not defenseless, but you are vulnerable."

"Why do you care so much? Weren't you occupied with Zahre?" I can't help but say.

Obsidian eyes meet mine as Darrius stalks closer. "Jealous, Starbright?"

"Hardly," I lie. "You seemed busy, that's all."

"She means nothing," he says, scraping a hand over his chin. "She was a possible alliance when I thought things would go differently."

"With your rejected soul-fated," I interject, tucking my dagger back into the harness wrapped around my thigh. "Ani told me."

The king lets out a humorless groan. "My sister can be painfully direct at times, and while I love her for her plain-speaking, this is not one of those moments." He bends and looks at me. "Why have you been weeping? Your eyes are red."

"I haven't," I whisper, but a lone tear trickles out, disproving my words.

"Please don't cry," he says softly. "None of this is what you think."

"Then what is it?" I swipe viciously at my cheek. "Gods, why do I *feel* like this?"

Eyeing me, he inches closer, each step making my lungs contract, though I refuse to move. "Do you know it is nearly impossible to break a soul-fated bond once a pair unites? At first, it's a chain reaction of alchemy and magic, biology and physiology. And then a fated bond becomes an irresistible force—there's no evading it once certain parameters are met."

"Like what?" I whisper. He's so close that we're sharing breath and body heat. I can feel my pulse hammering under my skin and see the refracted flecks of light in that midnight stare. His mesmerizing scent makes me dizzy.

A finger traces over my exposed collarbones. "Like sight and sound." He leans in to run his nose down my temple to my ear, making me shudder. "Scent, touch." He inhales, breathing me in, and then leans back. His tongue slips out to wet his lower lip, his voice a guttural rasp as his eyes devour me. His fingertip swipes at the tear on my cheek and he brings it to his mouth. "Taste."

My mouth dries at the hunger in his gaze. I can see his magic lashing toward me beneath his iron control of it, and I want his shadows to surround me . . . to consume me. I want to sink into them, into *him*. It's a dangerous desire. We are treading treacherous waters, and once we go past this point, there'll be no returning.

I fight through the fog of lust for reason. "What are you saying?" I ask hoarsely.

"We are written."

His eyes never leave mine. Something lances down to my bones—a coil of delicate awareness—at the oath that sounds too much like a sacred vow to ignore.

Stars above . . . is he . . . ? Are we . . . ?

Once more, I curse the cuffs on my wrists, impeding my magic and any ability to be sure about what is happening between us. That I'm not making a terrible mistake.

"Darrius, what if I'm not who you think I am?"

"I know *exactly* who you are." He stares balefully at the cuffs. "And you would, too, without them."

My heart climbs into my throat when his magic writhes over his skin as though his shadows are desperate to leap from him to me... and he's barely holding them at bay. He drops his guard entirely, letting them unravel in a river of darkness toward me. And then the epiphany hits with the force of a desert sandstorm.

I gape as tangible memories bloom, and then I squint at him—his shape, his frame, his size, and the unique *feel* of his magic.

Magic that I've felt many times before.

I gasp as realization hits. "It *was* you! All those times in my dreams? In Oryndhr. Did you come to me in my sleep?"

"Yes."

Those dark eyes hold me captive as his quiet admission makes heat explode in my veins.

Gods, he's seen me naked. *Touched* me. I'd always felt those dreams were much too visceral to be figments of a fervid imagination, and now I have my answer. "How?" My voice is strangled.

"One of my numena is dreamwalking. It takes an immense amount of magic to cross astral planes, but I could never resist your call."

"*My* call?"

"Your magic's call, Starbright. I am yours as you are mine."

The answer is there, rising out of the depths of my mind, but by the stars, I feel it in my bones, in my veins, at the core of my being.

"Because we're soul-fated," I whisper.

The realization is like the unveiling of a truth I have always known. It's the reason my magic recognizes his, the reason his manticore won't ever hurt me. His *mate*.

We are linked by the fates and the stars. My mind is racing, chasing over possibilities and mulling over our past interactions.

"You knew me?" I ask.

"The stars had spoken." The king exhales. "But I could not find you, not until I felt a glimmer when your magic ascended."

"My mama died," I say, connecting the timeline. "Her magic hid me from those who wished me harm. Without her life force, the protections diminished."

He nods. "I resisted, intending to reject the bond, but then you summoned me for the first time, and I could no sooner stay away than I could stop breathing."

Why would he want to reject the bond? Hurt fills me at that, but my cheeks burn as embarrassment is quick to follow. I know *exactly* what moment he's referring to.

I'd just turned twenty, and Laleh and I had celebrated with a little too much of her father's wine. We had climbed to the roof of my family's inn to count the stars, while lamenting my sad, solitary state and the fact that I was destined to die a virgin.

"Can't I find one good man in Coban?" I'd groused. "A girl has needs."

Laleh had giggled, still sated and flush from her adventures with not one but *two* lovers in the broom closet of the tavern. "There's always Cyrill."

"Bite your tongue, wench!"

With an eye roll, Laleh had mimicked kissing the air. "Then for tonight, I guess you'll have to be satisfied with your imagination. Maybe you should wish on a star for the best dream-railing of your life." And just then, on the heels of her words, a silver streak had arced across the heavens. "Star gods! Hear our plea for the sake of finicky virgins everywhere!"

"Laleh!"

I'd snorted as we dissolved into drunken giggles.

That had been the night—the very first night—I'd lain in bed and silently wished for the other half of my soul to appear in my dreams if I couldn't have him in reality and if he even existed. Embarrassed heat drizzles through me at the recollection. Because my perfect dream lover *had* come in bursts of starlight and shadow, and I'd woken shaken and spent... from a starsdamned dream.

Only it hadn't *just* been a dream.

"It was you," I say. "All those times."

"Yes." His intense focus is on my mouth. His shadows flutter around me, and I feel my own magic rise to their gentle touches. "I want to kiss you. I want to know if your lips taste the same as they do in all my darkest fantasies."

My core goes liquid.

Stars...

I have to be smart and strong—giving in to my desires and the melting invitation in his eyes won't get me the answers I seek. "But you said you intended to reject the bond. You didn't want this then, so don't pretend now." Anger douses the embers of lust. "You said so before."

Onyx eyes flash. "I was protecting you!"

"You were protecting yourself," I say, stepping sideways and walking to the window, where I can breathe air that isn't him. "You didn't want me."

He scrapes a hand through his hair. "I do want you, that's the fucking problem."

"You have a poor way of showing it." I narrow my eyes. "Why should I even believe you when all you've done is push me away? Why, Darrius?"

"Because as much as I crave this, you will be the fucking end of me!"

The bitter admission explodes between us, and my heart feels as if it has been torn from my chest. Gods, I can't breathe. "If I'm so fatal to you, why keep me here? Send me back home."

"Because you're not safe there."

"Good thing I'm not your problem," I snap.

He scowls, eyes flaring gold again. "Why couldn't you have stayed where you belonged? None of this would have happened if you hadn't come here."

"So it's my fault?" Hurt blooms beneath the blades of both our words. "Did I ruin your precious plans with your Aspačanā bride?"

"Gods, how are you this obtuse?"

I rear back. "I don't know. How are you such a fucking coward?"

The smallest flinch catches my eye. Guilt surges, but the hum of victory runs through me, too. The formidable, fearsome nightmare king is capable of being hurt. There's a foul power in it, but I revel nonetheless. That fathomless stare glitters, his shadows writhing as he stalks toward me. Chin aloft, I hold my ground in front of the windowsill even when he invades my space.

"Is that so?" he snarls, peering down at me, eyes dark with resentment, embittered lust, and fury as tenebrosity lashes like a knot of inky serpents around him.

A similar cocktail wars inside of me, only my starlight wants to burn everything to the ground. Sands, I'm sinking so deeply into an abyss of anguish and anger that it makes me heedless of the danger. "*Yes*. You'll tuck tail and run at the first sign of trouble. Darrius Nightsong, the craven king."

"You speak of things you do not know," he grinds out. "I. Am. Cursed!"

"And yet in spite of said curse, your manticore fights for what he wants. Can you say the same?"

In a flash, a powerful hand encircles my throat. It's a loose hold, but I go still nonetheless. Eyes on mine, he doesn't stop there. The king cages me against the sill with his body, lean hips imprisoning mine, and his free hand fisting in my loose hair. He pulls, making my back arch slightly, and desire burns through me at the press of his groin on my stomach. His *hard* groin. A depraved shudder runs through me.

Nostrils flaring, his lips part.

"Are you afraid of me, Starbright?" he rasps, that gravelly voice doing more to me than his controlling hold. His thumb caresses my hammering pulse.

I bare my teeth. "Never."

He bends, mouth ghosting over my jaw to my earlobe. He bites, and I wince even as lust shoots through my veins. Beneath my bodice, my nipples bud painfully, and a traitorous, throbbing heat gathers in my core. My magic rears up, runes unspooling down my arms as my bracers flare. That unsettling, predatory gaze flicks to the silvery coils and darkens even more. His tattoos writhe, snapping at my skin. Not for the first time, I wish the cuffs gone so he can feel the full answering force of *my* magic.

I'm far from unprotected, not as I yank my dagger from its holster and wedge my arm up between us to press the point of the blade to his throat. Shadows instantly wind around my forearm, but I keep my hand locked in place as a drop of blood swells. Sands, the sight of it shouldn't enflame my lust even more, nor should I have an indecent desire to taste the scarlet bead. Perhaps I am as much of a monster as he is.

I laugh coldly. "We all have demons, don't we?"

"*Not* like this," he says, his gold-sheened onyx stare drilling down into mine. "A god cursed me to never consummate my soul-fated bond that is my divine right. Anything I *feel* will trigger the curse, and when I claim my soul-fated, I will be condemned to the beast for eternity." He scoffs, an awful, derisive sound. "So you see, Starbright, my so-called demons herald my end. Can *you* say the same?" he asks mockingly.

Dazed, I blink at him, thoughts churning. Anything he feels? As in emotions or physical sensations? Is *that* why he has been pushing me away every time we get too close? Why he's been keeping me at a distance? Because he feels *too much*?

"Are you going to kill me, pátnī?" he murmurs, unaware of the chaos unspooling in my mind.

"What does that even mean?" I snap.

His eyes bore into mine like burning embers. "Wife."

"I'm not your wife." A shiver climbs my spine.

"The Royal Stars have decreed it so."

"Fuck them," I spew recklessly.

The king smiles slowly . . . a full one that curls his lips upward and makes starlight sparkle in those night-sky onyx eyes. My breath hitches when he laughs. *Laughs!* Sands, it's fucking beautiful. I don't think I've ever heard him sound like that, but one thing's for sure: I absolutely do not *ever* want to hear that again because of how utterly weak it makes me for him.

"That irreverent tongue of yours, Starbright, will earn you their wrath."

"Still obsessed with said appendage, I see." That saturnine gaze drops to my mouth. I lick my bottom lip, and his eyes dilate. "Infinitely."

My heart is still fluttering at the stupid effect of his laughter. His fist tightens, tugging my head back, the sting of my scalp riding the pleasure simmering in my veins. Looming over me, he presses down, and the tip of the blade sinks into his throat, the bead of blood becoming a small rivulet that runs into his collar.

"Don't."

"You think a mere blade can stop me?" he murmurs, and then groans as I lick my dry lips again. "I'd welcome any blade for a single taste of you. Let you bleed me dry. Tell me to stop, Suraya, and I will." His entire body shudders as if he's been holding himself back the whole time, as though he's about to climb out of his skin. "I am selfish and craven. And I fear I am not the least of what you deserve."

"But you're what I need," I whisper, lowering my arm and releasing the dagger so it clatters to the floor between us. "Exactly as you are."

His eyes widen with despair and hope, the shine of gold eclipsing the obsidian for a frenetic heartbeat before that beautiful jet stare returns. Desire rides him, as does the curse. His fingers on my throat tighten, drawing me up to my tiptoes. A small snarl escapes him as he angles me to where he wants me, and then his mouth crashes into mine.

Chapter Twenty-Six

The Night King

The first real taste of my soul-fated is sublime and dangerous, like a shot of the most potent aphrodisiac. I want to bring her to the ecstasy she can only reach at my hands. On my tongue. On my cock. I want to claim her. Mark her. Own her.

Fuck her senseless.

Driven by pure carnal instinct, my mouth ravages hers, the beast inside of me making his needs known as his primal consciousness rides mine. I force myself to calm, not wanting to lose myself to the curse too soon, but the softness of her lips, the decadent wellspring of her mouth, and those soft moans and whimpers of desire will be my undoing.

Gods...

I drag my mouth away, licking along the tender line of her jaw to her throat. I suck harder when she moans, desperate to see my mark on her gorgeous, lustrous skin. With my free hand, I yank up her skirts and lift her so that she can wrap her legs around my waist. When her hot core grinds again mine through the thin barrier of her undergarments, my knees nearly buckle.

I shift her back to the stone wall beside the window, relishing in the needy sound she makes when I circle my hips, my cock aching for friction and sweet relief.

"How wet are you for me, pátnī?" I growl. "Shall we find out?"

A dazed but lucid gaze burns into mine. "Not. Your. Wife."

"My soul-fated then."

"You're grasping at straws. You rejected that."

I chuckle. Defiant to the last. One day, I'll fuck the insolence from her lips, but for now, I'm too focused on discovering if she craves me as much as I crave her. I kiss my way down her chest and greedily lift her breasts from her bodice, delighting in the velvety pink-brown peaks that are practically begging for my attention. I scrape my teeth over her nipple, while pinching the other between my fingers. She whimpers but winds her fingers into my hair to yank my head to her other breast.

"Harder," she whispers.

Yes, my fiery little star loves the bite of pain with her pleasure. I oblige, sucking hard and nibbling over her delicious skin, leaving a trail of dark red marks behind. My beast practically purrs with satisfaction.

"Darrius," she moans. "I need to ... please."

"I'll give you what you need." I grasp her throat again, collaring her. "Say you're mine."

Even in the throes of desire, her mouth tightens. "No."

I grind my hips into hers, feeling the head of my cock push up through my waistband and notch into a sweet spot that makes her cry out. I mimic the act of fucking, rolling my pelvis up into hers and watching her pupils swallow the gray of her irises with each stroke. "Tell me, *wife*, who do you belong to?"

"Myself," she gasps, and glares at me, magic roiling in her eyes. Her fist, already tangled in my hair, pulls downward, dragging my face to hers. "Stop fucking teasing me, Dare, or I'll finish myself off."

Gods, she's a fucking queen who bows to no one.

She called me *Dare* . . .

Desire ignites, sending my shadows into a frenzy. They wind in her hair, shuttle up her legs, tug on her exposed breasts, exploring every inch of heated, fragrant skin they can touch. Her runes are incandescent, nearly blinding me. Ashes below, my magic loves them, darkness dancing over the radiant symbols with a profound reverence, coaxing them out to play even though her magic is inhibited by those cursed cuffs.

A spike of anger barrels through me—I'll eviscerate the fucking soul that dared to manacle her . . . that dared to subjugate my mate. My bones shudder and my skin tightens as the manticore claws against my insides. Impotent rage makes me fight the curse for a handful of agonizing seconds, but I refuse to lose myself to it before I can savor what is mine.

Calm, calm, calm.

Miraculously, the beast retreats almost with a strange sense of mutual understanding.

How?

But I'm too far gone to process why any of this is even possible—too grateful for the reprieve I've been granted. I need to grasp each moment I can before it's snatched away.

Nearly mindless with lust, I claim Suraya's lips in a drugging kiss while easing her legs to the ground. My soul-fated lets out a noise of discontent, but I snake my right hand between us, beneath the copious layers of skirts, and slide up her thigh to cup her mound. She's so starsdamned hot that I can feel her arousal pulsating through the gratifyingly damp fabric.

Tugging down her undergarments, I drag a finger through her drenched folds and groan at the silken sensation. "Fuck, Starbright. You're soaked."

She writhes helplessly against me, hips chasing the friction. My thumb settles on her clitoris, and she lets out a whimper, nails digging into my shoulder. I ease my middle finger into her and she grips me with that velvet heat. So fucking *tight*. So starsdamned *wet*. I add another finger, working both into her, relishing the sound of her desperate moans as she clenches hungrily around me.

I groan and sink my teeth into the bare flesh of her shoulder. I'm half on the edge already, cock aching with need as her warm arousal coats my fingers.

My mouth waters, the beast inside inciting me for a taste.

Patience, I caution him. *Good things will come to those who wait.*

Astonishingly, I can feel the depth of his urgency and the mating instinct riding him. But he acquiesces. I am shocked. We have never been connected—*united*—like this before. Is it her doing? I don't question it, I lean into it, not wanting him to take over if I lose myself.

"Darrius, don't stop . . ." she cries out, riding my hand in graceless jerks.

Now, now, now. I don't know if the chant is him or me, but I cannot resist the call any longer. I grip her hips and drop to my knees.

"What are you doing?" she gasps, blown-out pupils staring at me.

"Giving you what you need." My lips curl into a wicked smile as I lift one leg and throw it over my shoulder. I kiss the inside of her knee and position myself right in front of my glistening altar of worship. "Pátnī."

"I am not—" Gray eyes squeeze shut right as I swipe my tongue from entrance to clit and suck hard. I swirl my tongue and graze my teeth over her pulsing flesh. *"Fucking stars, Dare!"*

She comes with a strangled shriek, leg tightening and hips bucking into my mouth.

Gods, if her skin tasted sweet, her arousal is like the headiest, richest nectar, drenching my lips and sating my soul. Watching her come undone is like glimpsing a million shooting stars bursting across the heavens. A gift. A fucking marvel.

My cock releases as she writhes beneath my lips, offering me every drop of her pleasure. When her shudders lessen and cease, those brilliant, starlit eyes open and drag me down into their beautiful, dangerous depths.

"Are you mine now?" I ask, blowing on her soaked, tender folds.

"N . . . no."

I grin madly, incensed and challenged by the rebelliousness in her stubborn stare. I stand, taking her with me as she squeals, balancing her body on one shoulder and with my right hand. The scent of her intimate flesh surrounds me, intoxicating me. Gently, I set her on a nearby armchair and drag her plump ass to the edge, inhaling my new favorite fragrance.

"Darrius, what are you doing?" she squeaks.

I lift a brow as if to say, *This again,* before sinking to my knees, a position as king that I am unfamiliar with but now completely dedicated to. "You know what I'm doing. Kneeling before my queen. Making her admit whom she belongs to by showing her that *I* belong to *her*."

"I can't come again," she says, cheeks burning red as I position each of her legs lewdly over the armrests and admire my handiwork. I bite her inner thigh in punishment, her smothered whine rolling through me. Deep inside, the manticore purrs with approval and pride at the boneless, flushed state of our mate.

"You'll do what you're told. Now suck," I growl, sending a blunted pillar of shadow into her shocked, parted mouth, giving her something to occupy that ungovernable tongue. Then I descend to feast.

She is chaos and certain ruin.

But she is *mine*.

Chapter Twenty-Seven

"Are you well, Sura?" Laleh asks me from her cushioned seat to my right.

Blushing, I blink repeatedly and stare at my best friend. "Yes, why?"

"You're fidgeting, blinking like sand is in your eye, and your face is very red, like you've been stuck in a forge for hours hammering away at something. Do you have a fever?"

Lust fever, and I certainly want to be hammered by a sexy, vicious king who is much too good with his tongue. And his cursed shadows. I burn even hotter with mortification as I vehemently shake my head, banishing wicked visions of sucking off what had felt like a thick shadow-cock while he pleasured me to oblivion.

"I'm fine. It's just hot." Suddenly, a rotten stench wafts into my nose, and I cringe as it permeates the air. It reeks like the basilisk had. "Do you smell that?"

"Are you certain you're all right?" Laleh shoots me a quizzical look. "I don't smell anything, and it's nowhere near as hot as Coban."

She's not wrong. It's many degrees cooler than the desert at the height of midday, when you're wishing you can burrow into the hot sand just for a reprieve. But that kind of external heat isn't my problem; it's the one inside that's immolating me.

Pretending to be interested and paying attention to a grueling, highly competitive exhibition tournament for the sun god when I can still feel the king of Everlea devouring me between my legs has to be a new form of torture. I flush deeply for the thousandth time from my position of honor on a special dais and throne in the spectator stands, glad that no one around me, including my observant best friend, can sense my private thoughts.

You're blushing again, pátnī.

I scowl at the intrusion. Well, mostly private. I can't see him, but he's here somewhere.

I'm certain that Darrius is now calling me that name only to aggravate me, and it's working. I don't even deign to respond as I strengthen my mental walls and push his smug voice out. Though he has every reason to be smug—I've never come so many times in my life.

Much later on when I wasn't splayed open and held in his thrall, he had explained that his manticore had demanded half of it. I suppose it's a silver lining that he and his beast are at least of the same mind about something. That being *me*. Heat climbs up my spine at the deliciously filthy memory of being bent over my footboard and wolfed down from behind.

I'm nearly certain that I'd felt claws digging into my thighs at one point.

In truth, I'd been marked from top to bottom by the time the king had finally relented and taken pity on my sobbing, satiated state. Eventually, my magic had healed all the bites, bruises, and claw marks. A part of me missed them, something deeply primal blooming at the rough evidence of his claim mapped all over my body.

Heat sluices through me again.

Focus, Suraya, for ashes' sake.

I swallow, grabbing the fan in my lap and swishing it aggressively near my face. From the side, Ziba hands me a glass of water, and I drink it gratefully. To my horror, she had witnessed the proof of the king's lovemaking written all over me during my bath in the evening. She hadn't said a word, thank every star in the sky, but her eyes had glinted with what had looked oddly like relief. By this morning, when my skin was back to normal—thank you, suppressed but effective magical blood—she, too, had returned to her normal quiet and efficient self with no mention of my extracurricular activities with her beloved sovereign.

And beloved he is, contrary to Oryndhrian rumor.

Those who might not adore him respect him. Even the Aspačanā.

A wave of screaming overtakes the entire crowd, citizens from all over Everlea, including the horde clans. These tournament events will be followed by nights of frenetic feasting, which are central to the Gauntlet of Mithral—a fascinating combination of athletic games, sacred celebrations, and cultural spectacle.

The stands had been erected quickly at the intersection of the four territories belonging to Rakh, Shabra, Chamros, and Karkad. This is hallowed ground to them, the space where many of their communal rituals take place: the intersection of sky and earth is the center of their divine beliefs.

I don't miss the significance that my magic, embodied by the simurgh, is symbolic of the earth and sky connection as well. Which is probably why each of the Aspačanā leaders is focused on honoring my presence and wanted me here. That and the mistaken belief that I can cure the plague threatening their livelihoods. Not that I can do much without the full extent of my magic.

I swallow hard and gulp more water, very conscious of the hundreds of stares flicking to me from the onlookers who see me as some corporeal representation of their goddess.

Oxhorn drums start to beat, heralding the start of the procession. There is a visceral energy humming through the spectators, including nearly all the nobles from Verisia, who have never before been invited to the Gauntlet.

First, each of the Aspačanā leaders will be presented to me with their courts in a display of their primary elemental numen, and then the official tournament will begin. As I understand it, there is jousting, strength contests, hand-to-hand combat, and even chariot racing. I sit up, excited by the energy in the stands as everyone pitches forward to see the presentation spectacle in the open-air arena. Several dozen musicians follow the marching drummers, and ethereal panpipe melodies fill the arena.

Jaw agape, I stare, fascinated, when scores of beautifully dressed entertainers in bright clan colors emerge in their wake and start to dance, their supple bodies undulating like the numena they represent. The Rakh dancers twirl live flames in between their limbs, while the Karkad ones send ribbons of liquid up into the sky like tiny airborne rivers with each leap. I can't help observing that Zahre is front and center, clad in blue leather. Droplets of water roll across the voluptuous body I try not to notice.

He doesn't want her.

I despise the fact that I can't seem to control my jealousy. I have no reason to be, but Ani's words about the king's former lover echo poisonously in my brain. I drag my gaze away and focus on the Shabra performers, who are manipulating shiny rocks in a dazzling display of dexterity, while the Chamros dancers rise up, whirling into the air on magical wind currents.

I watch with wonder, along with everyone else. Even Laleh looks impressed. Each rais and raissa gallops onto the sands riding massive, decorated warhorses to roars and shrieks of their people. Rais Azes and Rais Masišta are bare-chested, their arms, legs, and torsos covered in tattoos, their big muscles oiled and glistening. Gold torcs adorn their necks.

Even the raissas, Tabiti and Karânî, have ornate gold jewelry hanging from thick armored collars over fitted tunics, their tattoos of various abstract animals like snarling cats, flying griffins, and horned rams also on ferocious display.

The four riders come to a sharp halt in front of the dais, bowing their heads in deference. I smile and cant my head in return, lifting the two fingers of my right hand to my chin and releasing them toward each leader, like I've been told to do by a very helpful and knowledgeable Ani, who is well-versed in Aspačanā culture and formal customs.

"Lady Suraya," Raissa Tabiti says as her horse dips down to its forelegs. "May your flame forever burn hot."

The nearly seven-foot Rais Masišta is next. His horse doesn't bow, but he draws his massive ax and holds it high. "May your waters never stop flowing."

"May the earth always provide," Raissa Karânî offers, her horse rearing up to its hind legs and pawing the air.

Last, Rais Azes eyes me, arrogance radiating from him in waves. "May the winds favor you."

There's one more competitor, and that's King Darrius Nightsong. There's complete silence as we await his entrance—no performers, no acrobats—and an entire realm holds its breath.

The sound of an azdaha screeching cuts through the air. Indira circles above everyone's heads with a cry and lands dead center on the ground. The king sits astride her back.

Glittering crimson azdaha eyes collide with mine.

Starkeeper, Indira greets me, and I bow my head in mutual respect.

How are your eggs? I ask. She bares her teeth in a happy grin that makes a few onlookers shriek.

Thriving, she says. *Razulek sends his regards and says to make sure this one doesn't murder too many of his subjects in a jealous rage.*

I laugh and then frown. Surely that's not going to happen.

Indira opens her mouth and roars, lowering a dark bloodred wing so her rider can dismount, and my mouth utterly dries. The king is bare-chested as well, gold dust shimmering over his oiled bronze-brown skin, and wearing tight black front-laced leathers that leave little to the imagination.

Gods . . .

His silver hair is caught up in a tail tied at intervals, the sides freshly shaved, an obsidian crown sitting on his head. His huge broadsword is strapped to his back, and the gorgeous art of runes, roses, and vines surrounding a snarling azdaha winds over the densely packed muscles of his chest and stomach. The runic script I'd seen before glistens with gold, and as he turns to pat Indira on the snout, I catch sight of breathtaking scarlet wings midflight in profile stretched over his back.

Interestingly, they remind me of the gold-veined red wings of his manticore.

Worry fills me. Will he be able to control his curse here?

He had with me, but that had been different. He'd pushed the line of extreme emotion, but he and the beast had had some internal agreement, at least when it came to pleasuring their mate. My cheeks heat at the worst time, and Darrius's midnight eyes snap to mine.

Stars, he shouldn't look so fucking edible.

And I shouldn't be thinking about eating him . . . or about him eating *me*.

Too late. His nostrils flare, and I cross my legs, definitely squirming in my chair as desire burns like wildfire through my stupid veins.

"Pátnī," he says loudly, pulling his sword free and holding it across both palms. My stomach swoops at the very possessive, very meaningful, and very *public* address even as I swallow a surge of dread. My ears burn, especially when the Aspačanā leaders gape and a volley of whispers makes its way through the avid audience.

Elegantly, I rise, expression neutral. "Not yet."

I expect him to be angry, but the conquering smile that cuts over his gorgeous face is anything but. No, instead it's elated as if he relishes every ounce of my fight. I suppose the predator in him loves the chase, and I'm not making it easy for him, no matter what his prophecies or the fates say.

I know from my reading that the consequences of refusing a soul-fated bond will mean a gradual withering, or worse, increasing volatility, of my magic. But sealing the bond is still a choice. *My* choice.

If and when I decide, it will be mine.

A vortex of shadows surrounds the king as his magic makes him reappear at my feet. People scramble out of the way, though many of the court nobles are well accustomed to his unique powers. He kneels and grins wickedly at me as his delicious scent absolutely demolishes my senses. To everyone else, a competitor is kneeling before the guest of honor, his sword aloft and flat in presentation. But it's more than that, especially when he licks his lips.

"My favorite position," he mouths. His shadows tease over my ankles and calves, one even daring to venture to my thighs, making me gasp.

"Stop," I warn. "And make your troth."

"My steel and soul are yours." His handsome face goes solemn, those fathomless eyes scouring mine and then dropping to the cuffs at my wrists. "May your starlight always burn." I think he's done when he rises and sheathes his sword, but he reaches for my trembling hand, bringing my knuckles to his lips. "May your simurgh always soar the skies. May truth always keep you from the lie."

And then he's gone in a whorl of darkness, the barest of kisses ghosting over my skin.

MUCH LATER, AT the evening feast, I sit at the edge of a long table and watch the horde children playing festival games. As with the adults, the competition is intense, and I cheer when a girl of about ten years of age bests one of the bigger boys at the archery targets.

Laleh sidles up to me, and I glance at my friend, nearly balking at her appearance. She looks drawn and pale with dark circles under her eyes—a far cry from her appearance earlier. Her hair is mussed, and for a moment I catch a thick line of bruising at her throat. "What's that?" I ask, pointing at her neck.

She looks at me, and her eyes take a second to focus as she draws her collar up. For a moment, it looks like spidery purplish veins are crawling below her lower lids, but when I blink, they're no longer visible. She smiles, though something about it feels oddly unnatural.

"Nothing," she says brightly. "An accident. One of my scarves got hooked on something. I'm so clumsy sometimes!" The bruise looks far too precise and thin to be caused by a scarf, but I don't press, sensing her discomfort.

A memory yanks hard at my brain, though when I try to follow the thread, all I get is a sea of empty space, as if that particular recollection doesn't want to be found. There are only a few of those gaps remaining, thankfully. But what could be so bad? Laleh is here and she has confirmed Amma and Papa are both safe and well. They're all I care about.

She shifts closer and peers at me. "What does *pátnī* mean?"

I knew the question was coming. "It means 'wife.'" I swallow and fight off another blush. I've always told my best friend everything, and now shouldn't be any different. "The king thinks I'm his soul-fated."

"Are you?" she asks.

"I think we might be." When those spidery dark violet markings under the thin skin of her eyes reappear, this time I know I'm not seeing things. "Laleh, your face!" I say, alarmed. "Are you feeling well? Are you having a bad reaction to something?"

She blinks rapidly. "Perhaps. My eyes were quite itchy earlier. It could be the cider."

"We should find a healer."

Laleh nods. "Good idea." She clears her throat. "But first, I need to tell you something. It's important. The oracle—"

But then, I hear the slight whoosh of an object and register a small green dart sticking out of the side of Laleh's neck. Before I can yell, or even duck out of the way, a sharp sting pierces me in the same spot. Within seconds, my limbs feel numb as some kind of nerve paralysis invades my bloodstream.

I know that my magic will sluggishly clear out whatever toxin it is, but Laleh isn't so lucky. In slow motion, I see and hear her head crash into the wood of the table as she collapses. I realize how extremely vulnerable I am when I try to cry for help and no sound comes out.

One by one, all my senses start to shut down. My hands remain useless in my lap, and I can do nothing as I feel my limp body start to slump. Desperate, I will my magic to heal me faster so I can fight, scream, or do anything but just lie helpless.

Use the bond, call for the king, my simurgh says.

Darrius!

But there's a strange wall between us. I feel it like a pulsing obstruction, a barrier of some kind refracting the projected thought back to me. It's not on my end but the king's. It feels foreign, like it doesn't belong . . . like someone has created a mental blockade.

But what psionic mage here has the power to do that to the *king*? And who would even dare to mentally attack him? Unless . . .

Could Darrius himself have done this?

Vivid images of the beautiful Zahre and the king fill my head, visions of them tangled together, her body undulating over his. What in the ever-loving stars? I don't know where the horrible hallucinations have come from, but they're *not* mine. Despite his many flaws, Darrius has not lied about the Karkad woman.

Recognizing my weakness with my mental walls down, especially with a powerful psionic magi in the mix, I slam them back up. My simurgh is enraged. *You are the Starkeeper. No mental magic is more powerful than ours. Break through it, Suraya!*

I try to no avail, feeling as though I'm being pushed underwater. I make one last-ditch effort, reaching for the azdahas, knowing their otherworldly senses won't be compromised by any magi.

Razulek! Indira! If you can hear me, we need you. Darrius and I are in trou—

But then something smashes into the back of my skull and pain explodes, my plea breaking off abruptly. I might be the Starkeeper, but I'm still housed in a castle made of mortal flesh and blood.

My eyes roll back in my head as oblivion strikes.

Chapter Twenty-Eight

It seems like an eternity until the toxins finally start to flush from my system. My eyelids flutter open to flashes of light. I try to touch the back of my head where there's still a dull throb, but my arms are tied. I can smell the metallic odor of blood, however... a lot of it. Mine?

My body jostles uncomfortably as I take stock of my position and realize I'm moving in a covered cart, with my hands and legs bound. I listen, the sound of horses accompanying the crunch of the cart wheels. A gag is tied over my mouth, but I inhale through my nose, scenting salt on the damp wind.

Painfully, I shift upward, peering through the gap in the back. A sparkling blue horizon greets me; we're on a cliff, and I can hear the sound of gulls and the crash of waves far below. Where am I, and how did I get here in this wagon?

Confusion drains away to be replaced by fury.

Someone fucking took me! And *hit* me! And... I glance around the cart, panic rising. Laleh isn't here.

Darrius! I scream mentally, half expecting the same barrier from earlier, but it isn't there.

Suraya, where are you? His internal voice sounds panicked even as relief fills me. *Indira came to me, told me what you said before you disappeared.*

Not sure. I see the ocean. Someone captured me.

Did they hurt you?

I'm alive.

Rage crackles down the bond. *I will find you.*

Darrius had been right to worry. I had not expected a brazen abduction during the feast, when all acts of war are supposedly forbidden. And now, I'm without a weapon, trussed up like a goose, and my magic is restrained. I am completely exposed and vulnerable.

I wiggle toward the opening at the back and wince. Rolling from a moving cart is going to hurt—but better than the alternative. And it's not like I haven't done it before.

I grit my teeth, roll to the edge, and brace for pain.

"She's awake," a raspy voice says, as the wagon stops abruptly, but it's low-pitched and distorted somehow.

"Already?" Now *that* deep voice I recognize. Masišta.

"I told you she's powerful," the disguised voice says. "Even basilisk venom won't stay long in her system. You are lucky she's magically cuffed."

Basilisk venom! Gods, is Laleh alive? The venom might not harm me, but it will definitely kill her. Footsteps approach and familiar green eyes assess me as she yanks the gag from my dry lips. "No worse for wear," Raissa Tabiti pronounces, and I want to kick her in her teeth. So I do, jerking my legs out toward her. She ducks the strike and grins.

"Where's Laleh?" I grit out. "What did you do with my friend?"

She ignores me. Dread pools in my stomach when Masišta joins her with a booming laugh. "The king will dismember you," I snarl.

"The king is drunk and fucking my daughter," he says smugly, and I suck in a breath. In our mental exchange, Darrius hadn't sounded drunk or distracted; he'd sounded unhinged. "As it was supposed to be," Masišta goes on.

"You need to hurry," the other voice commands. "Then deliver her through the portal as agreed."

Deliver me where? As agreed with *whom*? With a wild lurch, I fling myself off the edge of the cart to identify the speaker, groaning at the bite of stone, and peer around the side past the dozens of Karkad and Rakh warriors surrounding us on horseback. But the only thing I see instead of who is speaking is empty space. My simurgh roars inside of me as if she knows someone is hidden there.

An illusion!

"You're a dead magi, whoever you are," I shout loudly.

"Who's going to kill me, Oryndhrian? You?" Ghostly laughter echoes on the wind as the presence dissipates. I frown. Why did that sound *so* familiar?

I have no time to figure it out, recoiling in horror as Masišta approaches. I need to fight! I need to do something, anything! I struggle wildly, fighting against my bindings. Runes explode down my arms in a blinding explosion of light as my bracers flare, brutally suffocating my magic. My simurgh shrieks her fury at being so starsdamned powerless.

Tabiti crouches, a fingertip trailing over the iridescent runes on my arm. "Beautiful. Too bad. The oracle advised your magic would have been useful against the rot. But it's not as valuable as azdaha eggs or hatchlings. Our clans will ride the winds."

Who is this fucking oracle? Laleh had mentioned the same name before she'd been poisoned. Who had promised them such an impossible prize? Is it the owner of the other voice?

"You will never be worthy of them—azdahas choose their riders, they know their hearts," I say, tears of impotent rage spilling from the corners of my eyes. Unwilling to give up, I focus on surreptitiously working my thumb through the knot at my wrist. "This oracle is lying to you!"

An unholy roar echoes across the space, rattling my bones as a furious crimson azdaha smashes into the circle of Karkad and Rakh warriors, scattering them like pins. I can feel the seething vengeance of the rider on her back and a wild, hysterical laugh bubbles up inside of me.

My king is here.

The next thing I see is body parts rolling across the dusty ground, one head with sightless eyes staring up at the sky, right before it is devoured in a vengeful storm of shadows. Boils and pustules cover another handful of men as Indira's poison rains down. I could fucking weep with relief. My frantic attempts to loosen my bonds renew.

Shouts of the dying pierce the air as the remaining warriors desperately start to fight, ice and fire magic exploding. Darrius is a swirling vortex of shadows, magic blasting from him, even as he compels the men to turn on one another before dispatching them with his onyx blade.

Tabiti screams, a blazing fireball forming between her hands.

"Darrius, look out!" I yell as the knots securing my hands finally slacken and I tackle the ones on my feet.

Darrius dodges the missile and counters with a vicious ice blast. A deadly smile blooms as the darkness swarms around him, sucking in every point of natural light. His shadows promise death.

"You stole from me," he says in a multilayered voice that makes my insides quail, even though it's not directed at me.

"You do not know what is at stake," the raissa snarls. "The rot spreads to our herds. We had no choice."

"They don't care about that, their price was hatchlings, Dare," I say. "Azdaha babies. They're in danger!"

Indira screams with rage and immediately takes to the skies after the king gives her a nod. She must warn the other azdahas and protect her own precious clutch.

"Who?" Darrius says coldly, but Tabiti only laughs.

"The oracle foretells a new god, and soon, your reign will be at an end."

His lips curl. "So be it."

With a howl, she rushes toward him, her body engulfed in flames. The king doesn't hesitate. He disappears into a column of smoke, and I watch with rapt horror as it—*he*—pours down her throat until she's gasping and clutching at her neck.

By the maker...

Her eyes start to bulge, blackened blisters forming on her skin that bubble and expand, moving horrifically across her flesh. And then she explodes, leaving Darrius covered in the remnants of her blood, organs, and shattered bits of bone. I hear one of the few remaining men behind him vomit and the sound of horses galloping away. Rakh, if I had to guess.

Darrius cocks his head like a gore-covered fiend, silver hair scarlet and dripping. My heart pounds, but not with fear. He's a monster to everyone but me.

"One traitor down," he says softly. "One to go."

The ties around my ankles loosen, but then my body whips sideways as Masišta grabs me like a rag doll, pressing his knife to my jugular. A hundred ice shards dance in the air around me, ready to pierce every vulnerable point. "Move and she bleeds."

A bloody Darrius prowls closer, his face a dead mask, eyes empty like the abyss. "For every second of pain you cause her, I will exact a hundred times its measure from you." Magic pulses from him, his voice hypnotic with compulsion. "You will release her and turn that blade upon yourself."

Masišta barks a laugh, tilting his arm to show a rune carved into his skin. "My mind is guarded from manipulation."

I blink in shock. Is that the work of the psionic magi, too?

"You will suffer, I promise you, for touching what is *mine*," Darrius snarls, rage bleeding from him as his shadows form pointed spikes.

"And yet you have made no claim upon her," Masišta says, lowering his head to drag his nose down my neck. "Your bond is unsealed."

I have no doubt that Darrius can breach the walls around Masišta's mind, but he's careful now, unwilling to risk my safety. *Dare,* I tell him, *my simurgh will protect me from the worst of it. I will survive. Do what you must.*

But the king paces like a territorial animal, eyes locked on us, and I can feel the wrath emanating from him in malevolent waves. That black gaze shimmers from ebony to gold and back again, evidence that the curse of the manticore is riding him hard. If he changes to the beast, he will be without his magic. Not defenseless—the manticore is lethal—but in that form, he will be an easier target. His lips part and nostrils flare as he gulps air, striving for calm, but it's not working. His facial bones are sharpening, a feral look overtaking his expression.

Darrius, control.

I. Am. Trying. The growl in my head sounds savage.

Masišta snickers. "Ah, yes, I see it. The beast comes. I always thought that was a rumor. If I cut her, will that make you angrier?" The blade slices into my skin, blood dripping down my throat. I stiffen and try to keep any expression of pain from my face, so it doesn't send Darrius into a tailspin. But when the knife wedges deeper, I can't quite keep in my whimper.

"I will rip the limbs from your body and feed them to you," a seething Darrius promises.

"Temper, temper. Perhaps, but not before I carve through her pretty neck," my captor taunts. "Choose wisely, Your Majesty."

I exhale. My simurgh can't save me from a severed neck, but maybe I can hold Masišta off long enough for the king to strike. I'm no stranger to pain. I gather my magic, watching as Darrius splits into six identical versions of himself, surrounding us.

"Kill him!" Masišta bellows to his remaining men, at least the ones from Karkad who haven't fled yet.

The copies of Darrius might be illusions, but it's a testament to his vast wellspring of power that they are also able to wield magic. I've never seen anything like it as they take out the remaining Karkad warriors in a combined attack that is almost too quick to watch. Then they surround us in a menacing semicircle, looking so alike that I'm not sure at first glance which is the real king.

"Stay back or she dies!" Masišta bellows, panic lacing his tone as if he knows there's no way out for him.

Fingers tighten at my throat, and I conjure a magical shield inside me, turning my skin diamond hard. It won't last because of the cuffs, but it's something. Masišta snarls and squeezes harder as he drags me backward toward the cliff's edge. More ice spears form around me in every direction. I brace. Those are going to fucking hurt.

The standoff is interrupted as a popping noise bursts through the air and the smell of ash and ozone of a portal fills my nostrils. I frown when a nearby small army appears out of nowhere in my peripheral vision. But whose?

Don't the wards prevent portals into Everlea? Then again, Laleh came through as well—so maybe the wards are somehow vulnerable?

"Took you fucking long enough," Masišta crows.

I turn, the movement of my wounded throat making me yelp. And freeze as a familiar face comes into view. Gladness fills me to see my best friend alive and well, even though she, too, had been poisoned with the basilisk venom.

Laleh doesn't look too sickened, though her complexion is oddly waxy and those purplish lines beneath her eyes are evident in her ashen skin. Possibly, a reaction to the venom. I'm so busy checking her for signs of injury, deliriously grateful that she survived, that it takes me a moment to notice the imposing, gorgeous man standing beside her.

A man with a golden crown on his dark hair.

A rush of unexpected feelings invades my chest, tightening it impossibly.

So much love . . . and so much heartbreak. I wheeze a breath as a strange pressure around me builds and pops. Runes on the underside of my cuffs flare and the persistent fog in my mind fractures into stardust. It feels like a spell or enchantment has been lifted. And suddenly, a flood of memories rushes in to fill all the gaps in my brain.

I know *exactly* who the stranger is because I remember everything.

I remember who did this to me . . . the man standing right in front of me.

A man I once loved, Roshan Acharia, the king of Oryndhr.

Roshan stares at me with those beautiful, expressive brown eyes in his breathtakingly handsome face, and for a heart-stopping moment I can't control the deluge of conflicting emotions barreling through me.

Love, hate, hurt, anger.

Sorrow for everything lost.

"Starkeeper," someone whispers, and I flinch.

My gaze flicks to the people surrounding him, and I recognize many of the faces: Aran, Clem, Hamid, and my old guards. I cherished them once, too, but they all stood by and did nothing while their king put me in irons. Aran was my teacher, Clem was my friend, and Hamid was a mentor, until they chose *him* . . . and abandoned me. Bitter rage blooms on the heels of my recollection as my heart shatters anew.

And then my stare lands on Laleh—my very fucking *dead* best friend—who has been with me here in Everlea. My heart quails in my chest, and I'd lift my hand to rub at the phantom pain if the rais of Karkad weren't holding me in place.

"I saw you die," I whisper hoarsely, feeling my eyes burn and my mind fill with horror. Who would be so cruel to play a trick like this? "You *died*."

She laughs, the macabre sound chilling me to my bones. Her eyes, including the sclera, bleed to dark purple, those ugly veins stretching wider until she looks monstrous. "I suppose I *did*. But I have a new lease on life, thanks to a little corpus magic from this realm."

"Who?" Darrius is back to a single version of himself, his voice dark with fury.

"I'll never tell," she singsongs with a giggle.

Aghast, I stare, remembering what Ani had shared with me about the unlawful, dangerous side of necromancy, death magic, and re-animation. Laleh is nothing more than a fleshly husk, animated by corpus magic, not the girl she'd been. She's not alive and she has no soul.

"You're a revenant, not my Laleh," I say, my voice breaking on her name.

She pouts. "But I have *so* many of her memories. I thought we could be friends."

"My best friend is gone."

"But I am still here, darling Sura," she says. "I'm better and stronger thanks to the blessing of my lord Fero." I blanch at the ease of her admission, cold terror filling me. "You can be, too, you know. A goddess, if you just accept him, as you were meant to do. He will reward the faithful."

I gape in horror. Fero is *here*?

"No! What the fuck have you done?" I snap through my teeth. "I killed the queen and banished him!" My voice is wild, my hands balling into fists. "The god of death is the harbinger of eternal devastation, you stupid fucking fools."

In anger, I move toward her and belatedly realize that Masišta's arm is still banding me to him while I'm under the threat of his knife. "Let go of me!" I snarl.

"Release her," the king of Oryndhr commands, and I hate the way that deep baritone feathers over me, opening wounds I had thought closed. My chest burns.

Masišta sneers. "The oracle says the beasts are breeding. We had an arrangement. Her for the azdaha eggs."

Gasping, I blink in confusion that *he* had orchestrated that vile exchange, but then Roshan frowns. "I have no knowledge of that," he says sharply. "Now let her go and leave before I end your miserable life."

After a tense handful of seconds, Masišta shoves me to the ground and hurls himself off the cliff to the ocean below. For a moment I'm stunned. Then I remember that he controls water, so he will likely survive the fall into the sea.

Groaning, I push myself upright, wincing at the stones cutting into my knees as I stand. My magic heals me, but that doesn't mean I don't feel the bite of pain or the lingering numbness from the ropes. Darrius shifts closer, his posture stiff. This isn't a dissenter from his own kingdom; this is a king from a neighboring realm. Any aggression could be construed as an act of war. Including said king's act of showing up unannounced with a small army.

"You have come here," Darrius asks in a silky tone, "without a royal decree?"

"I was invited by Rais Masišta and Raissa Tabiti," Roshan says, and cocks his head, a dark purple flicker bleeding through his eyes. I study him, breath stalling in my lungs. I've seen that somewhere recently—*Razulek's memory!* And I'd seen it myself in Coban.

Suddenly, I realize why he'd stopped looking at me what seems like a lifetime ago in Kaldari. To hide that something foul had been consuming the Roshan I knew.

The same foulness present in Laleh...

Stars. Is it truly Fero?

"Both traitors to the crown," Darrius says. "Tabiti is dead, and Masišta soon will be. Why are you here, Acharia?"

"To reclaim my property," Roshan says in an inhuman, dissonant tone that raises chill bumps along my arms.

That's not his voice.

No, the man you loved was worthy of the gift of light you gave. I don't know if that's my simurgh talking or my conscience, but I do know one thing. Like Laleh, this isn't *my* Roshan.

"I belong to no man," I tell Not-Roshan, lifting my chin.

"Those cuffs say you do." That awful timbre grates like a serrated knife over delicate skin. He stares at his cousin and jerks his head. An unhappy-looking Aran obliges, and suddenly, the runes on the bracers ignite and my magic flares obediently, shimmering coils of light curling over my fingers. The sight of it, the violation of it, nearly breaks me.

"Stop," I hiss. "I am not a thing to be controlled. Take them off."

"Return to Kaldari with me and I will," the king says, stepping toward me, hand outstretched. "I'll forgive you for leaving if you only come back to me."

Incredulous, I stare at him. "You'll... forgive *me*?"

Not-Roshan stills and his eyelids flutter. It's as though a switch is flicked. The violet filaments in his eyes bleed away, leaving them clear. "Please, Sura, I'm begging you, do this for me," he says quietly, his voice shifting back to the warm cadence I know. "I love you. I've always loved you. Come home. *Please.*"

Darrius bristles at the declaration, and jealous umbrage echoes down our fragile bond. I spare a glance at him over my shoulder and notice that his irises are still gold bright. From his bloodless clenched fists, it looks like he's only holding on by a thread.

Stay with me, Dare.

I turn back to the Oryndhrian king. "No, Your Majesty, you are enamored with the *idea* of me. You love the Starkeeper. The weapon that can give you what you want: total dominion. I can't go back to being used as a tool of destruction. I won't."

In the blink of an eye, his gaze swirls with purple mist again, and I silently mourn the loss, the glimpse of the man I saw. Before I can move, he lunges forward and snatches hold of my hand. Darrius lets out a roar, and within seconds, his power obliterates all light, vicious ribbons of darkness ready to flay the Oryndhrian king alive. His shadows rip him away from me, tossing him into the air, and re-form like a pernicious mass hovering over him where he falls.

"Darrius, no!" I shout. "Regicide will start a war."

"He did this to you," he rasps hoarsely, as if he can barely speak.

Despite the gravity of the situation, I feel a tingle of warmth at his devotion, both his and the beast seething beneath his skin. "You can't murder everyone who hurts me, Dare."

Those eyes blaze a blinding gold. "Watch me."

"Everlea is not prepared for war, not when the Aspačanā are divided and your court is in chaos. Who knows what kind of trouble Masišta will stir up? You need to be smart, not rash." I turn to run my palm over his cheek, mindless of the dried blood caking his skin. "We both know where that leads. Your people need you." My voice lowers. "*I* need you."

Laleh skulks over to her furious king, who has leaped to his feet. I shudder at his eyes, now dark purple and furious. His men point their jādū-infused weapons at us. They might not have akasha, but those blades and bows can do tremendous damage. Without my magic and with Aran's control over my bracers, I'm exposed, and Darrius's curse is on the cusp of taking him.

We need to be sensible. Prudent.

"My lord, did I forget to mention that your archrival is the little Starkeeper's soul-fated?" Laleh's sweet tone sets my teeth on edge.

"But never fear, she's still undecided, and soul bonds can be broken with the right touch. The oracle told me—Fero can see to that."

"I'll never choose you or your fucking god," I say to the purple-eyed Not-Roshan.

"You stupid girl," he says with a dark laugh, and I recoil at the vitriol in his tone. Not-Roshan's evil laughter continues, and my chest aches. Is any of my prince in there? Is he lost for good? "The nightmare king wants you for the same reason I do. For *power*. But you're too enraptured by your precious bond to see it."

I smile without humor. "That's where you're wrong. He never wanted this." My jaw clenches. "He didn't tie me to him with false pretenses and false declarations, only to use me as a weapon for his personal ambitions. He has *never* used me."

That oily, violet-hued rot slithers in Not-Roshan's eyes, his voice growing thicker and deeper. His features sharpen, healthy flesh going sunken, as *something* wholly malevolent takes over. "You belong in Oryndhr at my side. As my queen and future vessel." His smile grows cruel teeth. "Or Aran will command those pretty cuffs to drain you until there's nothing left, and then I will torture you until you beg me to die." He slides his virulent gaze to Darrius. "And when my wayward progeny inevitably falls to his curse, then I will take Everlea and raze it to the ground. You can save the fate of thousands or be selfish and condemn them to the fate of the realm of Rothdar."

But my brain is stuck on one thing: *His* progeny? What does he mean?

"You can't bypass my wards," Darrius grinds through his teeth.

"How do you think we got here?" he says. "You have many enemies, boy. The wards protecting your little kingdom are the least of my concerns, not when they will be dismantled from within at my command."

"You dare threaten me in my own kingdom?" Darrius replies.

"Give me back what is mine!" Not-Roshan roars.

Darrius's magic bursts out of him in a violent eruption of shadows, his hold on his temper precarious. "She belongs to no one but herself."

Those words strengthen me.

"So be it." Not-Roshan flicks a hand, and I see Aran start to chant with a look of horrified shame, but as in the past, he doesn't do anything to fight whatever iniquitous hold his king has on him.

The runes on my cuffs brighten again and an eruption of agony drives me to the ground. My entire body feels like it's on fire as if my own magic is boiling me alive. My simurgh screams and screams as we're torn apart by an unseen force, and then we start to weaken, our magic being stripped like swatches of skin. Gods, I'm fucking dying. Whimpering, I tear at the bracers until blood pools across my skin, but nothing stops the onslaught. Dimly, I hear Darrius roaring my name before crashing down beside me.

"Had enough?" Not-Roshan taunts.

Shuddering, eyes wet with tears, I spit a mouthful of blood. "Fuck you."

"I suppose not then," he says, and searing pain crashes through me anew. "Aran, a portal, if you please."

"Your Majesty, we can't leave her like this," he grits out, staring helplessly at my contorted, crumpled form. "This is wrong."

"She made her choice. Don't worry, the defiant little star won't die. She'll wish she did, however."

Darrius cradles my face, tears running down his own cheeks and cutting paths through the dried blood there. This proud, impervious king is weeping because of my pain . . . because he can't take it away or fight these demons for me. His eyes are brilliant gold, his features sharpening with every second, and I know I'm about to lose him to the curse.

"Stay. With me. Dare," I sob brokenly. "Please . . ."

"Starbright, remember what Ve said," he whispers urgently, pressing his forehead to mine as I convulse uncontrollably. Sweet darkness flickers across my consciousness; I would welcome it. "You are both lock and key. You're the only one who can break these chains. I'd give my life to take the pain for you, but I cannot." He kisses me, his lips on mine, but I can barely feel them. "Please, Starbright, you must fight."

Darrius's beautiful voice fills me inside. *Pain is the greatest teacher in life; it is both a seed of courage and the root of strength. Without pain, there's no evolution, just like without darkness, there is no light. We are but a vessel. Fight and be reborn, pátnī.*

I can barely think through the torment saturating my senses, but the word—*that word*—filled with so much hope infuses me with a strength I didn't know I possessed. The bond between us pulses, and wondrously, I feel a surge of *vitality* as his magic bolsters mine. I dig deep into the wellspring of akasha in my blood to the core of my starlight power.

To my *soul*.

Swallowing my sobs of agony, I sink into the spell eating away at my essence and embrace it. I let the blistering paroxysm spread into every molecule, because from the ashes, my faithful simurgh and I can only rise. The pain is debilitating, but I was born to burn, and my own flames can never immolate me.

The runes on my arms erupt, my aura so blindingly bright that I have to close my eyes, and then *finally*, I feel my simurgh emerge from the embers like a drizzle of stardust kissing my skin. She lets out a war cry from our lips that makes everyone clap their hands over their ears.

Delving inward, I target the corrosion woven into the bracers like small lesions in the starlight of my magic, and I heal each of them one by one, purging the rot from within. These cuffs were created by *my* magic—corrupted, twisted magic used to overpower and oppress me—but it's still mine. I am the key.

Open.

The cuffs release, falling to the ground, and I collapse.

If I wasn't staring at the king of Oryndhr right at that minute, I would have missed it—a look of utter awe, so filled with love, pride, and heartbreak that it's like a punch to the gut. Unconsciously, I reach a hand out, a spiral of starlight ghosting over him.

I never wanted to hurt you, my starling.

My magic brightens, amplifying his thoughts. *Roshan?*

It's too late for me. Save them. Save everyone. You're the fiercest woman I know.

A sob wells in my throat. *Ro, are you with me?*

I'm always with you, Sura.

Clutching his head, my former love snarls like an animal, a grotesque undulation beneath his skin making his spine snap straight and his eyes bleed to a putrid mauve and then go frighteningly vacant. And suddenly, we are in the presence of something so evil that the stench of decay spreads everywhere. A dark purple film descends over his irises and spidery tendrils of rot branch over his cheekbones. He looks like something born of the abyss.

A monstrous, inhuman creature.

The entity that has taken over the king of Oryndhr hisses like a serpent as Aran hastily conjures a portal behind them. One by one, they disappear, but right before he enters, the god-king pauses, his voice like knives against the senses. "I'll see you soon, son, and next time, this realm will be mine."

"Son?" I mumble, wondering whom he's talking to.

His mouth curls into a gruesome rictus. "Oh, little Starkeeper. How much he has kept from you. Your precious fated is the heir of death himself."

Part III

Hopelessness is not without hope; the dawn always comes, even at the cusp of a starless night.

—Everlean proverb

Chapter Twenty-Nine

Darrius Nightsong is the son of the god of death.

Two truths that I know unequivocally now: One, he *is* my soul-fated. I can fully feel him, since the cuffs are gone. And two, he is a starsdamned deity, a fact that I cannot seem to come to terms with, no matter how hard I try. Not just because his father is a colossal prick, but because he's part fucking *god*.

"Fero is your father," I say to Ani for the dozenth time.

"I don't understand why this is such a point of obsession for you," she says, tugging on the ends of her hair in frustration and flushing with discomfort. "You're not exactly mortal, either."

I stare at her and scowl. "I can still die!"

"So can we."

"Why didn't you ever tell me that you're a baby-god, too? I thought we were friends."

She stares, and I lift my brows before she sighs again and capitulates. "We *are* friends, and I didn't tell you because who wants to publicly announce to the first person they actually like being around that their father is a merciless, sociopathic deity? And baby-gods are not a thing." She stabs at the open volumes in front of me with a finger—one on runes and one on the history of magic across the realms. "Happy? Now study."

Somewhat mollified, I direct my attention to the books, but I can't concentrate on the words. I can't help the gnawing hole of dread in the pit of my stomach. The resurgence of Fero and the perverted abominations he has made of Laleh and Roshan also weigh heavily upon me. We're not on the verge of a war between realms—we're on the verge of a war for life as we know it.

Again. Only this time, he already has an anchor.

Frowning, I chew my lip, my thoughts drifting to the king of Oryndhr. In the moments when I'd seen the *true* Roshan, I had sensed him in there, buried under the rot that is Fero. Is there a chance to save him before he's lost forever?

And the question that haunts me: How long has he been under Fero's influence? I think back to the moments when he'd been distant and callous, those purple flickers of flame the only sign that he'd become an ancient god's puppet. I think of how cruelly he'd betrayed me, forcing my own magic against me, and my heart feels like it's fracturing in my chest.

Because I *know* it wasn't him.

It was never him, which somehow makes everything better and worse at the same time. I'd seen glimpses of him—a gentle stare, a softened smile, those brown eyes that saw right to the heart of me—like sunlight through a stormy sky.

Gods, could I have done *more*? Seen signs of it earlier? Helped him somehow? Had I failed him before he failed me?

My throat feels tight as helpless emotions barrel through me. The thoughts are gutting, a marrow-deep sense of grief swirling through me at everything we'd built and lost through no fault of our own.

I never wanted to hurt you, my starling.

I'm always with you, Sura.

I don't realize I'm crying until I feel the wetness on my cheek. Hurriedly, I swipe it away before Ani can see it. I don't want her pity—she won't understand. I can feel my magic rising to comfort me, my simurgh's presence like a soothing balm to my jagged-edged sorrow. Without the bracers, I can feel her presence fully. I hadn't realized how suppressed and subdued she had become.

Frowning, I rub my bare wrists together. It's a relief to finally have the cuffs off, but at the same time, I'm also fearful that my magic will do something I can't control. It's like relearning to use an injured limb when you've taught yourself to exist without it. Everything is thrown out of balance in a terrifying way.

That's the reason Ani and I are starting slow with the most basic runes. My magic feels like an enormous reservoir inside of me, with my reborn, formidable simurgh waiting for the chance to flex her wings. I sense her more keenly now, like she's a true extension of my consciousness—part of me as she's always been, but also her own wholly sentient self. It's as though we've evolved into some ascendant version of ourselves.

What's more frightening, however, is just how much power we have . . . and the fact that my magic level—one known as sidereal—is above sovran, above the king himself, who is the only recorded sovran magi in Everlea. Though he's not technically a *magi* . . .

Secret starsdamned deities.

He, too, had been closemouthed about Fero. It's clear there's no love lost between his father and him, but I'm hopeful that when he returns from his palaver with the Aspačanā, he will be more willing to open up. He has been gone for the past week to manage the growing tensions after exposing Masišta's treachery. And there's still the matter of the traitor behind the theft of the azdaha eggs and the arrangement with the Aspačanā: the *oracle,* whom, now that I have my memories back, I remember as the mastermind of treachery in Oryndhr as well.

I glance up. "Ani?"

Her pencil stops scratching across the parchment. She's engrossed in translating yet another book from a language I don't recognize. "If it's not about history or practical magic, I don't want to hear it. And there's no such thing as baby-gods. Let it go."

I snort at her deadpan expression. "It *is* practical. Technically," I say, and she waves a hand for me to continue. "If a person was . . . contaminated . . . by a dark spirit, could it be expelled? Or is that person lost for good?"

"Is this about Laleh?" she asks, blue eyes sharpening. It's not, but I'm interested in what she has to say, so I nod. "Necromancy is powered by corpus magic and a blood enchantment. If the magic is removed, then her mortal body would decay." Her brow wrinkles when I flinch at the bluntness of her delivery. "Does that answer your question?"

"I suppose. I just can't get my mind around how real she seemed." I could see how people who had lost loved ones might be attracted by the idea of keeping them, but they're not who they were. "It was Fero's doing, I gather," I whisper, and wrap my arms around my middle.

"Or a powerful corpus magi." Ani tilts her head. "As Starkeeper, *you* could."

"I could never do anything like that."

She nods. "Good. Because the cost of sanguimancy is a little bit of your soul each time. It's like a drug: the more you use it, the more dependent you become on it." She purses her lips, looking perturbed. "We only have a few registered dominant corpus magi. It could have been any one of them. Necromancy takes a lot of power and skill."

"How do you just know all this?"

She rolls her eyes. "I like to read. So should you."

Oh, right. I stare sightlessly at the text in front of me. I make it a handful of minutes before I push back in my chair and clear my throat, earning myself a belabored groan from her.

"What now, for the love of Zora?"

"Could someone be saved if they've been taken over by the remnant of a god?"

"You're referring to the Oryndhrian king, I presume?" Ani asks, and when I nod, she frowns. "Why do you care? He's the one who bound you and tried to use your magic as a weapon. You should be happy that he's suffering."

I gape at her. "I don't think I can be happy that *anyone's* suffering, especially someone who didn't consent to be used. Yes, he's made mistakes and I've been hurt in the process, but he wouldn't do that if he wasn't coerced."

"How do you know?" Ani asks curiously. "People do unspeakable things for power."

I understand that more than anyone, and I would stake my life on the fact that the man I once loved—*might still love*—would never damn his people to an eternity of servitude and horror. "I just do. The Roshan I know would never welcome that. He fought against the crown for his people for years in hiding and . . . he died to save me. He's still there. I can feel it."

Ani's gaze is sharp, her eyes flicking away and then back to me, a blush forming on her cheeks. "Do you still love him? The king of Oryndhr?"

My breath shudders to a stop, that raw, unhealed wound tearing open again. It wouldn't hurt so much if I didn't still care. "I don't know," I say slowly.

"You don't know if you have feelings for him?" my friend prods.

I lick dry lips. "I . . . Maybe. It's not that simple."

The clatter of a helm falling onto the marble makes me swing around. Darrius is standing there, the fleeting look of hurt on his face making my stomach swoop. *Stars*. Did he overhear me? I push out of the chair and glare at Ani, who could have easily warned me he was there.

"Darrius," I say, trying to read his inscrutable expression. "You're back."

"Yes." His beautiful face is tired, with dark shadows under his eyes, and he smells of horses and leather like he hasn't had a proper bath in days, but the bond doesn't care. Light travels down my arms in stardust spirals to mingle with his shadows. As always, I feel a sense of awe seeing my natural magic in action. The cuffs had smothered so much. He watches their dance with a certain dispassion, as if oddly resentful that our magic is happy to see each other.

"How are the clans?" I ask.

"Chaotic."

I bend down to grab the fallen helm. "Any news on Masišta?"

"No."

"Is there a new rais?"

"Zahre."

His one-word answers grate. I glance over my shoulder, but Ani has made herself scarce. "Are you angry with me? If it's what you overheard before, I'm very confused about a lot of things since I got my memories and magic back. But my residual feelings for Roshan, even if they are real, have nothing to do with you and me."

His throat works. "Don't they?"

"Darrius," I say, placing a hand on his armored chest. "We are soul-fated. Our path is written in the stars."

He clenches his jaw. "We are still unbonded."

"Because I'm not ready." I try not to let my fear bleed through my frustration. "And you said it yourself—you're not ready, either. You just won't tell me why. War is coming whether we want it or not, and we both need to figure this"—I flick a hand between our bodies—"out before that happens."

"Whose side are you on, Suraya?" My heart flinches at the use of my name. It feels unfamiliar and wrong somehow, as if we are strangers.

"How can you ask me that? I'm here, am I not?"

His eyes grow hard. "How do I know you won't betray us to go back to him? What if your *confusing* feelings end up costing us everything?"

"That's not fair." I grit my teeth. "What if you decide that Zahre is the alliance you want after all? I don't fault you for having been with her. Am I jealous? Yes, of course I am, but that's a natural emotion. You've just spent so much of your life suppressing what it means to actually feel that you don't even know what's normal."

The king moves toward me, and instinctively, I move back. My breath tightens as he stalks me, and I match him step for step. I don't even realize I'm being herded into a small room with a circular table until he lifts a hand and his shadows slam the door shut.

"Do you know why that is?" he asks silkily.

I gulp. "Why what is?"

"Why I don't allow myself to feel?"

I blink at him, wary of the menace and slightly unhinged gleam in his eyes. That and the fact that he is slowly undoing his sword belt, letting it fall to the floor. Then go his epaulets. I'm torn between looking for an escape route and gazing hungrily at him as each piece of armor is detached. "Yes, you told me, it's your curse. You become the manticore."

The backs of my thighs hit the table as he closes the last of the distance, removing his crown and setting it on the polished surface. Darrius cages me between his arms, his rich scent musky and deepened but no less seductive. My entire body quivers as I brace my weight on the wood.

"Yes, love. I was cursed. And I have my father to thank for that," he says, winding a hand deftly into my hair. When his fingers catch on a knot, I let out an involuntary moan at the tiny bite of pain. His bottomless gaze is so inky that I can drown in it, the menace eclipsed by desire, but I can see the jealousy crowding the edges of it.

"H-he did?" Somehow, I'm not surprised to know it was Fero; the brutality tracks.

Darrius's fist tightens, yanking my head back, and he runs his nose up the column of my throat. "Yes. That was my punishment for betraying him, you see, for helping my uncle, Saru, in the War of the Gods. I helped banish my own sire to the void where he languished in his own rot for centuries. As a parting gift, he returned the favor. If I feel any emotion—sadness, anger, joy, bliss, lust—the beast would take over. And if I ever found my soul-fated, I could never *love* her, or the manticore would be my immutable future, forever damning us both."

I gasp when he sucks on my pulse hard enough to leave a mark. Shock at his words combines with lust at the movement of his wicked mouth, and I have trouble concentrating. "Are . . . aren't soul-fated bonds sacred? How could he do that?"

"Father of the century, isn't he?" Darrius mocks. "Technically, he didn't touch the bond. You see, he wanted to make sure I could never fall in love or I would become the beast forever, and you would be mated to a monster who would never be a man. Our bond would die. He didn't want me to unite our magic because it would make me stronger than him. Together, my soul-fated and I would be unstoppable." He rears back, a muscle beating in his cheek. He spins away from me with a noise of disgust, and I grip the edge of the table weakly. "Cruel, isn't it?" He laughs, but it's an empty sound.

I stare at him. "How do you know that loving me means you would become the manticore indefinitely?"

He glances over a shoulder at me, despair in his expression. "Each time, my transformation to the beast has been longer. I lose myself a little more. When you were with *him,* I shifted for weeks, lost to blood and hunger and madness."

Oh, sands. He means when I was with Roshan . . . intimately.

My face heats. Stars above, had he felt me bedding another man through the bond? I frown and think back to my first time in the aqueduct and the strange feelings I'd had reverberating through me, ones of hurt and displeasure. "You could feel . . . me?" I whisper.

His big frame shudders. "Always. But you chose him, and I could no more take that from you than I could stake my own claim. I would never condemn you to a future with a monster."

"That's also *my* choice to make," I say softly. "I happen to have a soft spot for that monster, you know."

My attempt at levity dies when he doesn't react, and I lift a hand to his heaving shoulder. He whirls, driving me backward, and wraps his large palm about my throat. Sands, it should be wrong, but I love when he collars me like this, when he stares at me like he can't get enough and I'm the only thing he needs to exist. "Didn't you hear a word I said? I won't condemn you to this. That's why I wanted to reject the bond."

"We don't know that will happen, Dare. Maybe the answer to the curse *is* the bond." I reach up to cup his face. "I have my magic back. We could try."

Hope flickers for the barest moment before it disappears. "No, I can't risk you. And I can't risk abandoning Everlea without a king with war on the horizon." He releases me so suddenly that I slump back. Anguish twists his features. "Gods, I'm sorry. I should take my leave. I've spent days with the Aspačanā, weeding out Karkad's treachery and the rot in my own court, and all I wanted to do was come back here . . . to you." He swipes angrily at his face. "Only to hear you say you love another."

"Loved," I reply softly. "Yes, I loved him. But you cannot fault me for that, Dare, for not knowing we were soul-fated. You had other lovers, too."

"That was sex, nothing more."

Jealousy and desire punch through me. "And the beast didn't take over?" When he shakes his head, resolve fills me. "Then have me like you did her. Without emotion."

"Suraya," he whispers.

"Will sex seal the bond?"

"Not entirely. There's a ritual." His lips part, pupils dilating with lust. "Is this what you want?"

"If we can't beat the curse, I think you need to practice your control with the manticore. You said it yourself: It's different now. With him. And he likes me."

"What if it doesn't work?"

"Last time, you connected with him and he ceded control to you. Don't push him away," I say, blushing wildly at the thought of our previous encounter. "He's part of you."

Holding his gaze, I reach for the straps of my dress and unfasten them, letting the soft fabric pool to the floor until I'm standing only in my undergarments. He lets out a groan, his shadows flickering about him, as I kick off my slippers and reach down to step out of my undergarments. I've never been much of an exhibitionist, but the idea of standing like this, *bare,* in front of him only makes me hotter.

"Fuck, Starbright. I'm covered in sweat, and you're perfect. I cannot . . ."

Gods, I love when he calls me that name.

"You can. I need you exactly like this." I lift my brows and point to his clothing, the rich, earthy scent of him doing maddening things to me. "Your turn."

He reaches for his belt and then stalls. "You don't know what you're asking for. I won't be gentle. I don't know how to be."

"I want you as you are." I walk toward him and put my hand over his, undoing his buckle and then the laces of his trousers. I'm unprepared for the size of his cock when it springs free at full attention. I've only ever seen one of these before, and while they are comparable in length, his is curved and thicker than I'm used to. A bead of fluid forms at the tip, and I bend to lick it off, moaning in my throat at the salty-sweet tang of him.

"Fuck," Darrius groans as I envelop the silky head with my lips. I fist him at the base and take him as far back in my mouth as I can. But when I glance up and his eyes roll back in his head, I suppose I'm doing something right. "Enough," he says, dragging me up to take my lips in a brutal kiss.

His tongue explores every inch of my mouth as he walks us back to the table, his erect cock pressed wickedly against my stomach. Stars, I'm so wet I can feel my arousal leaking down my inner thighs. He grips my chin, face harsh with tension. For a second, his eyes flash gold, and I wonder if we're making an irreversible mistake.

But every instinct inside of me says that we're not.

"Last chance, Starbright. Are you certain?"

I smirk up at him, reaching down and making him hiss when I stroke him. "You've done this before as a dreamwalker. Let's see if the real thing can match up." When he doesn't move, I squeeze hard. "Now fuck me like the god you are."

Stars, the *hunger* in his eyes is almost too much to take. His gaze fucking immolates.

He kisses me hard and turns me roughly, hand to my spine and pressing me down to the table. He spreads my legs and runs a palm over the plump curve of my ass. "Gods, look at you. You're fucking gorgeous like this."

I feel his fingers slip through my folds and hear his grunt of approval at the wetness he finds there before angling himself into place. And then he thrusts into me to the hilt. Even though I'm drenched, it's by no means an easy fit, the burn of the stretch making me gasp and shoving me to my tiptoes. His cock feels like it's splitting me in half, but I want this. I want to *feel* every inch of him. "Darrius..."

"Fuck, you were made for me. Let me in."

I quiver around him. He *isn't* in?

With a whimper, I wriggle back, wincing at the sublime stretch as another inch penetrates me. The king withdraws slightly, making me gasp, and then shoves in hard, bottoming out. Pinned beneath him, I'm so fucking full that I can barely breathe. I swear I can feel his cock in my throat.

"*Gods* . . ." he groans.

"Move, please," I beg, once my body adjusts, my walls fluttering around him.

I don't even have time to brace before he starts fucking me ruthlessly, fist at my hip and one in my hair—the sweet bite of pain knotting with ratcheting pleasure. His thick cock drags out and shuttles back in, slamming harder each time. And I desperately want more of that delicious friction. Whimpering, I match him stroke for stroke, hips bearing back relentlessly, *savagely,* like we're distilled down to the most basic versions of ourselves.

And by the maker, I want him fucking unhinged.

His shadows collar my throat and twine over my heavy breasts, pulling cruelly at my nipples before dragging both my wrists behind my back. I should hate being bound and used like this, but I love it. I love the feel of him, the crash of his thighs against my ass, his ragged breaths and desperate strokes as if he wants to burrow inside me forever. This isn't lovemaking—it's a brutal conquest of heat, light, fury, and shadow.

I've never been taken like this: all-consuming, raw, real, and everything I didn't know I needed. It's angry and primal, our magic spiraling and coiling, the bond between us snapping tight.

At times, I can almost feel what *he's* feeling, along with the immense hold he has over his emotions. And although there's a part of me that wants him to break and give himself over to me entirely, it will be at a cost that neither of us is prepared to pay.

"Dare, I need to come," I whimper as he impossibly speeds up, the erotic slapping of skin and our feral grunts of pleasure the only sounds in the room.

"Good," he snarls. "Give me all of you, Starbright."

His shadows snake between us, reaching my clit and vibrating against it. The pleasure builds to a crescendo and I'm screaming as my soul shatters into a million pieces, every single rune on my body lighting up and blasting outward in a brilliant detonation of light. As I convulse mindlessly around him, the orgasm prolonged by his merciless vibrating shadow magic, Dare's thrusts become erratic.

His palms slam down on the table on either side of me, razor-sharp claws sprouting from their tips and splintering through the wood. For a moment, his cock grows impossibly thicker inside of me before he withdraws—making me tumble into a second bone-shaking orgasm—and buries himself one final time before he comes with an unearthly roar. Pulse after pulse of his hot spend fills me, and I swear to the fucking stars, my orgasm goes on forever.

Darrius collapses over me, my body still quivering with violent aftershocks. But it isn't long before he pushes up, taking me with him, his shadows turning me helpfully so that he can take my lips in a tender kiss that makes my toes curl.

"Gods," he rasps eventually, lips ghosting over my jawline. "Are you well?"

Forming words takes actual effort. "Define 'well.'"

"Did I hurt you?"

"Far from it," I say, catching the tinge of worry in his tone. "Except for obliterating my brain, that is."

He chuckles and kisses me again. When we part, his irises gleam with the gold of his manticore. I glance over my shoulder at the deep claw marks marring the table's surface, and stroke his cheekbone with a fingertip.

"You didn't change fully."

"It was close," he admits.

Elated, I grin at him. "Then I suppose we simply need more practice." I feel our combined fluids drip out of me and my cheeks heat. "Stars, I need a bath."

Eyes glowing brighter, he nuzzles my neck with a soft rumble and holds me tighter. "The manticore likes you like this. Dripping in our seed."

At his words, a thought about contraception that I probably should have had much earlier occurs suddenly to me. I haven't renewed my annual inoculation, which would have been due about eight months after I received Javed's invitation. With everything that had happened, I hadn't given it any thought. Until now.

"Dare, you came inside. I can't . . . We can't . . . Stars, will I . . ."

"Don't worry," he says. "You won't." When I stare quizzically at him, he smiles. "God power."

I laugh, somewhat relieved, though also strangely disheartened, an emotion I have no desire to dissect. "That's handy. I suppose you don't want mini-baby-god despots running about."

He rears back in mock affront, a playful, unguarded grin on his face that stops me in my tracks. Stars, seeing him like this should be illegal. His shadow magic swirls to hoist me up, banding my arms behind my back and winding my legs around his waist like I'm nothing but a toy for him to play with. I blush at the lewd position, feeling his length rub against me. "Darrius . . ."

"You think me a tyrant?" he says.

I moan. "No?"

"You sound unsure, pátnī." His shadows swipe through my soaked folds, spreading me wide. I gasp as they dip inside, the wicked tendrils scissoring like a pair of fingers. I'm sore, but it feels too good to stop. "Should I teach this pretty little cunt a lesson?"

By the maker, he's so filthy. Pleasure ramping, I writhe shamelessly on him, moaning every time the crown of his cock hits my clit and his magic strokes a spot deep inside. "Still not your wife," I say, unsure why I'm protesting the endearment, other than to be contrary and to provoke him.

The denial works. His eyes glitter with vengeful promise as he notches his tip at my bruised entrance. "I have your soul and your body. I will conquer what's left until every part of you is irrevocably mine," he vows possessively. Then he sinks into me, snatching whatever useless reply I was about to make from my lips.

I'll make you forget him. The ferocious thought fades almost immediately, but I catch the jealous viciousness of it.

And then my god of night proceeds to absolutely ruin me.

Chapter Thirty

Smiling to myself, I dress in supple leathers and an armored vest, and wince at the delicious soreness between my thighs. Though I could have easily healed myself with magic, I want to feel him for as long as I can. Given his size, it's no surprise I still do. I have no illusions that what we've done repeatedly for the past week has strengthened our bond.

Though it still isn't complete, I can feel it, stretching like a magical tether between us. If I follow it with my magic, I sense the king in the war room with his council, strategizing on the wards and the defenses in place for the people of Everlea.

You need me, Starbright?

I blush at the caress in his mental voice. *No. I'm just about to head for my training with Karânî.*

Remember to keep your elbow high, he says. *And trust your magic.*
I will.

After eating a quick breakfast of a pastry filled with sweetened almond paste, I make my way down to the training fields. But I falter when I see a familiar, gorgeous redhead standing with Karânî.

"What is she doing here?" I ask, keeping my simmering feelings at bay. Darrius might trust that Zahre had nothing to do with her father's schemes, but I don't. I have more than enough experience dealing with ambitious women in a royal court. Though Zahre is not Helena, the similarities are too obvious to ignore.

Karânî spreads her hands. "Zahre is a much better fighter than I am in close combat with a dagger, which is your weapon of choice, so you will spar with her after our ride. Then you will fight both of us because war is unpredictable and you may have to face multiple enemies at once."

I narrow my eyes. "Did you clear this with the king?"

The tall blonde cants her head. "Of course. However, he said it would be up to you."

Frowning, I glance over at Zahre, loathing how confident, fit, and beautiful she looks, and absolutely reviling the knowledge that she has been the recipient of Dare's considerable skills in bed. But as I told him several nights ago, neither of us can be blamed for having a past.

In fact, while I scour the library in my scant free time for books on how to perform a magical expulsion without killing someone, Darrius has been the one to point me in the right direction. So he's trying. I want to be the bigger person, too.

"Very well," I say.

Nuadar arrives, leading a very large, unfamiliar horse toward us. The beastmaster hasn't warmed up to me—in fact, he even seems more antagonistic than ever. I eye the stallion just as warily when he flares his nostrils and paws the dirt. He's much bigger than the mare I've been learning on. "That is the king's warhorse," I tell him. "You have the wrong mount."

"I also requested a larger horse," Karânî informs me. "As the chosen rider of an azdaha, a small horse will not give you the correct practice or proficiency. And since we are not sky riders, the biggest horse we have will have to do."

"Stars, we're full of changes today, I see," I mutter.

I use magic to boost myself up into the saddle, feeling the massive beast prance beneath me. Karânî and Zahre mount their equally large warhorses with their intricate tack and bridles, holding themselves like they'd been born in the saddle. *They probably have*, I think sourly, and automatically loosen my stiff posture to mimic theirs.

"Stay relaxed, remember to let your hips swing and absorb his movement," Karânî reminds me, and I can't help my blush at the recollection of other rather indecent lessons. I exhale and clear my mind when she stares at me. "Keep your spine loose, chest open, and body upright."

We walk slowly at first so I can get used to the size and the gait of the horse. He's nothing like riding on Razulek, of course, but he's a well-trained animal, and my nerves soon settle at being so high off the ground. Besides, if I fall, now I have my magic to catch me.

Zahre nudges her mount closer to mine and clears her throat. "I want you to know how sorry I am for my father's actions," she says, surprising me. "They were unforgivable. As raissa, I hope to earn back your trust."

I nod. "Thank you."

"I know you may not believe me, but I did not know that the king had a soul-fated," she says quickly. "I would not have entertained a union otherwise. Soul-fated pairs are rare, even among the Aspačanā, blessed by the goddess, and are cherished."

"Thank you for telling me," I say to Zahre. "And I appreciate you offering to help train me."

"You're welcome." She smiles, a dimple glinting in her fierce face. "But you might not be thanking me later. I do not plan to go easy on you."

I grin back. "I hope you don't."

Karânî signals for us to move into a trot and then a canter, which I do with more ease than I expected, until we transition to a full-on gallop. The power beneath me is unbelievable. I hadn't realized just how much Karânî had been holding back her own horse while we'd been practicing with my smaller mare, because now we are flying across the meadow.

Exhilarated, I watch as she unhooks her feet from the stirrups to crouch atop the saddle before firing her bow toward a marked tree. Zahre does the same with as much finesse. I can't stand like they do, but I rise up and clench my thighs tight around the stallion's flanks. Focusing my magic, I grab my bow and nock an arrow. I remember to keep my elbow up, and just as we pass the target, I release, watching as it goes wide when my balance is jostled.

There's no time to wallow, however, as we come up to the next set of targets. Doing the same will be a hundred times harder on Razulek up in the sky. I keep calm and concentrate on making a clean slate with each new shot. I miss some and I hit others. By the time we come back to a stop at the training grounds, I'm breathless and high from adrenaline.

"You did well," Karânî says, "for your first time on that horse. Six out of ten targets."

"Not bad," Zahre congratulates me as she dismounts. "You eliminated six enemies. Pretend that your magic is nearing depletion. Let's see how good you are with a dagger."

Considering I've come close to being depleted twice—once with Roshan when he'd nearly died and then when I'd healed Razulek—I nod. Although my power feels like a bottomless well lately, both Ani and Darrius insist that akasha has to be replenished, especially if a magi uses too much. I need to be better at identifying when I'm nearing that point.

I pull my dagger from my sheath and meet Zahre in the ring. Some of the king's men gather to watch, and I feel my nerves take hold at the attention. "Don't focus on them," Zahre says. "Eyes on me."

She attacks first with a quick swipe toward my torso that I dodge.

I suspect that was merely a test of my reflexes, because the next one comes much faster. I spin out of the way, going for my own offense with a lunge and a thrust. She dodges me easily and then parries with a swift shuffle and spin combination that has me misjudging where her body will go. My balance wavers. I take precious seconds to reacquaint myself, time I'm well aware she could have used for a fatal strike.

Zahre moves like a dancer, similarities in her footwork, fluidity, and dexterity. I wonder if she'd looked so graceful when she danced with Darrius. The brief loss of focus costs me as a punch catches me in the stomach, and I gasp when her blade whines across my chest plate and nicks my arm.

"Shit!"

She lifts her brows. "You were distracted."

"I was thinking about how well you move," I say. "Like dancing."

Zahre slows down her footwork. "You have a good eye. Most fighters watch the feet and the hips to determine movement, so my style of fighting confuses them. My hips sway this way, and you automatically think that's where I'm going, but my center of gravity is a misdirection." She shakes her head with a smirk. "What you should watch are the knees."

I mimic her steps and feel like a fool when a wolf whistle from one of our spectators cuts through the air. A storm of shadows bears down out of nowhere and tosses the man into a pond, and I feel a bolt of possessiveness seething down the bond. I roll my eyes when Darrius materializes at the far end of the ring and the crowd instantly dissipates.

Jealous much?

He scowls. *I should cut out their eyes and feed them to Indira for even looking at you.*

You're so violent, my king.

Pleasure rumbles down the bond. *Call me that again.*

I turn and wink at him, being intentionally perverse. *Violent.*

"The king is here," Zahre remarks, interrupting our silent exchange. "Do you want to give him a demonstration?"

I balk. "Now?"

She grins a bit maniacally and waves over Karânî, who also enters the ring, her short sword in hand.

Bronze earth magic lights Karânî's blade while frost shines over Zahre's dagger. With excitement filling me, I glance down at the runes near the hilt of my dagger and call for my starlight. It whooshes down the steel in a glimmer of iridescence. I let my magic fill me and then fly into motion.

I lunge and parry, slice and thrust, catching my blade to each of theirs in showers of sparks and magic. I dodge the magical attacks, leaping out of the way when a fissure forms in the ground and attempts to swallow me, and evading a stream of ice that shoots from Zahre's direction. I respond with strikes of my own, coils of glowing starlight whipping out in multiple directions. Toying with them, I yank my foes off their feet and snatch their weapons. I push them off-balance and singe their clothing. Before, without magic, I was at a disadvantage, because Zahre is undoubtedly the better warrior with a blade, but with my magic, I am invincible.

I believe that right until I look down and see the hilt protruding from my chest just before I feel the pain.

Fuck, this is going to ruin my day.

Darrius's roar fills the air as he runs toward me, his shadows disarming everyone within striking range. I frown down at the curious lack of blood, but realize dully that the flesh around the blade is frozen. Shadow magic takes a screaming Zahre to the ground in vicious fury, a hairsbreadth away from ripping the bones from her body.

"Dare, no! It's not her blade." His attack stops, and she limps to retrieve her fallen dagger. I wheeze as my magic dulls the searing edge of the pain, pushing the blade out and healing the wound. "Someone else threw this."

Zahre's voice trembles as she kneels at my side, her nearly identical dagger visible in her palms. "That's my father's blade."

"Masišta," the king seethes, waving a hand at the dozen guards who have come running at his shout. "Find him! Get that snake and bring him to me." He glares at Zahre. "If you had anything to do with this, you will pay in blood."

"I didn't, Your Majesty." She taps the center of her brow. "You may look, I have nothing to hide from either of you."

I watch her carefully, sending out a tendril of my magic—and my nascent psionic abilities—into her mind. If she feels the intrusion, she gives no sign. It's surprisingly easy to sift through her thoughts, and nothing I see points to treachery. Everything she has said she has meant, which warms me considerably.

I searched her thoughts, I tell Darrius via our telepathic connection. *She's telling the truth.*

The look he sends me is one of utter astonishment. *Like her father, Zahre has a talisman that doesn't allow mind magic.*

I shrug, recalling how easy it had been, and flinch slightly. *I saw what I saw.*

I believe you.

THE NEXT FEW days pass in a flurry of preparation, while Darrius works diligently to ferret out the treason in his kingdom. Nearly all the nobles from Pix, Lora, Morien, and Solis have been summoned, given Verac root, and interrogated. In addition, all three of us—Darrius, Ani, and I—have also taken the root and consented to being questioned.

So now we have a handful of insurgents in the prison who were accomplices of Lord Donnan and paying for stolen azdaha eggs, but we have yet to identify a corpus magi powerful enough to perform necromancy who is working against the kingdom. So *who* is the traitor?

Because something *is* coming.

Signs of the rot are growing in Everlea, with more animals becoming feral as the basilisk I killed was, even nonmagical ones like cattle. We're doing everything we can to help, but if the infection spreads, it will become an uncontrollable plague.

Ani bustles into the library, where Darrius and I are scouring the texts for a cure. "Bad news, brother," she says, shoving her hair out of her eyes. She looks frazzled and upset, and is clearly not taking care of herself. Her thin frame is gaunter, her eyes sunken. "The Aspačanā have reported the rot is now spreading in their horses. It's taken hundreds so far."

"But how?" I ask. "Can we test the infected?"

Ani nods tiredly. "I'm working on it."

I remember the dark tendrils that had been on Laleh's skin and frown. "What if Fero is the source of the plague?" I ask. "Darrius, you said before that when you banished him, he languished in rot. His return can't be a coincidence. And somehow, a remnant of him has hooked into Roshan . . . like a parasite." My frown deepens. "Could he be the original source?"

Nodding his head, Darrius studies me. "That is probable. Most pathogens are spread by fluids, bites, or some kind of contact. Could it be vector-borne?" he asks his sister. "Like a sting?"

"Very possible," Ani says. "It could also be transmitted via blood or even a hex."

"What if the rot needs to be intentionally implanted from one host to the next like a seed or spore?" I say, thinking through the scenarios. "Sand tapeworms in Coban hatch in the intestines of hosts, and their eggs are passed on in undercooked meat or fecal matter. It could be similar." I shudder at the thought of the rot gestating inside of a body like larvae. "Or it could be as Ani says, something as simple as blood transfer."

Ani brightens, looking more enthusiastic than when she came in.

"I'll see what I can dig up. I have a few samples that I can test for each of those possible variants for the necrosis."

"Be careful," I tell her, and she nods, already distracted with her plans.

After the princess leaves, I turn to the king. "Are Raz and Indira and their eggs safe? I couldn't bear it if anything happened to them. They're family." When his face tightens as if he's hiding something, my heart free-falls. "*No . . .* not them."

"I just received word from Indira this morning," he says in a low, hard voice. "I wasn't sure how to tell you. It's Razulek. He's been quarantined in a remote cave for the roost's safety."

"Why didn't *he* tell me? How could I not feel it?" I ask, pressing a hand to my chest. But even as I ask the question, I already know. He's done it before to safeguard me from the worst of the pain he endured in Kaldari. A painful sob forms in my chest as I reach out and sense the connection with Raz closed off. "Dare, I have to see him. I know my magic can heal him. He saved my life. I won't let him die."

He nods and gathers me into his arms as I weep all over his chest. "The cave is high in the mountains, and we can't portal to it, as magic there is too unstable. We will have to fly."

"Won't Indira be with her eggs?" I ask.

He pulls back to cup my face in his large hands. "If you wish to see him, you will have to fly on me," he says, eyes flashing gold. "As the manticore. I can't risk taking any other animal too close to Razulek in his condition."

"Dare, what if you . . . can't turn back?"

"That's not how the curse works, thankfully." He tilts my chin up and kisses me. "As you said, he's family. He saved your life, so we owe him our help."

Chapter Thirty-One

We leave the castle library, and Darrius heads down to the enclosure where he's been locked away in the past while I make a quick detour to change out of my dress. I put on a gorgeous pair of black-and-gold leathers that Darrius had made for me, sewn from similar spelled fabric as my feast dress, which should provide a layer of warmth as well as protection. A hidden sheath for my dagger is sewn into the lower back so I can reach for it comfortably with my right hand. Lastly, I braid my hair back so it doesn't get tangled in flight.

I run into Ani on the way out in the courtyard, where she's talking to the head of the kingsguard.

I hurry over to her, and she eyes my gear. "Do you have training?" she asks, curious.

"No, Raz is sick. I'm going to see if there's anything I can do."

"Oh, no, I'm so sorry." Ani wraps her arm around me in an awkward sideways hug that's so *her* it makes me smile. After a moment, she brightens, reaching into a pocket and pulling out a vial of green powder. "This is dragon's bloom. You won't believe who came up with the idea. Nuadar. The man's a genius. It has similar properties to the sedative for my brother's beast."

Frowning, I take the vial. Just because I don't like the beastmaster doesn't mean he's not good at his job. "What does it do?"

"From our initial tests, it acts as a blocker and counteracts infection in close quarters. It might make you sleepy. I don't know that you'll need it, but it might be worth trying. How are you getting there? Portal?"

"Too unstable." I bite my lip. "Dare's taking me."

Her brows draw together. "How . . . *oh*."

"I know," I say softly.

"Sura . . ." Her worry for my safety is evident.

I squeeze her wrist. "I trust him, Ani. He won't let me get hurt."

She nods, but the worry in her eyes doesn't dissipate.

When I get to the paddock, Darrius is pacing back and forth. He looks grim, worry lining his solemn face. "We don't have to do this," I tell him.

"We do. I just don't want any harm to befall you, on my back or being exposed to Razulek."

"You won't, and don't worry," I say, digging into my pocket for the vial. "Ani has been working on a prevention of sorts. She says it should inhibit infection if we have to get close."

"That's good."

I watch as he sheds his outer layers of clothing, my pulse automatically beating quicker as his honed physique is revealed inch by inch. No matter how many times I see him, his utter perfection doesn't fail to take my breath away.

He smirks when he catches me. "See something you like, Starbright?"

"Always."

The unsealed bond between us flares. "Later, when we return," he growls, "I am going to edge you until you scream. Now step back."

Groaning at his wicked promise, I do as he says and watch in awe as he falls to his knees and his body shifts from man to manticore, bones snapping and cracking, fur and wings sprouting, and body quadrupling in mass. Within seconds, the manticore pads toward me, fangs on display and scorpion tail hovering menacingly. He butts my stomach with his huge head, and I run my fingers through his mane.

"Mate." The rumble is almost a purr.

"I've missed you. Are you sure you're up for this?" I ask him, knowing that despite everything, he and Darrius are two separate beings.

"Yes," he growls.

He lowers down onto his massive front paws tipped with razor-sharp talons and then bends a gold-veined carmine wing so that I can climb onto his broad, muscular back. I settle myself on the velvety section behind the base of his mane, hooking my legs under the tendons connecting to his wings for purchase. Without a saddle, I have to use my muscles to stay in place—thank the stars for my training with Karânî on the larger horses. It's not the same as riding on Razulek, either, with his bumpy ridges—the manticore's fur is slippery and soft.

Shifting to get comfortable, I wind my hands in his mane as he takes us outside, and then with a great heave and a beat of his powerful wings, we are airborne. I'm holding him so tightly that I might strangle him, and as we rise quickly into the air, I press my body down onto his, clinging like a spider monkey. It's only after a few minutes that I'm brave enough to sit up and watch the realm of Everlea fly by below.

We veer south from Verisia, and I catch sight of the rolling plains of Rakh and then Chamros, heading toward the huge rise of the Barrin Mountains. From the maps I've seen in the library, Nyriell and Droon are on the other side. Those are also unstable areas for jādū, so it doesn't surprise me that we can't portal there directly. When we had visited the azdahas, a portal was only viable in the lower mountain ranges near Deadman's Canyon for similar reasons.

"This is amazing," I shout out loud, loving the wind blowing into my face and the sun's radiance warming me. I hold my hands wide and close my eyes. The manticore gives a rumble of approval that I feel through my legs, each mighty beat of his wings propelling us forward at impossible speeds. When we begin to descend to the steep side of the highest mountain range, I hold tight again until we're on a ledge on the outside of a small cave.

I smell the same necrosis as the basilisk, even before I dismount.

"Should we take this?" I ask Dare, holding up the vial. "Just in case?"

He sniffs the bottle and bares his teeth. I put a tiny bit of the green powder on my tongue, wincing at the bitter taste, and then scoop a little into the cap for him. The manticore snarls but eventually sticks out his tongue, a whine rumbling from him as he swallows. Then we make our way into the cave. Light engulfs my palms as we press into the shadows.

Razulek is at the very back, curled into a tight ball. He doesn't look good, and the smell oozing from his pores is foul. There's no doubt he's infected, and the closer I get, the more I can see the festering blisters on his hide. Fuck. How long has he been like this? And why hadn't he told me? I barely suppress a sob as I inch closer. A feral beast, even a friend, can be dangerous, especially when in pain. My magic will protect me, but I don't want to hurt him more.

"Raz?" I whisper. "It's Sura."

One eye cracks open and it's covered in a dark purple film. I shift toward him and the manticore growls, nudging me back in warning, his tail flicking back and forth in aggravation.

"It's all right. He won't hurt me. I have to touch him for this to work. Can you shift back? It might be easier for both of us."

He shakes his head, his paralysis barb at the ready. I don't have time to argue. Perhaps he thinks he can protect us better in this form.

The azdaha doesn't even move as I get close enough to touch his unnaturally clammy snout. I can sense Dare's displeasure from his constant grumbling, but I can't let him distract me. Normally Raz is warm to the touch, but now his hide is dry, with patchy, flaking scales.

"I'm going to try to heal you, old friend. Just don't roast or bite me, please."

Although I'm perilously close to his teeth, I press a hand gently to his snout and reach for my magic, pushing into the mystical connection I have with him. His akasha is dull, making me think that he's close to the end. *No, no, no.* I send my healing magic into him, and he rears backward, crashing into the top of the cave and causing a small rockfall. He screams in pain, and I clap my hand over my ears.

"Stay," I shout to the manticore, who is in an aggressive lunge position, talons out and barbed tail ready to strike. "Stop, Dare! Darrius, if you're in there, *trust* me." He doesn't stop snarling, but at least he doesn't come any closer. "Thank you."

I turn my attention to the azdaha and use my magic, ribbons of light spooling out of me to band around Razulek's mouth and more to keep his limbs, wings, and tail in place. He thrashes, looking at me with baleful, glassy eyes that don't recognize me. It might seem inhumane, but he'll only hurt himself . . . and me.

"I'm sorry, Raz. It's going to hurt before you can heal. We have to burn the rot out."

I begin. He screams and screams, struggling against my magical hold as I weep, my corpus magic roaring through him and eradicating the rot with its light. As I study the spidery purple veins in my mind's eye, I frown.

I am even more convinced that the rot *is* Fero, latching on to the living like a leech. Then when the host eventually dies, would it take over and be reanimated by a corpus magi? Sands, what if he is building an army of revenants? It makes sense that he would target the magical creatures first, then—they are the most powerful. Next would be people...

Dear gods...

My heart drops as I now consider if the Scavs were part of the army stationed near the border of Oryndhr that Razulek had mentioned. They had to be. Because with an innumerable brigade of Scavs at his beck and call, Fero would have an inexhaustible supply of soldiers to invade Everlea. He'd need only one death magi to turn them... one proficient in necromancy.

The so-called *oracle*.

I blink, my mind racing. When I'd been in Kaldari, the oracle had been linked to the Scavs, too, as well as the mercenaries in Coban. What if it was a disgruntled Everlean magi who wanted to overthrow Darrius? A shiver runs through me as the dots start to connect. *Nuadar* is a dominant corpus magi *and* he has a particularly strong numen for toxins, which explains the serum he made to weaken the manticore. He could have just as easily made a contaminant from the rot.

If I'm right... so many people in the palace could be in danger! The king, Ani, Ziba, Maxur, all the guards, my handmaidens... Gods, does Darrius know of the snake in his house?

I exhale a breath, and the sudden silence of the cave is deafening.

"Dare?" I whirl in a panic, looking for my manticore, but he's nowhere to be seen.

Maybe he needed some air, or maybe the screaming was setting off his protective instincts. It could be anything. He'll be back.

Checking that Razulek's body is out of immediate danger and on the mend, his own natural healing magic kicking in after a significant boost from mine, I crawl my way to the front of the cave, weak from the expenditure of magic. I've never felt the drain this badly before, but I've brought Raz back from the brink of death. Not quite necromancy, but certainly a hefty level of healing. My eyelids are so heavy, fatigue setting in.

Stars, I want to sleep for a week.

But first, I have to find the king.

I make it outside, blinking in the bright sunlight as my eyes adjust from the gloom of the cave, and to my intense relief, I spot my manticore's tail. But then I realize he's panting uncontrollably. He turns his giant head, only to whine and collapse. What's wrong with him? Panic lodges in my stomach. I don't know if I have any more akasha left in me to heal him.

"Dare, are you well? Dare! *Darrius!*"

My own senses whirl, breaths coming in short bursts much like his, and then my legs give out. I'm so depleted, I can barely keep my eyes open. Even my simurgh has gone quiet. I know I shouldn't, but maybe just for a short while, I can rest.

Then I'll fix him . . . and myself.

YAWNING, I STRETCH my arms upward, and then frown at the sharp rocks cutting into my back. Where am I? Did I fall asleep on the floor of the forge? But when I crack open my eyelids, I see a twilight sky and the tops of thick evergreens. The sun is just finishing its descent, spearing red-gold fingers over the steep rises of the mountain. The last thing I remember is healing Razulek and falling asleep from sheer exhaustion. I blink and attempt to roll the cricks out of my neck with a wince.

Then I remember Dare, in manticore form, collapsing, and terror blasts through me as I come awake fully.

I scramble to my feet, looking for the cave and Dare and Razulek . . . but I'm somehow in a completely different location. I spin around, desperate to find any markings that might tell me where I am.

It's still the Barrin Mountains, as far as I can tell, but I'm on some type of plateau on one of the highest peaks. The view of Everlea is breathtaking, but when I swivel, I gasp, because Oryndhr is visible on the other side. I can see the edge of the flat Dustlands and even the start of the rolling desert dunes of my beloved Coban to the south.

"How nice of you to finally wake up," a voice I instantly recognize says from behind me.

Whirling, I reach for my dagger behind my back, but the handle is not where it should be. I don't remember removing it, which means that someone has disarmed me—perhaps the same person who brought me here.

But I don't *need* a weapon to defend myself.

Revenant Laleh stands on the other side of the plateau with a small army of spidery-eyed soldiers—all in various stages of decay.

And my father is slumped on his knees in front of her.

Oh, dear gods. *Papa.* I don't even care that I was right about the rot and the army. I just need to make sure that my father hasn't been harmed.

Or worse . . . isn't one of *them.*

Please no, please no, please no.

A guttural moan rips from him, but he won't lift his head, and I can't see any part of his skin or his eyes to know if he's been infected with the rot. I need to get closer! I snarl as knots of fear tighten in my stomach and lurch forward only to smash into an invisible barrier that nearly throws me onto my ass. Charcoal smoke blooms at the point of impact and then dissipates.

This must be part of Darrius's wards between Everlea and Oryndhr.

"Papa," I call out, crouching down. "Can you hear me?" But he doesn't look up or even act like he knows I'm here. I clench my teeth and meet Laleh's dead, purple-veined eyes. "If you've hurt him, I'm going to tear you apart and spread your corpse to the winds so you can never come back in one piece."

"You wound me, Starkeeper. I suppose I'll just have to retaliate the only way I can." She grins and kicks my father in the back. He groans and crumples into a heap.

Shit. I can't detect if he's breathing, and terror fills me. I pound at the barrier, more bursts of smoke appearing at the contact. "What do you want?"

"Take down the barrier or he dies."

"How do I even know it's him?" I counter. "It could be one of your revenants."

She stoops to yank on his hair, and his beloved bearded face comes into view. I exhale, searching for clues that she's manipulating me. It looks like him, without any marks of rot on his features, but she'd fooled me before, too.

Laleh nods thoughtfully. "He'll make a good soldier soon, I think, but not just yet. I want to have my fun first with this clever leader of the insurrectionists."

I blink in confusion before the realization dawns. There's rebellion in Oryndhr? And my father is leading it? I feel a spike of pride, but fear quickly erases it. Laleh will no doubt want to make an example of him.

She winks and grins. "Now, break the wards or I start with each of his teeth."

Horrified, I shake my head. "Only the king of Everlea can remove the wards."

"Not true, according to our loyal friends."

I sense people behind me on the Everlea side before I hear marching footsteps. My magic roars to my fingertips when Masišta and his merry band of Karkad assholes come through the trees. There are even a handful from Rakh and one or two from Chamros. I notice my dagger tucked into his waistband. So *he* had ferried me here.

"You snake, I should have fucking killed you," I say through my teeth and lift my palms, letting coils of starlight weave through my fingers. "But I can remedy that now."

"Put your claws away, Starkeeper, or I take a chunk out of the old man," Laleh chirps from where she stands. "I've become quite adept at removing bones from live bodies. Quite the surgical exercise, I tell you." She presses the tips of her fingers of one hand to her lips. "And the cries of pain are divine."

"You're sick," I say.

She nods sagely. "It's the rot. Eats away at any humanity. But it's better in the end, I think, to give in to our natural impulses. So freeing. You would love it, Sura."

Masišta sneers at me as the parody of my best friend lets out one of those annoying giggles. Gods, that sound grates on my nerves. My Laleh would never make such an asinine noise. Her laugh was full-bellied and real.

"Touch me and I promise you *will* die an excruciating death," I snarl to Masišta and his men before insolently giving them my back. My magic will warn me if they attack; I feel my simurgh casting a protective shield around me. "I don't know what you think you know, but I cannot break these wards. Only the king can."

"You're the king's soul-fated," Masišta says.

"We are not bonded," I say, and slap the invisible barrier for good measure. The air reverberates in ripples of pale gray smoke, but the wards stay active. "I don't have the power to do what you want."

"A pity," Laleh says, and puts her foot across my father's neck.

A groan emerges from him. "Peapod?"

The nickname makes me falter. Stars, maybe it really *is* him. Dread rushes in on the heels of doubt as she presses down harder on his spinal cord, making him cry out. Powerless fury lashes up my spine as my eyes sting with unshed tears. *Fuck!*

"Laleh, please," I beg. "If there's any of you left in there, don't do this. You don't have to do this. He loved you. He treated you like his own."

She cocks her head. "And why would I do you any favors? You left me to die in that tower, didn't you?"

I open my mouth, but no sound emerges. She's right. I saw Morvarid cut her throat, but maybe . . . is it possible she had survived? I hadn't even checked her body. I'd left her there when the tower collapsed. Guilt ravages me. "I'm so sorry. I thought you were gone. Please don't hurt him . . ."

"Break the wards."

With a half sob, I force my power into the barrier, but I'm still not recovered from healing Razulek, and the magic I have replenished is eaten up by the swirling smoke. I'm aware that I am weakening any chance I have to defend myself from the men at my back, but I can't let my father die. Or if he is already dead, I have to give him peace. I won't leave him to be defiled and corrupted. I scream, shoving more magic at the wards, but they don't budge.

"I can't!" I cry, feeling my shield flicker at the strain of magic. It's my only defense.

She removes a knife from her belt and grins. "This is going to hurt him, Sura. Badly. I hope you're prepared for what you're letting happen."

"Laleh, no!"

Darrius, wherever you are, I need you. Please.

I don't even know if he can hear me, as I'm not sure what happened to him after we'd both collapsed. But before Laleh can do anything, I barely process the arrow flying in my peripheral vision from the woods behind her that lodges right into my father's skull. An involuntary scream tears up my throat. *No!*

Only . . . it's *not* my father, but an illusion that shatters the minute the jādū-forged arrowhead explodes.

Another man wearing my father's face runs out of the forest, a bow in hand, followed by a dozen others. Stars, is *that* him? Or another illusion? Conflicting emotions war inside me as a scuffle breaks out between them and Laleh's revenant soldiers.

But I have my own problems to worry about when my magical shield alerts that Masišta and his men are moving closer in an attempt to surround me. Deflecting an ice blast, I release a starlit flare. I'm down to the dregs of my magic, but it's still strong enough to incinerate three of the men to my right.

"We need her alive!" Masišta roars as a pillar of fire fizzles against my weakening shield.

I spare a glance at the fight behind me and glean hope from the fact that my hopefully real father seems to have the advantage. Gritting my teeth, I try to pinpoint my attack, instead of wasting what little akasha I have. There could be more men hiding in the trees, and if I'm depleted, I'm doomed without a weapon.

Sending out a tendril like a lasso, I yank one of the men closest to me forward and obliterate him—but not before divesting him of his sword.

There, not so doomed.

"Cut off their heads and burn them with fire," I hear someone shout from the other side. Someone I *know*. That can't be . . .

But I am too busy deflecting an attack of ice spears to turn around. More horde warriors, as I suspected, slither out of the forest where they'd been hiding. My simurgh's shield will have to guard against the magical attacks, and I'll have to take these pricks out with my sword. The odds in my favor are not great, but I haven't trained for weeks to just give up now.

With a war cry, I eliminate two men with a series of quick thrusts before sliding into a lunge to wound a third across the backs of his ankles. Blood flies, spattering me like rainfall, but I'm lost to my battle instincts as I fight to stay out of their clutches.

A shout of pain that sounds too much like my father breaks me out of it, and I spin, just in time to see a half-dismembered revenant pierce a sword into my father's leg. In slow motion, I watch him stumble and fall, blood leaking from his lips.

Aran—I knew I'd recognized that voice—appears behind them, carving his weapon straight through the revenant's head and then sketching a fire rune over his decapitated skull. Instantly, it bursts into flames. He drops to his knees beside my father, and to my shock, he gathers him close and places his hand over the wound, trying to heal him.

Wait. *Why* is he helping him? Aran is Roshan's man. *Fero's* man.

Unless . . . he isn't. Is he with my father and the insurrectionists?

He doesn't see Laleh loom from behind them, a crossbow at the ready. She meets my eyes and grins evilly, releasing her arrow right into my father's stomach. I roar with helpless despair, unable to reach him through Darrius's wards. Rage overcomes me as my simurgh shrieks, a strange pressure reverberating in the air.

We are not powerless.

With that, my Starkeeper soul implodes like a supernova, creating a black hole of magic that sucks akasha from everywhere. Masišta screams along with his men as every single one of their bodies dries to a husk, their magic nourishing the dearth of mine.

It's both horrific and beautiful, frightening and sublime, when immense power claws up my body, through my bones, and the runes on my hands detonate. I feel the wings on my back expand wide as my spine bows with the influx, and the smirk on Laleh's face turns to shock and then alarm. I touch a shimmering finger to the barrier and it fractures in a smoky spiderweb of cracks.

We are your end, revenant.

The magical voice is a high-pitched, multilayered sound that makes the remaining humans clutch their ears. I step past the shattered wards, and I cock my head at the necrotic creatures the god of death created.

Tell your master we are coming.

"Sura, it's me," Laleh cries. "Your friend. Don't abandon me this time."

But even in my heightened ascended state, I know that my friend—my dearest, sweetest friend—died a long time ago. With a single flicker of thought, the revenant who stole her face liquifies to purple-red sludge.

My light dissipates as I crash to my knees. "Papa?"

"I'm here, peapod," he rasps, breaking the arrow with a grunt to remove the shaft. "Flesh wound."

Everything is spinning, but I fight the dizziness as I send magic to his bleeding injury. "Why have you come? It's dangerous. This war will leave nothing but rot and corpses in its wake. I need you and Amma to be safe."

"She *is* safe." He wheezes with a low laugh. "And well you know that I can't sit still or silent and let our people suffer. That abomination with Laleh's face came to Coban looking for you. I went to Kaldari for help, and the king's cousin made the portal for us to follow her."

I squint at Aran, who is staring at me with pleading, oddly hopeful eyes. "Why are you helping my father? You are an imperial runecaster on Roshan's side. *Fero's* side."

"No, I'm not. My cousin isn't lost," he rasps. "And I think you're the only one who can save him from the clutches of that *thing*."

"He's gone, Aran," I say. "His soul is corrupted. You saw what he did to me. What he made you do, too. To save him, you're going to need the might of a god, and we're in short supply of those, unless you have a connection to Saru no one knows about."

Tears leak from him, his remorse a tangible thing. "Ashes, Suraya, I know I don't deserve your forgiveness. But Roshan is fighting. He won't stop, not while your starlight still burns inside of him. And it does, I promise. Please, *please*. If you ever loved him at all, if you hold even a spark for him now, please don't let him go. Please don't let his struggle be for nothing."

Everything inside of me aches—my soul, my body, my heart—for the man I loved. Perhaps even still do, deep down where my heart is quietest. "I'll do my best," I say finally. "But, Aran, I can't promise anything. The rot is an unholy essence. I . . . I might not be strong enough to save him."

Relief floods his features. "I understand, Sura. Thank you for being willing to try."

Pressure in the glade builds as a storm of shadows descends. When they clear, an apoplectic Darrius is standing there, fury written in every line of his powerful frame. My chest swells, and I smile, my heart so full I can barely contain it. "You found me."

"I'll always find you," he says. His gaze flicks to my father and then Aran, darkening considerably at the latter. But then his voice lowers as I fall gladly into his embrace. "The manticore heard your call and knew you needed me. He shifted back and my magic healed us."

"I'm glad," I murmur. "Get my dagger? It's over there . . . Masišta . . . dead."

It's my last thought before I let myself sink into my beloved's shadows.

Chapter Thirty-Two

I sleep like the dead for three full days before my body—and simurgh—recovers from whatever it was that happened on that mountain. Despite the toxin I'd foolishly ingested, it had felt like some kind of augmentation . . . like an amplification of my magic, almost as if both my simurgh and I had become stronger.

The power I felt in that moment had been staggering in its intensity.

I think of the way my depleted wellspring had hunted the magic of the traitorous Aspačanā like a soul-eating vampire, how their bodies had turned into empty husks as I drank down their life essences, how the revenants had melted to sludge, and I shiver with equal amounts of fervor and dread.

Gods, the recollections make me want to never open my eyes, to stay gone and safe forever. The world would go on as it is meant to. People will survive. Unless the realms are ravaged by war—a *god* war—one they have no hope of winning. Then everyone I love will die. And everything I have done will be for nothing.

A groan escapes my lips.

"Starbright?"

The deep voice is a tether that I grasp on to. Darrius is my anchor, and yet, we still haven't completed the bond. Is he still afraid? Or am

I the one wavering because of what we might become? He's the son of a god . . . and I possess monstrous celestial abilities that no one should have any right to. Monstrous *cannibalistic* abilities. I shiver and squash down those feelings.

"My father?" I rasp. "Is he alive?"

Soft footfalls reach the bed. "He's here, and my best healers are with him."

I let out a relieved noise. "And Aran? Your shadows didn't pulverize him, did they?"

"Not yet."

I almost snort at the dangerous edge in his voice.

"What about Raz? Any word? I haven't been able to talk to him myself, though I can sense he's peaceful, with no pain or sickness."

"Still asleep but mending. Indira is beyond grateful." Darrius kisses my forehead and pours me a fresh glass of water from a nearby pitcher. I smile at him and drink it. "I retrieved your dagger."

"Thank you."

He moves behind me to drape his mother's necklace around my throat. The pendant rests comfortably in the hollow between my breasts. "This has protections in it."

"Dare, we need to complete the bond," I say softly before I lose my nerve. I feel the mattress dip as he sits at my side, his warm oud-and-smoke scent filling my nostrils. "If war is coming, we need to be prepared."

My eyelids flicker open, starved for that strikingly beautiful face. His wealth of silver hair is loose and curtains us from the world as he leans over me. "What happened up there?" he asks.

I inhale. "My magic . . . went feral."

"I felt it here," he says, rubbing his chest. "But you stayed in control."

"Barely. I . . . stole power from others. I drained Masišta and his men." I stare at him, reaching up to wind my fingers in his hair as if the small connection can keep me from fracturing apart at the admission of guilt. "Have you ever heard of anything like that?"

That inky gaze of his darkens even more. "I've only heard of magic sharing between soul-fated. But you're also the Starkeeper, so the depth and breadth of your power is unknown."

"It wasn't sharing," I whisper. "I *took* it. Forcibly."

His face goes hard, ruthlessness taking over. "Your magic defended you."

"Darrius, what do your legends here say of the Starkeeper?" I ask, thinking of the old Oryndhrian divination that has hung over me like a shroud. The fear that the weight of responsibility has thrown upon me. This feels a thousand times worse. "Indira told me that the sidereal rank is the same as what Oryndhrians call Setareh Framātāram. Master of the star. Is there a similar prophecy here?"

He shakes his head. "More of an old fable. A forgotten myth."

"Tell it to me, please."

His mouth firms. "Suraya, it's not—"

"There is power in myth, Dare. Even if it's bad, I need to know what has been written and what has been told."

"Very well." He kisses me, lips feathering softly over my chapped ones. "When the lightbreaker falls, darkness will abound, a king lost to chaos by star-cursed song. Such is the long shadow of day and the bright star of night, a soul-blooming spark tethered to both earth and sky. By the chosen's own hand, the ill-fated shall die . . . And as the night sky bleeds, a godslayer will rise."

Despite the knot in my belly, I roll my eyes and force a wry grin. "That makes everything *so* clear. Glad to see your Everlean ancestors were just as much assholes as mine. Who are the ill-fated? And am I this godslayer?" I swallow and frown. "You're a god. What if I am fated to kill you?"

"The fates are fickle," he says. "And you can't kill me, Starbright. You'd miss me too much."

Smiling unhappily, I ponder the fable and his words about the fates. "What if I'm just like your father? Monsters aren't born. They're made."

Darrius cups my face in his warm, strong hands. "Trust me. You're *nothing* like him. And you're wrong about that. Some monsters were created to be monstrous. Things that thrive in the darkness do so for a reason—they feed on foul thoughts and foul actions. They are not redeemable. They are not meant to be saved. They are meant to test *you*. To test your faith in yourself."

"What if I fail?" I ask in a small voice.

"The very fact that you are asking tells me that you will do everything in your power *not* to." Darrius pulls me up and situates me in his lap, his lips ghosting over my forehead. "If you want to complete the bond, we can."

"What about the curse?"

His expression softens. "You were right about what I needed to do with the manticore. I embraced that side of me, and I can feel him now, more than ever. He senses me, too. And that's all because of you."

"So is the curse broken?"

Those dark eyes flash gold. "No, and I'll never be free of it. My father thought he could break me by denying me my soul-fated and finding love, but what he didn't realize is that even a monster can be worthy of being loved, too. He didn't bet on you."

Chest swelling, I stare at him, knowing how much he has struggled. "I'm glad you're choosing to love yourself as you are, Dare."

He swats my ass and sighs with equal amounts of exasperation and affection. "I'm saying I love *you*, Starbright."

"Wait. You love *me*?" I whisper, and he nods.

"I was lost from the moment you told me I have too much, and I quote, *grumpy, asshole energy*," he says, lips quirking. "I have never wanted to laugh, fuck, or punish someone more."

My cheeks heat as butterflies explode in the pit of my stomach. "Who knew that I'd fall in love with the grumpiest god of all?"

"You did?"

"Unlucky me," I say teasingly, and kiss him. He mutters something vaguely threatening about bad girls getting fucked against my lips. Stars . . . *yes, please*—but I fight my surge of arousal, pulling back before he can deepen the kiss. "Wait, no tongue. I need to clean my teeth. And bathe before you get any wicked ideas about punishing me." His eyes glint mercilessly as I push off his lap. "Don't go anywhere."

"Only to get you something to eat," he says, standing to his full impressive height. I try very hard not to stare at the obvious bulge at his groin, but fail miserably. A vicious, moral-smelting smile breaks over that gorgeous face when I nearly stumble over my own two feet. "You'll need your strength, Starbright."

My core trembles, warmth filling every space inside of me at the promise and the threat tied into one. Sands, I *love* him. I don't even know when it happened . . . when I stopped hating him and when he became the air in my lungs, the hope in my heart, and my whole starsdamned night sky. For a second, I rub at my sternum, feeling the oddest hollowness that doesn't seem to belong in the midst of my happiness, like something—something *vital*—is still missing.

My magic, in its new ascendant form, feels untethered.

It doesn't take me long to feel refreshed after a quick bath. When I'm done, I clean my teeth and comb my wet hair, leaving it loose to dry. I grimace at the pile of my sweat-soaked garments, then wander into the nearby closet and grab one of Darrius's white tunics.

It fits me like a dress, so I don't bother with pants and roll the sleeves slightly. I suppose I could easily magic a set of my own clothing, but the idea of wearing his is just too tempting . . . and strangely soothing.

He must think so, too, because when I emerge from the bathing room, his eyes go wide and then darkly possessive. "Nice shirt."

"I thought so." My stomach growls, and I meet him at the table near the window, where there's a spread of different foods. To my surprise and delight, apart from fresh cut fruit and a basket of pastries, there's a dish that looks and smells suspiciously like my aunt's roasted and mashed tomato, eggplant, and herring, served with pieces of hot flatbread. I glance over at Darrius. "What is this?"

"Thought you might appreciate some comfort food. It might not be exactly like your aunt's, but I hope—" I don't even let him finish before I throw myself into his arms and plaster my mouth to his.

Once I'm done showing him my deep appreciation, I don't waste any time settling cross-legged into my seat and inhaling the deliciousness, sopping up every last drop from my plate with the flatbread. I lick each one of my fingers clean, making a noise of satisfaction in my throat, and look up to the other side of the table to see Darrius utterly mesmerized.

"What?" I ask self-consciously, wiping a drop of tomato juice from my mouth.

"Everything you do is such chaos," he says, but his tone is full of fondness tempered by wonder and a flash of desire when I lick my lips clean, too. "My beautiful, magnificent, unruly star. Devourer of darkness, defender of innocents."

At his words, suddenly I recall my thoughts about Nuadar on the mountain. "Darrius, I think Nuadar might be the oracle," I blurt out.

He goes still. "Why?" His reply is quiet, not defensive.

"It's only a hunch. He's a dominant corpus magi, but he's brewed your so-called sedative for years. What if he is involved somehow, making you progressively weaker or more susceptible to the shift? He also came up with the idea for the dragon's bloom, and I think that's what made us unconscious." I inhale, chewing the corner of my lip. I don't mention that the oracle had called me Oryndhrian, much like Nuadar had. "And I believe he might be colluding with the Oryndhrians from something Masišta said when we were on the cliffs . . . about the reproductive cycles of the azdaha and their egg count. Only a beastmaster knows that."

"He's been with my family for years," Darrius says, but then he stops and frowns as if the coincidences and timelines are too much to ignore. "I'll tell Maxur to investigate."

After I finish my meal, Darrius lifts a hand and a servant clears away the tray of food. He reaches for my hands across the top of the table, flipping them to stroke the lines on the inside. I sigh at the light touch. Our lives might be different, but traditions, prophecies, and beliefs cross paths and intersect across all realms.

"Can you read the lines?" I ask, turning my hands to flip his large palms upward.

"Chiromancy?" he replies, and I nod. "I know what they are, but I'm not a diviner by any means."

I trace the topmost line on his left hand with my fingertip, hearing him suck in his breath. "I've never read the palm of a deity before. Will you smite me if I steer you wrong?"

His shadows flare out of him to flick and tug on a lock of my hair. "Never."

The shadowy tendrils try to slink back to him, but I gather them with the softest tug of my magic and settle them in my lap as if they're cuddly creatures. Darrius's brows rise, but he doesn't pull them away, especially when he notices my utter lack of pants . . . or undergarments. As they nuzzle into the bare skin of my thighs, I peer at him, but he gazes back innocently.

Behave, I think to him.

His answering look is sinful.

I clear my suddenly dry throat and focus on my task. "Both hands are different. The nondominant hand is what is written by the fates and the dominant is what you change with your own will. This top line is your heart line. You see how it's very frayed at first but then strengthens? Your heart is very guarded. You were afraid, but you're not now."

I look to his right palm, where the heart line is smooth and deep, and smile. Darrius has always known his choice, even if his path wasn't clear. I stroke the second line of his left. "This is your head line. You're a man of discipline and order, though you can see from these smaller breaks that your mind goes in many directions at once. Your right is nearly solid—a testament to what you have achieved." I trace the curve around the fleshiest part of his left palm with a fingernail. "Your life line. There's a break here and here where others have influenced you. Perhaps sickness of some sort, maybe related to the curse." I glance at the right. "You can see the line on this palm is unbroken, showing your tenacity." Lastly, I stroke down the middle. "Your fate line is the same in both. Strong and unerring."

"Amazing," he whispers, midnight eyes holding mine.

"Darrius?" I ask, sliding my fingers through his. "What does performing the bonding ritual entail?"

"A true soul bond has four layers, much like the lines you just spoke about—head, heart, body, and fate—as well as seven points of connection, to each chakra in our bodies. While a physical connection can strengthen a soul-fated bond and an emotional one can deepen it, a mental oath—a meaningful vow—can seal it."

I frown in thought. "So, like marriage vows?"

"A soul bond transcends mortal rites," he says. "But yes, you will be my wife, and I will be your husband, as blessed by the fates."

I remember his nickname for me. "What's the male version of pátnī?"

"Páti," he says with a smile.

I taste the word soundlessly on my tongue and like how it feels. There's a certain sense of rightness—pátnī and páti. "How does the vow work? What do I say?"

Darrius stares at me, his handsome face solemn. "Are you certain,

Suraya? Once we do this, we will be eternally linked. We will share magic and a life force, and all our thoughts and our feelings. You will have power over me . . . and I will have the same over you."

Apprehension flickers, and I feel a peculiar wave of discomfort, as if some craven, selfish part of me *doesn't* want anyone to wield my magic. "But we will be stronger together?" I ask.

"Infinitely."

Darrius rises and pulls me up next to him. The difference in our heights is noticeable as he looms nearly a foot over me. He takes my small right hand and places it against the middle of his chest, aligned with his spine, and splays my fingers wide. Then he does the same to me, his right hand nestling between my breasts.

His voice is soft and grave. "The center of the palm rests over the anahata chakra—the heart bridge—which connects your throat, third eye, and crown chakras above, and the solar plexus, sacral, and root ones below." His left fingertip brushes over each point: the base of my neck, between my brows, the top of my skull, and then his knuckles slide down from between my ribs to my belly and lower, making me gasp.

Reverently, Darrius moves back up, ever so slowly, naming the purpose of each one from root to crown. "Survival, sexuality, identity, love, expression, intuition, and knowledge."

As he invokes each chakra, the energy sparks between them *and* between us. I can feel my magic flaring inside of me as if it knows what is about to happen. Despite my earlier trickle of apprehension, I sense no real doubt, only a pulse of certainty that this is our path.

Not our only path.

I blink at the unexpected words from my simurgh. *What do you mean?*

We are the passage between the earth and the sky, a conduit between the bright of the sun and the dark of the moon—both of your halves will be loved and anchored by kings.

Don't you mean king? I ask, frowning.

But the voice fades as my magic brims, my runes flaring with silvery iridescence as Darrius's shadows swirl along his arms. They meet in the middle where we are connected in a lover's dance, bursting upward like fountains of coiling light and darkness.

"Suraya Saab," he says in his deep voice that wraps around me like roughened silk. "I pledge to you my irrevocable oath to honor this soul-fated bond. As I offer you my hand, so I offer you my soul to keep from this moment forward."

My throat clogs with emotion, but I manage to repeat the same. "Darrius Nightsong, I pledge to you my irrevocable oath to honor this soul-fated bond. As I offer you my hand, so I offer you my soul to keep from this moment forward."

Every cell inside of me tightens as the vow settles into place like stardust. The magic between us seems to still for an infinitesimal moment before it blasts upward and outward, blanketing us both. I feel it the moment the bond seals, the tether between us glowing with otherworldly iridescence. Familiar magic that isn't mine fills my veins, and I watch in wonder as inky runic shadows wind up my arms and merge with the silvery ones already there.

"Fate marks," Darrius says, staring at his own arms, where a silvery pattern, reminiscent of the runes on my arms, has formed, intertwining with his shadow marks and sinking into his brown skin.

"Is this not normal?" I ask, when his brows draw together slightly as if he hadn't expected this.

He shakes his head. "Not in millennia. These are gods-touched bonds."

I pin my lips, but a strangled laugh bursts from me. "You're a god yourself, if you hadn't noticed, and I'm a warrior made with divine energy. It's only logical." I reach up, wind my fist into his collar, and grin before yanking him down. "You're stuck with me now, páti."

"Say it again," he says against my lips.

"*Páti* . . . husband."

The groan that leaves him makes something deeply satisfying, primal, and possessive flare inside of me. He's *mine*. Our kiss is transcendent, his mouth claiming mine as passionately as I claim his. I feel the bond humming between us. We kiss for what seems like hours, but eventually I pull away, albeit with great reluctance.

"As much as I want to stay here, I need to make sure Papa is well."

My king runs a hand through his mussed silver hair. His lips are red and swollen, his eyes gleaming. Surprisingly, a dark pink tinge washes over his cheekbones. "I understand, but we do, er, need to . . . consummate the bond in order to fully complete the ritual and seal the vows."

I lift my brows and grin at his adorably awkward expression. "Not that I am complaining, but don't previous times count?"

"No," he says. "We should be fine as long as it's not too long after."

"You can wait?"

My soul-fated kisses me softly. "I waited forever for you without any true hope of ever having you. What's a few more hours? You are worth infinite lifetimes, Suraya." His eyes burn with reverence, and it's a miracle my legs don't give out. "Go see your father. I have to check in with the kingsguard and the Aspačanā anyway. I'll see you tonight."

"I love you, Darrius," I tell him.

His eyelids flutter as if he's savoring the words . . . as if he never expected to hear them. In truth, that *is* what he's thinking, because I can feel every single one of his emotions through the bond. My heart swells as I say it again and he shudders.

"I love you with everything I am, Starbright."

The worship in his voice is only one part of the reason that I'm on a cloud by the time I make it to the healing wing. Despite the looming threat of war and the foreboding spread of Fero's rot . . . I feel light. *Hopeful*. It's the strangest thing, as if following fate had been the answer all along. Logically, I know it's not that easy, but for the first time, I feel like it could be.

Like Darrius and I could conquer everything.

With my renewed hope, I burst into my father's room. Ani is sitting with him. He looks like he's resting comfortably, eyes closed and chest rising rhythmically. The worry in my own chest loosens.

"Ani, how is he?"

My friend cocks her head, curious blue eyes studying me over the bed. "He's fine. Sleeping. What's going on with you? You look different."

I'm loath to share that Darrius and I had finally performed the bonding ritual. For some selfish reason, I want to keep the knowledge to myself for a little while longer. Once it's fully complete, I'll tell her, but for now, it's a special secret. "Nothing. I got some sleep."

She narrows her eyes, dissecting every inch of me. "No, it's something more." She stares me up and down as I try not to squirm in place, and then she makes a thoroughly disgusted face. "Oh, ashes. Did you and my brother finally do it?"

I snort with a blush I can't hide. "*Do it?* What are you, twelve? And none of your business." Ani stands with a shrug, face neutral, which makes my mirth fade. Is she upset? It's not as though she didn't know about the bond. "Is everything all right?"

"Of course. My brother must be very happy."

"We're both happy."

Her lashes dip. "Are you, though? Do you know what the bond entails?"

I blink. "Dare said we would share power."

A scoff leaves her lips. "Until he decides to take it. They can, you know? Drain you without your consent."

Something in her tone doesn't sound right. I peer at her eyes in a panic, trying to see if she has somehow accidentally infected herself, but her irises are clear. "Ani, is something the matter?"

"Ignore me. I am just tired." She reaches for a small vial sitting on the bedside table, and I wonder if it's the same dragon's bloom, but then I see that the contents are yellow, not green.

"Thank you for looking out for my father," I say, drawing closer to the side of the bed. "What have you given him?"

"A new serum," she says.

I nod thankfully . . . just as my father chokes and starts convulsing.

"Shit! Ani, something's wrong!" I reach for him, panic building as white foam froths at the corners of his mouth. "It's not working. Help him, please!" I throw myself on top of his large body to keep the spasms from harming him. *No, no, no.* This cannot be happening. "Ani, where—?"

I twist, looking over my shoulder to my friend. She stands beside the bed, deathly still, blue eyes like reflective glass. She looks sad. "As always, your timing could not be worse. A few minutes later would have been ideal for all."

"What?" I ask, confused, still trying to keep my father still. "Will he be all right?"

"No, of course not. He's dying."

The cavalier reply simply does not make sense. The words refuse to sink into my confused brain. "What?" I say again.

"You know, you can learn a lot about floramancy from books. It's wondrous, truly. Which plants secrete a sap that can make people lose consciousness, poultices to make infections disappear, herbs to make people tell the truth or ones effective against Verac root, which worked out well for me." She sighs, even as I gape at her in dawning horror. "Even what roots can kill a person slowly and painfully without a single trace. Clearly not as invisibly as I'd hoped, however."

"Ani . . . what . . . wait . . . did you . . . ?"

She tilts her head. "Yes, Sura? Use your words, please."

Her tone is condescending. My throat feels like there's an iron fist around it, suffocating me. "What are you doing? I don't understand. This is my *father*."

"I know," she says.

She *knows*? She's . . . done this on purpose? Fury washes away my confusion. I leap off the bed and face her, feeling my magic surge to my fingertips. "Fix it. Now."

Ani laughs. "Don't do anything stupid, Sura. There's only one antidote to this particular toxin, and not even your magic will be effective enough to save him. It's my special recipe—any application of magic and the toxin accelerates. Clever, no? So kill me, and your precious papa dies. He's in pain right now, but he still has time. Days . . . weeks even." She waves a finger in my face. "And don't even think of summoning my brother telepathically. Oh, I know how soul-fated bonds work. Trust me, that would be a bad idea."

I grit my teeth and stop myself from doing just that. "Why are you doing this, Ani? I thought we were friends."

"You didn't hate my brother as much as you should have," she replies. "And then when you got curious about soul bonds, I knew I had to work fast to put my plans in place."

Plans?

Much too slowly, realization trickles through me. Stars . . . it's been *Ani* all along . . .

"You're the oracle," I whisper. "You spread the rot."

"Don't feel bad, Sura," she says when she sees my aghast expression. "I poisoned my own brother, too, and you as well, I suppose. Sedated you with a slightly tweaked dragon's bloom, but even so, that didn't work as I expected it to." She releases a displeased noise. "Those Starkeeper gifts are tricky. Darrius should have stayed in his beast form, and *you* should not have been able to summon a drop of magic. And *neither* of you should have been able to consummate your bond. Alas, an alchemist's work is never done, truly."

"Why, Ani?" I ask weakly.

Ani smiles, an expression that makes my blood run cold. I realize it's the first real glimpse I've ever seen of the true her. "Do you know what it's like to be the firstborn but to be female? To be overlooked at every turn? To be viewed as weaker . . . as *lesser*," she says. "I was always smarter than him. I excelled at magic, was brilliant at diplomacy. And yet, nothing I did would ever reward me with the crown." Ani laughs. "I was named after a goddess, and yet, by nature of his gender, the throne of Everlea was his. Where's the fairness in that?"

"You'd start a war and destroy innocent lives to prove a point?" I ask. "That you're better than him? He trusted you, Ani."

She arches an imperious brow. "You're not listening. Not better, *worthier*. I am my father's daughter." Her mouth stretches into a grin that makes my skin crawl. "Didn't you like the gift I made for you? Your best friend? You should be thanking me."

My chest squeezes as if gripped in a giant fist, the pain making me wheeze. "You're a monster."

She shrugs. "She was useful, as you will be. You two have that in common."

"Darrius won't forgive you for this," I say, hands balling with impotent fury.

"It won't matter. And I don't need his forgiveness."

Chapter Thirty-Three

After flying the three of us to Kaldari over Deadman's Canyon on the largest griffin I've ever seen, Anahima—I can't bring myself to think of her as Ani anymore—forced me to take a potion that instantly deadened my mental connection to Darrius. And since her brother had trusted her to perform negotiations on his behalf, she can easily traverse the wards between the realms.

I'm alone now, and my father's survival is on the line.

It feels strange to be back in Kaldari. The throne room looks the same, but I am an entirely different person. I look around for Roshan, but he is nowhere to be seen. Instead, the deceitful princess is strutting about like she owns the place. My father, thankfully, is now resting comfortably in one of the bedchambers, even though he's sleeping the sleep of the dead.

Some of the courtiers seem familiar, while others don't. And they all seem very, *very* wary of the female magi at my side. Even the ones who come to take my father to a chamber where he will be cared for scurry away without meeting my eyes.

A thought brings ice to my veins: Has she *killed* Ro . . . the king of Oryndhr? That seems impossible, with Fero inside him. Is she planning to fully resurrect her father, then? Will she use me as Morvarid had tried to?

Loathing fills me. "If you think I will lie down and let Fero possess me, Anahima, you are dead fucking wrong."

She laughs, though her blue eyes flare at my emphasis of her given name. "Oh, I have plans for daddy dearest, don't you worry. He's a scourge, but a powerful one. I'm his true heir, after all." She waggles her fingers. "And then Dare won't be the only sovran magi in Everlea. In fact, with the power of a god in my veins, I'll be of sidereal rank, like you."

"You lied about your magic level," I say dully.

"Of course. How else could I have done everything I did? Form a—what do you call them?—revenant army with the power of my corpus sanguimancy. Control them with my psionic magic. Manipulate metal as a ferrokinetic or enhance my floramancy with heliokinesis. Fool everyone in the fucking palace our whole lives into believing that poor, bookish, gentle little Ani was never a threat to anyone." She shakes her head, smiling wildly. "And when I take my father's power, I can bring this entire castle down, if I choose."

Anahima has lost her mind . . . or this has been festering for a long time.

"You're not the only woman who has been underestimated and diminished in our realms," I say quietly, thinking back to how I'd felt when Javed had paraded me through the streets of Kaldari for our engagement like a pretty prize. Or how a man's value in Oryndhr had always held intrinsic worth, while a woman's was reduced to the marriage she made. I'd been profoundly lucky to have a father like mine, who had never raised me as less than, who had always taught me to *know* my own worth in a world that belittled it. "We have always been passed over and fighting for scraps. You're not the first in Endara, Ani, and you won't be the last."

She straightens to her full height—I'd never noticed how truly tall she is since she always hunched and made herself smaller on purpose—

and peers down the length of her nose at me. Sands, how much have I missed by taking her at face value? Like everyone else had?

Cold laughter bubbles from her lips. "Look at you, all this power, and still you bend to the whims of men. For what? *Love?* It's just another yoke of control."

"Not always," I say.

"You'll see," she says. "They make sweet promises at first. Trick you. Woo you." She runs a hand over the mantelpiece, watching me in the large mirror on the wall. "I had a soul-fated once, did you know?" I stare at her in shock while she nods, pursing her lips. "We did the ritual. I was besotted, you see. I thought he *loved* me." She turns then, and I can see the pure devastation written all over her before it's stamped out. "Then he drained me to the point of death and kept me there."

"Why?" I whisper, heart aching. "How?"

"Because I was useful. He wanted me for what I could give him. *Power.* Access to an exiled god." She snorts. "He almost had it, too. But one day, I found a way to free myself. I taught myself everything that sanguimancy had to offer." Ani's smile is a rictus. "Blood magic can be powerful and quiet. And then I stripped him of every drop of his magic and slit his throat, but that bastard survived. I never saw him again. Vogonis fled Everlea."

My vision tunnels. Could it be . . . ? It has to. I can still remember that awful neck laceration. He'd known *exactly* who and what I was when he'd slaughtered Javed . . . when he, too, sought to resurrect a god.

What are you doing, Vogon? the queen had screamed at the Scav general.

Taking what is mine . . .

"Vogon is dead," I say. "Morvarid killed him."

"I know. I felt him die," Ani says, thumping a fist over her breast. "I also know what my beloved became, building an army to defeat me. Ironic, isn't it, that said army is now mine."

I swallow, remembering what Darrius had said about the bond if one person dies. "But you didn't . . ."

"Follow my soul-fated into death? Hardly. My father saved me. He severed the bond for good, and the pain was unlike anything in this world, like having your soul shredded into pieces." She shrugs. "But it was worth it. Fero finally recognized my devotion and my value."

"So you did all this to hurt your brother?"

Anahima smiles. "My father hates him, you know. And gods can be infinitely patient."

The depth and intricacy of her deception sinks in. Ani's heart has been corrupted for so many years, a fact that becomes glaringly clear when I realize exactly how long she has been planning this coup.

"And what does the king of Oryndhr have to do with this?"

"Apart from anchoring the old man?" Anahima claps with glee. "Come look. All I need you to do is open a portal. Simple."

She leads me to a balcony that overlooks one of the back courtyards—and my knees nearly buckle at what I see there. A dozen Scavs, all of them revenants, identifiable by the state of rot and the tendrils of purplish decay beneath their eyelids. *Gods* . . . the stench is unbearable. I fight a rush of bile.

I remember General Vogon telling me that Jade made men perfect soldiers—now they're perfect soldiers who can't die . . . because they're already dead. The senseless loss of so many lives hurts my heart. And the Scavs are just the first to be sacrificed in the primary wave of Anahima's war. The people of Oryndhr aren't safe. And that's not even counting the unchecked spread of the rot through the realms.

"How did you do it?"

She knows what I'm asking even before I finish. "Blood connects us all."

Of course. The answer is usually the simplest.

My stomach sours. "So you want me to, what, let loose a plague on your own people? I can't open a portal for an infected army, Anahima. And even if I could, I won't."

She glares at me, blue eyes pale as death. "You can and you will. And besides, who do you think let the rot in? That feral basilisk? The azdahas? The cattle? My father was all too eager to share his powers of necrosis. And men like Donnan were all too eager to spread it to the people instead of feeding them. He did it for money. He was useful." She lets out an amused laugh. "I almost thought he would expose me that day in the throne room. Thank the gods I had the presence of mind to do a quick spell to keep him quiet."

I remember Donnan's face and the way he'd reached toward her.

"You let your brother kill him," I say.

She spreads her hands wide. "He made his choice. Men are so predictable. Donnan, Masišta . . . my brother. So easy to control. Even that weakling Prince Javed was so desperate to have an azdaha of his own . . . The stupid fool died before he could offer to trade the wounded male for an egg as I suggested."

I gasp at how deep her deception goes. "*You* handed Razulek over?"

Ani shrugs. "That stupid beast was meant to be *mine,* but he would not even look at me, as if I was too weak to be his rider."

"They're the oldest creatures in Endara, and when they pick their riders, it's about what's in their hearts. Clearly, he knew what was in yours wasn't worthy. That's why he didn't choose you, Anahima."

Her face hardens, mouth pulling into a sneer. "He deserved to be sent away. Even your silly Oryndhrian king—do you think his pathetic magi could even design the beast's bracers without *my* instruction for those runes? It was *my* idea to use the king's star-touched blood for yours." She preens. "I am the blessed oracle, after all."

Gods, I want to punch her in her smug face. "If you're so all-powerful, why can't *you* open a portal yourself?"

That earns me a hiss as if she doesn't like being told she's lacking in some way. "Are your ears painted on? I told you in the library—only a sovran in ergokinesis who can manipulate raw energy can open a portal across realms. It drains lesser magi, and I need to focus on executing my plans, not holding a portal open. And you, dear Starkeeper, have a well of power just waiting to be used."

There *has* to be a way out of this. I have no doubt that Darrius has discovered my absence by now. There's a strange feeling in my chest—a hollow that clenches from time to time—and I wonder if that's him tugging on the bond. Regret fills me. If we had fully sealed the ritual with consummation, would that have made any difference?

I grind my molars. "You'll have to kill me first."

Rage ripples over her. "You're being difficult."

"Am I?"

She sneers. "Perhaps it is simply incentive you need. I can just as easily speed up the toxin that will eat away at your father's organs as I can slow it down," she says. "Don't test me."

I blanch. That's the only breathing room out of any of this—Anahima has slowed the pace of deterioration, and if I cooperate, my father won't die. Nor is he in pain. But that can change on her whim.

Our standoff is interrupted by the arrival of the king and his entourage. Now these faces I know. Aran's expression immediately goes blank, but both Clem and Hamid, armed to the teeth, stare at me in surprise. Helena is also there, though my old nemesis looks like she hasn't slept in weeks. Her once glossy hair is stringy and dull, and her face is gaunt. I shouldn't feel pity for her, but I do. I'm not interested in her, however. I'm interested in the king who is staring at me with the strangest combination of yearning and hatred.

Dark purple mist swirls like poison in his eyes.

"Starkeeper, you look different," he rasps in the voice that isn't his. "Will she open the portal?" he asks Anahima.

She strolls over to Roshan, peering into his irises. "Hello, Father. How's the host? Still kicking in there? Don't worry, she will open it."

Ani smirks. "The Starkeeper will do as she's told. And each time she fails, I will destroy a city, starting with her little desert oasis. So much innocent blood will be on your hands, Suraya."

I feel myself start to shake as magic gathers inside of me. It would be so easy to kill them all in one fell swoop, to let my simurgh raze this entire palace to the ground—but there's no guarantee that I can save my father if Anahima is dead. Although, can I incapacitate her somehow? Buy some time? Gods! What if I miscalculate and doom my father? Everyone else? But I can't just stand here and do nothing!

Conflicted, I rub my chest at the heart chakra as that strange hollow feeling at the center intensifies, right as a massive shadow blots out the light overhead for the space of a prolonged wingbeat.

"Azdaha!" someone bellows from the courtyard.

Anahima's face darkens with rage as she shoves me onto the upper terrace, a dagger at my throat. The king of Oryndhr follows, surrounded by his guard.

"Brother!" my captor cries.

Indira circles above, and I can feel Darrius's shock from where he sits. Darkness takes over his form as he disappears into a storm of shadows and smoke to reappear in front of us in a seething whorl. The azdaha lands on top of a turret, stone crumbling beneath her talons as she settles in place.

"Anahima, what have you done?" he shouts, his eyes narrowing in confusion on his sister. "Release my wife."

I feel the stares of my former friends. "She poisoned my father and spread the rot," I blurt out. "She's your traitor. The one they call the oracle."

"Now you've ruined my surprise." Anahima pouts and peeks at her brother. "I'm going to enjoy sharing her with my army after you're dead." She pats my cheek with the edge of the blade. "I'll strip her magic, and then they'll tear your precious soul-fated apart. Brutes, the lot of them."

I know exactly what she's trying to do. The king of Everlea's virulent rage is a palpable thing, and I hear the ominous crackle of bones as the curse rises to the surface. He might have a tenuous truce with his beast, but the precious time he will lose could make all the difference between life and death. His features become leonine, eyes flashing a vicious gold.

"There he is," Anahima sings. "Let the beast out, brother. He hates it when anyone plays with his toys, doesn't he?"

"Mate," Darrius growls in the manticore's voice like he already has a mouthful of teeth he can't speak around.

"Only good mate is a dead mate," Anahima says brightly, then she attacks.

A blast of her magic crashes into Darrius, who lets out an inhuman roar. I feel the curse take hold and echo deep in my gut when a second blast hits me straight in the torso and sends me careening across the terrace to smash into the wall. *Fuck.* She's strong. I can feel at least a handful of broken ribs start to mend, but the pain still makes me wheeze.

Darrius starts to shake and shudder at the scent of my blood, his fear for me pushing him to the edge of the shift.

Dare, my love. Please stay calm. His head flicks to me, eyes warring between black and gold, fangs protruding over his lips. *She has my father in some floramancy stasis. Don't kill her. And don't change, it's what she wants. I'm not hurt, I promise.*

"Finally, some fun," Anahima says. She whistles, and the griffin we arrived on swoops down low to collect her right as she rips a huge piece of metal edging from the closest turret with her magic and hurls it at her brother. In a blink she wheels around, she and the griffin heading straight for Indira.

I deflect the flying metal with a thought and it lands with a boom several feet away. I run to Darrius; his face is back to normal, but his eyes are burning with a volatile cocktail of emotions. I kiss him fiercely, quickly. "Get Indira and deal with your sister. I'll handle the king."

"Are you sure?" he asks as his azdaha takes to the skies, talons out, narrowly dodging more metal projectiles.

"Yes, go before Indira gets hurt. She needs you."

He disappears into a swirl of shadows, rising upward to reappear on his azdaha's back. Magic explodes in the sky as the siblings collide. Dare is by far the better warrior, but Anahima is not to be underestimated, and I'm sure this is all part of some distraction . . . some master plan. She doesn't do anything without a reason, and though she'd seemed surprised when Darrius had arrived, she's not the kind of adversary to not meticulously prepare for every possible outcome.

Sensing the weapons pointed at me, I turn in slow motion as silvery runes flare up and down my arms. "I don't want to hurt you," I say to the kingsguard, a circle that includes Clem and Hamid. "Your jādū weapons are no match for me."

"Seize her," the Oryndhrian king commands.

Eight guards rush me as one, and iridescent ribbons of heat flare from my fingertips, sending them ricocheting backward. I'd rather not kill anyone, if I can help it. I snatch two dropped swords and fend off dual attacks at my front and back, spinning to parry one while thrusting toward another. The clash of steel fills the air, interspersed by the occasional screams from Indira and the griffin—but I can't look up. It's taking every bit of memory of my training with the Aspačanā raissas to fend off the highly skilled Oryndhrian kingsguard.

"Clem, why are you doing this?" I yell to my former friend when our blades crash. "Blindly following orders." I shoot a burst of magic out at the two guards creeping up behind me, sending them sprawling to their knees. "You know it's not him," I say, crashing my blade into hers hard enough to make her cry out.

"If I don't, someone else will," she pants. "Someone more ruthless than me."

I frown and slam into her side. "What do you mean?"

"At least this way I can save some people." Clem's eyes burn as she lowers her weapons, completely vulnerable before me. I blink in disbelief as Hamid does the same. "We're not all powerless and we control the things we can control. You taught me that."

They stayed to *disobey* orders?

A pained scream from above finally draws my gaze, and I suck in a breath as the griffin's claws rake across Indira's exposed belly and she goes into a wild spiral before catching herself midfall. Incensed, she flies at her enemy, talons outstretched to return the favor.

This needs to end.

I let my simurgh fly. The power that rides my fingertips makes me gasp. Luminescent tendrils fly out of me, latching on to every single person, holding them completely immobile. I pick my way through the magically bound guards, until I reach the king.

Him, I study with intensity. All the rage in the world is in those purple-hued eyes, brimming with hunger and hate. Killing him would be a mercy to the world . . . but if Roshan truly is in there, buried somewhere in the recesses of his own mind . . .

I made a promise that I would try.

The king's eyes widen when I reach out. "No, what are you doing?! Don't touch me, girl!"

"Roshan never talked this much."

I slam my palms over his temples and shove my magic inside of him, targeting each one of his chakras and the rot hiding there. It is the same approach I used with Razulek, only this is the source and it's going to be much harder.

I'm expelling so much magic, it hurts to breathe, but I focus and *push*, drilling down to the rotten pulsing core deep in his solar plexus—the chakra of ego, identity, power, and strength.

No wonder Fero has such a strong hold.

He howls as my light continues to burn away the spread, drawing attention from above. Out of the corner of my eye, I see Anahima shriek and dive down on her griffin, a panicked look on her face as she realizes what I'm doing. Darrius intervenes, cutting his sister off with bolts of magic, and I can hear her enraged roar.

Galvanized into action, I push my magic harder, reaching for every last drop of akasha. It's a wild, reckless move, but I don't stop. And slowly, inexorably, the king's gaze begins to clear of the miasma. His brown eyes—eyes I finally recognize—appear, tired but lucid. His body droops under my hands as if the god of death has drained the very life from him.

As he falls, Roshan grabs his dagger, and for a breathless moment, I think he's going to stab me with it. But he places the tip at his ribs, angling it up toward his heart.

"Kill. Me," he rasps as I keep pushing my waning magic into him. "Sura." My heart clenches at his words, at the despair in them. *"Please."*

"Roshan, stop," I tell him, swallowing the knot in my throat. "Trust me. I'm almost there."

He reaches up with his free hand to my face. "Always . . . love . . . you."

I can barely hear him, each strangled breath of air punching out of his lungs. Fuck, I'm losing him! Desperation grabs hold. *No, no, no.* I'm so close, but the last infernal clot holds fast like the parasite it is. Half sobbing, I slam more magic into it, aware that I'm using a dangerous amount . . . and that I don't know the consequences of pushing to my very limits . . .

Magic bleeds into me, and I can sense it as Darrius's.

Finish it, my soul-fated urges.

What about you? I yelp, just as a bolt of lightning nearly lifts him off of Indira, and the flow of magic falters for a second. I gasp as

Darrius turns to shadow and re-forms on the azdaha's back. He's safe—but Anahima is heading right for me.

I fling up a weakened shield much too late when a sheet of ice magic smashes into me, slamming me backward. My skull crashes into the stone of the courtyard and my bones shatter as my eyesight dims, blood thundering in my ears. It takes a moment too long for my already sluggish magic to heal me, and by the time my vision returns, Anahima is stooped over Roshan's supine body, chanting something. A blade flashes, but I can't see if she's hurt him or not.

Our eyes meet as brackish purple murk rises out of the king's mouth and disappears into Anahima's. Her expression is equal parts victorious and vicious as she grabs a screaming Helena and vanishes into a portal winking open behind her, taking her father's unholy essence with her. A second portal appears in the lower courtyard and the Scavs pour into it, but I can't worry about them right now.

On my hands and knees, I crawl dazedly over to the fallen king, feeling the blood leak down my back from my shattered skull. Aran is already beside him, casting his healing spells, though his face is abnormally ashen. "He's not responding," he cries.

"Roshan," I croak beside his limp body. A thin line of blood wells along his cheek that wasn't there before. Remembering the glint of the blade, I have no idea why Anahima would have cut him, but thankfully, it's not worse. "Roshan! Wake up!"

A vortex of shadows thuds down beside me, sending some of the men scattering, as my soul-fated gathers me into his arms. Lacerations and lightning burns litter his tattooed skin. "Starbright."

A garbled sob escapes me. "Darrius, he's dying. Can you save him?" Unfathomable midnight eyes meet mine, agony and indecision in them. I know what I'm asking, and I also know that he will deny me nothing, not while he has the strength to do it. *"Please."*

His eyes flutter shut, but then he nods once and removes his mother's necklace from my neck. A muscle tics in his jaw as he leans over my former lover and fastens the catch around the king of Oryndhr's throat.

"The opal contains the pure essence of my uncle," he says softly. "My mother was killed by Fero before she had a chance to use it. If anything can save him, this can. It will be up to Saru now."

Darrius . . . I can't get the words out, sorrow and gratitude choking me, but he feels my ragged emotions through our nearly complete bond anyway.

"I'll do anything for you, wife, even save another man. But are you certain this is what he wants?"

Roshan had asked me to kill him. But that was when Fero had nearly won. I also know what Dare is asking: using Saru's essence without Roshan's explicit consent, even to save him, is a gray area. Selfishly, I know what *I* would want . . . but it's not my permission to give.

Unsure, I glance at Aran, who nods without hesitation. "Yes. His heart endured only for you. If his soul accepts Saru's gift, it will still be his choice."

My throat closes up, eyes stinging, as the gem starts to glow when Darrius whispers an inaudible command. We hold our collective breath while the purest sliver of light from the pendant dissipates into the king's waxy, sallow skin. He's bathed in warm gold, a strange ethereal glow settling over him that brightens until we're forced to look away.

"Stay, Roshan, please," I whisper.

Aran is praying fervently to Saru, his lips moving and tears pouring down his cheeks. Everyone else in the kingsguard looks somber and scared, the waiting untenable.

And then I feel it . . . the slow dribble of akasha in his veins that quickly becomes a flood. I sit up and exchange a look with Darrius. He smiles, though his face carries a vulnerable hurt that he tries valiantly to hide.

I love you, I tell him firmly. *That will never change. Trust in us.*

Clem lets out a small noise, and Aran sucks in a breath as Roshan's chest rises once and then twice. His fingers twitch and his eyelids flutter. With a gasping inhale, he sits upright, eyes flying open and instantly finding me: brown with golden sunbursts at their centers, gleaming with life and Saru's otherworldly light. Brown and alive and full of so much love, my chest aches. There he is.

Gods . . .

Something inside of me—that aching hollow—yearns for completion.

I feel the moment when Darrius vanishes into a flurry of shadows, not because he wants to leave but because the curse is kicking in and he still has a kingdom to protect.

Dare, wait.

I need to run and clear my head.

Are you all right? I ask. I feel his torment through the bond.

I will always trust you, Starbright.

Chapter Thirty-Four

The Night King

Ours, the soul bond screams.

She is our sun—our *star*—our reason for living. Our happiness is her happiness.

And if that includes another, she is still *ours* to adore.

By the blood, I have never felt anything like this, my body struggling between killing every single soul that looks at my mate and destroying the world to give her everything she desires. And I know she still wants the Oryndhrian king. Still *loves* him. I can feel it through the bond, and the thought of losing her decimates me.

It's my greatest fear come to life.

I shift, unable to control my emotions.

As the manticore, we run and run and *run*. We run until our muscles are shivering and we're so exhausted that thinking is impossible. And then we sleep and do it all again. Run, hunt, sleep. Life exists simply by instinct.

When I eventually shift back and return to the palace, I recall the feel of her soul calling out to his, and his to hers. And now that he has the light of Saru burning inside of him like a living, divine flame, there's something there. A *bond*. It's frayed and worn and threadbare, but I can see it tethering them to each other. Not a soul-fated union, but a union nonetheless.

All it needs is a little care.

"I can destroy it," I whisper to myself.

"But will you?" a soft voice asks.

I turn to find Ve standing in my study, face wreathed in compassion, and I can't find it in myself to send them away with my usual rancor. "No. I could never hurt her."

"Even if she chooses someone else?" they prod.

I sigh. "Even so."

"Love makes space for everyone," Ve says sagely. "She won't love you less because she also loves another. You're a deity, you know this. You've seen all the wondrous shapes of the phenomenon of love in dozens of lifetimes."

They're not wrong. I *do* know this. Love is infinite, perfectly imperfect, and layered in its complexity. It might bring hardship and take sacrifice or work, but it never dies if nurtured. It endures through any storm. Love only fails if you give up on it.

"I saw that this path was written in her future," Ve remarks. "But I could not see how it would come together. I suppose that's up to you now."

I shake my head. "It will always be up to her. *Her* choice. If she chooses him, it doesn't change that my choice will forever be her in whatever capacity she will accept me."

"And him?" the guardian of the Royal Stars asks, white eyes glittering like a nebula.

"If he loves her as she deserves, then he shall have my greatest esteem."

Ve laughs. "That's rather enlightened of you."

"I am the son of a *god,* Ve," I scoff. "If we aren't more evolved than mortals, then the realms have a lot more to worry about than two people daring to love the same woman."

"That is very true, Your Majesty. And what will you do about your sister? She craves the power to wield the touch of death."

"Anahima has always been ambitious," I say, though my heart aches at the thought of my sister hiding so much from me for so long. "And she has grown strong. I knew she felt cast aside as a child, but I never realized it had festered for so long."

"The men in her life have always disappointed her," Ve says. "Her father, her soul-fated. Even you, by taking the role she felt was hers by birth."

"I would have gladly given it to her," I burst out. "I never wanted a crown. She was the one born to rule, not me." A hitched breath leaves my lungs. "This is my fault. I should have seen what she was going through. Even with Vogonis . . . I should have hunted that bastard down and killed him. I can't even think of what such a betrayal would be like . . . the devastation."

"She's angry," Ve says.

"And a threat to all of Endara."

Ve frowns, eyes going vacant as though contemplating the different threads of the future. "Yes, she is a powerful sovran, and with your father's stolen power, she is dangerous, with magic equal to the Starkeeper's. You will need to complete the bond."

"I am aware." I exhale. "Either way, I suppose I will have to face him and end him."

"Can you?"

"I don't know," I murmur. "Even the worst of us can be worthy of redemption. Sura taught me that."

"Well said." Ve props their long frame on the edge of a couch. "So back to the other thing. How's this going to work with two royal swords in the mix? Sandwich style? Pyramid? Spit-roasted? Oh, *she* might enjoy that."

I shoot them a mock glare with no heat in it. "Don't you have somewhere else to be?"

"Why, Darrius, I was so certain we were having a moment," Ve says, and then winks wickedly. "Very well. Don't do anything I wouldn't."

"Go," I growl.

"Spoilsport." Ve cackles. "Fine, I'm going..."

Chapter Thirty-Five

Roshan Acharia, King of Oryndhr

My heart feels so full and so bright. It beats the song of perpetual hope, and each beat is for her. The one whose fierce, benevolent spirit I crushed with *his* cruelty.

The love of my life.

Stars above, I remember everything: her laughter, her joy, her divinity when she shattered in my arms, her passion, the adoration in her beautiful gray eyes, and, *by the maker,* her *love* . . . and then her confusion, her sorrow, the way she looked when I shackled her, her hurt, her pain, her disappointment . . . and finally, her loathing for the monstrous creature I embodied.

And then she ran.

He had been furious, but I'd been secretly victorious.

My desert starling deserved to be free.

I cursed the rot that ate away at my humanity, and every day as I grew smaller, I guarded the spark she'd given me with everything I had. I would hold on to my Starkeeper's precious light to the last—she would be the final and only thing I saw until death took me.

And then she came and drew the rot out. Saved me . . . again.

But she is no longer mine.

She is . . . *his*.

Pain blooms like razor-petaled roses.

He's the one who gave you my power so you could live, a voice says, and I shiver at the sheer divine might of it.

"Saru?" I whisper, and rub at my bare chest. I look down at the golden starburst that had appeared out of nowhere—the god of light's symbol—as it glows softly. I'm still getting used to my new form, a form that feels slightly less mortal. While the god of death's rot devoured me, the god of creation's light empowers me.

In part, yes.

"I thank you for your gift."

Thank my nephew, he says. *Darrius would not have done it if he did not believe you were worthy of it. Nor would you have been able to accept my gift without akasha of your own.*

Shocked, I blink. "I have magic?"

Your parents were soul-fated—one blessed by Huma and one blessed by me. Sometimes our bloodlines are dormant for reasons beyond our comprehension. Saru sighs softly. *But now, you will survive because of it and return to your Starkeeper, who also found you worthy. Twice.*

My throat thickens. "That's just it, I'm *not* worthy." Sorrow makes my voice break. "Not of her, at least. I've hurt her irreparably."

My twin's power is hard to defeat. Even I was cast into god-sleep when I banished him.

"I should have fought harder."

Fight now. Fight for the future you both deserve.

I frown. "But she chose him."

The god's laughter echoes like bells. *No, child. Darrius is her soul-fated, they were chosen for each other by their magic and the Royal Stars. But love isn't always fated; love can also be a choice. You were freely hers.* I feel his light cast warmly over me. *So choose her in return.*

"How?" My frown deepens, hope and despair twining within. "I don't understand. How can I share her with another? I can't fight a soul-fated bond."

Do you love her?

"Yes."

Does she love you?

"I hope she does."

Then that is all that matters. There is no sharing. There is only giving.

It feels strange to be back in the palace in Kaldari.

Even stranger to be in full possession of myself as king.

My heels tap along the marble floors as people bow, their expressions still fearful as if they expect the monster to return at any point. It hurts my heart to see how I've lost the trust of even the servants who have worked in the palace since I was a boy.

When Fero had been in my body, it had felt like I had become nothing but a passenger. Or more aptly, a hostage, who was incapable of resisting.

I remember everything clearly, which makes my actions hard to conceive and forgive. There are times when I *wish* I could forget how vicious and ruthless he was, when he removed his opposition—nobles and aldermen I had known for years—simply because they spoke up against me. Or when I used her . . . like a tool. A weapon of destruction.

Gods . . .

I find my way back to our shared bedchamber and stare at the bed where we'd held hands and confessed our dreams and our darkest secrets, whispered our fears and our fragile hopes for the future. Where we'd kissed and made love endlessly, and I'd proven my heartfelt dedication over every inch of that perfect body. Where we'd been wrapped in each other's arms and murmured cherished words of adoration and love.

Stroking the silken counterpane, I exhale and press against my chest, the ache there almost too much to bear. I remember her sweet, unhinged laughter when I tickled her and the wicked promises in her eyes when she threatened to get me back . . . her magic torturing me for hours in the center of this very bed. I recall the devotion in her eyes as she curled up and spoke of her beloved family, and the ephemeral warmth of those iridescent ribbons—dancing and playful—a complete, natural extension of her.

I ruined those things. *Lost* those things. I feel my eyes burn with the shame of it, a pounding taking up residence between my temples. She had stayed for so long, even while I'd become a monster worse than my brother had been . . . until I had given her no choice but to run from me. Ashes, could I have fucked this up any more?

I love her . . . but will she be able to ever love me back? Ever *forgive* me?

"Roshan?"

Her voice is low, and I let the rich sound of it fill me and give me courage. Sometimes the only way past something is through. Fero's actions might not have been mine, but she had still been hurt because of them.

I swallow and turn. Slowly, reverentially, I let *my* eyes drift over her: the light on her beautiful face, the luminous glow of her skin, the wild, tumbling wealth of silver-streaked hair, and that tremulous smile. Stars, I've missed her.

"Starling," I whisper, mapping every single one of her beloved features and drinking her in as if she's my sole reason for living. She is. She has always been.

"What are you doing?" she asks, walking over to me. "You're going to be late to address your council."

"There's something I need to say to you first," I say, voice thick.

Compassion blooms in those pretty gray eyes—there she is again, trying to safeguard me from myself, trying to absolve me. "I know, Ro. I felt it all. You don't have to relive any of it."

"I want to." I reach for her palms and wait for her to place them in mine. I stroke their warm centers, grazing lines I've traced a thousand times. "You were always my spark of light when I was lost in the darkness. I'm so sorry for everything. I tried, you know. To fight him. I just couldn't win. Thank you for believing in me."

She bites her lip, cheeks flushing. "I'm not that selfless, Ro. Don't make me out to be some kind of martyr. I thought you were lost. I gave up."

"And I gave you no choice. Sometimes you have to let go of a sinking stone or risk being submerged yourself. I'm glad you did." I swallow past the thickening knot in my throat, my voice cracking. "I'm glad you found someone whom you deserve . . . who deserves you."

A frown forms on her brow. "What do you mean?"

"You're married now," I say. "Soul-fated to the king of Everlea, the man who saved my life. Or did I get that wrong?"

"You didn't," she replies quietly.

"Do you love him?"

Her eyelashes flutter. "Yes."

A stabbing sort of agony pierces my chest at the thought of her in the arms of someone else . . . in the arms of a king who isn't me . . . laughing with him . . . *loving* him. A person whom the fates and the gods had chosen for her. But Saru had said that I still have a chance.

Real love doesn't have limits or constraints.

Love is whatever one needs it to be.

Tentatively, I pull her closer, reading her cues with trepidation, but she comes willingly and lets out a contented sigh once she's cradled against my chest. It feels *so* good to hold her. Her sweet jasmine scent blooms in my nose, and I breathe her in like she's the only air I need to exist.

I tip her chin up, fingers feathering over her smooth jaw. "I hope we can find our way back to each other one day. Even if I might not deserve your forgiveness, even if I am much too late to make amends, I won't stop trying."

"It was never truly *you* doing those horrible things, Ro," she whispers, those beautiful gray eyes holding mine. "There's nothing to forgive." She rises onto her toes and presses her lips to mine in a sweet, chaste kiss for the briefest of seconds before she pulls away. "I'm sorry, I shouldn't have done that," she says, blushing when she sees my astonishment.

"Why?" I ask hoarsely.

"I don't even know if this is what you want . . ."

"Make no mistake, my starling, I'll *always* want."

Pressing her flush against me with a groan, I cup her jaw in both hands, threading my fingers through the mass of her hair, thumbs brushing over her cheekbones. Her lips part in unconscious invitation, and I claim her mouth with all the love and hope I have in my heart. She moans as her tongue sweeps hungrily along mine, and I devour her taste like a man starved.

The kiss feels like coming home.

Chapter Thirty-Six

Heat bursts between my legs and I squirm in my seat for the dozenth time.

This bond is relentless.

Not to mention watching two commanding and equally attractive kings preside over war strategy for the realms of Everlea and Oryndhr at each end of an enormous table.

On one side of the room, Roshan sits with his hands steepled, his handsome face somber. There's no sign of the evil god remnant that had been controlling him. He's the old Roshan and the man I fell in love with. The man I *still* love.

Perhaps, like him, I'd never truly let go of the spark between us... and the fact that I'd given him part of my soul so he could live binds us together even now. The greatest poets say you never forget your first love. And that's true, but mine is also eternally linked to me by the choice I'd made. A choice I stand by even now.

Even *after* everything.

Each day, a handwritten note is delivered to my chambers from the king of Oryndhr, some with earnest intentions to win back my love, some with sweet, poetic nothings, some with his favorite memories of us—the day he first saw me, our first kiss, when we made love—and others with the thoughts of me that had sustained him while he was under the influence of Fero. They come without fail, and I am eager to read each one.

He is determined to keep his promises and earn my forgiveness one day at a time.

But the truth is . . . I've already forgiven him. An offense is only unforgiveable if one is lacking in remorse and repentance, and Roshan has proven that he will do everything in his power to right his wrongs. As he has said, a true king will accept the consequences of his actions, even if they were steered by another's hand. He is responsible for his people and for guiding them down the right path.

The deep sense of nobility I admired about him hasn't changed, nor has his honor or integrity been irrevocably corrupted by Fero. Surreptitiously, I peer at him, drinking in his golden good looks that have only become more so in the months we've been apart.

His deep brown hair has grown longer, curling over his collar in a way that makes my fingers itch to touch it, and without the god of death eating away at him, his beautiful features hold a serenity that I haven't seen in an age. He's leaner, but no less strong—those wide shoulders and tapered waist still combining to make me breathless.

The memory of that sculpted body from Nyriell is firmly lodged in my brain. At the thought of my first time, my chest squeezes. Roshan has always been an attentive, careful lover. Would he be the same now?

At that wickedly provocative notion, my gaze shifts to my soulfated. My heart gives a quiver behind my ribs at the sight of Darrius, as it usually does. Impressive and kingly, he sprawls in his chair, silver hair fashioned into a warbraid, sides of his skull shaved short and with that spiky onyx crown resting fiercely on his brow. My mouth waters at the strength in that honed, preternaturally still form, like an apex predator lying in wait.

Little do the people know that beneath that mortal skin, a manticore prowls. His perfect face is carved in ruthless authority, the curve of his stern but sultry mouth pulled tight, his intense gaze directed to the map at the center of the table. I want that brutal midnight stare on me . . . undressing me, promising all the deliciously filthy things he will do to me later.

Stop, wife. Or I will fuck you in front of everyone on this table and let them watch.

I inhale audibly, a heated tremor pulsing at my core—gods, I wouldn't say no—and my cheeks burn at the admission, right before slamming down my mental walls. Being watched isn't one of my proclivities, but if it means getting my king inside me, I could be persuaded.

Especially if Roshan is watching . . . or participating.

The rush of heat accompanying that image is extreme.

By the gods, Starbright, I can scent your desire.

I blush hard. *I'm sorry. I'll try to keep a better hold on my emotions.*

An amused growl comes down the bond. *In any other situation I wouldn't mind, but I am unable to stand at the moment, lest I put my raging erection on display.*

Eyes fluttering shut at the sudden inclination to destroy the table blocking my view—and the equally violent urge to climb beneath it—I swallow. *Sorry, it's the bond.*

But it isn't just the bond, because I want Roshan, too.

And that terrifies me, because I don't want to have to choose between them.

"Are you well?" Clem whispers from where she's sitting on my right, her gaze concerned. "You're very flushed."

I nod and summon a pulse of ice magic to cool my overheated body. *There.* "There are a lot of people in here."

"It is quite warm," she agrees.

The war room is big, but it's definitely filled to capacity with Darrius and his small council, Roshan and his entourage, including the alderman of each city in Oryndhr, and the Aspačanā, as well as a few high nobles of Everlean cities.

My father would be here with Aran and their merry band of rebels, but he's currently sleeping in my old room in the castle. Miracle of miracles, Nuadar, of all people, had been the one to administer the healing tonic, specially brewed to counter Anahima's, that was saving him. I can't believe I thought he was the oracle.

Although I am being gracious to Clem, Aran, and Hamid, I'm more cautious in my goodwill. While Roshan had an evil ancient god manipulating him, they were obeying him without any such manipulation. To a degree, I can empathize, as I also did monstrous things out of loyalty to my king. But it will take time to trust them fully, I suspect.

Tell them the azdaha will fly for our riders.

The familiar, beloved voice nearly makes me leap from my seat. *Raz! How are you feeling?*

Ready for war, little queen.

I blow out an anxious breath. *Maybe you should sit this one out.*

And maybe you should go—how do you mortals say it again?—kick a rock.

Ouch, Raz. Solid burn. I laugh out loud, drawing a few angry looks as whoever was speaking thought I was laughing at them. *I better go. Things are getting wild here.*

By the time I finish talking to Raz, the noise in the war room has risen to a loud pitch as the Aspačanā leaders argue about how to handle Anahima and her revenant army. Karânî and Zahre are not letting any rais or nobleman silence them. I try to listen as Zahre argues with the new rais of Rakh that he should focus his forces on any attacks that might come from the sea.

He's shouting back that he doesn't want Rakh to be cut out of the battle. I rub my temples when Karânî argues that it's not a matter of being left out, it's a matter of covering all points of entry and vulnerability. He roars at her for Shabra to do it, and she bares her teeth at his aggression.

Darrius clears his throat, his shadows flaring out. Ink crawls up the walls, blanketing everything in darkness like a violent tide before receding and leaving silence in their wake. No one makes a sound, no one even moves, but every cell in my body comes furiously alive.

"You will be respectful, Batis," he says softly, coldly.

The rais bows his head. "Of course, Your Majesty. Raissa Karânî, I apologize."

The king's shadows settle back into his skin and creep over his thick throat. I want to lick them. I want to *bite* into that strong cord of muscle, trace my tongue over those collarbones. Another stab of arousal makes me nearly swallow my tongue as I envision those tendrils writhing over every needy inch of my skin.

Gods . . . what is wrong with me? I close my eyes and fight for calm.

Concentrate, Sura, I growl at myself.

"I agree that we should defend any potential access to Everlea," the king is saying, and I try hard not to notice his deep, smoky baritone. "Princess Anahima is one of, if not *the* cleverest minds in the realm. She will use every avenue to her advantage." He glances at Roshan. "How many men are in that Scav army?"

Roshan frowns. "Several thousand, maybe more. But she has been planning this for months. There are already infiltrators in many of your cities." He nods to the Aspačanā. "Your hordes, as you saw with Masišta." Zahre flinches at that, but composes herself as Roshan continues. "You will have the swords of my royal army, loyal to me."

Darrius glances at his nobles, representatives from Pix, Lora, Morien, and Solis. "Tend to your houses, root out any treachery, and fortify your borders." They all nod somberly as he repeats the same to the hordes. "Morien makes the most logical sense for a larger-scale assault since she has likely circumvented the wards there already. Anahima will leverage the forest beyond Pix for cover, but that valley is where she will make her stand. It's where I would."

"She needs a portal between the two realms," I say, drawing every eye in the room. "That is what she wanted me to do for her."

Darrius's mouth tightens. "With Fero's power, it may be possible for her to create it herself, but she will need a conduit and constant energy to keep it open."

"The azdahas have said they will fly with their riders," I say, passing on Razulek's message. I don't miss the relieved looks on some of the faces. We won't stand a chance without them.

Darrius exhales with a grim look. "You all have your orders. Post extra guards in Morien and Pix. Report back on any activity. I'll reinforce the wards while we amass our legion. Make sure the young and elderly are in the castle or any strongholds. And prepare yourselves for war."

DINNER IS SUBDUED, given the circumstances.

After the earlier chaos, we opt to take it in Darrius's private dining room. On a whim, I decided to invite Roshan, which I'm now thinking was a mistake, considering the two men have done nothing but stab at their plates and try to glare each other into submission. In public, they are united. In private, however, their mutual enmity over the elephant in the room is evident.

The elephant being me.

The tension is so thick it would take an ax to cleave through it, but I am determined to find some common ground before the blades make an appearance.

Darrius had reluctantly promised not to put his magic on display, but that doesn't stop him from sending his wicked shadows to wind around my ankles and calves under the table as if to remind me of their—and his—claim. I almost moan when one of them grazes the overly sensitive skin behind my knee, and admonish him with a glare.

Stop, I tell him.

I can't help it. They love you.

He knows I'd never reject them. So I resign myself to ignoring their little caresses and touches, warning Darrius with my eyes not to allow them to go higher. The mutinous, possessive look in his stare makes me sigh.

"How is the food?" I ask. "I had the royal cook prepare some dishes from Kaldari and also from Coban, as well as some authentic to Verisia."

Both men mumble "good" at the same time.

"Such high praise," I say with a laugh. "I'll be sure to pass on your appreciation."

Roshan looks up, his gaze softening. "It is delicious and very thoughtful of you, starling. Thank you."

Darrius visibly bristles at the nickname, but I send a warning pulse of magic toward him. "Yes, thank you, wife," he says, in a tender tone that both titillates and annoys me, mostly because he knows how cruel it is to flaunt that status in front of Roshan.

The king of Oryndhr sets down his fork to take a sip of his wine, a flicker of hurt flashing over his face before he conceals it. "It still astounds me that you are married."

"Soul-fated," I say softly. "We exchanged vows, but we have one more rite to complete before it is sealed."

He opens his mouth to ask what the rite is and then snaps it shut when he sees Darrius's smirking expression.

"If you don't stop acting like a child this instant, I will refuse to seal this bond," I growl at the Night King, erasing the leer from his face.

"You wouldn't," Darrius says.

I set my jaw. "Try me."

We resume eating, though Roshan seems to have gained a little more vigor to his movements, and Darrius has been suitably chastened. At least enough for us to dine in less fraught silence. When the servants clear the course, dessert and sweet wine are brought in.

"Will you stay in the castle?" Roshan asks. "When we ride out to meet Anahima?"

I lift my brows, spoon arrested halfway to my lips. "Why would I?"

Darrius lets out a deprecating laugh. "She's the Starkeeper," he scoffs. "The most powerful magic user in all of Endara. Why would we keep her here?"

"You would put her in danger and let her fight in front of you? What if she gets hurt?" Roshan asks. "What kind of man are you?"

"One who recognizes the might of his queen," Darrius shoots back. "And yes, she will fight beside me on the battlefield, where she belongs."

"If you love her as you claim, wouldn't you want to protect her? To keep her safe?"

"By suffocating her? She's not a damsel or a weakling."

"I never said she was," Roshan volleys.

Darrius laughs. "That was always your problem, Acharia. You can't shackle a creature meant to soar."

Dead silence blankets the room at the allusion to my old bracers. A muscle flexes in Roshan's cheek as he stares at me with so much remorse brimming in those gold-flecked brown eyes. "I know, you're right." He swallows hard and faces me. "And I am deeply sorry I had any part in that. I will beg your forgiveness every day for the rest of my life if I have to."

"I've already forgiven you, Ro," I say softly.

He shudders visibly. "I don't think you're weak. You're magnificent. What you did with Morvarid and Vogon, no one else could ever do. You saved Oryndhr. Saved *me*. I suppose I just want to protect you like you protected everyone else."

"I understand," I say. "I feel the same about you and Darrius. I want you safe, too. And the idea of either of you in danger or getting hurt is something I refuse to contemplate." I wink at him. "And by the same token, no, I will not remain here. I will stand between the two of you on the battleground, protecting both of your sexy but lesser asses."

Roshan blinks owlishly at me as if trying to parse the sultriness in my voice.

"We are soul-fated," Darrius says arrogantly, making me want to kick him. "She is meant to be at my side."

I open my mouth, but Roshan beats me to it, a smirk spreading on his full lips. "And she *chose* me. I'll always be her first love."

"And I will be her last," Darrius growls, shooting to his feet.

Roshan does the same. "That's not your decision."

Runes flaring, I stand slowly, extending my magic in silvery ribbons toward each of them. "Enough, both of you!"

Standing, they're both of a height, towering over me, and the thought of being pressed between them makes me nearly choke and swallow a decadent whimper. If they don't get their shit together, I'm going to have to take matters into my own hands.

Maybe I *should*.

Deliberately, I block the bond, feeling Darrius's flicker of surprise. I watch in my peripheral vision as my magic winds around their throats, sending other ribbons to bind their arms behind their backs and dragging them back into their seats. Coils wrap around their wide chests and finally slide over their mouths. Roshan's eyes are wide with lust, while Darrius's promise a host of retribution—the wickedest kind.

"I'm in charge now," I say. "You speak when spoken to, and you do not move unless I command it. No magical shadows, either. You do not question your queen. Do you consent? If you don't, I will not fault you for it. We can pretend this never happened. But I need this, and I need both of you to cooperate." When they nod in turn, I remove the magical gags from their lips. "Words, please."

"Yes," the king of Oryndhr says huskily. "Anything, always."

The king of Everlea's gaze flashes black to gold and back again. "As you wish, pátnī," he rasps.

Gratified, I put the magical muzzles back in place and take my seat. With a single thought, my dress vanishes into embers, leaving me in the lacy, barely there undergarments I wore for this purpose.

Well, perhaps not for this *exact* purpose.

Nostrils flaring, Darrius strains against his bonds, tattoos roiling on his skin, though obediently stays put. Excitement lights Roshan's eyes, his pulse pounding erratically at his neck. Their gazes are fastened on me—one burning gold-brown starburst that promises to set me ablaze, and one bottomless obsidian abyss that vows to devour me whole.

I shake with arousal, wetness seeping between my thighs.

Gods, I'm *feral* for them.

I throw my head back and dance my fingertips down the column of my neck, walking them downward until they land between my breasts. I magic away the covering, gasping as the cool air pebbles my nipples. I feel their combined stares, sense their desire, bask in their shortened breaths, but I don't acknowledge them. With both hands, I pluck at the taut peaks as my arousal starts to builds.

Stars, I never thought being watched would be so provocative.

But having these two powerful kings at my mercy, mesmerized by me, is a heady feeling.

Keeping my left hand on my breast, my right wanders down the flat of my stomach to the embroidered edge of my undergarment. A masculine groan from one end of the table echoes a grunt from the other. I have no idea who made which sound, and I don't care. I'm much too focused on the swollen, *soaked* part of me that is desperate to be stroked.

Suddenly, without warning, the table is gone and my legs are gently spread over the arms of my chair. I gasp at the new position, and then stare at Darrius, whose expression is savage with lust.

"That's cheating," I tell him, fingers halting and lifting his gag.

"You said we couldn't move," he rumbles. "I did not. The table moved. It was blocking my view."

I can't fault him, considering how I wanted to demolish the table in the war room earlier. "I'll concede this once, but only if you are both in agreement. Otherwise, this stops."

I might die if it does stop, but rules are rules. A queen can't be seen as a rule-breaking pushover because she craves an orgasm.

"I agree it is a technicality," Roshan rasps out. "Removal of an obstruction."

"Very well," I say, hiding my smile. "But no more interference."

I continue my teasing movements, inching over the damp lace to the gusset, where the fabric is drenched. With one hand, I slip the seam to the side, exposing myself, my fingertip slowly dragging down the center. I whimper as I slip through the silken wetness, my spine arching in place as sensation barrels through me.

"What shall I do?" I ask, removing the bindings from their mouths. "Tell me."

"Circle that pretty clit," Darrius says immediately. I do as he says and moan, almost as if it's his hand instead of mine.

"Fuck," Roshan groans. "Now slip a finger inside you. Tell me, how does it feel?"

I do as he says, writhing against the intrusion. "Hot, wet, like velvet."

"Add another." The harsh command is from Darrius. "If you're going to take our cocks later, you need to prepare yourself."

Our. Cocks. The gods save me . . . or *not*.

I groan as my fingers obey and split to stretch me. Roshan, not to be outdone, lets out an approving sound. "Now curl your fingers and find that spot, the one that drives you crazy. That's it," he says when I whine and writhe. "Imagine us filling you in turn and hitting that place inside you with every stroke."

"Fuck," I gasp, imagining them having their filthy way with me to complete ruination. "Yes, please. More."

My hands move faster, my thumb rubbing my clit as my pleasure pulses and spikes. Gods, I'm so close, I'm going to shatter.

"Stop."

The expression on my soul-fated's face is wicked and cruel. The breath rushes out of me as my hands falter and shudder in place. My climax is just out of reach. *No.*

"Darrius," I whimper, and watch as the two kings exchange a look, one of perfect accord. My core twinges in anticipation.

"You set the rules, my queen," Roshan says. "Now open your mouth and lick those fingers clean."

"How does it taste?" my ruthless soul-fated asks, when I immediately do as commanded.

I wrap my tongue around my fingers, lapping up my arousal. "Sweet."

"Good girl," he growls, and I viscerally writhe at the husky praise in his voice. "Get every drop."

Roshan lets out a moan when I suck hard, licking each of my fingers. "Now spread your lips for us. Let us see that pretty pussy."

The position is so deliciously depraved I can feel the fluids trickling down my inner thighs. "Please," I beg. "*Please* let me come. Tell me to come." The last four words are subconsciously layered with psionic compulsion . . . a sidereal command of the Starkeeper.

"Come," they both say at the same time, and I don't hesitate.

My fingers fly to my throbbing clitoris, my arousal so heightened that it barely takes a touch before my climax is cresting and cresting and *cresting,* and then it crashes through me like a tsunami as I shatter with a scream. My magic blasts out of me, stardust falling everywhere in a silvery mist, as quakes rock through every muscle in my body.

Fuck, fuck, fuck. Stars fill my vision, and I think I black out for a moment before the shudders racking me start to lessen. That has to have been the hottest thing I've ever experienced in my life, and neither of them touched me.

Gods. What will happen when they do?

Time to find out.

Chapter Thirty-Seven

Roshan Acharia, King of Oryndhr

The woman I love stands before me, clad in nothing but a transparent robe and those damnable lace undergarments from earlier. Stars above, but she is beautiful. Those bright iridescent locks woven through her wild, dark curls are shimmering, and her gorgeous gray eyes are full of joy and mischief.

She's a Starkeeper who has come into her magic with the grace of a queen, and yet so much of the loyal, strong-willed woman I knew is still there. As much as I hate what Fero did to her through me, sands, she has truly become something to behold. She forged herself into something resilient.

Powerful. Confident. Dauntless.

Seeing her pleasure herself like a siren in front of me had been a gift I'll never forget. I'd felt faintly discomfited at the thought of her in a sensual, erotic display for anyone else. But then I remembered Saru's words: *There is no sharing. There is only giving.* And if this is what she wants—the both of us—I am happy to try.

For her.

To be fair, I hadn't expected that giving her sexual commands with Nightsong would be so fucking erotic or that seeing her unravel so spectacularly because of both of us would nearly make me spend in my trousers. In fact, given the damp state of them, I'm not certain that I *didn't* come a little. Even now, my erection is rock hard and undaunted by the appearance of its competition, so to speak.

Not that I have anything to fear from Darrius Nightsong. I've made my starling sing, and I'll make her sing again.

"Are you ready to fly, Starbright?" a bare-chested king of Everlea asks, prowling nearer to her from the other side of the room. Her mouth falls open with a moan when he reaches her and his hand wraps around her throat as he presses his front to her back. She *melts*.

Her utter submission makes me impossibly hard, and when she turns those limpid gray eyes to me and urges me closer with a crook of her finger, my entire body tightens in response, my cock throbbing with instant, explicit need.

With haste, I remove my boots and unbutton my shirt. I want to make this perfect and memorable for her, no matter what it takes. I follow the silent summons, blanketing her with my front as she lets out a long sigh of pleasure at being pressed between our two bodies. I know how small she is, but when she's in front of Nightsong, held against him like that, she looks so delicate.

And yet, the power in my starling's petite body could decimate an entire realm.

I meet Nightsong's stare, and he gives me a small nod that he is here for whatever our queen wants. I nod in return. He's a difficult man to read at normal times . . . and this is uncharted territory for both of us, it seems. His black eyes flash gold for a second, and I frown, wondering at the change. Is that part of his magic? But it's something to worry about later.

For now, I want to drown myself in Suraya.

Groaning at the sweet vanilla and jasmine scent of her, I sink to my knees and untie the belt of her robe, parting the fabric in the middle so it reveals everything, my eyes snagging on her luscious upturned breasts and then diving to that decadent gathering of creamy lace between her thighs. I lean my head against her belly and drag my nose down to the edge of the lace, inhaling deeply, my eyes nearly rolling back in my head at that intoxicating scent. They're still soaked from her earlier orgasm, her rich fragrance flooding my senses. My mouth fills with water when she lets out the breathiest moan. By the maker, I could eat her alive.

"Roshan," she whispers.

I glance up, noticing that Nightsong has angled her head so that he is kissing and nibbling the tender skin below her ear, his free hand dropping to caress the breast I bared. The sight of her with her mouth parted, whimpering with pleasure as he fondles her, is sultrier than it should be. And suddenly I want to do my part to make her moan. "Yes, love?"

"Touch me, please," she begs, that thundercloud gaze fastened to me.

Teasingly, I run the backs of my knuckles over her mound, delighting in the lurch of her hips. "Here?"

She bites her lip. "Yes."

"As my mistress commands," I say, something I'd said to her during our first time together. She smiles in recognition, and I'm dying to taste her again. Hooking my fingers into the edge of her undergarments, I ease them down her legs, baring her to my greedy gaze. I blink at the neatly groomed expanse of glistening brown skin, nearly bare of any maidenhair. Now *that's* different from last time.

She sees my fascination, her cheeks flaring dark red. "One of my handmaidens said it would be more sensitive. It's easy to remove with magic."

"No complaints here," I say. "I love seeing every exquisite inch of you."

She groans as I run the tip of my nose down her slit. Above me, Nightsong plays with her nipples, pinching hard, but her hips jerk in desperate need every time he does. The scent of her is maddening, and I waste no time in setting my mouth to her, licking from entrance to clit with the flat of my tongue and swirling the tip around her bud and sucking. The moan that leaves her is music to my ears, and I push her legs wider, trying to wedge myself between them.

I peer up, watching while she drags Nightsong down to her mouth for a sloppy kiss, her spine arching as she shoves her lower lips into my mouth. I oblige happily, kissing, licking, and nibbling until her legs start to shake and her hips start to roll more insistently. I push two of my fingers up into her, delighting in her strangled sounds, sucking on her clit hard until her body seizes and convulses. I can feel her walls undulating on my fingers as Nightsong swallows her soft cries. I gorge myself on her pleasure until my face is gleaming with her release.

Stars, she's stunning.

I rise slowly, trailing heated kisses up her abdomen, pressing them softly to the inner curve of each of her breasts. When I finally stand, I bend my head to press my lips to hers, claiming her. My eyes meet Nightsong's obsidian ones over her crown; his pupils are blown out with lust as I'm certain mine are. He smirks, his mouth swollen from the intensity of her kisses.

"I need one of you to fuck me," our fierce queen demands, glaring up at us as if either of us will deny her. *"Now."*

We share a grin at her adorable display of temper.

"How is this going to work?" I ask the king of Everlea. "Do you want to ... go first?"

His irises flash that strange amber color again. "You," he growls gutturally, and I swear I see fangs. "Between the bond and the beast, my instincts are territorial enough. If I fuck her first, I may not be able to control myself after."

"Beast?" I ask, eyes narrowing in confusion.

"It's his curse." Suraya grabs my face and kisses me ferociously. "Don't worry, Dare won't hurt you," she says with a smile that doesn't appease me in the least. She detaches from us and climbs onto the bed, wiggling her delicious ass. "Roshan, I need you inside me."

Nearly mindless with lust, I can't shuck off my trousers fast enough, freeing my engorged cock from its tight confines. I give it one pump, hissing at the sensitivity. Reverently, I notch my crown to her wet entrance and push slowly into her, groaning at the silky feel that not even so many months of separation could make me forget. It's a snug fit, and I work for every single inch.

"Fuck, starling, you feel so good. Like home," I growl when I'm seated. It feels like I'm finally where I belong.

"You do, too." She moans as I withdraw ever so slowly, taking my time and drawing out every bit of the torturous friction. "Darrius, come here."

If she's able to talk, I must not be doing my job very well. I slam back in, making her yelp as I bury myself to the hilt. Obediently, Nightsong shifts to the base of the bed, where he drinks in the sight of her perfect face as I deepen my thrusts. Her body is angled on a diagonal at the edge of the bed.

"Take my mouth," she tells him on a shuddering breath, and I shiver at the throaty lust in her voice. "Make me choke."

Fuck...

Grasping her hips, I feel my eyes roll back in my head at the sublime clench.

Nightsong discards his trousers, and she accepts him between her lips with a garbled groan, while I increase my pace from behind. I have no idea why the idea of her sucking him off while I'm taking her at the same time is so fucking hot, but it is.

I want to make her come so hard that she flies to the moon and the stars she loves so much.

"Ro," she whines, and I warm at the nickname before her mouth is stuffed full again.

"I know, love, I've got you," I say, reaching around to rub her clit. Her body starts to quiver, and I feel my own orgasm start to build at the base of my spine.

She pulls off Nightsong long enough to say, "Come inside me."

Sands. The husky sound of her is like a fucking drug. I thrust faster, slapping wetly against her ass, and pinch her swollen clit as she screams her release. Once more, a shower of starlight bursts from her skin, the runes on her arms glowing an incandescent silver. I come on the heels of her climax with an agonized grunt, drilling myself as far as I can go, her body milking every last drop of me, even as I stare in wonder at the star that is mine.

The Night King

By the fucking blood, I need her now.

The pull of the bond is impossible to resist, and the manticore is savage beneath my skin, growling for completion . . . howling to claim what is *ours*. Hearing her desperate moans, seeing her beautiful face contort with so much bliss even as she chokes on my cock while Acharia takes her to the brink, is like nothing I expected.

I have to give credit where credit is due. The young buck knows how to wring every drop of pleasure from her, and for that alone, I am mollified. If he had been a selfish lover, I would not have been so kind.

The manticore would have devoured him.

Maybe.

Thankfully, the look of radiant satisfaction on her face is a thing to savor. Her movements over my cock are sloppy and uncoordinated, her eyes glassy with tears and her chin wet with drool, but she has never looked lovelier. I ease my crown from her mouth and pass my thumb over her swollen lips, wiping the saliva away.

"Are you all right?" I ask her, pulling her into my arms and kissing her softly on the mouth. Sitting on the edge of the bed, I pull her onto my lap and stroke her hair gently, my magic trailing over her body and checking in with hers. "Too tired? Sore?"

Her smile is so bright and beatific, it's almost blinding. "Not at all."

She reaches for Acharia, who is lying on his stomach across the bed, and feathers her hand through his damp hair. He lets out a soft sound of contentment that I, strangely, don't even feel jealous about. Nor about the fact that he's the reason my wife is so sated and boneless right now. I stroke a fingertip down her bare body, circling the tight buds of her nipples, enjoying the way she arches in my arms.

"You're a vision, Starbright," I whisper softly, my fingers trailing down each rib and over the luscious curve of her hip.

Her thick lashes rise to reveal shining gray eyes lit by haloes of her iridescent power. "I want to seal the bond, Dare. I'm ready. I want to feel you deep inside me and deep in my magic. I want us to be one."

Are you certain? I ask carefully, my rigid control fraying. *It will be rough. The manticore...*

She silences me with her mouth. *I've never been more certain of anything in my life. And I can handle everything you are, Dare. Just give me all of you, that's what I desire. I need the man, the god, and the monster.*

"Say stop if you want it to end," I growl, watching her eyes dilate as I place her on the bed and loom over her with one knee on the mattress like a vengeful beast about to take his prize. The king of Oryndhr moves to prop himself against the headboard, his eyes fastened to our stunning prize, whose body is shaking with desire.

I fist my cock as my shadows writhe with anticipation. Her beautiful gray irises blow out with lust, her stare fastened to my hand while I brutally work myself. I swipe the drop of pearlescent fluid at the tip with my thumb and coat it across her bottom lip, my hunger deepening as she licks it off with a moan.

"Dare..."

My mouth twists with ruthless purpose. Time to see my wife beautifully bound, begging for release, and at my mercy. I set my shadows free, watching as my magic glides up her body, savoring the soft satiny feel of her skin, nestling into every nook and hollow, and coasting over every succulent peak and slope. And when they've painted every inch, then they start to wind and tighten in a series of intricate knots and patterns. I take my time, relishing every moan over each sensitive point, the bond open and mirroring every sensation.

She squirms when my shadows outline the edges of her sex, and *I* shiver.

It's fucking torture, as though I'm the one tied in place.

Two thicker tendrils are held aloft by my will, hoisting my masterpiece a few inches off the bed while the rest gather below, lashing over her breasts and pulling tight enough over her nipples that she moans. Her wrists are layered over each other behind her back, shadows binding them in elaborate loops, and her ankles are cinched to the backs of her thighs. Dual coils hinge her knees apart to her elbows, leaving her beautiful sex bare, parted, and glossy with arousal.

She is art in motion. *Magical.*

And she is mine.

Well, *ours* for as long as she decrees it to be so.

I glance at Acharia, who is watching us with interest, his expression fascinated at the display of magic and the gratifyingly submissive position my stunning Starkeeper finds herself in. Admiring my handiwork, I spin her for our perusal, her rich, luminous brown skin blanketed and crisscrossed in obsidian lines. I move beside her to where she is suspended in the air by my magic and draw a fingernail down her arched throat as her pretty bound thighs come to my eye level. My gums ache as the manticore's fangs push through. He wants to bite—to *mark*.

"Do it," she whimpers, and I realize his need has trickled down through the bond.

Soon.

Roughly, I fist her loose hair that is hanging down nearly to the bed and bend to crush my lips to hers, delving deep into the sweetness of her mouth. Her tongue duels with mine, swirling and sucking me deeper. Splayed wide as she is, she's desperate for the connection, for the friction, anywhere she can get it, even if it's just from my tongue lashing against hers.

"So beautiful," Acharia murmurs, shifting close enough to stroke a finger over the inky bindings across her plump ass.

"She's a fucking goddess like this," I agree and loosen the ties over her legs just enough to pull her knees apart.

Suraya whimpers a needy whine as my shadows draw her to me, spreading her wide over my hips. To my satisfaction, her exposed folds glisten with desire. I knew she would love it! Gratified at her body's response, I stare down at my work of art, appreciating the sublime flow of those generous curves and the swathes of smooth, kissable skin punctuated by my glimmering bands of onyx, all laid out like the most succulent offering.

To her god...

To *me*.

Kneeling, I situate myself at her entrance and slam home in a single thrust, my eyes nearly rolling back in my head at the exquisite snugness of the cunt that was made for me. Her scream of pleasure edged by pain fills me with savage delight as I start to move. The arched position makes me hit a spot inside of her that causes her body to contort even more. Her eyes snap open as her core starts to flutter, her thighs straining and trembling.

"I'm going to...Darrius...fuck...I can't..."

"Let it happen, Starbright, I have you," I purr. Her body tenses, blood flushing every inch of her skin as her magic lights up every single rune, and then I release each of the knotted tethers at once. The rush of both her blood and her orgasm floods the bond as she splinters apart, and *gods,* the feeling of her climax echoing through me transcends anything I've ever felt.

Lowering her to the bed, I fuck her through it, her body thrashing beneath mine as the orgasm rolls into another. My eyes flash and my mouth crowds with teeth as I feel the beast, and in a panic, I force him back.

"No, let him through," she says, wrapping her legs around me. "I need *all* of you."

The shift is partial, but I can feel the fur sprouting as my fangs lengthen and my buried cock thickens. Suraya writhes, her body stretching to accommodate us and her reassurance flowing through the bond. *I can take you, don't stop.*

"What the fuck?" the king of Oryndhr blurts. Through the manticore's otherworldly sight, I can see his body outlined in a curious film of gilded radiance.

"It's all right, Roshan," my wife says. "He's mine, too."

I fuck her faster and meet her eyes. "He wants to bite."

"Then bite," she pants, head falling back in bliss.

She reaches out blindly for Acharia, her fingers tangling with his as she yanks him toward her to claim his mouth. The bond is wide open, her deep-rooted emotions for him also flowing down it, and oddly, I don't feel any rancor.

Her love is pure and beautiful and *real*.

But I can also feel her love for *me*, and that remains undiminished and true.

"Páti," she whispers, and I shiver at the claim. Her eyes are glowing with silvery filaments, the streaks through her mass of dark hair luminous with iridescence. I can feel my thundering pulse everywhere—in my chest, in my head, in my cock—as our magic intertwines.

"It's time," I tell her.

Suraya Saab, Starkeeper

Gods, I have never felt so full.

The pressure of my king's half shift is otherworldly. Somewhere deep down, I'm aware that I'm fucking a monster, but he's *my* monster and that's all that matters.

I reach for Roshan, who is still staring with wide eyes at Darrius's sharpened face, the sprouted mane, and the mouth full of fangs, though his expression has morphed from concern to interest, more so because of my enthusiastic participation. Grinning, I pull his mouth to mine and bury my tongue inside, coaxing his out to suck on it.

Stars, he tastes so good, like honey and iron, making me think of delicious desserts and hot forges. He kisses me back, hand moving to fondle my breast. With a moan, I reach for his hardening cock and pump my fingers from root to tip. Between the marvelous efforts of my two lovers, the sensation is nearly overwhelming, my mind already starting to fracture with bliss. I can't recall how many times I've climaxed. There was one point where my orgasm seemed unending, one flowing into the other.

Darrius quickens his pace, rolling his thumb over my clit, and everything starts to ratchet anew between us. He fucks me harder, and I pump Roshan in time with his thrusts. There's a synchronicity to our movements, the cadence of our breaths, and our magic dancing in a play of light and shadow.

"Harder, starling," Roshan moans, and I squeeze firmly just as Darrius snarls and hitches my leg high to claim an extra inch, slamming so deep my vision wobbles. He leans over, eyes gleaming bright gold, one strong arm planted on the bed beside my head, and I feel the graze of sharp teeth where my neck meets my shoulder.

I bare my throat in perfect trust. *Mate.*

Everything happens in glorious succession. Fangs sink into me, the bite of pain preceding an obscene rush of pleasure that obliterates me as I bear down on Roshan, who comes with a savage snarl, his gaze never leaving mine. Darrius's filthy groans are a balm to my heart when he explodes with a roar, the sound multilayered with man and beast, spilling his seed into me as his shadows devour the entire room.

Whimpering at the onslaught of my endless orgasm, my magic erupts through his darkness like a maelstrom of shooting stars, and as he collapses on the bed next to me, the soul bond seals between us—the beautiful tether glittering like a piece of the night sky.

But that's not what makes me gasp in wonder.

It's the shadows swirling with stardust and edged by the golden light of the sun that surround the three of us. I've never seen anything so ethereal, so godsdamned *magical*. I turn to Roshan, who is *glowing* with lambent golden light . . . a light that winds up my forearms to coil with the black and silvery runes already embedded there.

The interplay of the three—shadow, starlight, and sunlight—takes my breath away. My two halves . . . my two loves. At the realization, something vital locks into place, a feeling of completion in my soul. A sense of rightness.

Only now do I understand the prophetic words of my simurgh: *We are the passage between the earth and the sky, a conduit between the bright of the sun and the dark of the moon—both of your halves will be loved and anchored by kings.*

Darrius, the darkness of my night sky, and Roshan, the radiance of my rising sun.

My soul-fated *and* my chosen.

Chapter Thirty-Eight

The attack comes within a week, much sooner than we expected.

But Anahima isn't one to dawdle—she's a planner and she's methodical—she would not have moved unless all her playing pieces were in place. I feel a twinge in my gut at the thought of my friend's betrayal, though I can't even imagine what Darrius is feeling.

This is his *sister*, his right hand, the one he trusted most in the world.

My heart breaks for him. For both of them.

The king of Everlea left at the crack of dawn to meet with his war council and ready the Aspačanā. Roshan departed for Oryndhr a handful of days ago so that he could gather his army, and while the thought of him being so far away from me forms a huge knot in my chest—mostly because I can't feel him like I do Darrius via our soul bond—I know he'll be careful. Still, it feels like my heart is walking around unprotected outside of my body and I hate it.

"Don't you dare do anything stupid like die," I'd warned Roshan as I peppered him with kisses before he entered the portal to Kaldari. "If you do, I will be forced to reanimate you with sanguimancy magic and then murder you slowly."

He had smiled, tucking my hair behind my ear. "So vicious."

"I mean it. I didn't get you back only to lose you."

"You won't lose me, my starling. I promise."

Darrius had stood behind me, his strength the only thing keeping me upright as one half of my heart left for another realm. "He has the power of Saru, Starbright," he had whispered. "I suspect he might be immortal. In fact, I'm certain of it. The manticore saw a divine light around his aura."

That insight had given me a small measure of peace, but until Roshan is back here with me, I remain anxious.

The plan is to bring his army to Everlea via a portal in Solis. With Rakh guarding the sea-facing borders and Shabra, Karkad, and Chamros defending the west, as well as Darrius's army covering the north, Roshan will be well placed for any attacks from the east. We will have a defense on all fronts, or at least that is the idea. I'm sure that Anahima has a contingency plan in place, and my stomach is roiling with dread.

I pop into my old bedroom to check on my father. He's asleep, but he has been able to stay awake now for hours at a time. Nuadar is the reason my father is still alive. After Maxur's prompt interrogation, the beastmaster had made no effort to conceal his mind from his king's psionic magic, proving his loyalty.

I'm not too proud to admit that I might have judged him unfairly.

In truth, without his help, the deadly serum would have kept eating away at my father until he was too weak to live. But now, his sleep cycle will return to normal and the lethargy from the toxin will leave his muscles. Papa will have to undergo some special healing for any atrophying of his body, but according to Nuadar, he's going to be just fine.

"Did you know Anahima was a sovran-level magi?" I ask Ziba as she helps me into my leathers and armor in Darrius's quarters.

Ziba lets out a telling sigh. "As a child that girl had a jealous streak a mile long, but she hid it well. Everyone in the castle knew the princess had power, but when she tested, she was mestial or dominant at best."

"She told me the same," I say, wincing as she draws the buckles as tight as possible.

"It was part of her outer mask," Ziba says. "Downplay her strengths, pretend to be a healer while secretly studying how to use advanced corpus magic in poisons and toxins, not to mention her dabbling in death and blood magic. If anyone caught her, she manipulated their memories with them none the wiser."

I let out an exhale. "She could do that?"

Ziba nods. "A sovran-level psionic magi can do that and more. Some as powerful as Princess Anahima and the king can create whole illusions that aren't real, that exist only in the minds of those affected. For a long time, I thought only King Darrius possessed that power."

"Gods," I whisper, alarm rising at the thought of Anahima controlling me or anyone I love. I recall some of the images with Zahre and Darrius I'd envisioned at the Mithral feast that had never felt like mine. Instinctively, I strengthen my mental shield. "Are you afraid?"

Her face is grim, but she smiles. "Not with our king. And not with the Starkeeper by his side."

That's a lot of faith to have to carry, not just for one realm but two. I hug Ziba tightly, emotion clogging my throat, wondering if it will be the last time I see her. "You'll be safe, won't you?"

She bows reverently, tears misting her eyes. "Of course, my queen. As will you."

It's not the first time I have been called a queen, but it is the first time that I feel it, a destiny written into the marrow of my bones. I stand with not one but two powerful kings at my sides: Darrius's magic humming down the bond to empower me and Roshan's devoted heart grounding and tethering me. I am the conduit between the earth and sky. My simurgh flexes her wings, ready for what is coming and ready to defend both of the kingdoms under her watch.

Darrius, are you well? I'm going to Solis now.

His reply is immediate, apprehension and affection tumbling down the bond. *Yes, pátnī. Please be vigilant. I love you.*

Always am. I love you, too.

Chest squeezing, I make my way downstairs to the courtyard, where a small contingent of Darrius's kingsguard is waiting, led by Maxur. His face is hard, and I feel a pulse of pity. He'd also been blindsided by Anahima's betrayal, a revelation that must hurt, considering their on-again, off-again intimacy. She'd used him, too, to keep track of the king's movements and any decisions made in the war council. Darrius had trusted her, but she preferred to have all her bets covered. The general gives me a grim nod.

This is personal for him. It's personal for all of us.

With a deep breath, I pull on my magic to conjure the portal to Solis. Something tickles the back of my mind and my eyes catch the slightest shimmer of something before the smell of ozone hits my nose and the iridescent oval of my portal forms. Darrius had taken me to Solis via his own portal a few days ago so I could see exactly where I needed to be. Maxur directs five of his men to go first. I follow, knowing he will bring up the rear with the rest.

As I step through, the portal shimmers an odd color, and I feel it the second the magic envelops me—it's *not* mine.

But there's nothing I can do—I'm already through.

Heart pounding, I emerge in a cobblestone courtyard with a looming black castle behind me and *not* the open air of Solis. The awful sight of five dead bodies greets me . . . the ones of my guard who had stepped through before me. I grasp for the bond.

Darrius, the portal failed. I peer up. *I'm in a black-stoned fortress with spires.*

Morien? Fuck. Get out of there. You're—

His voice cuts off as a blast of magic douses our connection. I whirl around, but before I can reverse my steps, the portal is gone. My own power lashes over my arms in a defensive position in the empty courtyard as a sole pair of footsteps breaks the silence.

"Hello, my friend," Anahima says, and I blink in shock. She looks ghoulish. Her black hair is lank and greasy, her face haggard and gaunt. She was always thin, but her bones are in stark relief, her blue eyes burning like festering violet flames. Has Fero done this to her? The answer is obvious when my magic brushes against a twisted, malevolent energy.

It's Anahima . . . but not.

"What did you do?" I whisper in horror.

Her head cocks. "What's meant to be."

I shudder and try to stay calm at the utter *acceptance* in her voice. "Whatever that thing is, it's not your father." In some of the ancient texts I'd read, Fero had been described as a ruthless but impartial god, one who was the necessary balance to Saru. "That remnant is corrupt."

"I know," Anahima says calmly. "Did you know that in our prophecies, the lightbreaker dies so true darkness can rise? They also say that the godslayer will bring about the birth of a *new* god."

I frown. Is she talking about the same Everlean prophecy Darrius had told me? Is *she* the purported godslayer, if she means to kill her father? Then who is the lightbreaker?

Anahima lets out a condescending sniff as if she can read my chaotic thoughts. "Ashes below, you were always so slow, Sura."

"My name is Suraya."

She ignores me. "Allow me to break it down into child-sized

pieces for you. In the old days, they called Darrius the *lightbreaker* because of his power over the shadows." She sneers. "As firstborn, that power should have been mine. And you will help me take it back."

My fists curl and tighten. "I could end you right now and stop this madness." I gather my magic, though I know it won't be easy. Anahima is not to be misjudged, and if she tinkered with the portal to bring me here, it's because she wants me here.

A dangerous dark violet haze clouds her irises. "Very well. But I have your precious king. Your move, Sura."

"You don't," I say confidently, sensing no strain on the bond.

"Not *that* king, silly girl. The Oryndhrian." Her smile is a rictus, filling me with dread.

No, she's bluffing. Roshan is in Kaldari, waiting for me to bring him to Solis. "You're lying."

"Am I? I know everything that goes on in *my* castle. I didn't think you had it in you, my sweet, depraved little Starkeeper. Did you enjoy them fucking you like a common city slag?" I know what she's doing—deflection is one of her favorite tools. When I don't respond to her taunting, she sighs theatrically. "Fine, follow me."

I gather my magic like a shield, simurgh at the ready, and do as she says. She's a master of deception and she's been a dozen steps ahead for months now. We descend a stone staircase, and my lungs constrict as we come to a stop. I see Roshan bound and in a large cage in the center of the room. He's surrounded by venomous snakes. They're coiling restlessly around him, like a deadly whirlpool.

I remember how Laleh had tricked me with my father on the mountaintop. I won't fall for that ruse. "Try again. That's an illusion."

She rolls her eyes. "Go see for yourself."

Scowling, I walk forward and grasp the bars, the iron cold against my fingertips. My magic senses more of Anahima's wards, and I burn through them, only to find layers more. I tear through them, too, until I finally feel him. His blood sings to mine in the way it always has. No illusion would be able to replicate that.

He's real. *Fuck.*

"Roshan?"

His brown eyes snap open. "Get away from here, Sura! It's a trap! The snakes are tied to her life. That conniving—"

Anahima makes a tutting sound, Roshan's eyes going wide with alarm as the snakes writhe and hiss in terrifying unison. I reach down and touch one through the bars, recoiling at the dry coolness of its scales under my fingertips. They're real, too.

"I'll get you out of here, I promise," I say.

"Don't worry about me," Roshan says urgently. "Get to Darrius."

"What do you want?" I say to Anahima over my shoulder.

She shrugs and gestures upward. "A portal, that's all. As I asked from the beginning."

Steadying my mind, I walk out of the dungeon without looking back, because right now, I need to think about what my actions will do. If I open a portal for Anahima's revenants, that will bring war *and* the rot of the void to Everlea's doorstep.

Both are already here, my simurgh points out. She's not wrong.

Darrius, his army, and the Aspačanā have magic. If I open the portal for only a small amount of time, they should be able to contain the first wave while I figure out a way to get Roshan to safety. My magic can handle the portal and obliterate those fucking snakes. I'll just have to be careful to not let Anahima figure out what I'm doing. Once Roshan is free, I can end her once and for all.

She leads me up to a tower that overlooks the northern valley stretching toward Pix and Verisia. To my dismay, as we climb to the ramparts, the distant sounds of combat and the clash of steel reach my ears. I peer down in horror as a quake rocks the foundation of the castle, a fissure cracking through nearly half of the valley below.

A battle is already in motion, hundreds of soldiers on horses clashing with armed foot soldiers on the field. I can see the sparks of kinetic magic—fire bombs and ice blasts on both sides smashing into each other. Anahima must have recruited Everleans to her cause, because the magic isn't one-sided. Azdahas, griffins, chimeras, and rocs fly and swoop in the distance, but I don't see one that looks like Indira, or Razulek, for that matter.

Is he still in Solis, waiting for me as planned?

The glow of a portal at the base of the hill of the fortress is letting out a steady but narrow stream of revenant Scavs. If portals take huge amounts of energy, who is keeping it open? Frowning, I trace the thread of magic to where we are, and I gasp as I see it tied to Helena, who is sitting off to the side. A jādū collar surrounds her neck and heavy bracelets sit at her wrists, amplifying whatever is inside of her to maintain the narrow portal down below. A score of dead bodies are withered to husks beside her. I recoil in horror.

"What have you done?" I whisper to Anahima. "You're killing her."

She shrugs. "Yes, well, we're not all like you, Starkeeper. But all Oryndhrians, even if they don't believe in the gods, have akasha, some more than others. You can save her, if you want. Simply create another portal and release her from hers. Call on my brother's magic."

I stoop down. "Helena, are you well?"

Her glazed eyes are threaded with deep mauve lines, and she doesn't respond. *Shit.* With a nasty look at Anahima, I focus on the bond I have with Darrius and reach for his shadow magic. Theoretically, I know we can share magic and even combine our power, but it's not like I've had a lot of spare time to practice. I feel like I'm taking a stab in the dark.

Imagining the feel of his shadows, I call to them tentatively, summoning his magic to me. The resulting surge of power nearly knocks me off my feet, just from that one small tug, and I gasp, my skin feeling like I'm bursting at the seams.

Gods, he's strong. The inky ribbons on my arms come alive with his power inside me. It feels cold, unlike the heat of my own magic, like the darkness that sleeps in the dead of a winter night. Like death itself.

"Good," Anahima purrs. "Now, pour that into my portal like a good little Starkeeper."

"Fuck you," I seethe, longing to slam the cold power into *her* instead. My simurgh is raging to do just that, but I hold her back. As much as I dislike Helena, she doesn't deserve to die when I can save her life. And Roshan's . . .

Soon, I promise myself.

I focus on the portal that Helena's life force is tethered to and pour Darrius's magic into it, widening it slowly until it's nearly the width of the valley. Helena slumps over, breathing hard when I snap her connection. My eyes widen with horror when *thousands* of Scavs pour out, and my hold on the portal wavers.

Anahima makes a disappointed noise. "You can do better than that. Think of your unfortunate lover and all those angry serpents."

Rage bubbles at the threat, but I dig deep, and I draw on the bond again. *Forgive me, Darrius.* More power rushes into my veins, and the portal brightens and widens as I feed into it. But as fast as it comes, the power I'm drawing fizzles and the portal winks out. Something is blocking me. Not something, *someone*.

I feel my soul-fated before I see him, Indira's terrifying screech echoing across the valley as he arrows toward the fortress. Razulek is not far behind them. A small group of Anahima's followers attacks them in midair, and Razulek dives to blow a stream of fire at a griffin while Darrius sends a vortex of shadows to pulverize another. They continue toward me.

Suddenly, they both stop in midair, unable to come any closer. Dark purpose brews in my king's eyes as he prepares to blast through whatever shield is in place with his magic to get to me. In a panic, I wave and shake my arms wildly, telling him to stop. I have no idea what Anahima will do to Roshan, but Darrius still can't hear me.

"Stop! Roshan is here. He's in danger!"

Darrius shoots me a quizzical look, then points to Razulek.

Raz, who is carrying the king of Oryndhr on his back... hale and alive and *not* trapped in a cage of starsdamned snakes.

Chapter Thirty-Nine

I blink and squint in disbelief. It *is* Roshan, dressed in his royal armor with a golden crown on his dark hair. I watch as Razulek flies him down to where his army is marching.

Then who the fuck was that in the dungeon? I *sensed* Roshan's blood.

I whirl as Anahima starts cackling. "Gods, you truly are fucking gullible. They say the weakest minds are the easiest to convince. I expected more, Starkeeper. My acting was truly spectacular—*'Don't worry about me. Get to Darrius. Get away from here, Sura!'*" She says the last in a desperate singsong copy of Roshan's voice that makes me flinch.

That should have been my first glaring red flag. Roshan calls him Nightsong, not Darrius. But I'd been sucked in by Anahima's complex illusion. *Stupid, stupid, stupid.*

"How did you get his blood?" I ask.

"A single drop is all it takes," she says. "One nick on his pretty little face. Did you like the scar I left you?"

"I'm going to kill you," I say, power rushing to my fingertips. Now that both Papa and Roshan are out of her clutches, she has no collateral.

"You can try."

Anahima's stare is taunting as I launch the hottest blast of starlight I can amass at her, screaming in rage . . . and it passes straight through her body. Another fucking illusion!

"Where the fuck are you, Anahima?" I shout. "Face me and fight me. Or are you too cowardly to do so?"

Her response is to set the entire spire on fire. I immediately conjure ice magic to douse it, but it only grows stronger and turns blue. I try a gust of air, and it doubles in size. It's magical, feeding on counter-magic.

I hurry over to Helena, who doesn't look good. "Let's get you out of here."

"I'm not going to make it, Suraya," she whispers.

"You will." I pick her up and hoist her over my shoulder, rushing to the edge of the parapet as the unnatural bluish-yellow flames grow bigger. I could try a portal, but my brain is too scattered and too many things could go wrong. Besides, I don't trust that Anahima hasn't spelled this entire tower in some way to fuck with my magic like she did earlier.

Razulek!

The now riderless azdaha banks on his powerful wings, soaring just below the spire that's engulfed with fire. *Jump, little queen. I will catch you.*

Easy for him to say! Gritting my teeth, I close my eyes and leap as I feel the lick of flames on my neck, landing right on Raz's back. Luckily, I have the wherewithal to use magic to stabilize us, especially since Helena has passed out. *Thank you, old friend. You saved me.*

From what? he rumbles.

The fire, I say.

I feel his confusion. *There's no fire.*

Baffled, I blink and look over my shoulder. Sure enough, the spire is free of any flames. Stars, had I just imagined that? Or did Anahima somehow construct that whole intricate vision in my head? Gods, it had felt so real! I shove my mental shields up so hard that I nearly get whiplash, and I swear I hear the sound of mocking laughter.

Focus on what you need to, my simurgh cautions, *then you can hunt her down.*

The ferocity of the battle below us has grown, now that the massive revenant Scav forces—who are very hard to kill—have come through the portal. Thanks to me. But regret is a useless emotion without action. I have to help drive them back or kill them.

Raz directs a huge stream of fire at an ugly chimera when it gets too close for comfort with its talons and fire breath of its own. It lets out an earsplitting screech and tumbles from the sky, its wings shriveling to embers.

Brutal, Raz, I say.

This is war, Starkeeper. It's us or them.

We need to do something to stop it. I peer down at the bodies, seeing so many fallen on the field. The death toll is enormous, the sight of slaughtered horses and mutilated warriors making my eyes sting and nausea rise in my throat. *Where are my kings?*

The king of Oryndhr is with his army, fending off the dead ones from the east. And King Darrius . . . He goes quiet. *I see my mate but not her rider.*

Heart pounding, I focus inward and follow the bond to find Darrius on the ground, his magic a vicious, ravenous whorl of shadows. He's taking out whole lines of the enemy, but there are too many of them and he is expelling a huge amount of magic. But what makes it exponentially worse is that even though the king is pulverizing the dead to dust, the rot is alive and latching on to anything . . . including slain Aspačanā and Everlean soldiers.

I stare in horror as Karânî ruthlessly removes the head of one of her own horde who has come back to life . . . and that's not the only one.

The rot is spreading like a plague, just as Anahima had intended.

Raz and I swoop low to hand Helena off to one of Darrius's guards before I leap off to land at Darrius's side. My incandescent magic flares out in tandem with his to incinerate the revenants marching toward us. But the more we kill, the more they seem to spawn.

A blood-spattered kingsguard comes toward me, eyes riddled with purple smoke.

Fuck! I duck his swing and release a blast that bores a hole in his torso, and he still keeps coming. Maxur, in partially shifted wolf form, appears from nowhere and cleaves off his head. I exhale and nod my thanks. He jerks his head in return and disappears back into the fray with a battle cry of rage.

"Dare, we need to kill the source of the rot magic," I shout with a gasp. "We have to find Anahima."

"You're right. Hold on," Darrius says, snatching me about the waist and pulling me back against him. In seconds, we are enveloped by shadow, time and space rushing by, before we materialize on Indira's broad back, and then suddenly everything goes preternaturally quiet.

The sound of clashing steel dissolves into a pregnant sort of silence, one that portends horrors unknown. The hairs on my arms stand straight, goose bumps rushing over my skin. A terrible roar pierces the air, and a three-headed flying nightmare appears.

"What the fuck is that?" I yell, watching the huge beast fly toward us.

Darrius stiffens behind me, arm flexing around my middle as if to keep me close. "An azhi, a demon I thought was dead. And my sister."

"A *demon*?" I choke out.

"Summoned from the abyss."

Sure enough, Anahima is on the middle head of the massive creature, which has to be five times the size of Indira. "Is it an azdaha?"

Indira lets out a derisive snort. *That thing is as much one of us as an ogre can be called a mortal. It is a merciless, ill-fated monster that only knows how to kill.*

At her words, I stare at the incoming aberration, chills erupting all over my body. My breaths start to come hard and fast, and I force myself to calm. Panicking isn't going to help any of us survive the next few minutes. But the terror sinks into my bones anyway.

"So, mindless and monstrous," I say, going for bravado. "Got it. How do *we* kill *it*?"

Darrius grinds his teeth, frustration evident. "There's only one thing that can harm that creature and it's a god-touched sword. The center head is immortal."

Of course it is.

"Let me guess," I say, dread spreading through me. "We don't have one."

He nods. "The last one was lost during the hundred years' war."

"So what do we do?"

His expression is grim. "Survive."

The closer the azhi gets, the more terrifying it is.

Those fangs crowding each of its mouths have to be as long as my legs, and the myriad spines on its necks are tapered to lethal points. Its wingspan is massive, and it moves gracefully despite its considerable bulk. Designed for death, I have no doubt it will be formidable in battle.

As it nears, I can see bumps and oozing boils marring its greenish-gray body, leading down to twin spade-edged tails and four legs capped with talons resembling curved scimitars. But it's the deep purple tendrils of rot I can see that make alarm curdle in my gut. I feel my simurgh rise inside me, magic curling along my spine. If it's being controlled by Fero's corrupted rot, who knows what it's capable of.

I stare at its gaping mouths. "Does it breathe fire or poison like you, Indira?"

Indira chuffs. *Worse. One breathes a corrosive acid gas that eats away anything from steel to scales to bones, one blows out a nightmare plume that causes hallucinations and delusions, and the last and worst is the nullifying breath that erases all magical powers.*

I blink at the last. "Null? For good?"

It depends on the strength of the magi.

"Is it immune to magic?" I ask.

"The middle head is to most numena," Darrius says. "Kinetic magic fuels it, so we have to avoid elemental attacks, or it will become stronger, reviving the two other heads. All three are resistant to psionic magic."

I grit my teeth. "So we can't attack it, we can't control it, and we need a lost god-sword to even have a chance. What the fuck can we do?"

Behind me, Darrius rolls his neck, the deity in him coming to the fore. "The best we can hope to do is weaken it by working together in a collective approach. Evade the breath attacks, aim physical assaults at its underbelly and its wings. If we can take it down first, even better. Indira, call to your kin—our fight will be in the air, while the Aspačanā and King Roshan's forces keep the focus on the ground. Tell your azdaha army no magic."

I belatedly realize that Indira must be alpha of the azdahas when she lets out a trumpeting call that nearly makes my eardrums explode and echoes across the valley. Answering cries come back and dozens of azdahas, a few with riders and most without, join our ranks. My jaw falls open, eyes widening in wonder. If we weren't fighting for our lives in battle, it would be the most beautiful sight I've ever seen.

Azdahas in every gemlike color of the rainbow, blotting out the sky, their wings gliding on the wind—some delicate and ethereal like butterflies', and others spinier and batlike but no less majestic. There are tiny azdahas and huge ones, a few with long, frilled tails and some with thorns and spikes and barbs. And they all united at Indira's call.

"Gods..." I say. "There are so many."

Darrius leans into me. "When this is over, I'll take you to visit their largest adult colony on the Lost Isles in the northwest."

"I'd love that."

If we survive...

I don't see Razulek, but maybe he's still fighting down below. Fire is one of the only things that seems to kill the revenants and keep the rot plague from spreading.

I glance down to where most of the revenant forces have resumed movement, and I hope that Roshan can hold his own, because we are going to have our hands full up here.

As Indira swoops in, I send a test blast of star magic toward the beast. My power is unique and might lend us a small advantage, if it doesn't feed the monster. But Anahima dodges the blast at the last moment, the azhi moving nimbly under her command. She sends back several bolts of lightning that Indira narrowly manages to evade.

"She's an electrokinetic, too?" I shout in surprise, peering up at Darrius.

"Looks like my sister was hiding many things."

Raz, where are you? I reach out for the azdaha, sensing him near. *I need you.*

"Dare, we will be better off separate," I tell him. I twist around, kissing him soundly. He barely has time to return it before I'm leaping from Indira's back with a war cry; Razulek passes below, catching me easily on his back.

We zoom off to the right and bank sharply, aiming for the azhi's underbelly. Darrius and Indira attack from the left, his shadow magic pouring from him in a dark, viscous tangle of deadly ribbons and his obsidian sword cutting a path along the azhi's left head, blinding it temporarily. Buoyed by hope, I shoot a burst of starlight as Raz lets out a scream and swings his barbed tail into the monster's wing. We both make contact and the azhi roars, but the damage from our strikes is instantly healed.

That has to be Anahima's corpus magic.

Other azdahas dive, slashing with talons and snapping with teeth, but the injury they're inflicting is minimal. The middle head blows out a stream of gas that catches one bright blue azdaha dead in its sights, and it screams piteously when its scaled hide immediately starts to dissolve. The first head catches another with its nightmare breath, and I see the moment the delusions start when the azdaha and its rider turn on one of their own, launching an arc of fire that takes out a nearby griffin. The hallucinating rider—clearly an ice numen—sends several bolts toward Indira.

Darrius, behind you!

Luckily, they evade the attack, but there's no help for the azdaha or the rider as Darrius's shadows make quick work of them. Our eyes meet, mine wide with sorrow and horror.

This isn't working, I tell him. *Anahima is healing any physical wounds as fast as we can inflict them.*

Darrius nods grimly. *We need to unseat her.*

But how?

Digging deep into my well of power, I send bolt after bolt of starlight toward the azhi, hoping to keep it distracted while Darrius comes in from above, his shadow magic aiming for his sister. But it's as though Anahima has eyes on the back of her head; she turns the beast at the last moment. And in slow motion, I see the third head release a white cloud heading straight for the king.

"Darrius!" I scream, nudging Razulek into a spinning dive.

At the last second, I feel the azhi's breath crash into me instead of Darrius, and the dearth of magic that instantly takes over my entire mind feels like I've been submerged underwater. Everything is muted, the sound of my heartbeat thunderous as my magic is abruptly silenced.

Starbright, what the fuck did you do?

I gasp in a breath, trying to keep the panic at bay *and* hide it from my soul-fated. I need him focused on his sister, not me. *Better me than you. I can feel my magic coming back already,* I lie. *Don't worry about me, get Anahima!*

We circle around for another round, hearing hideous screams as two more azdahas get caught by the corrosive breath, blood spraying everywhere. Darrius evades another breath attack—this time the nightmare one—and my relief is huge. I don't even want to imagine the destruction he could cause if his powerful godly mind was affected by hallucinations. He'd wipe out half of our forces.

Reaching inward, I try to draw on my magic. But there's nothing, not even a spark. It's like I've lost a limb. What if it *doesn't* come back? This isn't like the cuffs, it's much worse. I can't even feel my simurgh, who's a constant presence in my chest. Instead, it's hollow and empty where she should be, like a gaping hole.

Lightning bolts spear toward us, and I barely hold on as Razulek attempts to dodge, but the last blast catches the top of his wing and we start to spiral. My heart is screaming with terror when we plunge downward in a sickening death spin. Maker above, I don't even have magic to heal him! Or to save us! Tears spring from my eyes as nerve-racking horror sets in.

Raz! I scream.

Hold on, little queen.

The ground comes toward us much too quickly as he aims for a clearing of trees. At the last moment, Razulek bucks me off and flips his entire body to catch me between his wings, which wrap securely around us. He takes the brunt of the fall on his back as we smash into the trees, sliding fifty feet before we stop. Mostly unharmed with the wind knocked out of me, I catch my breath, gently easing Razulek's limp wings off.

Fuck, Raz! Are you hurt?

His chest is rising and falling, but he's unresponsive. My cheeks are wet with tears, but I don't have time to deal with my emotions as the person I last expect to see appears in a blur of dark smoke.

Anahima . . . and she looks furious.

Chapter Forty

I clutch my dagger as my enemy stalks toward me.

She pulls an old sheet of parchment from her pocket that looks like it has been ripped from one of the library books she'd been studying. "What a windfall! Time to bind your powers for good, little Starkeeper. Can't have you interfering in my plans, but I need you alive so that I can make sure brother dearest succumbs to the curse when I cut you to pieces."

"He's your blood," I say, trying to buy time. Terrified, I reach deep. *Come on, simurgh, wake up.*

"I'm crowning a new queen," she says. "And he never cared about me, so why should I care about him? He had everything, and I was rewarded with the crumbs."

"Ani, he loves you. You know that."

She scoffs. "There's that word again. You throw it around a lot, do you realize? The only thing that is good for"—she taps her chin—"is nothing."

"I know Vogon hurt you—"

"Do *not* speak his name," she hisses, and then relaxes her expression with a speed that has me reeling. "Where were we?"

She begins to chant and ice slivers through my veins. Whatever she is summoning is powerful and dark. I can feel it brewing like a malevolent cloud. I lurch forward with my dagger, prepared to strike her in the heart, but a burst of magic from her palms sends me sprawling. My head smashes into a rock and my ankle twists painfully. Shaking off the darkness devouring my vision, I crawl for my dagger, blood dripping down my temple.

I don't even have the magic to heal myself.

Time to use the only weapon left at my disposal . . . my wits.

"Poor little forgotten daughter, feeling so sorry for yourself that you have to hurt others to make yourself feel good," I say. "So needy that you still crave dear daddy's approval, even if you were never the one he chose." I know goading her while I don't have any magic probably isn't in my best interests, but have nothing to lose—especially if she completes her spell before my magic returns. "And now, you've become the thing you detest the most . . . weak and subservient."

She hisses as that taunt disrupts her from her chant, but only stares at me. "Your insults won't work on me, Sura. I have magic and you don't, and soon, I'll strip you of every last drop. And once I have no more need of you, I'll kill you. Only now, I promise to make it hurt."

A hideous screech from above has us both looking up. I think I see Darrius and Indira flying around the azhi, but I can't be sure. Pieces of something—half a feathered griffin's body—are falling from the sky, while the other half is ripped apart and gobbled between two of the azhi's mouths.

"My azhi is a hungry beast," Anahima says, watching my grief-stricken expression with glee. "He loves fresh meat. *Especially* azdaha. I wonder how yours will taste? He should have died from the rot, but I'll get him sooner or later."

I sneer back. "You're a monster, just like your demon."

Swallowing, I stare up, hoping beyond hope that the azhi will be weakening from all the attacks, but it only shows signs of getting stronger. How is that possible?

The gentlest touch of my simurgh strokes across my senses. It's not much, but for a moment, I can see through her eyes. Thousands of filaments like a huge magical web creep from the revenants to the azhi, and the more of them there are, the stronger it gets.

I breathe out. "They're all connected."

"Not so stupid after all," Anahima says. "Though I sense the nullifying effects lessening, and we can't have that."

Darrius, if you can hear me now, target the revenants. They're strengthening the azhi. If you eliminate them, we might have a chance.

No response comes back, and my heart sinks.

Needing to do something, I lurch forward, hobbling with my injured foot. Anahima snarls and raises her hand, lightning gathering. Unable to leap out of the way with an aching ankle that isn't healing, I brace for impact, but a blur crashes into her, taking her unawares and sending them both tumbling to the ground.

Zahre!

The fierce raissa throws a huge blast of frost toward Anahima, encasing her in a tower of ice. She burns free easily, but that doesn't stop Zahre. Ice spears race toward Anahima, only to crash into a hasty shield she throws up. The raissa spins, her saber coming down close to Anahima's torso and then reversing direction to catch a thick section of her hair.

Anahima growls with rage, lightning sparking on the tips of her fingers as she fires several sizzling bolts in Zahre's direction, but the raissa jumps and spins, her body moving like liquid as she deftly avoids Anahima's attacks. Not losing an inch of ground, she lunges again with her saber, this time getting a strike at the back of her opponent's thigh. Anahima roars, her eyes turning violet, a mass of dark purple rot pouring out of her toward us like a pulsating wave.

I can feel its malice ... its hatred and hunger.

"Zahre!" I yell. "Run!"

Her eyes widen, but she listens and vanishes into the woods. The rot retreats back into Anahima's body, and I can only stare at her in mute shock. "I hate interruptions," she says.

"What have you done to yourself, Ani?" I whisper. "That . . . thing, whatever that void magic is, it's not natural."

"Power comes at a cost," she says.

"Whatever trade you made with Fero is not worth it, I promise you that."

She laughs. "Fero is gone. I absorbed his remnant and ate his power. The rot is mine, and Darrius's shadows will be mine. I will bring the abyss to Endara."

Dread fills me. "Ani, this isn't you."

Her smile is soft. "What do you know? You fell for my strongest illusion, sweet Sura. I was so angry, so alone, so lost. Do you know the rot eats all emotion? It takes away all the pain and the sadness and everything that makes you weak. You'll understand. Maybe that will be my gift to you, instead of death. I can make you like me." She waves an arm to her army. "Like us."

"I would rather face the azhi," I say, the idea of my free will being eaten away one I could never embrace.

Another bellow makes us both look to the sky. This time it's from the demon. The princess lets out a wild howl of fury when the beast takes a brutal hit to its wing and starts to spin in circles and plummet. I have no idea if Darrius heard me and if he directed some of the azdaha to the ground forces, but when I focus my magical sight, there is hardly any of the web left.

It's working!

I stifle my hope and call to my simurgh again. I can feel her more strongly! Magic, only the barest sliver before, feels like a steadier stream. Working unobtrusively, I use my psionic abilities to craft my own illusion—a weak and broken Suraya—even though my ankle is healing and the wound on my head is no longer bleeding. Anahima is a master illusionist, so I pour more magic into the version of me I want her to see.

An invisible leash wraps around my neck, and she drags me with her toward the middle of the field. "You hurt mine, I hurt yours," she screams to her brother, her voice magically amplified.

In the sky, Darrius directs Indira toward us, his face that stony mask of the vicious king who wields his weapon with cold precision.

Ani laughs, holding me up by my throat. "It's your turn, brother. Don't worry, I might even let her visit you as the manticore. She's into beast play, isn't she?"

Iron projectiles appear out of nowhere, all pointed toward me, and I brace. There's a chance that I could die from that many punctures before I can heal myself, but I grip the hilt of my concealed dagger in one palm, cautioning myself not to strike too soon.

Slowly, *quietly*, I let my magic infuse my blade, and I feel the starlight warm my skin.

I'm nowhere near full strength, and I'll have only one chance to make it count. My breath throttles as the azhi swoops down, talons extended to rip into Indira's back. She shrieks, contorting in agony, and Darrius loses his balance, toppling off. But he shifts to shadow, a seething mass aiming toward us.

It's now or never.

I pretend to stumble as if too weak to stand, and my captor scowls, shaking me roughly.

"Wake up, Sura," Anahima purrs. "Don't want you to miss out on this part."

Summoning every last ounce of my strength and my magic, I wobble and slump against her before striking as precisely as I can, my iridescent blade glowing white-hot as it slips between her ribs straight into her heart—even as I am impaled by a dozen iron stakes.

Agony pulses through me, the pain so excruciating I can barely think. My vision darkens, but I fight to keep conscious, sensing Anahima trying to heal herself against my blow. With the last of my strength, I shove all the starfire I have in me through the dagger.

Blood froths from my mouth as glittering starlight burns from me to the jādū-forged blade lodged in Anahima's side, and I keep it there and twist with the last of my fading strength until I hear the scrape of steel on bone.

Her skin starts to flake as she incinerates from the inside out, starting with her heart. A pair of incredulous purple-hazed eyes collide with mine, and I swear, for a heartbeat, there's a glimmer of something—admiration?—in them before they roll back. Her flesh darkens to the color of ash as iridescent starfire erupts from her eye sockets, crackling through her hair and making every strand stand on end.

I make myself watch. Not because she deserves a witness, but to honor every single life she took. And when I can see the outline of her bones beneath her incandescent, immolating skin, I sob through the hot blood bubbling between my lips.

In a way, I'd loved her, too.

Darrius...

Starbright, hold on. I can hear the desperation in his voice.

I try valiantly to do as he says, but the pain is unbearable. I don't hear Darrius's roar when I slip into darkness for a few seconds, nor do I see the curse take hold, his bones cracking and the howl of a manticore rumbling over the valley.

Starkeeper.

I hear Razulek's weak voice and relief fills me. *Raz, thank the stars you're alive.*

Weakly, I feel the tremor of his fear. *You're hurt.*

It was inevitable. My thoughts feel fragmented and faint, but I force myself to concentrate. *You know I read in a book once that your* kind were called "dragons" by the storytellers. *They were fierce and valiant and bathed their enemies in fire. You are the king of dragons, my friend.* My simurgh lets out a soft keen. *Take care of your hatchlings. I wish I could have seen them.*

Stay, little queen...

But my ability to think fractures and fades. Someone falls to the ground beside me and gathers me into their arms. It's Roshan, my Oryndhrian king—I can smell his bergamot and smelted-iron scent that always makes me think of home. Of Coban.

I curl into him. "Ro . . . you fought so well. Take care of him."

"Sura, no, no, no, stay with me, please."

Weak from blood and magic loss, I feel my punctured organs start to fail, my lungs desperately trying to give me air, my heart laboring to beat, and my simurgh desperately trying to heal the worst of it. But Anahima—devious, lying Anahima—poisoned the iron bolts, too. I feel her special soporific toxin burning through my veins as my drained magic tries to eviscerate it and tend my wounds at the same time.

Gods, I'm so tired . . .

A roughened tongue licks my face, and I rub my cheek against the soft, velvety muzzle of my manticore mate. "Dare, not sure I'm going to get out of this one." I reach up with my free hand to scratch his soft ears. "Will you let me say goodbye to Darrius?"

We are so wrapped up in each other that none of us notice the dark purplish rot from the blood that had dripped out of Anahima's body creeping toward me like ravenous maggots—until it's too late. They latch on to my calf muscle like blood-sucking worms, and my vision wavers when I feel hundreds of tiny teeth. My eyes flutter shut when I feel them start to chew and burrow.

"Suraya, no!" It sounds like Darrius. "Fuck!"

And then he cups my face and kisses my dry lips, and I feel my soul-fated's magic burst through me as I arch upward, my body shuddering from the influx of so much power. My dauntless, ruthless deity. But he's not done—that beautiful fool summons the rot toward him with his magic, meaning to take it into his own body.

I push upward and shove him away. My eyelids crack open as I stare woozily at the open, pulsing wound on my leg.

"We can't let that loose, Starbright," he whispers.

"Then kill it," I say.

That midnight gaze darkens in a way that says he's going to tell me something I'm not going to like. "It's ancient and can't be killed in that form. I need to take it from you, and you can bind me."

"I've got this," a voice says, and my gaze lands on my gorgeous gardener-prince. "I can do it."

Clearly, I am in love with two beautiful fools who don't value their own lives.

"No," I say. If I've learned anything from fighting against dark forces the first time and the true purpose of the Starkeeper, it's sacrifice. And for the people I love, I'm willing to do whatever it takes to keep them safe. "I'm more powerful than both of you. I should be the one to bind the remnant. My starlight will be its cage for eternity."

"You're damning yourself to eternal torment," Darrius says. "It won't go quietly."

I reach a hand up to his chest, feeling his shadows envelop my fingers. "Neither will I. This is what I was born for, Dare. To safeguard the realms. Both of them." Tears brim in my eyes. "Look after Raz, will you? And tell Indira we couldn't have done it without either of them." My gaze swings between my two beloveds, my heart rupturing. "Gods, how I wish we had more time."

"Starling..."

I turn and let my palm cup Roshan's jaw before threading my fingers through the silky dark curls that flop onto his brow. Maker above, he's so handsome he takes my breath away. "He stole so much from us, Ro. I can't risk losing you or Darrius. Tell Amma and my father I love them."

Those brown eyes flash with a stubborn expression I recognize. "Tell them yourself."

I'm not fast enough to stop Roshan from gripping my leg and absorbing the mass. His veins turn inky purple, and his eyes burn a deep violet, much worse than before, and for a moment, I'm frozen in terrified shock.

"Acharia, what have you done?" Darrius whispers.

He doesn't answer... those unholy dark violet lines creeping outward into his umber skin as if they'd never left. But then his brown eyes glimmer with gilded flecks that grow brighter and brighter, and a soft golden light covers him, becoming more brilliant until he's nearly ablaze. My simurgh kneels, and my lips part in awe, as if my magic unconsciously recognizes that it's in the presence of something divine.

Time stops in the presence of all the gods... and the glow is blinding.

Celestial.

The glow explodes, and when the light clears, Roshan is standing there... unhurt and untouched, with no signs of the rot.

"What was that?" I whisper in wonder.

"Saru's light," he says. "Turns out nothing from the abyss can live in my body. Or so he says, anyway. Now that I'm immortal. Looks like my parents left me with a legacy of akasha after all."

"Good to know," Darrius says, clapping him on the shoulder, relief clear on his face.

I sigh and hide my grin. "Great. Two arrogant deities. How did a girl get so lucky?"

My joy is short-lived, however, when I hear a deafening screech and a gust of corrosive gas misses us by inches. We stumble out of the way, running for the cover of the trees. The azhi lands, its bulk shaking the ground as it towers over us. One of the heads nudges the dead Anahima and then gobbles her down.

Foul.

But my disgust aside, I remember too late that blood is power, especially death magic—and sure enough the lesions and wounds on its body all start to heal, and before my eyes, it gets even bigger.

We narrowly dodge a combined breath attack, watching as the remaining Aspačanā hordes and the armies of the two kings gather at its back. They dodge a flick of its twin tails, weapons at the ready and waiting for our signal. The beast roars; it won't be long before its ruined wing repairs and it will be able to fly again.

"We only have a small chance while it's grounded," my soul-fated says.

"What do we do?" I ask.

Darrius grips my hand. "We do this together."

I feel the bond between us hum as my refilled wellspring of power expands and my simurgh rises. I realize what he intends when I feel our magic start to flow and combine. I'm scared to see what becomes of us, but I trust him completely. Shadow intertwines with starlight into a brilliant plume of shimmering night. He glances at me with so much love that my knees weaken. "I love you, Starbright."

"I love you, too."

"Now burn like the star you are," he says. "I've got you."

Silvery runes and tattooed markings light in tandem as the iridescent wings of my simurgh burst out of my back. Black shadow wings flare as he tightens his grasp on my hand, and together we aim our magic toward the azhi. Our combined magic blasts the two smaller heads, which explode in bursts of ash and embers. Only the middle head remains. The azhi roars in fury, sucking down the magic of the remaining revenants and whatever it stole from its mistress in a desperate bid to regenerate itself.

If we don't eliminate the last and most powerful head before the other two return, then we will have to start all over again. It's a matter of careful timing, constant pressure, and a whole lot of luck. Blood thunders in my ears, each passing second fraught with fear that the window of opportunity will close . . . that it will leap into the skies. We focus our power on the main head's eyes, blinding it temporarily, and it shrieks, attacking wildly but without coherence.

This is it . . .

Darrius retrieves his massive obsidian sword and tosses it to Roshan with a wink. "Show us what you've got, Sunshine."

Roshan grins back, and I watch in awe when he jumps on a horse and races toward the belly of the beast. The king and his mount move like magic, an aureate iridescence surrounding them both. My breath lodges in my throat when he gracefully dodges a stream of acid breath and a vicious swipe of the azhi's talons. It's only a testament to his skill as a rider that he doesn't get unseated. And then he leaps off at the last minute to roll beneath the creature's massive legs.

The sword—Darrius's sword—ignites, bright light blazing along its obsidian edges right as Roshan cleaves it through the azhi's belly like a hot knife through butter. The scream the demon releases is horrific as its entire body splits in half and flakes to ash within seconds.

Stupefied, I turn to Darrius. "Did you know your sword was god-touched?"

"It's not. But *Acharia* is. It's his akasha that made it so."

The Everlean prophecy floats to mind: *By the chosen's own hand, the ill-fated shall die . . .*

Tears spring to my eyes as the entire valley goes up in cheers and shouts of victory, the men and women of Endara who had fought and bled together lifting a victorious Roshan up onto their shoulders. Of course. A *god-touched* sword. I can't believe I didn't think of it.

"Stars, is it finally over?" I say, half expecting the demon to rise again for one last unholy hurrah. But it doesn't, thankfully.

Darrius nods, wrapping his arms around me. "It's finally over, my love."

"What do we do now?"

Roshan smiles. He's broken away from the crowd and made his way over to kiss my cheek. "Whatever we want."

Covered in blood and gore and gods know what else, I laugh at the two loves of my life, my heart so full it feels like it's going to burst. I like the sound of that. I like it a lot.

Chapter Forty-One

Whatever we want unfortunately has to give way to duty, which is what happens when two kingdoms and two kings are involved. Not to mention paying our respects to those who died in battle as well as making sure that the rot from the corrupted remnant of Fero is completely eradicated in both Oryndhr and Everlea.

As Aran had explained to me, Fero isn't *gone*—the gods exist in balance, after all, but his brothers and sisters have made sure that his ancient godly essence remains in exile until he realizes the errors of his ways. For a power-hungry god, that could be another several millennia. I'm not holding my breath.

"Ziba?" I ask as I fasten the last of my leathers. "Do you know where my husband is?"

Her expression drops for a moment. "He's in Princess Anahima's quarters again."

Needless to say, Darrius has taken the loss of his sister harder than expected, even with all her deception. I find the king of Everlea in the next wing of the castle, standing at the entrance to Ani's chambers. They've been cleaned as if she were expected back from the library or her study at any moment. But she won't be coming back.

I touch Darrius's shoulder with my magic before I reach him. "Are you well, my love?" I ask him, slipping my arms around his middle.

His body relaxes slightly, though his big shoulders remain hunched when I rest my cheek against the middle of his back. "I just wish she had come to me. I could have helped. I could have done something to save her. I failed in my duty as king and as her brother."

"She didn't want help, Dare," I say, stroking his stomach. "And you didn't fail. Her actions are her own. She could have chosen a different path, but she did not."

"I should have been there for her," he says brokenly.

The truth is Ani was lost by the end. The remnant had corrupted her beyond redemption. In fact, it was a mercy she was gone. While Roshan had hung on to the last of his humanity with everything inside of him, Ani had abandoned hers. That's the only reason he'd been able to come back from the very brink. Well, that and Saru's grace.

But I think about that every day . . . What if he had embraced Fero fully?

Not even Saru's light would have been enough.

Darrius nods. "I've been thinking of building a school for magical studies in her name. For budding magi."

"That would be a lovely way to honor her memory," I tell him, spreading my wings and wrapping my magic around him in a full-bodied hug.

"She was the smartest person I ever knew." He laughs sadly. "Even as a child, that brain of hers had the power to change the world. She would have made a strong queen, if our laws of primogeniture had been different and she had been nurtured to the role."

"So change them. That would be an even better way to honor her."

He huffs another laugh. "Just like that?"

"Change is inevitable, Darrius, if we want to become better people," I say quietly, spinning him to face me and studying his beautiful, somber face. "But we have to make the effort when we see that old ways are not working. We have to leave the world a better place than we found it. Otherwise, what are we here for?"

My king cups my jaw and strokes my cheek with his thumb. "That's true."

"Ani wasn't alone, you know, in the way she felt, that she was overlooked and undervalued. I admit there were times in Coban when I felt the same, that my only value was in my dowry and my ability to bear children." I bite my lip with a shrug. "I suppose that's why I rebelled and became a bladesmith. But I was also lucky because my father never forced me into traditional roles. He let me do what I loved."

"We need more men like him," Darrius murmurs, gathering me into his arms.

"You *are* like him. You've never made me feel less than or that I needed saving." I loop my arms around his neck, feeling his shadows come alive to tangle with my ribbons of light. "And if you truly intend to do something about it, then we should talk to the women of this realm. In a sense, the Aspačanā have the right of it. They might have their problems, but their women's voices hold the same weight as their men's."

He lets out a heavy exhale as he detaches from my embrace to lead us to the door. "Do you think Ani hated me?"

"I think she hated who she became," I say. "You were simply a convenient target."

He shakes his head. "It feels wrong to be sad after everything she did."

"It's all right to grieve, Dare. She was your sister. Your feelings will always be real, but you can't blame yourself for the path she chose. I've been where she was, so consumed by anger and pain that I couldn't see anything else. I had to make the choice between the truth and the lie, and sometimes the lie is easier because it's what we want to believe. Truth means looking inward at ourselves . . . and sometimes acknowledging that we don't like what we see. That is never easy—it takes great courage."

"You're very wise, my wife," he says.

I close the distance between us to kiss him soundly. "Don't you forget it."

Taking his hand, I lead him out of the castle and to the courtyard, where Maxur and his kingsguard are waiting near a portal that opens to the plains. But I stop Darrius as he heads toward it. The Aspačanā have their own traditions to honor their dead as well as rituals and feasting to celebrate them in their next lives. The king and queen of Everlea are expected to attend.

"We're taking a small detour," I say to Maxur. "The king and I will meet you at the burial grounds shortly."

Darrius frowns. "Where are we going?"

"It's a surprise."

I form a portal of my own and drag him through. Within seconds, we emerge on a plateau overlooking Deadman's Canyon, where a dozen azdahas are soaring the clear blue skies above us. I'm grateful that so many of them survived the azhi, including Razulek, Indira, and their two hatchlings.

As if my thoughts have summoned them, we are suddenly accosted by two gamboling baby azdahas that are the cutest things I've ever seen. One, a female, is a luminous silver, and the other, a male, is a vibrant green, just like his sire, though he has beautiful crimson markings over the nubs of his horns. I've never seen a prouder father than Razulek, who is perched a few feet away on a rocky outcropping.

I glance at my king. "You needed some adorable baby therapy, and Raz said they needed some playtime."

"When did they hatch?" Darrius asks, a tender expression taking over his face, one that makes me feel distinctly warm on the inside.

A fortnight ago, Razulek says.

"How's Indira?" I ask.

My mate is taking a well-deserved rest.

I giggle when the two babies crash into each other, their tiny wings flapping hard as they go tumbling over the ground, snapping their fang-filled mouths at each other. "They're already so big."

Azdahas mature at a faster rate as hatchlings. Our growth slows as adolescents.

"Can they fly?"

They will soon. For now, they can hover and glide very short distances.

I grin at Darrius, who has a look of utter astonishment when the naughtier of the two mischievous hatchlings hops into the air and blows a stream of frosty mist right at his head. The king conjures a blast of fire that snuffs out the ice before it can get anywhere near him.

"Cease that at once," he says in a tone that demands obedience, and the tiny silver azdaha falters in her tracks. Big icy blue eyes widen, but a defiant plume of smoke curls from her nostrils as she sizes up her much bigger opponent. After a beat of tension, she thinks twice of it before belching up a puff of frost and hopping away with obvious disdain. The smile on Darrius's face is worth everything.

I burst into laughter. "She's going to be a handful, I see."

Razulek sighs. *You have no idea, little queen. Already causing trouble in the roost. There are a few older hatchlings, and she has already established herself as alpha.*

"Like mother, like daughter. What are their names?"

The green is called Tiri, and she is Niloo.

"They're beautiful. What do they mean?"

Tiri means "swift one," and Niloo means "lotus flower."

I crouch down, putting a hand out for the smaller male. After a moment of consideration, cocking his little red-nubbed head to the side, he hops over to me and nuzzles his snout against my palm. A spark of akasha flows between us, and for a second, I can feel his emotions crowding mine. No words yet, just a wild stream of thoughts and consciousness, mostly love for his sibling and his parents, curiosity over the newcomers, and that he might be hungry.

"What's his ability?" I ask, scooping him up as he cuddles into my side.

Razulek leaps upright, huge wings flaring wide, and I go still, wondering what I've done wrong, which I realize the moment I look down. My hands, my arms, and the middle of my body have disappeared, including the tiny azdaha I'm holding. I can still feel Tiri in my hands, but I can't see him. He chuffs as if pleased with himself.

Tiri hasn't quite gotten used to wielding it yet, Razulek says.

"Invisibility is a rare power," Darrius says, grinning at me and trying to contain his amusement. "Useful for both him and any rider."

We play with the babies for a little while, and then we take our leave to go to the plains, as we don't want to delay too much longer. I can already tell that Darrius feels much lighter of spirit, which was my intent.

Loss is hard, but time has a way of healing all wounds.

Time . . . and baby azdahas.

"How were the burial services?" Roshan asks me the next day as I meet him in the private antechamber beside the Kaldarian throne room.

We are alone for the moment, but I know he is planning to speak with Aran, Clem, and Hamid, as well as most of the aldermen of the Oryndhrian houses. Like Darrius, I expect he intends to put new policies in place and make some changes.

"Interesting," I reply. "The Aspačanā bury their dead with their saddles and jewelry for them to take into their next lives. It's quite an intriguing ritual. And the feasting . . . well, that went well into the dawn hours."

"And the rot?"

I wrinkle my nose. "They've lost almost half their herds and a good number of their horses. Zahre confided to me that Ani had been the one to tell her father that the rot could only be cured by the Starkeeper and that Darrius had been keeping me from them on purpose."

Roshan frowns as he tugs on the cuffs of his ceremonial robes. "Why would she do that?"

"She wanted to sow mistrust between the clans and the king to serve her end goal of dethroning him. She even convinced them to call for the Gauntlet of Mithral as a distraction from what she was doing with Fero," I explain. "If she could create enough discord within Everlea, he would be less able to handle a simultaneous war on his borders with Oryndhr."

"That's very tactical," Roshan says, brows raising.

"She was one of the most brilliant people I've ever met," I say. "Darrius is not taking her death well."

"It's hard to lose a sibling." Roshan's voice is quiet, and I wonder if he felt the same after Javed was killed. Then again, his brother had treated him terribly—there had never been any love lost between them. An eternity ago when we first met, Roshan had quoted an old book: "The blood of the covenant is thicker than the water of the womb"—meaning the people we choose to let in . . . they are the important ones.

To wipe the solemnity from his face, I let a tendril of my magic creep up his leg and wind around his thigh. He exhales sharply, pretty brown eyes widening. "We've missed our little intrigues," I tell him.

A slow smirk curls the corner of his lips. "Have you?"

My magic drifts wickedly up his muscular ass, squeezing and caressing those firm globes before slipping around to the front and cupping him boldly. My handsome king sucks in air, every inch of him responding deliciously. "Though, it's much more fun in public when everyone can see the proud king of Oryndhr squirm."

"Don't you dare!" he says with a breathless chuckle. "Sura, as much as I want this and to bury myself inside you, Aran will walk in here any second with my small council. And trust me, no one wants to see their king with a raging mongrel in his trousers."

"I want to see it," I tease, going a bit short of breath myself at his provocative words. But with one wicked stroke along his length that makes him groan, I relent. "Fine, be no fun."

"I'll make it up to you, I promise."

"So what did you want to talk to me about?" I slip my hand into his.

Adjusting his groin with the heel of his palm, he inhales several deep breaths. When he's sufficiently collected—though the red flags in his cheeks remain, to my gratification—his face goes serious. "I've been thinking about this for a while now, what this realm needs and what will be in the best interest of the people. I want to abdicate."

I blink in shock. "Abdicate? As in . . . give up the crown?"

"Yes. This was always my end goal, even from the time I was leading the Dahaka—to free our realm from the monarchy."

Wide-eyed, I stare at him, slightly stunned at the timing. But as I think about it, I realize I'm not surprised. Roshan has never truly been interested in ruling, even when he led the rebellion. He'd taken the throne only to avoid the houses ripping themselves apart to seat a new monarch.

"What about Aran? Isn't he next in line?"

"Yes, he is," he says slowly, uncertainty swimming in his gaze. "But he has no interest, either. I was thinking of ceding control to the people. Making the realm a republic."

"Is that what you want?" I ask carefully. "The Imperial House is your family's legacy."

Roshan makes a scoffing noise. "My family's legacy is not something anyone should be proud of. Oryndhr needs something new and it's time for change. It was obvious when I was leader of the Dahaka that the monarchy was fundamentally flawed." He shakes his head. "I can't fix centuries of mistakes, and the truth is I don't want to. The people don't trust me because of my role with the Dahaka, and they begrudge my family name." He stares at me, regret and shame on his face. "I was also present enough over the last few months to know that ruling by fear only leads to mistrust and resentment. Allowing my people to self-govern is the best way for a real future."

"You know I will support whatever you choose to do," I say.

"Do you think I'm doing the right thing?" he asks, the expression in those brown eyes more vulnerable than I've ever seen it.

Gods, I feel such fierce love for my valiant, honorable king that I can barely speak. "The hallmark of a great ruler is love for your people, first and foremost, and caring for their well-being. And it sounds to me like you have the best intentions of the people of Oryndhr at heart."

Stars above, I am so proud of him. If there ever was a moment cementing my forgiveness of Roshan, this was it. A true despot would keep power no matter the cost; he would never put the interests of his people first. But I've always known in my heart of hearts that the man I fell in love with would prevail.

A knock on the door interrupts us, and Aran announces that the council is ready. Roshan takes my arm, and we both walk into the throne room together. It's full of aldermen from each of the houses and noble representatives from nearly every city, as well as the full dozen of his kingsguard lining the perimeter. When I see that Roshan looks nervous, I send him a reassuring smile.

With that, Roshan rises to stand before his people. "I've always believed that a king needs to live in service of the crown. His role is to serve you, not the other way around." The air in the chamber becomes electric in anticipation of his next words, and he takes a fortifying breath. "In Oryndhr, we have known war and peace, prosperity and hardship. We have seen dark times, and we have the Starkeeper to thank for keeping us safe."

I don't flinch when all the stares in the massive hall flick to me. I keep my gaze calm and focused on Roshan.

"We have always been a people of strength, courage, and resilience, and I urge you to consider those things now."

The king reaches up to grasp the golden crown upon his head and removes it.

At once, the room explodes into gasps and whispers, and Roshan lifts a hand to quiet them. "My great-grandfather wore this crown, I inherited it from my brother by blood, and now, I shall be the last of this bloodline—of any bloodline—to wear it. Oryndhr needs to move forward in the hands of its people. Therefore I, King Roshan Acharia, am renouncing my title. It's time for the people to rule."

The hall erupts into utter chaos, but Roshan stays calm, his spine straight. He looks like a tremendous weight has been lifted off his shoulders. As might be expected, not everyone is happy. Naturally, there are one or two noblemen in Regulus who feel like they are deserving of the throne, but the majority of the representatives seem positive and hopeful, and open to change.

"Keep order," Hamid roars loudly, "or you will be removed."

"We have prepared a formal document for the proposed governing structure," Aran says over the continued rumblings that eventually quiet down. "It outlines a transfer of political power to the four houses. The former king will stay on in an advisory role, as will the Starkeeper. But all decisions with respect to the governance of Oryndhr will be via an elected body."

With that, Aran clears his throat and begins to run through the finer points of the plan for the peaceful transition of power.

"Well done," I whisper to Roshan when he takes the seat beside me. "So now that you're a king without a throne, what will you do?"

His lips tip up as he winks wickedly. "Not to brag, but I do have some skills as a tree trimmer."

Epilogue

In the aftermath of both realms adjusting to new policies, Darrius eventually took some of the wards down, and new trade agreements between Everlea and Oryndhr were negotiated. While Roshan is no longer king, he still advises the new council in an official capacity, which works well for everyone. It's the start of a prosperous, mutually beneficial, peaceful relationship between two formerly feuding realms.

The hope is that magic will eventually return to Oryndhr.

My Starkeeper magic also came in handy to build a permanent portal bridge between the palace in Kaldari and the one in Verisia. It's like walking from one room to another, and the convenience is wonderful when it comes to practicality and accessibility. I did the same from Kaldari to Coban so that my father and Amma can always visit.

Now fully recovered thanks to Nuadar—who despite my groveling *still* hasn't quite warmed up to me, though I'm determined to win him over one day—Papa has announced that once things settle down and go back to normal, he and Amma will be getting married in Coban.

And finally, after weeks of preparation, the time of the wedding has arrived.

I'm excited to have Darrius visit the place where I grew up, for

Roshan to see it anew and certainly not while under the influence of a dark god. Needless to say, the village is in a fraught state now that the king and former king of two realms will be in attendance.

When Darrius arrives, he causes quite a few young women and men to swoon, which isn't surprising. Those dark good looks, his onyx crown over moon-kissed hair, and his towering build will weaken the legs of anyone with a working pulse. I restrain my territorial urges to snarl at anyone staring too long, and instead try to behave like the gracious queen I am.

You're not fooling anyone, pátnī. His honeyed rasp makes shivers coast down my spine. *I can feel your jealousy down the bond.*

I am trying to be a demure, well-behaved lady.

Even from where he stands on the other side of the crowded square with the alderman of House Aldebaran, his eyes glimmer gold. *You know I like you wild.*

My blush is impossible to hide. *Yes, I do know that.*

When Roshan arrives, the fanfare is just as uncontrolled, perhaps even more so—he's their former king, now simply just a prince, who saved their kingdom. With his thick dark hair, tawny-golden eyes, and athletic form, he doesn't even need a crown to look regal.

My prince greets me warmly, lifting me up and spinning me around. "Gods, starling, I've missed you," he says reverently, kissing me without care for anyone watching. He has made his claim of the Starkeeper more than clear.

"Ro, I was gone for two hours," I say, blushing at the scandalous thrust of his tongue and hoping my father isn't anywhere in the receiving room.

He grins. "That's two hours more than I could take. When can I get you alone?"

"After the reception. Now be a good boy or the magical tendrils will come out."

"Promise, promises." Roshan cants his head, but his eyes glint wickedly, making me let out a laugh. "Where's Nightsong? Ah, never mind, I see the fawning crowds over yonder."

"You know they're fascinated by him," I say. "The nightmare king of Everlea. He has a terrible reputation."

"One he secretly adores," Roshan says, lifting my hand to nibble my fingertips.

"Stop that," I tell him breathlessly, though the feelings spawning in my core definitely don't want him to stop. I love when he touches me like this. "Come on, we need to go."

The chapel is small, and only family and close friends are in attendance. Darrius joins us to sit on one side of me, while Roshan sits on the other. I hold both their hands as I watch my father marry my aunt, and as they promise to love and cherish each other, I can't stop the tear that slips down my cheek at how happy they seem. My father is handsome and dashing in his formal clothing, and Amma looks like a goddess in red and gold. I feel something brush my brow, and I smile at the gentle touch, knowing that my mother is watching with the other Royal Stars and that she approves wholeheartedly that these two are finally taking the leap.

It's about time, I think I hear her say, her laughter like bells.

Amma must hear her sister, too, because a radiant smile blooms over her lips.

When the service is over, we congratulate them and make our way to the reception hall, which is really the market square right outside the Saab Inn covered with tents and fabrics since so many people are here. Everyone wants to celebrate one of the most beloved couples in Coban. We feast, drink, and dance until my stomach is ready to burst and my feet feel like they are going to fall off. It's a far cry from a fancy ball at either palace, but so much more significant.

By the end of the night, Darrius has lost his crown, his shirt is unbuttoned, and his silver hair is deliciously tousled from dancing. He doesn't seem to care one whit that he's shredding his cold king reputation with every genuine smile that creeps across his face. And there have been a few.

Roshan is flushed and bright-eyed in the middle of the remaining dancers, and his old golden crown has been appropriated by Amma of all people.

She deserves it—she can be queen if she wants.

Darrius joins me where I'm sitting in my quiet corner and hands me a glass of water. He nuzzles my neck and draws me into his lap, kissing away my mumbled protests of propriety and prying eyes. But no one is paying us much attention. After hours of festivities, most of the crowd has dissipated, with only a few determined stragglers remaining to celebrate to the very end. Laleh would be among them, if she were here—she would have stayed to the last. I lift my glass and toast my best friend, hoping somewhere she, too, is watching and happy.

A sweaty Roshan comes to flop beside us and plants a sloppy kiss on my lips before stealing my water and guzzling it. "Hey! That was mine."

"What's yours is mine and what's mine is yours." He glances up at Darrius. "His, too, I suppose."

Darrius snorts. "Not yours, Acharia. Only hers."

Gods, he can still be so growly and possessive, and I love it. Another glass of water appears in a whorl of shadows. "Thank you, páti."

I feel his delight at the endearment. "You're welcome, Starbright."

I take a sip and then hand Roshan the glass, which he accepts with a sheepish grin. After quenching his thirst, he turns me sideways and lifts my legs, drawing them over his knees while I'm still sitting on Darrius. Then he removes my slippers and proceeds to rub my sore feet, which I relish with a silent, appreciative groan. I danced too much tonight, and while I could have easily used magic to heal them, sometimes it's good to feel things fully . . . even the uncomfortable things. Sore feet are a marker of my time well spent.

"Should we return to the palace?" Roshan asks, glancing over at us. "Sura wants to go to Kaldari tonight. She has a surprise for you, Nightsong."

An imperious eyebrow arches. "For me?" Darrius asks.

I nod, turning my cheek into his chest and breathing in his delicious smoke-and-oud scent. I love how they both smell so different, and yet, each of them feels like home to me. Roshan's scent makes me think of warm forges and hot summer days, and Darrius's makes me think of starlight and crisp winter nights. My sun and my night sky.

"Yes, we want to show you Nyriell, and the underground aqueduct."

Your special aqueduct? Darrius asks silently, his surprise filtering down the bond.

The very same, I say.

Isn't that important to the two of you? I can hear the uncertainty in his mental voice. *I wouldn't want to . . . intrude.*

It was Roshan's idea.

"Shall we depart then?" Darrius asks aloud, his voice thick with emotion.

"Soon." I watch my father draw Amma into his arms, their eyes only for each other as they spin beneath the twinkling stars of the night sky. "I'm so happy for them," I murmur. "I'm glad they have each other."

Easing to my feet, despite both their protests, I stand and walk over to the far side of the market square, climbing the steps to a terrace where I can just see the dawn's rays cresting over the tops of the highest dunes. The coming sunrise already has the promise of being majestic.

A familiar presence materializes beside me, and though they take no earthly form, I can feel them just the same.

"Ve," I greet my old guardian.

The ethereal outline inclines their head. "Setareh Framātāram."

"I was hoping I'd see you tonight." I turn to the glimmering Royal Star. "I wanted to thank you for not giving up on me. For helping me find the place I was always meant to be."

I sense their smile. "You found your own way, child. And we are so proud of who you have become."

I lift my palm, staring at the slightly glowing marks. "I suppose you were right about my destiny. Love is such a strange thing, isn't it? Those fated to us and those we choose . . . love at first sight and love after a lifetime . . ."

Ve peers at me. "Like anything worth keeping, love takes trust, patience, and communication. It can challenge you, break you, and test your every limit, but the journey is worth it in the end."

My grin is wide. "My, my, look at you, Ve, talking without cryptic riddles for once! Seems like we're both finally finding our way."

"Always so cheeky." They giggle, and I feel a playful pinch on my cheek and then the loving warmth of their embrace. "Be happy, child. In the end, that is the only thing that matters."

After Ve leaves, I think about what they said about love.

I think of Roshan and our tumultuous path, and despite the heartache, I wouldn't change a moment of it, because our love has been forged in fire and blood, like a sword hammered and folded until it's nearly unbreakable. And my beloved Darrius, who fought so valiantly to reject our soul-fated bond for years, simply to protect me from being tied to a monster. Though he's not a monster—no part of him is.

I feel a lighthearted growl through the bond and I grin. Well, Dare might be . . .

But together, we fought the *real* monsters and we won.

Biting my lip, I glance over my shoulder at each of my loves—my chosen and my soul-fated—one touched by light and the other born in shadow. My silence and my storm... my beating heart and my starlit soul. My simurgh flexes her wings in utter contentment, and the tricolored runes on my arms—silver, obsidian, and gold—shimmer.

We are bound by the earth and the sky, blessed by akasha, and we will forge a new path forward, one of our own making.

A future we deserve... one we are worthy of.

If your spirit is not fit to see the Simurgh, neither will your heart be a bright mirror, fit to reflect him. It is true that no eye is able to contemplate and marvel at his beauty, nor is it capable of understanding; one cannot feel towards the Simurgh as one feels towards the beauty of this world. But by his abounding grace he has given us a mirror to reflect himself, and this mirror is the heart. Look into your heart and there you will see his image.

—Farid ud-Din Attar, Persian poet, *The Conference of the Birds*

Glossary

Akasha: the infinite ether of the universe and source of raw magic

Amr'ita: immortality in the ancient language of the gods

Aspačanā: gender-neutral nomadic horse clans of the steppe in Everlea, divided by elemental magic and led by a rais or raissa

Azdaha: a gigantic, winged, snakelike mythological monster, resembling a dragon or wyvern

Azhi: a flying three-headed demon with magical powers for each head; can regenerate

Basic: lowest level magical rank; possesses minor abilities

Chamros: air magic horde clan of the steppe

Coban: a poor Oryndhrian desert city

Dahaka: the rebellion and separatist militia opposed to the Oryndhrian monarchy

Deadman's Canyon: heated chasm where the azdaha roost to lay their eggs

Dominant: high-level magical rank; possesses significant abilities

Droon: an abandoned city drowned by lava from an active volcano

Dustlands: an expanse of arid wasteland at the center of Oryndhr, inhabited by Scavs

Eloni: a wealthy Oryndhrian city, second richest to the capital city

Jade: a hallucinogenic drug distilled from jādū crystals that causes euphoria and temporary immunity to pain

Jādū: crystal remnants of magic, used to imbue weapons with elemental magic, open portals, and send communications; also used for Jade

Jaxx: a poorer forested city in west Oryndhr

Kaldari: the capital city of the kingdom of Oryndhr

Karkad: water magic horde clan of the steppe

Lora: a wealthy shipping port city on the northeastern corner of Everlea

Lost Isles: home to the adult azdaha colony

GLOSSARY

Magi: an akasha-blooded practitioner of magic; formerly a member of the outlawed Order of the Magi

Manticore: a mythical man-eating monster with the head of a lion, leathery wings, and a deadly scorpion tail

Mestial: average, mid-level magical rank; possesses satisfactory abilities

Morien: city in Everlea and home of Lord Donnan

Nyriell: a hidden underground city and the secret home of the houseless; protected by the Dahaka

Páti: *husband* in the ancient language of the gods

Pátnī: *wife* in the ancient language of the gods

Pix: a small landlocked city in Everlea

Rakh: fire magic horde clan of the steppe

Royal Stars: minor deities, hands of the gods, and creators of the Starkeeper

Runecaster: an official handler of jādū crystals for magic and portal use, usually part of the Imperial House

Scav: nomadic outlaws who live in the Dustlands and are addicted to Jade

Setareh Framātāram: master of the star

Glossary

Shabra: earth magic horde clan of the steppe

Sidereal: magical rank above sovran; incomparable abilities

Simurgh: a benevolent mythological creature with the head of a dog and the body of a giant bird, reminiscent of a phoenix or a firebird, generally female

Solis: a wealthy city on the eastern coast of Everlea

Soul-fated: a fate-ordained bond between two magic users, which acts as both an anchor as well as an amplifier of magic once the bond is sealed

Sovran: highest magical rank; possesses exceptional abilities

Starkeeper: a celestial warrior created by the Royal Stars to save the realm of men during the War of the Gods

Veniar: a wealthy Oryndhrian city, third wealthiest after Eloni

Verisia: capital city of Everlea, home to the king's castle

Xersten: a small Oryndhrian city nestled in an isolated mountain range

Acknowledgments

Writing this book was such an incredible ride, a flying-on-an-azdaha-over-the-ocean kind of ride—exhilarating, scary, and breathlessly awesome! I wanted to bring the most epic vibes to the page and make this story fun, thoughtful, action-packed, and deeply romantic while staying true to some of my favorite tropes, like enemies-to-lovers, forced proximity, found family, and forbidden love.

For anyone curious, the Aspačanā were inspired by the Scythians, nomadic warriors on the Eurasian steppe, from Persia to Russia, between 900 BCE and 200 BCE who were known for their horsemanship and their ferocity in warfare, especially with mounted archery. Typically blue-eyed with blond or red hair, their arms, legs, and upper chests were heavily tattooed with dots, birds, and fighting animals. Feasting was a huge part of their culture, and they loved being intoxicated. Truly fascinating research!

And now it's gratitude time!

To Priyanka Krishnan, editor extraordinaire, thank you for everything. Your insight, notes, and incredible suggestions ("Why not both?" shall forever be iconic in the genesis of this story) really made this book shine and took it to the next level. I am so grateful for you.

To my incomparable agent, Thao Le, thank you to the stars and beyond. I adore you, and none of this would be possible without your guidance, support, friendship, and constant advocacy.

Huge thanks to the entire production, design, sales, and publicity teams at HarperCollins for all your efforts behind the scenes. In particular, I want to thank Emily Dansky, Michelle Lecumberry, and DJ DeSmyter for their amazing enthusiasm and care for this series.

To all the reviewers, booksellers, librarians, educators, writer friends, extended family, and close friends who support me and spread the word about my books, thank you so very much. Your support means the world.

To my husband, Cameron, who is my anchor, thank you for always being there to keep me from floating off into the ether. And to our three children, Connor, Noah, and Olivia, thank you for giving me all my undoubtedly *magical* silver hairs.

Last but most important, dearest reader, thank YOU for reading, and spending some of your precious time in the world of Endara. I would not be here doing what I love without you. If you're new to the Amalieverse (I also write historical romance as well as science fiction and fantasy for teens and younger readers), thanks for giving me a chance. Happy reading, my friends!

About the Author

AMALIE HOWARD is a *USA Today* and *Publishers Weekly* bestselling romance author. She is also the author of several award-winning young adult novels. Her books have been featured in *The Hollywood Reporter*, *Entertainment Weekly*, and *Seventeen*. When she's not writing, she can usually be found reading, being the president of her one-woman Harley-Davidson motorcycle club, or power-napping. She lives in Colorado with her family.

Read more from
AMALIE HOWARD

A bladesmith with the power of the stars in her blood and a prince with a dangerous secret will fight to save their kingdom in this spicy and spellbinding romantasy inspired by Persian and Indian mythology.

> "My newest obsession! A breathtaking, sexy romantasy full of twists and adventure."
> —Rebecca Yarros,
> #1 *New York Times* bestselling author of *Fourth Wing*

DISCOVER GREAT AUTHORS, EXCLUSIVE OFFERS, AND MORE AT HC.COM.